Soul of the Sky

C. G. Carter

Soul of the Sky

Olympia Publishers
London

www.olympiapublishers.com
OLYMPIA PAPERBACK EDITION

Copyright © C. G. Carter 2024

The right of C. G. Carter to be identified as author of
this work has been asserted in accordance with sections 77 and 78 of the
Copyright, Designs and Patents Act 1988.

All Rights Reserved

No reproduction, copy or transmission of this publication
may be made without written permission.
No paragraph of this publication may be reproduced,
copied or transmitted save with the written permission of the publisher, or in
accordance with the provisions
of the Copyright Act 1956 (as amended).

Any person who commits any unauthorised act in relation to
this publication may be liable to criminal
prosecution and civil claims for damage.

A CIP catalogue record for this title is
available from the British Library.

ISBN: 978-1-80439-697-1

This is a work of fiction.
Names, characters, places and incidents originate from the writer's imagination.
Any resemblance to actual persons, living or dead, is purely coincidental.

First Published in 2024

Olympia Publishers
Tallis House
2 Tallis Street
London
EC4Y 0AB

Printed in Great Britain

Dedication

Davie, I'm sorry you never got to see this book completed.

Acknowledgements

Jess and Max, thank you for all your support through this process.

August 17, 2723

An'Gonye

The thing I remember most is that deafening sound of silence.

It wasn't the screams ripping through the air as I cowered behind a barrel that stuck with me. Nor was it the pounding of my own heart inside my eardrums as I locked gazes with the corpse-colored eyes. It wasn't even the sound of my footsteps squelching through my mother's brain matter. What I remember most was that, for the first time in my life, the tribe's lands were *silent*.

The day I met with An'Gonye, I was starving.

Hunger didn't feel like an emptiness. Hunger felt like you were two seconds away from choking on a cold, slimy serpent that stretched from your esophagus, through your intestine, stifling your breath and choking your movement.

I was hungry, so hungry that my arms shook when I raised them to wipe the dust from my cheek. I couldn't move my legs to even walk over to the dumpster.

A shaky breath caught in the hole of my throat. I couldn't even cry. I couldn't summon the tears to my eyelids.

I blinked until my eyes got too heavy to open. Then I hallucinated.

I hallucinated the man again. I knew he wasn't real. I knew I wasn't crouched behind a barrel in my basement, watching the man dressed in all white leave scarlet tracks across the hearth. I knew I wasn't really seeing him push a gloved hand through his lemon-yellow hair and chuckle as he said, "We barely participated." My gaze traced the line of his neck from his clean shaved jaw to that perfectly sculpted collar bone popping out of his unbuttoned white shirt. He was so calm, so nonchalant.

I hallucinated that feeling of blood, rushing beneath my flesh, a barely there itch. I hallucinated the electricity burning my nerves, frying my veins and muscles until they convulsed and rooted me to the spot. My stifled breath came in short, fast pumps, in and out of my nose. The air stung my eyelids, opened so wide tears welled along the bottom lid.

Even in that alley, with the smell of mold and garbage, I could still smell the tangy scent of iron that clung to that man, churning my stomach in nausea.

At the time, I had a moment of hope that maybe they were paramedics and they were going to help us.

I was fourteen when I learned hope was a fool's game.

I only remembered what the boy's eyes looked like. When he stared straight into me, my body went rigged and cold at the unfeeling eyes the color of rotted flesh. They had no light inside them, even with the piercing evening sun drenching the room in brilliant amber. Those were not the eyes of a man who healed. They were the eyes of a monster.

My scars itched under the bandages wrapped around my forearm. Sixty-two of the sixty-three vertical cuts tingled and burned with phantom pain. I clenched my jaw and reminded myself *scar tissue heals stronger.*

I forced my eyes open. I forced them to look at the grimy brick alley, at the OCHI EDO scratched into the brick across from me. I forced myself back to reality, away from all those thoughts.

I didn't see the boy with chocolate eyes until I smelled the warm sandwich. I wanted it so badly I almost puked. I'll always recall his deep voice, scratchy with dehydration, as he said, "Here, if you'd like," as if I would do anything other than grab the offered food and swallow it whole.

I still remember his laugh, the open-mouthed smile with the left incisor slightly overlapping its neighbor. It was enchanting. Maybe that's because I associated it with the two slices of sourdough with cured ham, spinach, and appenzeller shoved between them.

"You've got the same coin as me," he said. He touched the matching coin that he had strung around a chain on his own neck. His fingers were calloused and clean. I think he may have wanted to touch my own, if the minute flinch of his forearm was anything to go off of.

"Elonqua gave it to me," I choked out.

I wiped my hands on my shorts, the bread crumbs falling off onto the ground. "Thanks," I mentioned, "for the sandwich."

"Don't mention it," the boy said. "I'm An'Gonye." He didn't give me a surname.

"Ainsley." I didn't give him my surname, either.

The boy with the chocolate eyes looked to the side of our alley. He had an attractive nose and a strong jawline. A splattering of cocoa freckles splashed across his walnut skin like stars.

"Have you found them yet?" he asked, straight brows furrowed with concentration. He had checked for people. He had made sure we were alone.

I shook my head. The North Wind. The people this coin represented. Some society. I had been given only the instruction: "Find them." I pointed to the scratched Greek letters on the wall behind the chocolate eyed boy.

He studied the wall for a moment before turning back to me with a shrug. "Me neither. Elonqua didn't give me anything. Well, he didn't give me anything other than this dumb coin."

I smirked. "He?" I questioned. "My Elonqua was a woman. She wore a pink hat."

The boy with the chocolate eyes rolled back to sit instead of crouch, his palms making little divots where they pressed into the dirt. His nostrils flared and his lips pressed out in the center. "Huh," he expressed. "Weird."

I blinked once and pulled my knees up to my chest. My arms wrapped loosely around them.

I studied the boy closely. His relaxed posture, the almost imperceptible pink scar on his jaw, his well-defined body that was at least half a head taller than mine. His hair was much curlier than mine and popped out of his head in all directions. He had this relaxed look on his face, like everything would work out for him again.

"Where are you from?" he asked, his eyes catching my own again. He looked, maybe, a year... two years older than me.

"The Glass City," I answered. "You?"

"Oh, I heard about that place. They have these glass makers there, this little tribe."

I swallowed around the lump in my throat and fought back the bitter taste of bile. I nodded. "Yeah," I agreed. "The glass was really beautiful." So beautiful that they were killed for it. I brought a shaky hand up to twirl around the ring of glass on my neck, with ten little snaking points stretching outward from the loop

"I'm from Navij'Biem," the boy with the chocolate eyes continued. "You know, the place that specializes in skin grafting?"

I nodded. "I've heard of it."

"Why don't we look together from here on out?" he asked brightly.

"For the North Wind, I mean. It would be nice to have a partner."

I think, when I looked at him, I liked how he looked at me: Like I was just another kid. In that dark alleyway, where he had given me that warm sandwich, where he had looked for the same thing as me, he saw me as an equal.

I wasn't meant for affection and kindness. Not after what I did to my brother four months ago. "No," I mumbled. "I'm good, thanks."

The boy with the chocolate eyes started, then shyly rubbed the back of his neck. "Ah, that's fine. I hope we meet again at the finish line."

I didn't say anything as he pushed himself from the ground and walked over to the entrance to the alley. He looked over his shoulder and waved. "Well, see ya, then." Just like that, he was gone.

That's right, a voice inside me nagged. *You didn't deserve his kindness.*

My fingers gripped my shorts so tightly that I tore the fabric. I shut my eyes tight. *I'm so sorry, Jace,* I thought to myself. *I'm so sorry I told you to go play that day. If I hadn't told you I would set the table, you'd still be alive.*

But An'Gonye hadn't known that. Otherwise, he never would have given me that sandwich.

But Jace, I swear to you, I thought. I thumbed at the brass clamp around my wrist, the same brass clamp that had a partner buried six feet below, wrapped around the wrist of a boy who died when he was nine. *I will find the North Wind and I will get you justice.*

October 4, 2724

Yonten

My eyes scanned the map in my hands. I would need to go west bound to get to the nearby coordinate.

It seemed to me that I should have been able to see something on my way here, if there was even anything to even look at. However, some small part of me wanted to take the extra time to check, afraid that I would miss whatever it is I was looking for.

I thought briefly to the boy I had met with the little scar on his jaw and the dark freckles. It had been a little more than half a year since we had our encounter; I hoped he made it to the place we were both looking for.

He had a strong accent and I thought the common tongue felt misplaced with it. He probably thought the same thing about me.

I thought I spoke perfectly, but when people heard me speak, they always asked which Region I came from. I spent a lot of time with my dad, practicing common tongue with him so that I didn't have an accent; sadly enough, it didn't seem to work.

A loud whistle came from ahead.

My heart rate quickened, the shrill sound spiking my adrenaline. My eyes darted up to a group of three men about twenty paces in front of me. They were hooting loudly enough to let me know they were the source of that whistle.

One of them had hair done up in spikes. He had a pronounced forehead and a far-off gaze. Another was tall, like a Podocarpus shrub, and just as prickly, covered in lots of stubble and body hair. The third looked plain, someone who could fade into the background and never be noticed if he refrained from speaking.

With a sinking feeling in my gut, I realized they were looking back at me. I also realized just how empty the alley I was walking through was. I crinkled the map and stuck it in my shirt pocket right away. I sped my pace, despite the afternoon fatigue I felt.

A shiver slowly traced its way down my spine and I did not want to stick around to find out why.

"Hey, kid, you lost?" the plain one called out. His friends laughed when he said that, like it held some secret meaning between the three of them. Perhaps it did. They stood in a semi-circle, leaning against alley walls, shoulders hunched and spines curved.

I took a deep breath. I would not convey any sign of weakness to them, not vocally, not physically. I clenched my fists so they wouldn't shake and I turned my head up to show confidence. "I know where I'm going." There was no quiver in my voice.

The tall one stuck his hands into the front pockets of his baggy brown pants. They hung off his hips like they were hand-me-downs from someone even taller. He began walking down the alley, straight toward me, that hunched posture never changing.

My feet faltered slightly when he slurred, "Don't be like that, we're just — we wanna be friendly with ya. You don' look like a local."

"I don't need any help finding my way, thank you," I reiterated, quickening my pace. My heart skipped a few beats and my palms and neck felt clammy.

The other two walked over to their friend slowly, bull-headed confidence in each step taken. Despite the slurring, I didn't believe them to be drunk, based off the smoothness of their movement.

I stopped. I took one step back.

With a start, I realized I had let my mask slip. I showed hesitation. My chest tightened and my breathing accelerated.

I moved to take another step back. The yank on my wrist from the one with the spiky blond hair kept me in place. I winced and my eyes darted between his hand and his body. I tugged a little, but his hand was firm. It felt warm. Too warm.

"Hey, we're being polite. You should know when to be polite yourself," he said as his index finger tapped the soft side of my wrist, where the veins showed through the skin. He had a strange smile on his face that wasn't really a smile. It, unlike his hand, was colder than falling snow.

I didn't want to beg, but I knew I couldn't take all three of them in a fight. "I have — in my bag, I have money. It's yours," I told them, looking at the three in turn.

The one holding my wrist guffawed in a way that made my stomach drop. "We don't want your money," he told me.

My breath caught in my lungs.

The blond's other hand came up to my shoulder, pushing me back. The unforgiving wall stung my spine as I was shoved into it.

It shouldn't matter what they did to me, because I existed only for one reason. My life, my experiences, should mean nothing to me. As I stared down the inevitable future, I realized that I hadn't been able to push aside myself just yet; I still did care.

"Please," I tried, pushing with my free hand against his chest as he drew closer to me. The plain friend grabbed the hand that was pushing. I started to kick. "Let me go!" I yelled.

I wasn't an idiot. I knew what happened at this point. I knew how much it would hurt and that it would probably take me a long time to get over it.

My leg was pinned down, too. Three against one wasn't a fair fight, but it was the card I was dealt. I felt a cool breeze of air on my abdomen and a warm hand reach up into my shirt, just as a different hand clamped over my mouth. I squirmed as much as I could, but there wasn't much I could do.

The blond made a hushing sound. "Don't worry, I'll be gentle." He said it like he was doing me a favor.

I closed my eyes. I could still get out. I thrashed, but only felt the heat intensify as they pressed closer. I squeezed my eyes shut.

Ia, Arrakaul dves Psoe, meriv jjeskje. A prayer I hadn't spoken in a long time. I couldn't speak it now, but I could think it. Please, Sun God, protect me. I had lost faith in her when my people were killed, but even if it was slim, there was a chance she existed and that she would protect me, if only this once.

I felt hot breath on my neck, smelled the smoky scent of tobacco. A wet muscle writhed against my neck with suction and I screamed. It came out muffled and quiet from beyond the hand.

"You're such a pretty boy," he muttered lowly against my flesh. If we were in public, and there was no hand covering my mouth, I would say, *Stop touching me. Get off me. Leave me alone. I'm not a toy.* The hand under my shirt tracked higher.

And then, all at once, they were off me. The stones beneath me slammed into my knees and a tender ache laced my bones. I was shaking and I was breathing hard and I was sore from all of my muscles clenching.

A fourth person had joined the trio. I missed where he had come from. I couldn't see his face, for his back was to me, forming a bright orange barrier between me and the men who had been on me a moment ago.

The plain man had ended up on the ground, the tall one slouched on the wall opposite me, and the blond standing at a pace away.

My fingers gripped onto the bricks behind me tightly, using it to help me stand.

I felt numb.

"You bastard," the blond man said, his fists balling up and his stance widening.

The man between us was more still than a mountain and calmer than stone, unflinching against the threatening figures.

A lump grew in my throat. He saved me. *He saved me.*

Time seemed to slow, then. The tall one pushed himself away from the wall and the plain one hobbled to his feet.

First the tall one lunged forward, but the man caught his outstretched hand, leading him in a circle, nearly close enough to touch me, and slamming him into the blond. They both fell on the impact.

The plain one tried to uppercut the man. He moved his head to the side just enough for the punch to miss. Quick as a viper, the man in orange jabbed the plain man in the indent just above the collar bones. He fell to his knees gasping for air.

The blonde had gotten up and was running at the man in orange now, while his back was turned, but the man snapped his back leg out and sent the blond flying into the wall, a wheeze accompanying the smacking sound of head slamming against brick.

The tall one was staggering to his feet, but the man in orange kicked him between the legs in an almost comical way.

All three of the men who had attacked me were on the floor, groaning or gasping in some form.

It was then that the man turned to me and I caught the first glimpses of his face.

He was older than I by decades, I could tell, yet his wrinkles were thin. He had a round and kindly face and his monolid eyes crinkled at the corners. But by far, the most noticeable thing about him was the disfiguration on the left side of his face, where his skin had pattern of raised and wrinkled lines, that hung over his flesh like a wet cloth. I tracked that burn down his throat and across his shoulders until it was obscured by the collar of his orange tunic.

Everything about him seemed dangerous. The marked body, the incredible violence he just displayed. Still, when I looked at him, I didn't feel danger clawing at my skin from inside me. Instead, I took a shaky breath of relief. My muscles unclenched.

I walked toward him. I wrapped my arms around his middle and pressed my face into his chest. My body shook and I took in big breaths of air, grateful for the unexpected appearance of a stranger.

He patted me on the back gently. He smelled of jasmine and a river bank.

Thank you, I wanted to say. I didn't have the energy to say anything right now. I think he understood that.

He gently pushed me away, his hands light on my shoulders. "I would like you to come with me," he articulated, voice without tone or pitch. "Will you?"

He gave me an option, put me back in control of things.

I nodded. It was the only thing I could do.

He turned and began his graceful path, stepping over the limp and groaning bodies of the blonde and the shrub man. I moved to follow.

The man in orange robes didn't talk to me on the way back. If I were being honest, I couldn't think of anything to say to him either.

He led me out of town and into the woods. I probably shouldn't have followed him, not after seeing what he could do, but I did.

Far be it from me to believe the cliche about the enlightened hermit, but the man seemed to fit the mold. He was withdrawn, wore strange attire, and seemed to live in the small cave he took me to.

The mouth was barely taller than me with my arms stretched above my head. There was a small area of twigs encircled by rocks, a propped-up pot hung above the remains of those wood hunks. There was also a mound of cloth, strewn about near the rock circle: sleeping gear. Clothes hung from a line, hastily pinned between a rock grouping and a pole stuck into the dirt. A bow and quiver sat propped up by the mouth of the cave, along with dried bags of corn and beans. It was a hovel, tidy, though it was.

The man took a seat by the mound of blankets, his feet tucked beneath him. His eyes closed and he breathed deeply. In. Out. I waited, in vain, for him to say something.

"What is your name? Why did you offer that I come with you? Do you have a vested interest in helping out kids?" I asked, finally feeling the need to end the uncomfortable silence.

He chuckled, like he knew a secret I wasn't privy to, and said to me, "You speak an awful lot for one who has nothing to say."

My face burned and my jaw clenched. I gritted my teeth together and inhaled deeply.

"I am Yonten, but this was not always my name." He sounded far, though he was only a meter away.

Yonten looked into my eyes with his own. They were dark and mellow like carved obsidian.

His lips twitched up. Calmly, he closed his eyes once more, as if he were about to sleep. "Give up your quest, young one," he advised. "There is no light at the end of your tunnel."

In that moment, I knew he had been a sentry, guarding another of the *ochi edo* stones, waiting for someone like me to come looking for it.

Those who knew could tell when they looked at us: We were dirty and starved. We traveled alone, with stuffed packs and sallow eyes. We looked like the departed, not yet ready to leave this earth. When I caught glimpses of myself in still waters, a ghost looked back at me.

An icy feeling crept into my fingers and toes, spreading into my core.

I felt the need to yell, to scream, and to cause this man pain. How could he tell me to give up? How could he know the pain of losing everyone? How could he know the desire to make things right? How did he know me well enough to comment on my life?

"You are trying to find the North Wind, right?" he asked, that perplexing calmness clinging to him like dew on a spider's web.

He closed his eyes and folded his palms in his lap. "Give up," he instructed.

I swallowed. "What?" I snapped at him.

"Give up." He was unrelenting as steel.

I clenched my teeth together. I tried to keep my voice low and monotone this time as I argued, "I can't."

If I gave up now, it would be telling my tribe I had moved on. It would be saying goodbye to the elders and saying goodbye to the aunties and uncles that made up my support system. It would be saying goodbye to Dad and Mom and Jace and Farrah.

And I wasn't ready to say goodbye yet.

Yonten sighed and his shoulders heaved up and down. He pushed himself up from his seat at the ground and began a steady walk toward me. His neck was hunched over, pointed toward the ground. His hands lovingly clutched at one another.

I noticed a tear on his left sleeve, the color black peeking through about where his wrist would be.

He stopped when he was next to me. I turned to face him, blood still crunching beneath my skin. "They call themselves Gods, you know."

Gods? I would like to be a God, if only for a short while, if it could get my brother justice.

Before I could tell him as such, Yonten quoted, "*O ánthropos pou ischyrízetai óti eínai Theós eínai pio kontá se énan daímona.*" People make a distinct voice when they quote things from memory. It's a little curt and lacks the intonation of immediate thought. It also comes out much slower, as if a rhythm for the words has already been established.

"The man who claims to be a God is closer a demon," he said. It was pointed and he turned his head enough to make contact out of the corner of his eye.

Yeah, *really* fitting of the whole wise, enlightened hermit.

But he was wrong. I had seen demons. I had seen them talk about death as if it were the weather. I had seen the carnage they wrought and felt the pain and the guilt of being alive in their wake. I had asked myself why it could not have been someone else to survive, hoping I would hear an answer that never came.

Those demons left behind a shell of a human. If I had to fill that shell with a demon of my own, I would do it without hesitation.

I pushed my lips together in a flat line and clenched my fists. It had been a little over a year and I still had rage filled to the brim.

My vision went red and hard nails cut into the palms of my hands. I knew I could not fight him, so I was forced to stand with muscles tensed, breathing ragged, and brows furrowed until I shook. I was reckless and naïve teenager, yes, but I was smart enough at that time to know to know when action was required and when words were.

"At least I'm doing something," I bit. I spoke a little too loud and a little too fast and with a little too much spite.

I could almost feel the warmth leave my body as anger wrapped its cool tendrils around my heart. This was the first true manifestation of my cold, fiery rage. Years later, I loathed myself for feeling it toward a man I grew to admire.

"Yeah, maybe I won't make much of a difference, but that doesn't release me of the obligation to try." My voice wavered and cracked and I flinched when it's broken sound hit my ears. I was dangerously close to crying. I blinked back the blurriness in my eyes. "I'm trying! Every day I am trying to right what I can because I can't just sit around waiting for things to get better; I have to do *something!*"

Tendrils of ice squeezed my heart, making my chest throb. The breath left my lungs and I was ready to fight, but there was no fight I could logically take.

Something akin to surprise glistened in Yonten's eye.

Let him see my resolve, I thought, wishing that Jace could hear me from wherever he ended up. I hoped there was a brilliant fire burning in my eyes, showing my passion and my anger and my dedication. I knew better than that. My eyes were cold and dark.

I will do something, I thought again. *I'll get you justice. That's a promise.*

Yonten turned his head to look at me directly. "How old are you?" he demanded. I saw nothing on his face to indicate his intentions.

"What is your scar from?" I asked him, in turn. He did not get to demand something of me without compensation.

He chuckled, and it made me distinctly more shaky when I found he took my anger lightly.

"We all have scars," he said. I would get no answer from him.

My left arm prickled. I moved to run my thumb over the scars that were hidden beneath a series of bandages. I supposed that was true. I had a great many.

I had the ones on my arm. I had the scar on my shin from a climbing accident when I was young. I even had a scar on my finger because I had been stupid enough to challenge Emil to touch a hot pan with me and be the last one to let go. I had won, but my finger had been immobile for weeks (looking back, the younger me was a moron).

The ice and the anger dissipated like fog receding after a wind, knowing, logically, it would not help me get what I wanted. My body unclenched and I looked away from him. "I turned sixteen a few days ago," I mumbled.

I pulled my feet closer together and unclenched my fists. Sticky beads of moisture rolled slowly down my palms onto my fingers. I didn't look at that sticky liquid to see the color. I knew what it was. I could smell the iron and rust.

"What is your name?"

I should have been rude and left.

"Ainsley."

He hummed and looked away. "I have a proposition for you, Ainsley," Yonten mused.

He began to walk. I moved to follow.

"I get the next two years of your life, until you turn eighteen."

The dirt was hard underfoot and reverberated through me as my heels impacted the stiff ground. My lips tugged downward and my eyebrows knit together. "And what do I get for that?" I was not in the business of brokering deals.

"I will tell you where to find the North Wind and I will teach you to be one of them."

My breath caught in my throat. There was no veritable guarantee that he would uphold his end of the bargain, especially with his adamance that I quit. I exhaled.

"Why?" *Why would you do that when you obviously disapprove?*

"I think I can change your mind in two years."

I pursed my lips. This man did not know me well enough to know how stubborn I was, that I would not change my mind because my family and my tribe still deserved salvation in the wake of their genocide.

I said nothing.

I followed him through bushes and brambles. The forest here was a strange combination. Evergreen trees and cracking dirt. It was like all the moisture was sucked into the wood, leaving none for grass to grow. My light blue sneakers get caked in that slightly reddish dust. The air here smelled dry, but the temperature was cold.

I could hear a lone bird calling out and could see it circling above us, creating the only sound in the valley. I had learned the forest was never quiet, nor the desert, nor the sea.

The hairs on the back of my neck stood on edge and my heart beat a little faster. The landscape began to change. It was no longer those dry evergreens, with the red soil. No, it was different. These trees had trunks of white and bright blue leaves that almost blended with the sky. The ground was a bright yellow, the color of lemons. It looked unnatural.

"Why are we here?" I demanded, coming to a stop at the edge of that clearing.

He laughed. "Where you are going, you will need to learn to school your expressions."

"Why?" I asked, trying to force the scowl I had down to a more neutral expression.

"Because emotions portray desire. And desire can be a weapon used against you."

I pulled air into my lungs and let it out. My face slowly relaxed. My tongue pressed into the insides of my cheeks, stretching them out to relieve the tension that still remained.

Yonten sat with his legs crossed and tugged back his long orange sleeves.

Within the next five years, I'd try really hard to remember him like that, from a time before I lost control of myself, before I was tainted. But I couldn't freeze an image in my brain. Eventually the perception blurred and I couldn't pick out the details. I would be able to picture Yonten, but I wouldn't be able to picture how the wind brushed the tips of the treetops, or the sound of them rustle. I wouldn't be able to picture the litter of small rocks on the ground.

"I accept your offer," I announced.

Yonten closed his eyed and let out a puff of air. I saw his left eyebrow twitch. I think it was the first sign of frustration I had seen him show. It marred his face in the way trout stands out against the grey rock bottom of a stream.

"You are a fool." His words had gone as soon as the syllables reached my ears, dissipated like smoke.

My bottom lip twitched, pulling down ever so slightly before I consciously brought it back up again.

He shook his head and schooled his own face. "Look, kid," he deadpanned, "there are a lot of people with less to lose then you. Those are the people who you'll find where you're headed. If you have anyone, *anyone* you care about, your weakness will hurt them. They will rip those people from your grasp permanently."

I smiled, the kind of smile that you only make when you're not really smiling at all. "It's a good thing there's no one left for me to lose."

Yonten sized me up then, with his coal-black eyes. He stood and walked over to me. "Then, we start here tomorrow." He raised his hand and brought it close to clasp my shoulder tightly. He squeezed.

The squeeze was a little too tight. A little too warm. A little too familiar.

I didn't see Yonten's hand. I saw *his*. The man with the spiky hair, the one who grabbed my wrist. The overwhelming desire to run hit me and my hand reflexively shot up, knocking Yonten's own away.

My body convulsed and I fell backward, clutching at the yellow dirt and gravel rapidly as I tried to scramble away. The ground made a home under my nails and muddled with the sweat that had broken out over my skin. I heaved uneven breaths, in and out, in and out, *in and out, in and out, inandoutinandout.*

Then I saw Yonten's face, calm and sad, looking at me like I was glass. *Don't,* I thought. *Don't look at me like that.*

This time I was calmer, the desire to take care of myself overruling the physical sensations. The tension released from my body like a pulled rope cut loose. "I'm not weak, I—"

"We all have scars," he cut me off. "There are the ones that mark your left arm, that you try so desperately to keep hidden, and there are the ones in your mind, that move your body without consent."

Shame clawed at my spine from inside my skin. I should have more self-control. I was not a toddler. I should be able to think before I act. A deep pit of discomfort grew in my stomach.

I clenched my hands tightly and pushed myself up from the ground. I felt my nails biting into my palms and I shook all over. I couldn't bring myself to look at Yonten.

"And you have many in your heart," he continued.

I froze. My muscles tightened again and I forced myself to meet his gaze.

"You will gain scars until the day you die, Ainsley," he said, turning away from me, "it would do you well to make peace with them." He began to walk away without me.

This time, I couldn't follow, the pride I desperately clung to rooting me to the earth until the sun set below the horizon, just to prove I could look past my fears, look past the weakness I had just displayed.

I pushed one foot in front of the other, walking toward a trunk of a tree. I stared at the bark, looked at all of the uneven lines and swirls. I don't think I was really seeing them; I was seeing myself in an alley where no one had come to rescue me.

I watched my fist press itself to the tree harshly. My skin stung and my knuckles ached. I did it a second time, more quickly than the first. I watched as my knuckles left trails of red on the white.

I didn't feel the pain that laced splinters in my skin. I didn't feel like I was in my body.

I watched the images of my tribe's corpses, the image of that alleyway flash in my mind.

Make peace with them.

June 19, 2725

Yaya

When I was little, I used to lay in the dry dirt during high summer. I would run my fingers through the fine powder and feel the orange and brown dust stain my skin. I thought, *dirt is soft*.

That perspective, that dirt is soft, changes the second a retired assassin throws your body into dirt.

I stood and balanced on the balls of my feet. As I scuffed the back of my right hand against my cheek to clean off that dirt, it occurred to me that I was most likely just rubbing more on. I shook my head, trying to stop my spinning vision.

Think only on the present, I reminded myself.

I bent my knees and pushed forward with my toes. I tensed the muscle in my left bicep, drawing back for an uppercut to Yonten's chin that was quickly becoming reachable. I wasn't as tall as I would have liked to be at seventeen, so I aimed low.

Yonten pushed his right arm out and nudged my wrist past his body. My knuckles grazed the orange sleeve on his shoulder. He could have dodged completely, but he didn't. I knew why when the bruising snap of Yonten's own knuckles collided with my cheek.

I was no stranger to pain, but pain was a funny thing. It was funny because, no matter how much you experienced, certain physical reactions could not be controlled. A blow to the nose always made my eyes water, just as the blow to the cheek I just received would always make my teeth collide and my skull rattle.

So, when the fist bruised the skin on my cheek, my teeth did collide and my head tried to turn away from the point of impact. This, in turn, prevented me from noticing and avoiding a knee to my own stomach. It stole the breath from my lungs and brought a tenderness to my abs.

A second thing that was funny: The more you get hit, the more you get hit.

I hunched over as Yonten's elbow impacted my spine. My back arched and the ground pulled out from under my feet.

The dirt was unrelenting when I met it again. I could feel the purple marks forming on my skin as I hacked up mucus.

"Remember the rule?" I heard from above me.

I groaned and pushed myself off the ground. I staggered to full height and pushed my shoulders back. *Get up,* was the rule. *Get up until you cannot move any more.* It did not matter how many times I was knocked down, so long as I was not the one to stay down.

I was told that the first day. Desperate to prove myself, I went the whole day taking blow after blow until I collapsed. Yonten had left me in the clearing. When I woke up, I had walked myself back to base, a slight limp in my steps. He was awake, waiting with a smirk that said with no words, 'You alone are responsible for moving yourself.'

I panted, lacing my cold and sore throat with the heavy tension of air. My chest was cold, in spite of the warm summer weather. It spread, encroaching on my every nerve ending. It was the frigid winter, taking over and thinking for me.

I knew how to win.

I crouched and lunged forward.

Yonten widened his stance, to offer himself stability. *Good,* I thought.

I let my feet slip off the ground and my body followed, sliding across the top of the dirt between his legs. My sneakers dug into the yellow dust and I tucked my head toward them. I twisted my core and threw all my weight into my shoulder and pushed it into his lower back.

Yonten yelped. I supposed even he, too, must be surprised from time to time.

I would never beat him head on, not while he knew how to redirect my attacks, when I hadn't learned how to redirect his. He had said he would only teach me once I could knock him off his feet.

Today was the day I did that.

Yonten stumbled forward. I swung the heel of my foot in a low circle and thrust the palm of my hand into his shoulder.

I watched as his body twisted and his feet lifted from the ground. He came crashing down with the same force he had let me hit the earth with.

I breathed heavily and squared my body once more. I understood why he wanted me to knock him down before he taught me anything else. He wanted me to strategize, to outsmart a stronger opponent.

"Don't you want to take it easy on an old man?" he joked.

I smirked as I relaxed my stance, tilting my head to the side and my chin up. "I don't know," I mused. "Did you ever get tired of going hard on me?"

"Never!" he responded with a false offense. He raised his eyebrows high and pressed lines into his forehead. He may have been joking, but he wasn't lying when he answered "never." He didn't get tired of going hard on me because he was upholding his promise. Yonten never pulled his punches and I didn't want him to. I didn't want to scrape by because he was going easy on me.

I knew the people who had decimated my tribe were skilled, too skilled to just be serial killers. It was carnage, but it was organized carnage. In order to combat that, I would need to take advantage of every blow. I wanted Yonten to push me further than I could go alone.

You're almost there, the phantom in my head explained. *Just a little further and you'll get them justice.*

My fists moved in front of my face and I widened my stance as he had before. "There is your answer," I breathed out.

I could take a beating. That, at least, I could do. Months' worth of scrapes, sweat, and bruises had taught me that.

Yonten moved like the shadow of a whip. He was fluid and smooth, and gave the promise of cracking power if he were to strike. And he moved like that toward me, seeming to hover across the ground, his shoulders never once bouncing with his stride.

"You knocked my feet off the ground," he informed, his cheeks drawn up in a smile akin to pride.

My face heated. Would my parents take pride in me for this in the same way he did? I knew they wouldn't be proud of me for dropping out of primary school.

Yonten slowly moved his head to the side, to look toward the wide creek of shallow water that ran through the area. "Go stand on that pillar," he told me. The water ran in translucent rivulets over the tops of pebbles no bigger than my fist, of varying shapes and colors. The stream would barely reach above my ankle, were I to stand in the deepest part.

I knew which rock he was referring to. It was more of a pillar that was carved into stone. I looked between him and the pillar, hoping he was joking. He wasn't.

I heaved a sigh and walked over. I had to wade in the water to get to the pillar. The water seeped into my shoes slowly, then all at once, squelching as I moved in them.

My face screwed up in a grimace. All socks were awful, but wet socks were the worst.

The base was a little bigger than my spread hand, and it felt rough and sharp. It would skin my hand if I pressed down and rubbed against it. It only reached my knee. I placed my left foot atop the pillar and pushed off the rocky ground with my right, balancing on a bent knee. I placed my toe down and centered my feet. I wobbled a little, feeling the weight of my own body without anything to hold it in place.

My hips wobbled a little, waiting for something. "What now?" I asked.

"Close your eyes," he instructed. I did. The sounds around me became more noticeable when I wasn't focused on what I could see. Sounds grew sharper and the feeling of my own body became more noticeable. It was harder to balance with my eyes closed, because I could feel every quake of my knees with nothing to root myself to the spot.

A strong force pushed my chest, knocking the air out of me and collapsing my body around the point of impact. My eyelids opened and my stomach dropped. The rocky bottom of the shallow river rose up to meet me and placed pinpricks of pain all across the bottom of my skin. The water instantly drenched me, cold and heavy.

My head snapped up to meet him and I forgot that my face was supposed to be still. I was sure the frustration could be seen in the drawn-up brows and the pinched mouth I fought to push off my face.

"What was that for?" I grunted.

He closed his eyes and smiled. "An old man needs to be petty."

"Ah, of course. That's how you dinosaurs keep your bones from eroding to sand, right?" I retorted.

He smirked. He did that a lot when he didn't want to verbally acknowledge my jibes.

I raised my hands up in surrender and flashed a crooked smirk of my own. "Seems fair to me."

I placed my hands on the rocky bottom and pushed myself up, ready to stand on the pillar again. It was harder to balance with the weight of the water pressed into my clothes. "Get off of there, we have to refill supplies,"

Yonten called out.

My head snapped up to look at him. "Why did you have me stand up here if it was only going to be once?" I asked.

He turned away from me. "I thought it would be funny!" he called over his shoulder, as he walked away.

A breathy chuckle left my lips. I should have expected as much from him.

"Are you crazy, that's ridiculous. Last month, this bag was half the price," Yonten argued with the sales clerk.

She looked like she wanted to hit him and had to pinch the bridge of her nose to keep from doing so. "Sir, there was a shortage in the last shipment due to a drought in the supplier region," she said. "You can wait until next season or you can check with a new vendor."

"But then I wouldn't get to see you, my dear," Yonten admonished.

She sighed. I snorted.

Yonten was actually a massive pervert. I had expected him to be reserved and at peace with himself when I had first met him. Instead, there were many layers: the layer of a teacher, the layer of a minimalist, the layer of a pervert who flirts with the forty-year-old sales clerk that worked the general store.

Even a sage has faults.

My snort drew his attention to me. He shot me a look. It was the *Scram, kid, you're messing with my chances look*. He didn't have a chance with the sales clerk regardless of my presence.

Although I had grown used to the idyllic scenery of the forest, the city was a nice trip, too. And this city was particularly striking. It was like an outcropping of beige buildings, reaching upward to the sky, topped with orange shingles and lined with patterned blue tiles. There were raised sidewalks and hand painted street signs that gave directions. The smell of the ocean occasionally drifted inland toward us, but the day always retained its stagnant and balmy air. The dust kicked up in the streets and muddled its dry scent with the earthy smell of turmeric.

I walked past the shaded alley I had met Yonten in a little more than a year ago.

When I thought about it, I could still feel the breath on my neck, the too warm hand on my stomach. The thought made a shiver run down my back and a feeling of slime crawled across my skin.

Most days I didn't think about it, most days that memory was buried so far in the back of my skull that it never saw light. But it was never gone. It was always sleeping until I came back, waking up just long enough to shoot tar across my flesh and tell me, *you're disgusting.*

I saw the scene of what had happened to me through an outside lens, a third person perspective, playing like an old reel in my mind. I often wondered if I was seeing what Yonten had, if I had spent so much time with him that I had somehow tapped into his memories because they were easier than my own. I wondered if I had changed at all since then, if I could do anything to stop something like that from happening again.

A force hit my left leg. I turned to look at what had hit me, my fists instinctively balling up and adrenaline tensing my muscles. A warm pressure wrapped around my waist. I saw a little girl hugging me with everything she had.

I took in a sharp inhale of air. My hands moved dumbly to touch her shoulders, to apply a light, but firm pressure against them, trying to push her away.

"You looked lonely, Tiz," she said as she gripped tighter. Her voice shook; she was lying.

I pushed more firmly at her shoulders to force her away from me.

The girl took a step back, but bunches of my beige shorts still popped from the spaces between her fingers.

She removed one of her hands and tugged at a strand of green hair, nervously. She didn't look up to meet my gaze.

"Hey," I tried. "Can you tell me what's wrong?"

I understood that tight clench of her hands, the need to root herself to anything that breathes. It's the feeling of powerlessness, trying to grab onto a rope when drowning. I had felt it twice in my life: the day I met Yonten and the day I buried my brother.

I grabbed her small shaky hand in mine, watched quiver as I pried it away from my shorts. I crouched down to kneel before her, bringing us to eye level.

She finally looked to me, her green eye peeking out vibrantly against her dark skin.

I thought *eye* instead of *eyes* because only one was visible. The other had swollen eyelids covering it, with cracking makeup intended to hide the purple bruising. She had a dainty nose, a nose that had a pink scar against the corner, right where the nose met the flat of her face. Her thin lip had a dark red line slightly left of center, evidence it had been badly busted.

She could not have been more than eight years old.

"Can I look at your lip?" I asked her. I made sure to move slowly when I let go of her hand.

Her eye grew wide and she looked over her shoulders rapidly, as if scanning for someone. I looked too, trying to see if anyone's gaze was focused on us for too long.

"Yes," she mumbled.

I nodded and held my right hand up for her to look at. I watched her eye trace the lines of my fingers, deeming it safe to allow near her face.

"What is your name?" I asked to distract her as my thumb reached close to her lip to feel the edges of the red line. I pressed in slightly and she winced. It was deep, like the scab had formed inside her skin. It must be painful under pressure.

"Yaya," she answered.

I pulled my hand back. "I'm Ainsley. What types of games do you like to play, Yaya?"

I kept looking around us, to make sure no one was watching. We didn't look related and she didn't seem to want to draw too much attention to herself. My eyes found Yonten's orange robed figure, still haggling over the price of a bag of beans.

"I like to play board games." Yaya's small voice brought me back. "Like Komikan."

I look back to her. "Very cool," I acknowledged. "My favorite board game is Senet. Have you ever played that?"

She shook her head.

"It's very fun, you should try it one day."

Yaya paced between her feet, scratching at her arm nervously. She wasn't quite ready for the question I wanted to ask her, still not comfortable with me. "Now it's your turn to ask me a question," I stated instead.

She nodded and reached a small hand out. It touched the top of my head, her fingers getting caught in the perpetually messy curls. "It's like the snow, like an old man's. Why is your hair like that?" Children were always quick to point out looks.

I tried to smile at her. "My mother's hair was white, so mine is, too," I told her. "Why is your hair green?"

She smiled a little at that, her eyes lighting up. Yaya leaned forward a little. "My hair is from my mommy, too. She has much longer hair than me, but hers is always kept up in pleats around the top of her head. I don't like my hair braided."

I nodded at her. "Well, that makes sense. It's more fun to keep hair down."

She hummed in agreement. Her shoulders were more relaxed now, less tense. I checked behind her again, no one was staring for too long. I think she was ready to be asked.

"Can I ask you another question, Yaya?"

"Sure, Ainsley!" It was like her personality had done a complete turnaround.

"How did your lip and your eye get like that?" I asked.

I watched the smile slowly dissipate from her face and the tension slip back into her stance. She looked down at the ground. *That's common with victims of abuse, the fear and the shame.*

"I promise it will be our little secret, just between you and me. No one else will ever know you told me," I whispered, holding my smallest finger out toward her. "Pinky promise."

I didn't want to hear the words she would say, not really, but I needed to hear them. I felt my breath catch in my throat and the muscles in my back tighten. She looked fragile, like a sparrow.

She hummed and bit her lip. She shifted her weight again, from foot to foot. She looked over her shoulder again. I looked with her. Finally, she took my smallest finger in her own. She leaned forward and whispered back, "My daddy."

I waited for her to elaborate. I held out my free hand. Hers was half the size of mine when she placed her own in it. I gave her a little squeeze. *I'm here.* It was all I could be for her. *Here.*

"He hurts me — he hurts me and my mommy. My mommy — she doesn't — she stays hidden in the house. Sometimes she can't help me — she just falls asleep."

A chord snapped within me, too cold to maintain its elasticity. It's splintered pieces stung.

"I appreciate you sharing," I thanked her.

She nodded, but she still looked uncertain.

"Would you like to get some ice cream with me?" I asked her. I wanted to take her mind off of our conversation and off of the person I was nearly certain she had been running from when she ran into my leg. "I know a place with stretchy ice cream that you would love."

She nodded. I pulled my little finger out of hers and stood. Immediately, I felt a tight squeeze on the hand she still held. I didn't pull that one out of her grasp.

I was reminded, vaguely, of Jace when he was scared. Jace was one year older than Yaya looked when he was killed. He would always cling to my hand, like I had the power to make his fears go away, to protect him from anything the world could throw at us.

That day, I had failed Jace. I had stayed in place, like mom had told me to, while she went out to find Dad and Jace. I should have gone with her. Maybe I could have held Jace's tiny hand in my own and gotten him out of there, hidden him away behind the barrels with me. But I hadn't. And Jace was dead because of that.

I squeezed Yaya's hand a little tighter. I would not fail her in the same way.

"What grade are you in?" I asked her.

"Third year of primary."

I kept asking her questions to the ice cream stand and while we sat on the town square's fountain rim.

I had ulterior motives other than cheering her up. I asked Yaya questions about her dad and his habits, her mom and her habits, and where they all lived. I told her that if she heard noises tonight, she had to stay in her room, and that me telling her to do that had to be our secret, just like the one we made earlier. She told me she could keep that secret because I bought her a treat.

I had decided that the split lip, the scratched nose, and the black eye were the last blows Yaya would receive from her father.

I sat perched on the roof of the building next to Yaya's apartment complex. I had a straight view of the doorway inside her home, from my window-viewing vantage. Inside the poorly lit house was quite a nice white couch, and a large dining table. Their family was upper-middle class, if I had to estimate.

Yaya was right when she told me about her mother. She wore her green hair up in pleats on her head. She was a squirrely woman, trying to keep everything in pristine condition. I could guess why.

I tugged the face covering up over my nose and tugged on my utility belt with my thumb to make sure it was tight.

I waited in the dark for their front door to crack and for Yaya's father to come home. When he finally did, I wasn't surprised at what he looked like. A short man with an even shorter temper, rounded with days wasted away at a desk job.

Sitting there watching him take out his anger on Yaya's mom was hard for me to do. I wanted to jump forward and grab his wrist before it landed another blow. I stopped myself. I needed there to be no witnesses, and it was highly unlikely that this would be the night his hand killed her. It was a calculated risk, and the odds were stacked in my favor if Yaya's mother were not a part of the equation. So, I waited, grinding my teeth until the woman stopped getting up.

The man waddled over to the couch, like he hadn't just beat his wife unconscious. *He favors his left side,* I noted.

I breathed out a puff of cold air into the late summer's humid night. This time, all of me, every inch, every nerve firing off, seemed to be made of a contained blizzard.

I heaved myself over the side of the roof and climbed down the drainage pipe. I was lucky the pipes of this old city were thick enough to hold my weight (most modern ones were not, as I had learned). Then I worked my way up the side of their building, peeking into the window when I made it into the top.

I could see more clearly now what he looked like. His face was clean shaven, with lines around the mouth that stretched downward like a bow. He had thick eyebrows that framed shadowed eyes and a hooked nose. He would have been attractive, in his younger years, which is probably why Yaya's mother had married him, why she may have been willing to overlook the warning signs.

I pulled a thin, metal pry bar from my belt and pushed it softly into the window's frame. I applied pressure to the back end and the window slid up, just enough for my fingers to grab hold underneath. I put the pry bar back on my belt and grabbed hold of the window with my right hand, careful to grasp tight to the pipe with my left.

I was thankful when I opened the window fully, for the temperate summer night, which would go unnoticed in the comfortably cool household. If it were warm inside and cold outside, I would have been caught in a moment. I was even more thankful for the silent city, which slept from dark until daybreak. It meant the only concern I needed to have as I slipped inside was falling silently on the floor.

I closed the window behind me.

My feet barely made a *pat pat* as they hit the beige tiles and the sound was muted by the television set the man had his eyes glued to. I untied the scarf from my waist and held it in both hands, pulling the fabric taut.

Everything happened so fast I couldn't really piece together how I felt or what I was thinking in those moments. I remembered wrapping the cloth around his face and forced it between his teeth, muffling his screams. I remember him thrashing, violently, back and forth, while I just pulled it tighter. I remember my eyes tearing up and wetness blooming on my face when the back of his skull hit my nose. I remember clocking him in the base of his skull, right where the brain stem would be.

When he lost consciousness, I was brought back to my body. I tied the string behind his head, firm enough that it would not slip, my fingers sure and unflinching. I walked around to his side of the couch and heaved him up so that I could drag him to the dining table, stepping around the woman's body he had left on the floor.

The carpet was soft underfoot as I propped the man up in a chair. I grabbed the rope I had attached to my belt and used it to tie his arms. The rope was scratchy and used, so I hoped, silently, that it would not hurt him.

But you don't actually care if it does, the voice in my head reminded me. *After all, you came here to hurt him, to teach him a lesson. Pain won't kill the man. It certainly didn't kill you.* I pulled the string a little tighter.

I patted his cheeks with my hands, trying to bring him back to consciousness. It took a few moments before he groaned and groggily blinked his eyes, his head bobbing back and forth. His eyebrows crossed in confusion before his brown eyes grew wide. His eyes looked the same as Yaya's. Different colors, but distinctly the same.

"I saw you beat your wife tonight."

I don't know if I was expecting a response to tumble out of him, a shake of the head or a sharp gasp. He was surprisingly calm, unmoving.

Maybe it wasn't calm. Some people froze with fear. I was well-acquainted with that freezing, and I still remembered the helplessness that

I felt when I had sat frozen, holding a hand over my mouth and nose, as I prayed to my god that she wouldn't let the man in white see me.

I took a deep breath and raised a hand to my cowl to make sure my hair was still tucked inside. I reached that hand down to tap the smallest finger on his left hand. "That won't happen again," I declared. "Think about this visit as incentive."

When I was younger, I watched a lot of mobster movies with my friends. My favorite part was always the shake down scenes, when the mob blackmails someone who crossed them. I think, when I took his little finger in my fist and snapped it quickly to the right, hearing the sound of the bones break, that must be how the mobsters felt: a strange combination of dangerous, appalled, and vulnerable.

He inhaled sharply and I had to look away from his face. I looked at his hand instead, saw the steady purple forming on his olive skin. It was a revolting color. He grappled with a scream and created a bastardized grunt.

"Did you know that it's more painful the further down a hand we go?" I asked.

He whined behind the cloth that I had shoved in his mouth. I looked back up, briefly, and watched tears stream down his cheeks, wetting that cloth, turning the beige a translucent sheer.

I tapped my index finger against the area of the hand closest to the wrist, over a bone I had come to learn was called the hamate. "This one hurts a lot," I murmured, tapping it. "It would make it hard to hurt your daughter and wife, for a while."

A pit in my stomach swelled.

I didn't know if the statement about his daughter and wife was to make myself feel better, to justify what I was doing.

Most people viewed morality as a sliding scale of greys. They say that life isn't black and white, that things are more complex than a binary solution. *I cheated because my spouse doesn't satisfy my emotional needs* or *I stole because I wanted to pay off my loans.* There's always some excuse that takes the guilt, the blame, the transgression away.

That's bullshit. Life *is* black and white. Humans just prefer to see it in shades of grey to make it easier to cope with regrettable actions. They can't handle the thought that they may have done something wrong.

I'd rather weigh my options knowing they are black and white, than delude myself into believing that they're grey to make myself feel better.

I could see clearly that the situation I was in was black and white: I had the power to stop this man from hurting his daughter and wife any more. Yes, it was evil to harm him, but it is far more evil to allow him to harm a child. In this circumstance, I was doing the right thing.

That did not mean I took delight in pulling the ice pick from my belt. The steel was cool and heavy in my hands with the weight of what I was about to do.

"If I were you," I advised, "I would bite down really hard on that cloth."

I slammed the blunt back of the ice pick down onto his hand and watched it force in the skin. I heard a crack as resistance gave away underneath the point of impact. A sharp and quick scream ripped through the man's throat. It hurt my ear; he didn't bite down on the cloth like I told him to.

He moaned and breathed heavily through his nose, like he was running a marathon. Snot ran down his upper lip.

It was hard to watch him, his head lolling back and forth, fighting off unconsciousness. He was brave enough to not shut down while the fear and pain made him lame. I could give him that acknowledgement; I would give him nothing else.

With shaky fingers, I grabbed a hold of his hair and yanked his head to the side. I pushed my face close to his ear, close enough I could feel his warmth on my cheek and his breath on my neck. I could smell the tang of sweat sticking to his skin. I used my free hand to tug down the mask I wore over my mouth. I wanted to speak without leaving room for misunderstanding.

"If you ever lay a hand on your wife or your child again, this moment will be a fond memory," I promised, low and steady. It wasn't a threat; it was a promise.

I felt him nod rapidly, felt him shake. He was right to fear it.

I pulled my mask up before pushing myself back and releasing his head.

As I watched his body go limp, I thought to myself how disgusting I was, looking at him like he was less than a dung beetle, when I was no different. We both used fear and intimidation to get what we wanted. I was just a little better it.

I scoffed, pulling myself away from that line of thought and walking myself over to the window. I took one last look at the scene, to stain into my memory what I had done, to live with the burden.

I fled. I ran through the darkened streets quietly as I could. My mind had gone blank, and my body was acting on instinct. That was a good sign. It was a sign that all of the sore mornings that my muscles burned and my skin ached were for moments like these.

It only took me ten minutes to get back to camp, where the night fire burned and Yonten quietly ate his meal. I stopped running far enough away that I thought he wouldn't be able to tell my footfalls. I stilled my breathing.

Yonten knew, he always knew, if things were abnormal. I felt a sinking feeling when I opened my mouth to talk and I felt the mask pulled up on the lower half of my face.

I had been careless. It did not matter how still my breath, nor how calm I looked. Yonten was the one who had given me the advice to always conceal my identity; he would know I had done something. I quickly pulled it down, hoping he had not yet seen it.

He stood from his cross-legged position and stalked over to me. His eyebrows were drawn together and his movements were more jagged than usual, like the flight path of a dragonfly instead of the flight path of a bee.

"Where were you?" he demanded, voice stifled with worry.

I froze. It was the first time his voice had displayed any consideration. He was good at concealing his voice, not his face.

I shook my head and shrugged my shoulders. "I was out." I didn't want to elaborate, hoping he would drop it. I was tired. All I really wanted was to roll up on my bag and drift off into the uneasy sleep I knew, dreaming of my family and the man in white.

As he came to stand in front of me, I saw the worry lines disappear to be replaced with a new look of shock. It was the kind of shock someone shows when a politician gets caught engaging in bribery.

"What is on your upper lip?" he asked, reaching his hand forward before stopping it in midair.

I touched my skin with my left fingers, feeling a sticky substance right below my nose. Parts of were dried and flaked and stuck under my nail. I looked down to confirm what I knew it was. I rub the crimson mess on my finger, staining my pale skin rouge. It must have happened when I was headbutted.

I looked up to Yonten's black eyes, piercing into me with a silent plea. I didn't know what he was pleading for.

I don't lie unless I need to, I reminded myself. It was a rule that I had set for myself when I was young. I would lie to people when my safety or the safety of others was in danger, never more. I could be a thief, I could be an assaulter, but I would never be a liar. I would not to lie to Yonten.

I tugged the mask down and took in a breath with an open mouth. "It's blood," I exhaled.

I saw his face contorted in agony, then in rage. I watched as his right hand drew up and came down, whip-like once more. I could have made a move to dodge it, for I knew it was coming.

Hitting a kid to punish them is why you got into this mess in the first place, I argued to myself. I didn't approve of Yonten hitting me, but I didn't move because this was probably the only punishment that I would get for what I did to that man.

I had spent a year being beaten up by Yonten, but the sting of his slap hurt more than any other injury he had given me. It made me want to hit him back, to show him that he wasn't my keeper. I wouldn't. I would never hit someone in rage. It wasn't who I was. And no matter how much it irked me to lay back and take a beating I didn't believe I deserved, I would not retaliate.

Instead, I let the face slip. I let the cool, rational, and calm face I had worked so hard to curate fall off of me like weights. My jaw clenched and my eyebrows drew together. I was angry. So angry that the blizzard inside me burned too cold for my flesh to contain.

I said nothing. I didn't need to. My face and my clenched fists said what I couldn't in words.

Yonten matched my rage, shaking with a fury like I'd never seen on him. His breathing was ragged and his body was stiff. His back was hunched, as if ready to pounce.

"You are a fool," he spat at me, his usually immobile scarred skin drawing up with the force of his movement. "You are a fool and a child and a bully."

I tried my best not to flinch at those. I would not allow myself to feel guilt over his projected shortcomings. He was the fool. He was the child. He was the bully that raised a hand against me without asking me the reason I had blood on my face.

I let him tear into me, a monsoon crashing against my wooden ship.

"How dare you take what I have taught you and use it to hurt someone else," Yonten continued, words like a pyre. "It is not your place to impose your will upon humans in the way you did. It was wrong."

Words ran across the tip of my tongue, ready to argue, ready to say that he was wrong, that didn't know what he was talking about. Because he didn't. He didn't see Yaya's eye so swollen that she couldn't even open it. He didn't feel a cut so deep in that girl's lip that it would be a permanent scar. He didn't hear her voice quiver with fear when she thought her father would punish her for telling someone about the abuse.

That little girl would now sleep safely for days, maybe weeks, perhaps two or three months because of what I had done. Yaya would not have to live in fear of her father's broken hand the way she had of his sturdy one. She would be safe for a time, and her father would think twice before raising a hand to her once more.

I didn't say any of this. I did not regret my actions. I did not need to justify them.

Yonten's hand reached out quickly and fisted in my shirt. I could have ducked, but I made no move against it. I felt the pull of fabric against my back as he brought me closer, I felt his warm breath on my face as he yelled, "You are not a god; do not play at being one!"

I do not need to be a god to play the role of one, I thought.

His hand shook from how tightly he held it. I brought my own hand up to cover his and pushed it away. I had taken the punishment my teacher had doled out. I refused to be pushed around any more.

I took a step back, maintaining my face once more.

"I'm spending the night somewhere else," I informed him, my voice was stone. "Calm yourself down while I'm gone."

Yonten looked at the ground, his breathing steadying and the tension in his shoulders beginning to fade. I think he didn't bring up my disrespectful tone because, deep down, he hated that he had put his hands on me. So he stood there, and took my disrespect, a slap in itself.

His face slipped away from the press of eyebrows, the contortion of lips, and faded into melancholy.

Yonten brought his right palm up to his forehead and pressed in with the heel of his hand. He ran that hand back, like he was pushing non-existent hair from his eyes. "I wish you would cast aside your hatred," he murmured. "People were not meant for such things."

I wasn't sure if I was supposed to hear him.

It is not hatred that burns inside me, old man, I thought bitterly.

I had told him so much about me, every little detail of my past, but he would never understand my desire to protect those without the means to fight their own battles, like I had *wished* someone had done for my tribe. *And I will never share that with you.*

I had no more energy. I was a husk, walking, watching, waiting, but never feeling. My anger had dried. I wondered briefly if that was a bad thing. Did it mean I had grown so tired of feeling that my default setting had become ennui?

I turned on my heels and looked into the dark of the forest. To a normal person, they would have lost their dark green hue and become blue or a black. I saw them green. I saw things as they were.

"I'll be at the clearing tomorrow," I breathed out. "For training." I heard the crunch of my feet on the ground before I felt myself moving. I didn't know where I was headed, I just knew I needed to go somewhere, to hit something.

I hit a tree until my knuckles were wet with the slick of my blood a year ago. Maybe another tree would like the taste of my blood.

Earlier in the day, I had wondered if I had become better.

I had. I was strong enough to protect people now.

September 23, 2725

Elonqua

I packed my bag for the first time in a while. I balled up the keepsakes at the bottom in a spare shirt, put my medical supplies and my snacks in after that, strapped my water skin on the side, and bundled the sleeping bag on top.

"Have you changed your mind?"

Yonten had asked me that question every morning, without fail, for over two years. He knew by now that I wouldn't change my mind, that I was too stubborn to answer him in the way he wanted me to. Maybe he asked out of habit.

I pushed myself up from the ground and slung the pack over my shoulder before I turned to look him. I tried to memorize the curves of his face: The dainty nose and the rounded jaw, the monolid black eyes and the thin lips lined with the marks of a smile, the burn scar running across his face in uneven ridges.

More than what he looked like, I was trying to memorize his presence. He felt like the eye of a storm. The last bit of calm I'd see for a while.

Yonten had told me never to show emotion, unless it was a smirk. A smirk, he had told me, was an indicator of confidence and control. I offered him one as I answered the same way I had answered every day, without fail, for over two years, "No, I haven't."

We both knew that was going to be my answer.

Seven months ago, I asked him why he had defected from the North Wind. Yonten had told me that after he joined, he met a woman who worked as a server in an area he worked. He told me he loved her after that first night. He told me that he met with her in secret and they had a child. He told me that both the wife and the child had been killed when they were discovered. He told me *that* was when he defected.

If they ever found him, they would kill him, too. When I asked him if that was why he lived in this cave, he had laughed and said that he preferred it to living in a place that wasn't his home.

I understood that. Some places are better to leave as memories.

He sighed, and I watched his shoulders sag and his hands grasp themselves tighter. I could read it in his posture that Yonten believed he had failed me because he had not been able to change my mind.

I wished I could tell him he didn't fail me, that I was never going to change my mind because I made a promise. I knew the words would be empty; we differed in opinion too much for them to mean anything to him.

He walked close to me, and placed a heavy hand on my right shoulder. I felt tension as he squeezed. "Don't let them know what you want," he advised me, for what may have been the last time. "They will use it against you."

I nodded. Keep desires locked deep inside. I could do that.

His eyes searched my face, looking for something. When his hand moved from my shoulder to my cheek, was it an indicator he found what he was looking for? I didn't like the weight of him touching me softly, looking at me in the way he did, with sorrow and preemptive longing. I don't know anyone who enjoyed goodbyes.

He took a deep breath, his chest expanding and falling in a fluid motion. Always whip-like. "You can find them at forty-three point one-eight-seven-two degrees North, four point eight-two-one-five degrees West. It looks like a mountain, you'll want the tallest one. Climb the trail marked with a skull and a landslide warning. It is meant to keep casual hikers away."

I felt the fluttering in my stomach once more. I was only a single sea away from where that place was located.

"I will write to you using the P.O. box, but only when I am away. I won't get caught. I'm smart," I promised.

"I know you are," he chuckled. His hand slipped away and he buried it in those stupid orange robes of his. "You're an adult, by all accounts now."

He was right. A few years was all it took to lose my baby fat and grow into an adult. I became limber and toned, with a decent amount of strength. That would be enough. I would make it be enough.

Yonten pulled me into a hug. Warmth pressed against my front and weight fell against my back. His squeeze was firm. It was the second time we had hugged.

I lifted my arms to hold him back, punctuating with a tight squeeze. He wasn't perfect; Yonten was flawed and made mistakes. But he forged me in flames and metal, and those flaws seemed negligible when compared to that.

When Yonten pulled back, his eyes were wet. He wouldn't let the tears fall, but I could see them for what they were.

"I'll be going now," I told him. "Thank you for everything."

"Pounce like a jackal," he advised. His hands shook beneath the colored fabric of his sleeves.

I nodded. After more than three years of waiting, I knew what I had to do.

I didn't look back as I left Yonten behind. My goals had not changed; dwelling on him, missing him, would not change my mind. I would board that ship, sail across the Ardïnatne Sea, and make my way to the mountain peak I had been aiming for.

It occurred to me when I boarded the ship, that I had never traveled across water before. The ground seemed to sink beneath my feet. I couldn't tell if I liked the feeling or disliked it, though I knew the sensation would only intensify as the ship reached open waters.

Many of the sailors, I noticed as I leaned against the railing in a spot away from the freighters, wore light colored garbs. They all had quite a bit of hair. Not a single man had shaved his beard and not a single woman had shaved her legs. The general impression I got was that the week-long voyage wouldn't afford a chance to wash, so upkeeping looks was a moot point.

The briny air chapped my lips when the cargo ship did set sail, hoisting up large white sheets that I'm sure were more for show than for anything else. The breeze felt nice on my skin and the salty air warmed my lungs. I could get used to a life like this. Maybe in another life I had been a sailor or, more dangerously, a pirate. Maybe I still could take that path.

No, I thought with a bitter taste coating my tongue, *I was always meant to be here and that's where I'll stay.* 'Here' to me, wasn't the ship. 'Here' to me, was wrist deep in the blood of the man in white.

"You 'ave a light?" a sailor with a heavy accent inquired as he came to perch beside me, leaning on his elbows against the ship railing. I couldn't fathom why he looked inward at the ship when he could look out at the light chartreuse waters that sparkled like innumerable gems.

I shook my head. "I don't smoke," I rasped, throat a little dry from the lack of water I had that day.

"Rats," he said. He had an accent that didn't pronounce his vowels completely, hopping gutturally from consonant to consonant. His skin was leathered from sun exposure, and his hands were rough and worn. I looked back to the sea.

"Why a cargo ship?" he asked.

I shrugged. I didn't feel like talking. He didn't seem to mind. "I got this lassie back home," he said. "I told 'er the sea was my lady, and that I can only ever love 'er on the side." He laughed at his words, though I didn't think they were particularly funny.

I decided then that I liked him. He was cheerful and friendly.

"I'm rethinking that now," he mumbled. Then, more clearly, "It used tah be a more pleasant trip. Ol' Ruttherford used tah play the fiddle tah pass the time. Now it's just quiet and dull."

I looked back to him. I had played the viola in my younger years. I wondered if the fiddle was anything similar. "What happened to him?" I asked.

"'E passed 'alf a year, nay, a little more than tha,' ago."

I looked back down to watch the cerulean waters lap up the sides of the ship, rocking us back and forth. My people pledged themselves to a sun god. I wondered if the sailors pledged themselves to a sea god. I wondered if Ruttherford prayed to that sea god before he died.

"My condolences."

The sailor hacked and spit out a wad of mucus over the railing and into the water. "Don't. 'E was quite the bastard, really. Only good thing about the fella was 'is music. 'Is fiddle still sits 'ere."

I thought to offer to try to play for him, before I realized that it wouldn't matter if I did. I was just a temporary fixture in their lives, a disposable lightbulb waiting to be changed out. If I played the fiddle for them, they would still make the return trip in the tuneless cacophony of the sea.

Besides, I hadn't played in years. I doubted very much I could successfully play a new instrument without practice, no matter how much of a prodigy I was in my younger years.

"You play the fiddle?" he asked, like he was reading my mind.

I took a breath of the air and closed my eyes, letting the sounds of the waves and the crying birds splash into my ears.

"No," I answered, "I have never played the fiddle."

The path was marked, just as Yonten had said it would be, marked with a *Danger* sign. I ignored the warning to keep away and continued up the mountainside, nervous for what I would meet.

My left hand twiddled with the twine necklace around my neck. It found the sharp edges of my mother's pendant and the smooth edges of the pierced coin the woman with a convex hooked nose had given me.

The lines in the trees started to break. They were oddly shaped trees, with red and white twisting trunks, leaves cast off from branches in every direction. They were stained red and orange, with muted imitations littering the floor. They crunched under my feet and offered a smell that was neither crisp nor fresh, but some distinctive musky cross of the two, carried on the stagnant breeze that rose hairs across my skin. The world was quiet on overcast days like this.

There was a cave ahead of me, with a little fire outside the lip center of it. A woman in grey and brown rags sat near the fire, warming her hands on its rolling heat. She was made to look like a beggar, but her forearms were too muscular to have belonged to a hermit and where her rags were tied at the waist, the trimmed outline her abdomen was visible.

The Gatekeeper, she would have been called.

I approached her slowly. She didn't show physical recognition in her movement to indicate she heard me approaching, but I felt her sideways glance sizing me up.

"Elonqua sent me," I told her. I reached into my shirt and pulled the twine from it. I heard the clinking of glass on metal as I jostled the string.

It was then that the woman looked to me. She had lines that ringed the corners of her face from frowning, but crow's feet forming at the corners of her eyes from laughter. Her eyes had no light inside them. What I was most drawn to was her jaw, rough and pulled back like a man's.

Her mud-colored eyes searched the pierced coin, watching it dangle in the wind. Without a word she nodded, and turned to look at the cave behind her, indicating with her head that this was not the end of my trip.

"Thank you."

I walked into the lip of the cave and crossed the boundary of its dark shadows, placing my feet down on the floor carefully, trying not to make sound. Dim sconces lit the walls, leading me deeper and deeper into the mountain.

The mountain's tunnel had walls of shadows, streaked with racing rivers of cream and honey. It smelled of water and musk, and I felt cold in the stagnant air. Despite my efforts to silence their cadence, my feet echoed across the unrelenting walls of the tunnel.

I didn't really know what I had been expecting. I certainly hadn't expected a giant sign that said, 'Secret Society meetings: Once every year, on the Autumnal Equinox!' On the other hand, I also was not expecting a clandestine abode, deep within a carved-out mountain in the abandoned wilds.

It had taken me over three years to get here, to finally be on the knife's edge of justice for the sixty-two of the thin pink scars that lined my left arm.

Farrah, are you cheering for me? She'd be old enough to do it now. She would have been three, had she not died that day. *I'm sorry the world mourned me instead of you, but I'll get you justice.*

A pit of tension began to build at the base of my skull, an arrow of nerves mingling with my spine. It was pride, I think, that I had finally made it here.

I imagined if the sun god were real, she would be proud of me, too. She would say to me, *Ainsley, you have only a little more to go. Don't disappoint me; don't disappoint them.*

But she did not exist. Gods are carried in belief. When the Psoe Nepsul died out, she died with them.

So, I would have to find pride in myself until I killed the man in white, until I killed everyone he had worked with. I would finish that mission. I would finish it or die trying. That had been my promise.

And I have never broken a promise.

A stream of noise, multiple overlapping breaths, trickled out of the circle of light in the distance. An end to the tunnel. The light was yellow and unnatural, meaning I was still within the mountain.

I noticed my palms were a little oily when I clenched my fists. I quickly wiped them on my shorts and took a deep breath to calm my nerves. I did a mental check to ensure I would enter that light, enter the area of chattering, as the person I wanted them to see me as: I squared my shoulders, widened my gait, steeled my face.

The room was a dodecagon, with arcs in each of the corners converging down toward a pointed, carved trumeau that hung just above a waist high goblet that contained dancing green fire. There were pointed pyres at each of the twelve corners, casting finnicky shadows up the walls with their green flames.

Copper sulfate, my mind recalled. *That is what turns flames green.*

A set of double doors on the opposite wall from the entrance, bearing the same carving of the bronze coin. A mountain with drifting clouds and a celestial body, though I still didn't know if it was the sun or moon, encased in twelve lines, like the markings of a clock.

As I made my way to a corner of the wall, I studied the others in the room. Varying backgrounds, varying looks, varying sizes. I tried to count. I got to thirty-two before I realized that I had forgotten which ones I had actually counted and which ones I hadn't. Humans looked remarkably similar, for all their differences.

I did try to look into the posture of the people who were there. Were they carrying themselves with confidence? Did they favor their left or their right foot? What marks marred their bodies and what would indicate how they got them? I ran through the lists in my head, eyes darting from person to person.

Yonten had told me only twelve would pass the trials.

I looked at a young woman, whose eyes looked through the floor she gazed at, and wondered what she had lost. We all came to Asgard for the same reason: We believed it was our only option. When it came down to it, would the loss of the woman with inked flowers across her jaw outweigh mine?

I heard the footsteps and swishing of clothes behind me, and stepped to the left. I didn't step far enough. I was jostled by the unrelenting motion of an outside force. I glanced at the figure that had done it, before stepping further to the left. I didn't need that to happen again.

The man who couldn't utter the phrase, 'Excuse me' was the size of a house. Easily six and a half feet of solid muscle, probably weighing in at two hundred and forty pounds. His nose was crooked, and his jaw favored the left side over the right. He looked like someone who did cage fighting, if the busted brow with a butterfly bandage was any indicator.

A surge of bitterness rose in my throat and I hoped the rude man wouldn't pass. Not because he could throw me against a wall with no effort, but because the concept of trying to play nice with someone like that made me want to hurl.

I backed myself up until I felt the cool press of stone wall against my back, bleeding cold in through my shirt. I closed my eyes and crossed my arms, relaxing against the wall. I took a deep breath. I crossed my left leg over my right and opened my eyes. The air in here felt humid. Too many bodies, too little space.

In the corner of my eye, I saw another figure enter the room. She was small and fairy-like, with dainty ankles and a gait like a gazelle.

I waited, counting. *One, two, three.* I wanted to see how high I could get. I knew that we had until sunset. I had shown up two hours before the sun would set, by the rough count of my hand. *Twenty-five, twenty-six, twenty-seven.*

More people trickled in as time progressed, though the space between them spread further and further the closer we got to the deadline. By the time I had reached the count of six thousand, eight hundred and forty-five, six more people had entered the room.

The last to enter the room was a man in green robes. He shut the door behind him with a clang and cleared his throat for attention. Not that he needed to, no one was talking, not even the people who clearly came together.

His voice was shaky when he spoke and I wondered why. He didn't look older than forty and he looked in top physical condition. He rubbed his jawline beneath his beard and had a blank expression on his face.

"Only a certain number of those coins you all bear have been released into the world, meaning the Elonquas have deemed you worthy to be here," he spoke, "You've all been vetted. However, this only entitles you to take the entry trial."

Instead of looking at the man with the pink beard and snub nose, I looked around at the people looking at him instead. I tried to find the others looking around as well. Those people would be the ones I saw again; I'd place money on that.

I heard the man take a few steps forward before he began to speak again. "In a few moments those doors will open, and there will be other members on the other side. Please, pick one and they will lead you to the location of the trial phase."

My stomach flipped.

"So, yeah," he mumbled under his breath, so quietly that I was certain only the people closest to him heard. "Best of luck."

My shoulders raised and fell with a deep breath.

The doors in the back opened, exposing two lines of people in green robes. Immediately, those closest to the door began to shove their way to the front. I stayed in place to watch the exodus.

When the crowd began to thin, I moved. I kept tight to the wall and tried to make myself as unnoticeable as possible.

I drew up to one of the people in green. She was just shorter than me and looked like she was ready to kill someone, with a face of stone and a stance of iron. "Looks like we're together for this thing," I said to her, trying to ease the tension.

She nodded, unrelenting. "Come with me," she deadpanned. She swiveled and stalked off, her stride wide and intentioned. She led me down corridor after corridor, so fast that I didn't have time to mentally catalog the details before I was turned down another, identical hallway.

Eventually she led me down a set of stone steps that spiraled into an unlit cave, with a sliver of a hole cut into one face of the rock. It smelled damp and dry simultaneously, and it stung my nose and made me want to sneeze. I scrunched up my face to hold it back.

"I'm leaving you here for some time. You will receive water once daily and you will not receive any food," she informed.

I glanced around the area. It wasn't a cell, per say, because there were no bars. But it was a prison, complete with a wooden door that locked at the top of the stairs, and chains in the wall that would bind me to one area.

Before the war, they had used places like this to get information. I never really thought too much on torture; the third war had made it practically obsolete.

Only now, psychological torture would be used to ask me: How much can you take before you snap?

"We will not tell you when you have passed," she told me. Her bow lips did not twitch, her arched brows did not raise. Despite this, I knew she was lying. I don't know how I knew she was lying, and it wasn't yet a perfected skill, but I had gotten better at calling bullshit for what it was in my four years in the real world.

I smirked and held out my two wrists to her, exposing the tender flesh on the inside. "Have at it," I said, tasting the cold air of the ice inside me, rolling off my tongue like liquid nitrogen. I squinted at her in mock amusement, "I can't wait to lose a few pounds."

If the gut intuition I got wasn't enough to tell me she didn't think I was funny, the too rough clasping of cold metal on my wrists was.

"The rules are simple," she recited, "be one of the final twelve to withdraw."

Tension bled into my trapezoids, tugging at the muscles beneath my skin. It would leave me sore afterward. Sore in a way that only sleep could bring relief to. My discomfort didn't matter. I would deal with anything they threw at me; I had made up my mind about that long ago.

The cold of the room bit through my clothing and a shiver trailed across my spine, nipping and biting at me and warning me that it wouldn't be easy, no matter what I had decided on.

The girl came to stand in front of me. The green robes that she wore were billowy. They reminded me of the robes that Yonten wore. I thought, briefly, how different they were from the commonplace garb of the rest of the world. They were out of place and ancient and had spirals of gold designs that traced their edges and the outline of the spine on the back.

Modern clothes usually had loose fitting pants with many pockets and a many belts to hang utilities from. Shirts were usually in layers. An undershirt that was thin and clung to the body, and a looser shirt over that. Modern clothes were always very plain and only had symbols during certain ceremonies, like a birth or a marriage.

She cleared her throat. She moved like an otter, slick and quick, when she brought her hand to cover her mouth. She spoke like an eel, "Let us know when you fail. We will hear." *When*, she had said.

I nodded and flashed her a crooked smile. "See you on the other side," I said, knowing it would bite into her, irritate her in a way only cockiness could.

I watched her leave, her long brown hair fanning out behind her like a sheet as she walked briskly away.

I tugged on the chains a little. They were unrelenting. At least, I thought, I did not have to stand. They were loose enough that I could sit on the bench of cave wall behind me.

I wasn't a moron. I knew that isolation was never good for the human mind. If I were to be chained in a dark area for a long time, I would need mental fortitude.

It will not be that bad, I deluded myself, *there are much worse things than being alone.*

I lowered myself to the stone bench, felt the slightly damp surface of the hard earth, and tipped my head back to try to make out the shapes on the ceiling.

The lamp of the lone light would have been too dim for a normal human to see much from. It would have only been there to give them something to focus on. For me, with my tribe's genetic mutation, the light clearly illuminated the room, and I could see all of the arcs of black rock that formed the canyons of the ceiling.

I took a deep breath and started counting.

September 30, 2725–October 11, 2725

Ma'at

The waiting was the worst part: Endless moments of nothingness stretched infinitely before me, like some twisted purgatory.

Sweat spilled from the tip of my nose, falling against the dark floor that made up the fortress. It was dark inside the little cell, only a dimly lit lantern on the other side of the cell, just out of reach, a flickering flame that leapt across the jagged walls. The cuffs rubbed red divots into my wrists, bound by unrelenting metal.

When kept in darkness like this, the human sleep cycle changes. It goes from eight hours of sleep for every sixteen spent awake to twelve hours of sleep for every thirty-six awake. After a few hours with no external stimuli, humans get restless and emotional. Then we hallucinate. After thirty days, we will have trouble reintegrating normally to society.

I had no idea how much time had passed since the girl left me here.

I had passed the restless stage already. I had decided it best to talk to myself, meaningful ramblings to keep my mind sharp. I talked to my brother, my mother, my father. I told them my favorite memories that we shared and I told them who I had become in the past few years. I had become a polyglot, a survivalist, and a tracker. I had learned to fight tactfully and strategize flawlessly. I became who I needed to be.

I imagined what they would say to me. My father would ask me what it would cost me.

In my mind, I would hallucinate. I hallucinated running out into the open, counting bodies in my head until I found the two I was looking for. In my mind, I could see Dad who was curled protectively around Jace, turned black and mottled in the attempt he had made to protect my little brother from whatever it was that burned them. It hadn't worked. In life he had looked different than us, with his brown hair and his brown eyes and his brown skin; he looked the same as all the others when his body was burnt to a crisp. I had unclasped the scorched metal watch from his wrist and clicked it shut around my own.

Then, in real time, I would reply, "There is no price that can be demanded I am not willing to pay."

My mother would weep and tell me I am wasting my life.

Again, I would hallucinate. I hallucinated stumbling out from behind the barrel my mom had tucked me behind after the pair had left. I had run up the basement stairs to find my mom covered in blood on our kitchen floor. Her arms were twisted in the wrong places, purple and scrapped. Half of her head had been smashed in, and chunks of mottled red spilled out in a sickening half halo about that side of her face. Organs spilled from her middle, staining the yellow robe she had been wearing. I had peeled the necklace off of her throat and tied it around my own.

I would argue, "I found purpose in a meaningless existence."

My brother would ask me if I were happy.

I hallucinated extracting Jace's tiny body from my dad's arms, only the brass band that matched my own making him identifiable, watching his skin crumble to black ash against mine. I could smell the distinctive smell of burnt flesh as I whispered in my brother's ear, "You're fifty-three." I had carried him with me while I finished counting the other bodies, hoping he would gasp, inhale, and I would rush him to the hospital, hoping he was alive and that I wasn't alone. I hadn't let Jace out of my sight the whole two weeks that it took me to bury my tribe. He never inhaled.

"I will be."

I didn't really experience emotional instability like others may have. I think that was because I only had one true emotion left in me, one that I concealed, but never forgot.

My rage wasn't a fire, burning unchecked to destroy my life as it expanded. My rage was a frost, slowly creeping into the areas of my life I needed it to, retracting as I willed it. My rage was not a puppet master that could use me; I had no problems maintaining it during my isolation.

I *did* hallucinate.

At first, I was speaking both the parts of my conversations. Then I noticed I was only speaking for myself. I could hear, in their voices, the words my family spoke, as if they were actually with me, standing just out of my view. It was then that I knew I could no longer talk to them if I wanted to keep my mind stable.

I started to solve mathematical equations. "If the wind current is twelve miles per hour southbound and I am firing an arrow with a weight of half a pound downward at a forty-five-degree angle, how much distance will I have to adjust my aim to if I am west of my target?"

I kept cycling back to diseases I had come across and tried to relay them to the symptoms they would display. "Pain in the abdomen or muscles, coupled with fainting, fatigue, low blood pressure, sweating, nausea or vomiting, darkening of the skin, and excess urination is a sign of Addison's disease, which is a result of adrenal insufficiencies."

I recited words from books I had read, things I could remember. "In all the realities we could have shared, I was fated to know you as I do now, in the world where we must kill one another." Sometimes I could remember the titles of the books. Other times I didn't remember the titles, just the words, emerging from a blurred print of my memory.

It was easier for me to use my brain like this than it was for me to have conversations with my dead family, but my mind often drifted.

The chilling dripping sounds were once again brought to my immediate attention. My mind noted them by count... *one... two... three... four... five... six... seven... eight... nine... ten... eleven... twelve...* and then the counting would start over, another set of twelve, an endless cycle, as everything was. It helped to think in terms of twelve because it was a reminder that I only had to be the twelfth contender to pass the exam.

My teacher came into my mind then, a vivid memory of Yonten knocking me to the ground unrelentingly. *"Get up,"* the man would spit at me. The man, hard as steel and the best fighter in the world, would demand more of me than I was capable of. *"You can bear any pain for a small amount of time, you can fight for any small amount of time. Then bear it again."*

The tiredness had sunk deeper and deeper, past layers of muscle, sinew, and bone. The cloth touching my too hot skin brought the overwhelming desire to sleep.

I'll bear it, became my mantra. It allowed the anger to spread over my heart and mind, hardening me against the discomfort. *I'll bear it because now is too early to fail.*

The ice whispered haunting nothings as it encroached further into me. Promises of justice, swift and immediate, filled my mind. *You know what is demanded of you,* the ice whispered to me, showing faceless men and women in its glassy sheen. The ice grew stronger, thicker, more brazen. *You must end them the way they ended your kind.*

"I will."

Footsteps in the corridor, descending the spiral stairs. Stairs of stone, stairs which helped to create and echo the persistent drips. The sounds halted. No more footsteps, no more drips. It was silent, but for the pulsing of my heartbeat that thrummed under my flesh.

"You are not as worthless as I had thought," an eel-like voice pierced through the darkness.

I kept my head down. For some reason, I thought seeing someone, even someone like her, would make being alone again far worse.

"You are one of the top twelve; congratulations. Now you only remain to prove yourself. Resign at any time; we will hear you."

I made it.

I didn't move, did not allow my face to indicate my relief. I could do better. I could *be* better.

"Do not disappoint, my friend." With that, her footsteps receded away, leaving me once more to the solitude of the cell.

I turned my gaze up, to peer at the sliver of light that the lantern gave off.

I knew it was pride and pride alone that made my lips pressed tight together. I looked back to the stone floor. My eyes fluttered shut and a steady breath left my opened mouth and shaky lips.

Waiting was the worst part.

One... two... three... four... five... six... seven... eight... nine... ten... eleven... twelve...

I gave up three sleep cycles and four days later when I dry heaved my stomach acid out of my body. With a heavy heart, I spoke to the empty and dark cell, "I concede."

For a while, I was left there, the smell of my own bile rising from the ground to fill my nose with an acidity that made my lips purse in disgust. I felt weak, inside and out. My body could take almost no more and my mind was so very tired of itself.

This time, there were no warning footsteps to alert me of the woman's presence. "You lasted longer than many," the same empty voice told me. She said nothing else, but got to work on the cuffs that encircled my hands. I heard the snapping of metal and felt the sting of it as it moved across my bloody wrists.

I moved to hold my hands gingerly and survey the damage. They were shaky. I had low blood sugar and my body was going into starvation mode, resulting in cramps along my legs and back. I noticed my arms looked smaller, my stomach, too. I would need something to eat before I could clean myself off.

"How long?" I asked her, my throat scratchy and sore. I finally looked to her, searching her doe eyes for any judgement, any sign that I wasn't a failure.

"Sixteen days, five hours, forty-two minutes, and three seconds," she said. I had not been informed when the others dropped out, but sixteen days seemed like a lot.

She turned swiftly and started for the stairs. I followed her wordlessly. She moved silently as an unwanted child, ever present as a member of the background. I wondered if she was happy here.

The drag of my legs up the spiraled stairs was torture and my muscles ached in retaliation.

The hallways she took me through were dark and dim, lit only by sconces and lanterns. It was like looking through into the past, a cold and unrelenting relic that had been born of determination before me and would last long after me. Our feet echoed softly through the stone walls and there was no exit to be seen, just endless, unfeeling stone corridors.

I could make out her image now, green robes lined with silver and long brown hair that brushed her waist.

She stopped suddenly and fully, and in my exhausted state, I almost ran into her. She pushed a wooden door open. It was a small room that looked much like an inn, with a bed, a table, a tub, and a chest. My pack was propped up against one of the bedposts. Laying on the bed was a set of green robes that matched the ones she wore, a silent statement of my inclusion. She only gestured with her hand inward.

"Bathe, rest, change, and eat. Your belongings are in the chest. I will collect you soon," she spoke, leaving no room for argument.

I entered the room and the door was closed behind me with a clink. Immediately, I stripped, shedding the summer cloth that I wore. I had bartered for the light blue overshirt, the white tank top, and the cargo shorts. The worn red shoes I had bought. Shoes were too expensive now to trade labor for. It was with great sadness I handed over the coin for it, the last of the denarii I had stolen from the tribe's houses, but the soles had served me well.

The clothes were damp with my sweat. I bet they smelled. No showering for a little over two weeks was not a recipe for a decent scent.

I slipped into the hot water in the basin, feeling the tension leak from my body. I couldn't remember the last time I used a tub instead of a secluded stream.

I grabbed my clothes from the floor and held them under the same water. There was soap. I used it to scrub my body and my clothes. Despite the fact that I would now be provided for, with silk green robes that fit properly, I didn't want to leave these to be thrown away. I had worked hard for them, and they had value to me for the remainder of the season, when I would trade them for a set of slightly warmer clothes.

Once I was sufficiently impressed at the squeaking feel of my skin, I got out of the bath and used the towel to dry off. I hung my clothes on the rack chest the towel had lain on.

There was a small vanity in the room; they wanted us to look nice. I caught a glimpse of myself in the mirror. My cheeks looked sallow and my muscles had much less tone than when I had first come. Starvation did a number on me. I wouldn't be at full strength for a while.

That wasn't the part of myself I was fixating on. I was fixating on the fact that I had grown to be a perfect combination of my mother and my father in features. I even looked like they did now: dead. I was a ghost walking, all white, with piercing eyes of gold hellfire. I recoiled into myself and turned sharply away from the mirror. There was a reason mankind was blessed to never see themselves.

You were dead long before today, I was reminded. *Don't be upset that you now look the part.*

I dressed quickly into the robes. They didn't hurt the skin that had been made raw around my wrists. I ate quickly, too, a small amount so as to not make myself sick. I grabbed my toothbrush and gave my mouth a good scrub. I crawled atop the bed in the room, it was hard and uncomfortable.

The room was too bright with flames; I knew I wouldn't actually sleep well. Nevertheless, I whispered, "Farrah" to the empty room as my eyelids fell heavy against my cheeks and I curled in on myself, praying for some kind of reprieve.

The room had no clocks, no windows, and no way to leave, other than the door that had been locked when I first entered. I was effectively a prisoner for another day and a half.

I didn't get much sleep for the duration of my stay. It wasn't the bright lighting of the room that made sleeping hard, it was the ringing.

I had maybe three hours of rest before it pierced through the veil of unconsciousness, rousing me. It was faint enough that it didn't hurt, but loud enough that I couldn't block it out. The message was clear: I wouldn't rest until the trials were finished.

The thought invaded my mind that I must have been one of the first to give up, if the trials were still ongoing.

Disgruntled with the state of affairs I found myself in, I ate some more. I read the books I had stolen and I practiced the forms they showed. I put my clothes into my bag, then pulled everything from the bag out and reorganized it because it was too chaotic now. I used the scissors placed on the vanity to hack off my hair until it was at a reasonable length.

I was immensely relieved when the eel-tongued girl came to grab me two days later.

I heard the churning of the lock and my eyes jolted open. The door pushed inward slowly.

She smiled at me, but it never reached her eyes. I was one of many she had seen before and would probably see again.

"The trials have ended, my friend."

I nodded. It felt like a solemn moment when I stood, when I grabbed my bag, when I followed her without a word. It felt solemn in a way that left me knowing this was one of the memories I would be able to recall as vividly as the day it happened.

The walls were the same as they were when I last saw the outside of the room: cold and unforgiving. I tried to mentally picture a map in my head as we walked counting paces. Twenty-two steps, left. Thirteen steps, right. Thirteen again, right again. I lost count by the time we made it to the two large double doors.

They were tall, shaped like two halves of a flower petal. They were made of wood, stained red, not natural. And they had ornate arcs of silver etching in an ivy pattern around the rims and from the bottom, holding a bronze circle in the middle, twelve marks around it in a ring. The bronze hoop was split in the middle where the door was, but the crack was so faint that if I squinted it looked to be one unit.

The girl stood off to the side. I looked to her. She nodded toward the door. \

"What shall I call you?" I had never asked her name. Most likely because she did not matter to me.

"Kubaba, my friend." She was curt in her words, straight to the point, and did not ask my name in return. It seemed I did not matter to her either.

I took a deep breath and let my shoulders sag. I pressed my lips together and the pushed the doors open quickly.

There was a grand hall, lit by five blazers, set up two to the left of the door and two to the right. The largest of the five sat at the back of the room, up a set of steps. The room was the shape of a dodecagon, coming up in a domed structure. The corners of the room had pillars that stretched decoratively to arch inward toward the center, just like the room I had entered before the trials.

There were twelve figures in the room, all wearing scarlet robes with silver finish. *They match the door* I thought. The carpet, too, was a red and silver bridge, meant to lead me across the stone floor.

I took a hesitant step forward, then another, feeling trapped within my own skin.

The twelve spoke as one, as if rehearsed a thousand times. "Do you wish to wash off the past? To work for just cause of order?"

Order was not the only just cause to pursue.

My throat was dry, and when I swallowed, my esophagus clenched around nothing. I was aware of every inch of myself, felt the blood in my veins and the sinews of my ligaments where they rest.

"I wish to join the North Wind," I answered around their question. My voice was steel, cold and unrelenting

"Come forth."

Just as the twelve Gods presided over Olympus, the twelve leaders presided over this room.

I walked to them, keeping my eyes and chin up. I stopped just ahead of them. My gut instinct told me to kneel and I did, falling to the red and gold carpet softly. My gut intuition also told me to drop my gaze. I did not, I stared defiantly at their white masks, the last vestiges of my pride refusing to give them an indicator of submission.

"You may never reveal your past self to another living person. You shed who you were tonight," they state. "These are the terms."

I didn't have a choice, not really, not when this was the way to my salvation. "I am aware of the terms." I was careful not to say I accepted the terms.

One of the twelve stepped forward, the one to the immediate right of the flame. The figures in stood in front of me, tall and surreal. I faced its mask; crimson veins traced through the shapeless white. This time, the person spoke alone. "We let you keep one reminder. What did you want most of all before today?"

I did not need time to search for my desires. "Justice." I would get justice for Farrah, who had taken my place on the death records; for my tribe, who were now an extinct race; and for my family, who I was not competent enough to save.

Another stepped forward, to the left of the flame. "Not vengeance?" it asked.

I took a sharp breath in, deliberating my words carefully. "Justice comes in many forms," I decided on. I was not naive enough to confuse the pair. Justice is what happens when retribution befalls those to balance the world. Vengeance goes beyond retribution. What I craved was justice, I was certain of it. To me, an eye for an eye was a proper system. It was the system I had grown up with, and a system that worked.

And, by the blood in my veins, I would get my family justice.

Still, the self-conscious need to hide the bandages on my left arm, hide my past and my future, filled my stomach, writhing like a serpent. I refrained from moving; motion would only draw attention to the arm.

"You shall be Ma'at, Egyptian God of Justice. It will be the only piece of your identity you keep." The first turned away at those words, returning to its position at the right of the blaze.

You are wrong, I thought. I made no vows to them yet; I was careful. Therefore, I was only honor-bound to one promise: The one I made at my brother's grave.

"You may choose where you will be marked." *Branded,* they meant.

I had never thought about marking myself more than the scars I already had. But really, what was one more voluntary scar on my body? It would heal.

"My right shoulder blade, please." My back was fairly easy to cover.

The second to emerge grabbed a prong from within the pit, glowing a blinding orange. I could make out the shape that was on the door on the branding iron: A circle with twelve equidistant notches reaching inward.

Two more members, from the ends of the chain, walked toward me. They grabbed my arms gently, but their hands were unrelenting. Some people in the past must have struggled.

I made a silent vow to not make them restrain me; I could restrain myself.

The second walked around to my back and tugged the corner of the silk robe off of my shoulder, exposing my skin to the cold air that only the inside of a mountain could have. "Ma'at of Justice," it proclaimed, "you are henceforth North Wind."

At first, I could feel all of the twelve prongs in the hoop as it pressed into my flesh, ripping and rebinding the skin to itself permanently. I smelled the burned scent of skin before the pain began to spread, blistering my skin and severing my nerves. My eyes watered, and begged to be shut tightly, as if shutting them could keep the pain of hot metal away; I refused to let them close completely.

I clenched my jaw and my vision went red. I refused to move, to make noise, to be seen as weak. I sat there, counting the seconds until the brand was taken off of me. I inhaled sharply, unaware I had been holding my breath before my lungs relieved themselves.

Those around me resumed their positions in the line of twelve. I pushed myself to my feet, careful not to shake, not to stagger.

The room seemed darker now. I looked over my shoulder. The four fires behind me had gone out.

When I looked back to the twelve, they stood with their palms extended in front of them, as if holding an invisible tray for me to take. "Welcome," they said in unison once more. They pulled their right hands to gesture to the left of me, slow and steady. I turned my head to follow.

A small door, made of stone like the walls, was visible, a barely there outline, only now visible because of the torches by its sides that seemed to have lit themselves. I noticed there were others like it, all lining the sides of the room, faintly. I went toward it.

I pushed inward and took a deep breath. I was beginning to tire of all these rooms with no windows.

It led me down a hallway, dark but for the soft orange glow of metal lanterns overhead. There was only one door in the hallway, at the other end.

When I entered the door at the end of the tunnel, there were already ten others wearing the same green robes as me in the room. I was eleventh to enter.

I couldn't articulate why I knew that I had lasted longer than these ten individuals, but it was apparent in an instant, in how they looked at one another, in how they looked at me.

I grimaced to myself. *Only one person beat me?* How was the difference between that person and me so large when it the trial got exponentially harder? Just what kind of a God came in first?

The room was quiet and tense. Many of those who sat near each other did not carry out even a whisper of communication.

Many looked around my age, two looked much younger, three older.

I joined them against the wall, crossing my ankles. My eyes stayed pinned to the door I had come through, not wanting to miss the face of the person who came out on top of a trial that got exponentially harder as time progressed.

Two minutes passed before the door creaked open. For some reason, I expected a real deity to befall my sight, but the champion seemed a normal man, made of flesh and bone and blood. He looked older than me, but that was the only difference I could ascertain. Just a man, a mortal.

A man entered behind the first. This one was middle aged and had the distinctive appearance of being ill-kept. He had a scruffy peppered beard lining his jaw and neck and his hair dangled around him in unbrushed wads. His skin-tight black suit looked stiff, like some substance had dried on it before he had the chance to wash it.

"I'm Pluto, I'll be something of counsellor for you all, but don't tell me about your feelings because I don't care," the man in black's voice was scratchy and low. I liked it, I decided, and I liked him for his brutal honesty.

Pluto pulled a hand up to scratch at his scruffy face. "My humor is wasted on you," he mumbled. Then, louder, he announced, "You all have one week to recover. Familiarize yourselves with our property and resources and with each other."

When Pluto took a few steps forward, there was a slight hesitation in his right foot, as if an injury had left him disabled. His black eyes flashed in when he crossed the light of the fire that crackled in the corner of the room.

"This is the common area, where you will dine and gather." He pointed to the left. "Bathrooms." To the right. "Bedrooms."

Pluto paused, seemingly searching his mind for something beyond his reach. Graphite eyes darted from left to right, scanning memory stores. "That's all." He must have remembered nothing. Pluto turned and left the room without acknowledgement we had heard him.

At once, everyone surged up and toward the rooms. I couldn't blame them. Everyone here had to be exhausted. We had spent days in our own personal little hells, nothing but our minds to keep us company. That wasn't exactly a leisurely vacation.

I stayed propped against the wall instead, taking in the fine details of my location. It looked almost like a lodge, in a way, neat and homey at once.

I was closest to the living area, complete one large sofa, and three arm chairs, all arranged in a semicircle around a coffee table (the lacquer of which was chipped, revealing multiple shades of oak), facing toward a grand fire. The fire was a nice, heartwarming touch to the otherwise foreboding stone building, I thought.

There was a nice collection of books framing the northern and southern doors that lead into the room, set into the walls, just so. On the south side, further from me, was the dining table and twelve chairs, with gold plates on the backs.

I smiled to myself. I may actually enjoy my time here... if I didn't feel like I was being watched.

I shifted my weight and picked myself up from the wall, making my way over to the northside shelf closest to me, looking over the brown leather coverings and their written titles.

The collection was quite diverse. Not only were there books in a multitude of dead languages, but the North Wind kept a variety of subjects in their records. One was an archive on twenty-first century warfare, another a compendium of poisonous plants found in the humid tropics of Perajath.

My eyes kept skimming until I found one that piqued my interest: A book on how to track people using their location pings.

I was careful and light with my fingers when I tugged the book from its place. It was small and the pages were crisp in my grasp. I took it with me to the brown armchair, the one closest to the fire, and sat down, leaving my pack by my feet.

I didn't get far into reading before I felt a presence at my shoulder.

"Can I help you?" I asked, without looking up from my page.

A silky chuckle met my ears. "Quite perceptive of you to notice me." He came and sat down on the coffee table in front of me. I still didn't look up from my page, but I could tell from the cockiness of the tone who it was. "I notice you didn't go to the rooms like the rest of us."

I lifted my head slightly to meet his gaze. Never in my life have I been so compelled to assault someone. He had a crooked smile on his Octavian lips, knowing, as if he had bested me by observing my actions.

"I noticed that you pretended to go to the rooms and waited in the archway to watch me leaf through the collection," I retorted with a quirk of my left brow. I had felt a gaze on me, it was a calculated risk to assume it was his.

The cocky demeanor he held when he first spoke at me disappeared almost instantly, replaced by a light and cheerful one. It was as if he had been trying to intimidate me, and when he realized it wouldn't work, switched his tune.

"Was I that obvious?" he asked in that falsified tone. "Sorry, I guess I just wondered why you didn't go meet your roomies." I was always good with probability.

He extended a hand. It bore a nearly black metal ring with a tropical blue hued stone inlaid in the center.

I studied his face, looking at the curves for deception. I saw nothing. He was an incredible liar, and an even better actor. His thick brows were straight and his almond eyes were crinkled at just the right angle. Even the smile lines visible around his mouth had just enough asymmetry not to look forced.

I extended my own to grab his. "They gave me the name Ma'at," I stated firmly, fitting easily into the mold that had been created for me.

"Oh, it looks like we're bunk mates, then," he said with a lilt in his voice as he shook our clasped hands. He was trying to hide it, but he already noticed his room was missing one person. What did he gain from hiding his intelligence? "I'm the top, though."

My stomach churned in unease. I didn't trust this one, my instincts telling me to be wary.

"I'm Iktomi now. The other two with us are Sancus and Kali. They're still settling in." He dropped my hand. It warmed in the absence of his cold skin.

I looked him up and down. I didn't really know how to respond to that information because I didn't actually care who the others were or what they were doing. "I see," I settled on.

Iktomi smiled crookedly once more, though it wasn't as cocky as last time. This time, I didn't feel the surge of immense annoyance it gave me last time. "Why that one?" he asked, nodding his head toward the book.

The change of conversation suited me more. I shrugged before letting my head lull back to the paper pages, hoping he picked up my hint to leave me be.

"I see," Iktomi mumbled.

From my peripheral vision, I saw him leave the table. I looked up once more when he returned a short moment later.

He shrugged and gave a third smile, one that didn't give me the sensation of a spider crawling up my neck. "Good idea." He held a book in his left hand, the one without the ring. He sat in the armchair next to mine and began reading.

We read late into the night, without another word spoken between us. The noise from the rooms became quiet after a while, everyone succumbing to their own exhaustion from our trials.

My eyelids felt heavy, too, the first time in nearly three weeks that sleep had come without struggle.

"Farrah," I whispered to myself, knowing that I wouldn't be able to make it to bed that night.

I pulled my legs up to my body and leaned my head against the soft, worn leather of the chair, content to let the fire's heat pull me into unconsciousness. I inhaled the scent of wood varnish and moist stone,

"Ma'at?" Iktomi's silent whisper came.

"Yes?"

There was silence for a moment. I thought that he had fallen asleep, too. "Would you like to be friends?"

My breath caught in my lungs. Iktomi had immediately rubbed me wrong, had ground my gears so thoroughly they became a fine powder. Additionally, he barely seemed fatigued from the trial.

But when he asked that question, his voice sounded so meek and unsure that I had no other choice than to believe that was what he truly wanted.

It was stupid of him to want to make friends here. Childish. Impractical.

"Yeah," I replied. "I'd like that."

January 1, 2727

Abbadon

She was a retired police sketch artist. I told her I wanted a picture of someone from my past. I said I could describe him. She said it would cost me twenty denarii. I paid.

He had blond hair, like a faded lemon. It went past his shoulders, down to his collarbone. He had the kind of neck that ran into his face. It was a diamond shaped face, with a pronounced jaw. His lips were downward turned and he always had a little stubble above them. His nose was bulbous, crooked near the top. His eyes were... cold, murderous...? Droopy, but lively. He had a large forehead, his hair slicked back into a low pony tail. He looked like he was a guitar player in a band that plays in pubs.

After a few clarifying questions, she drew him perfectly. An exact replica to the memory in my head. She asked me if I were certain this was what he looked like, told me if it wasn't, she would fix it. I told her it was him.

I've only had three dreams since I left home. They recurred without any regularity. One, the one that I've had the most, is of the man in white. I hadn't forgotten his face.

Seeing that man, my vision going crimson when I looked at his white suit and his slicked back lemon yellow hair, made my stomach coil and my breath come in quick hot shallow puffs. Staring at the man in white again, after dreaming about him all those years, filled me with the same crest of fear I had felt on the day I had first seen him.

It was naive of me to ever have believed I could train fear out of myself. I had deluded myself into thinking I was stronger than my part. I was not. But even when fear left me tensed, jaw clenched, pupils dilated, I could push past all of that. I could *move.* That was enough.

To my dismay, Abbadon was actually a decent person. He spent one day a week at the hospital, reading to the sick kids for no less than ten hours. On his way home from his part time work at a local coffee shop, he would stop by a flower stand, buy the brightest colored bouquet they had and proceeded to hand it to the first elderly person he came across. On Thursday mornings, he would take an hour-long stroll, stop at a park bench, and throw out bird seed.

I couldn't tell if this was retirement for him or if he was just waiting for another request before he shed the humble bachelor routine and donned the red mask of an assassin once more.

Did he dream of me the way I dreamed of him?

My mind told me *No, he never saw you. That's why you're alive.*

Abbadon traveled regularly. He stayed, always, at a small inn in in the small town he happened to be visiting that Saturday night. I knew this because I had checked his bank records. This week, he had booked a room in a place called The Little Bird in a town nestled between two mountains. I paid in all cash for a room in the bed and breakfast across town.

Yet, I took my food and drink in the same dining area as he did, the small restaurant on the first floor of The Little Bird.

I was careful with my gaze, kept it short and drifting, for Abbadon should have been very aware of someone looking at him, given his profession. It was harder to track his movements like that.

Waiting for him to tire himself out and retreat to his room had my stomach twisting itself into wires, endlessly sparking and tangling in heated coils. I remembered that same feeling from the time I first saw the man in white, being completely at the mercy of it.

I had staved off my obligations for years; it was time to ensure no more children felt that way.

I guess I wasn't a child any more. No, I was nineteen now. That was plenty old to take on the responsibility I had staved off for years.

After what seemed like ages, Abbadon wiped the corner of his mouth with the tip of the violet table napkin and stood. He walked gracefully across the hall, heading for the arch in the back that led up to the rooms. It was decorated with floral accents, etched into the wood with a careful hand.

For a moment, I hesitated to stand. Was there any possibility I had the wrong man?

No. There was no way. I dreamt of his face so much. I had stained his likeness into my memory. I knew his face better than my own. So how could the man who did such horrendous things fill the role of friendly neighbor so spectacularly? How many people can one person be?

I pushed myself up from the bar and headed toward the arch Abbadon had gone through. I felt like my feet were shaking the ground, feeling the hollow feeling surge up through my legs. I tried to make my feet fall lighter.

I peeked my head in only slightly, enough to see him get off on the second floor instead of the third. I followed, up the creaking wooden steps, listening to where his footsteps fell above me. He stopped mid-way through. Fifth support pillar. Then the noises disappeared. He had gone into a room.

There were two possibilities. Left or right.

So, of course, the next logical step was to climb up to the third floor and walk to the fire escape at the end of the hall. One, two, three, four, five, six, seven, eight, nine, ten, eleven, twelve, thirteen paces from the fifth pillar. Before I stepped out into the frigid night air, I stripped out of my overclothes to the dark blue layers beneath. I pulled the fabric bunched at my neck over my mouth.

I left the clothes on the floor, tucked behind a plant. I'd pick them up later. Or maybe I wouldn't. No one could trace the white hair that clung to the fabric back to me.

I pried open the window and hopped out onto the fire escape. It creaked in the night breeze, was orange with rust, and offered unencumbered access to the roof. I climbed onto the railing and pulled my body onto the shingled top. The sound of stone scraping stone rung out, making me flinch.

I was more careful with my weights as I crawled to the edge, counting the distance, to the fifth pillar. I peeked over, looking for the faint light that came from the windows. When I saw it, I pulled a carabiner off my utility belt and attached it to the drainage pipe. *Ia,* I requested to no one in particular, *ikka djewoc je.* Please, let it hold.

I pulled the rope I had brought with me from my back, stringing it through the metal carabiner. My stomach settled against the cold, winter worn stone and my legs folded over the edge until the toes of my boots hit the side of the building. For a moment, my stomach dropped beneath me.

I couldn't fall; I wasn't done yet.

I wrapped the rope tight around my right hand and threw it over my head to rest around my hamstrings. I grabbed the loose end with my left hand and leaned back. The taste of copper singed my tongue when my left hand let the rope slack and I began my descent.

The light was dim enough to insinuate only a bedside lamp or a candle had been lit. But that dim candle was enough to make out the man in white, the prominent cut of his jaw, the angled brow, furrowed over a book he held.

I took a deep breath of damp air and pushed with my legs. My body shifted sideways and the force of my kick shattered the window around my heel.

My fingertips burned, even beneath the gloves, as they slid against the wooden planks. My left leg slid extended; the right pulled toward my body. I used the right to push up to full height.

My eyes never left the man in white.

His eyes widened in shock and his stubble-lined jaw clenched hard. His skin lost color. He stood and immediately widened his stance. Something changed in those droopy eyes of his, like a spark going off before a mine explosion.

I didn't wait for him to make the first move. I pulled a knife from my belt and threw it at his shoulder. I lunged forward as he shifted to the side. It just nicked his shoulder.

You're not tall, I remembered Yonten telling me. *So don't waste your time trying to be.*

I bent over into a lunge to his right, the side he had leaned toward. Grasping my right fist in my left hand, I levered a quick push of my elbow into his rib cage from below. I felt the crack and immediately pulled back, jumping to the side. I wouldn't stick around to feel his own elbow come down on my back.

The man in white had me beat in height and bulk; I could tell when my elbow impacted his ribs. Age had not crippled him.

He hunched slightly. He used the movement to aim a fist up at my jaw. I grabbed his wrist with my left hand and pulled it toward me, right past my own ribs and into open air. My body shifted its weight onto the left leg and twisted toward the right, my elbow coming up once more, this time to make contact with his cheek.

I realized my mistake as I turned my back to him. My body convulsed in slow motion, a grunt ripping through my throat when Abbadon's palm struck the L1 vertebrae on my back. The air was ripped from me like a tornado rips pipes from the soil.

The pain blinded me until a forceful thigh came up to the junction where my hip met my ribs, hitting the muscle there.

My body folded. I lost my hold on his wrist as the ground met me. I didn't think I had any more air to lose, but another puff left my lungs as we collided.

I gasped. My vision swam around me. I saw a flash of white.

My body moved for me, forcing me to roll to the left, out of the way of the heel of Abbadon's shoe. My hands fell flat on the wood planks and I forced myself into a crouch. I spun on my hands, flicking out my left leg to sweep at his ankles. Abbadon jumped back, and my kick missed, but it gave me enough time to jump up to standing again.

I lunged again, attempting the same move. He pivoted. My lungs collapsed around his quad and my body was lifted off the floor. I hacked, my throat tightening and eyes bulging. I fell to the ground again, feeling the splintered wood pierce my cheeks upon impact, leaving a stinging and sticky mess.

His hand was on my shoulder rolling me over. He looked like a crazed man, hair slipping from its careful ponytail. His mouth was ajar and his slim shoulders heaved up and down. His hand moved to the front of my shirt and pulled me up. His right hand drew back and tightened into a fist.

I flinched as it collided with my nose. The world splintered into a series of multicolored dots around me. A wetness filled the mask and my eyes watered. I smelled the tangy scent of ferrous oxide. I blinked away the tears and brought the flat of my hand to the side of his exposed ear.

He let out a grunt of pain and dropped me as his ear drum popped.

I scrambled back and away.

He used the metal frame of the bed to pull himself up. Then, with a strength I had never seen, he tore a rod off.

"I don't know who the hell you are," he said, "but you—" Abbadon didn't get to finish his sentence. He tripped over my foot and fell forward.

My body moved before my mind could register what was going on. I tightened my core and leaned onto my knees before lifting the right one and throwing it onto his back to push down on the thoracic spine. It was his turn to gasp.

I pulled another knife out of my belt and leaned forward to press the blade to his neck. My breath came in huffs and blood rushed in my ears. It was over.

I slowly moved off his back and pulled him by the hair to a seated position, kneeling behind him. He grunted in protest, but didn't resist.

My jaw clenched and my teeth ground together. He could have easily ended my life if he hadn't been unlucky enough to slip and fall. I had believed the North Wind to be the most skilled warriors in the world; he shattered those thoughts in an instant. I couldn't make a mistake like that again.

I steeled my face and forced my heart rate to slow so I could maximize my stimuli reception again.

I was a fugitive now. I was guilty of assault, battery, and soon, murder. *There isn't room for another mistake,* I thought desperately.

"I have two rules: Answer my questions honestly and do not scream."

I was taking a gamble with this. He could lie. He could shout. I clenched my teeth once more, but willed my hands to be steady.

I would kill him regardless of his behavior. I couldn't break my promise. I would not fall short in my devotion. *Abbadon will not leave this room unless it's in a body bag.*

"Do you understand?" I questioned.

His Adam's apple bobbed as he swallowed.

I moved the knife slightly, just enough to let him know I wanted him to answer verbally.

"Yes." He sounded calm. His composure was beyond any I had ever witnessed, considering the circumstances. It made my face screw in knots and my vision turn red.

"Four years ago. There was a small village. The people had white hair and gold eyes," I spoke with a steely tone. "You were there, correct?"

There was a shock-still silence. "No," he lied. I could tell the slight tensing of the muscles in his neck and the sharp hitch of breath that was barely audible. I pressed the blade in slightly, just enough to pierce the skin and let the man know I was serious. I watched the blood stain the white collar of his shirt a tie-dye pattern when it mingled with his sweat.

I leaned forward enough to whisper in his ear, "That was your final warning."

I felt his Adam's apple bob once more. He sighed in defeat. "Yes, I was there. I only remember because I can see your eyes through that mask of yours." He only remembered because my people had been easily identifiable? How many people did he kill that he couldn't remember? Tension coiled in my stomach and spread through my back. I leaned back from his ear, satisfied with that answer. "You wore a completely white suit on that day, too, correct?"

"How did you—?"

I gripped his yellow hair tighter in my fist and pull his head back to cut him off. "Correct?" I demanded.

He grunted in pain and surprise. I couldn't see his face, but I could imagine it. It was a chiseled thing, etched full of confusion. He was wracking his memories trying to see if I was there. The dead-eyed boy had not spoken of me, then. That may explain why Abbadon paled at the sight of me; he may have thought I was a ghost.

"Yes," he choked out. I loosened my grip slightly, to better hear the next answer.

"How many of you were there that day?"

"Ten." I wanted to ask how many of those who were present were still alive. That would only give away my intention to kill him and I doubted he would answer any more of my questions if he knew my plan for him.

"Why were you there?"

"We were sent to kill everyone in that tribe," he stated slowly. Only now, with his life in the balance did it occur to him that this may have been a mistake.

I breathed in and out before clarifying my question. "You misunderstand. Nothing was taken from the tribe, so you were not looters or raiders. I know your intent was strictly extermination. Why were you ten, specifically, the ones who were there?"

His muscles tensed up once more: shock. "We are assassins by trade," he explained. His breathing did not change and the pulsing inside his jugular did not fluctuate—He was being honest. "The most elite in the world."

So, then, it was an organized unit, acting as a group.

I thought briefly to the North Wind. Some of my current clan took on jobs to kill people, but those were typically mass murderers and felons that posed a threat to society. I could rationalize their deaths by believing they needed to be removed to allow others the best chance at life.

But your tribe was not full of criminals, a voice hissed maliciously.

"Does your group of assassins have a name?"

Abbadon paused.

I understood how he felt. I was forbidden to mention the North Wind to any outsider. He was probably in a similar situation with his group. I empathized with the man strongly in that moment, but my loathing burned deeper, an insatiable fire that would scorch my mind until the day I got justice in the stead of those who couldn't grasp it themselves.

"We call ourselves Rabum Giru, from the Akkadian *great fire*."

A fire destroys, but it also cleanses and renews. That would indicate those in the Rabum Giru thought themselves judge, jury, and executioner. I ignored the similarities between the Rabum Giru and the North Wind.

"What price did you demand?" *What price were my people worth to you?*

"Three thousand. Three thousand for each person there."

They killed sixty-two. One hundred and eighty-six thousand denarii. I didn't know the life of a person was worth so little.

My chest froze. "Who ordered the hit?" I breathed out.

"I don't—" the man stuttered, noticing a shift in my voice. "I don't know his name."

My grip around the knife's hilt tightened. "Don't screw with me!" I yelled. His left hand flinched slightly, but his head and neck remained motionless.

That was bad. I had lost my composure. It was a dangerous thing to reveal emotion to an enemy.

Be careful! You can't afford any more mistakes.

"Who sent you?" I asked more calmly.

"I'm being honest, I don't know," he stated, bluntly. "Only the boss knows. He was the one who led the mission." There was no quiver in his voice. He wasn't lying.

My heart sped. I thought the man in white was the boss. I had seen his face for years, thinking that he was the answer to all of my problems. Frustration ate at my throat. *Damn it.* I still had to find the boss, then.

"How many of the ten who were there…" I inhaled a little too harshly. My everything hurt. "Are still alive today, Abbadon?"

"Nine. M-myself included." The stutter indicated he knew where this was going. I had what information I really needed from him anyway.

I hummed. An eye for an eye was always more convenient when there were less eyes to be taken. "Names?"

He let out a strangled chuckle, his head pulling more harshly away from my hand that held his hair. I tightened my grip and yanked his head back.

"I won't tell you that shit," he spat, his blue eyes locking with my own and a cruel smirk twisting his features. "I won't sell out my brothers."

I had known he wouldn't tell me. Looking back, I think I only asked because I wanted to prolong what came next: taking a life.

In my tribe, if someone is wronged, they are allowed to return the action to the person who wronged them. It is a system of balances that reflects intent. Since my tribe could not seek this balance, this justice, I had to be the one to enact it for them; I was the only one who could.

The world is black and white, I told myself. *Don't delude yourself into believing it's gray. Abbadon's death will help set things straight.*

I kept my eyes open as wide as I could, looking at the reflection they cast in the window, dark and faded. If I was to become a monster, I would watch myself slip into depravity.

It was an out of body experience as I watched my reflection cut his throat open, heard him choking on blood. I dropped the knife and pressed my hand over his mouth, to muffle the sounds. I held his body tight to my own, felt it convulse against my skin.

I wasn't there. I watched Abbadon die through a hazy mist.

And when his body went limp, I set it gently on the ground.

Red flowers blossomed across his shirt. There were crimson raindrops on the wooden floor. There were tracts of mahogany across Abbadon's chest. The coppery, cloying scent made me want to hurl.

I swallowed hard, flexing my fingers. I was in control of myself, but it was delayed, like walking against a strong wind. It felt like that when I picked up the knife again. It felt like that when I pressed it into his wrist. It felt like that when I began to saw, side to side, hearing the squelching of muscle and blood and tendon sinews.

I grabbed his hand with my own and tugged while I cut away the last half, separating his hand from his body. I lay it on the ground. Then I worked on the other one, mindlessly sawing and pulling until it came off.

A knock at the door echoed in the room. "Sir, are you all right?" a mousy voice called out. "We heard some noises and wanted to make sure you didn't fall."

My heartbeat didn't speed up. I didn't react at all. I didn't even look up from his corpse.

I lowered my voice as best as I could and let out a hearty chuckle, forced and fraudulent. "I'm quite all right," I announced in a husky tone, trying to match Abbadon's bellowing sound. "I was exercising. My apologies if it disturbed the other patrons."

"Very good, sir," the voice said. "Enjoy your evening." I listened for the sound of feet to disappear. When they did, I blinked rapidly, before standing. I walked over to Abbadon's head, eyes already glazed over.

I began the task of cutting through the neck, layer after layer of flesh. It wasn't as easy as the hands; the tendons were stronger and they snapped and made popping sounds when I cut through them. But I succeeded.

The head and hands were both removed. The hands were taken for impure action. The head for impure intent. Actus rea. Mens rea.

It was then that I faded into my body once more, witnessing myself through my own eyes once again. I saw my hands, dyed with slimy, caking blood. This time, I knew I wouldn't just *feel* sick.

I pushed myself up and ran to the tub at the corner of the room. My diaphragm contracted and warm bile rose in my throat. My mouth flew open and I emptied myself into the basin. The smell of acidity pricked at my nose and made me hurl again, vomit splattering against the side of the tub with a wet splat.

My arms shook as I pushed myself up. I turned the faucet and let the water wash away the vomit. I scrubbed the sides of the basin with the bar of soap that sat on the rim. Once the tub was clean, I plugged the bottom of the basin, watching the water slowly rise.

I felt empty. Maybe when the water filled up, I would feel full, too.

I turned off the faucet when the water was high enough and stepped inside, my clothes still on. I gripped the white soap hard, and rubbed it against my hands first. The water began to turn rosy and bubbly. I scrubbed the rest of myself with that soap, too. My hair, my face, my clothes, anything that may have the smell of copper on it. I pulled the plug and let the water drain. Then I plugged it back up and filled it again. I scrubbed myself all over a second time. I still didn't seem clean enough.

I stepped out of the basin and grabbed a towel. I stripped off the wet clothes and rang them over the drain, watching as grime floated across the smooth surface of white porcelain. I didn't drain it this time. It wasn't colored red any more.

I lay my clothes out to dry over the sink before toweling myself off.

The towel was fluffy, light, pure.

October 30, 2725

Kali

If I were able to mention Yonten, I would have asked if Neto was his brother, despite how very different the two were. They bore no physical resemblance. Neto was bigger, with a more trapezoid shape to Yonten's rectangle. Neto had hair, though balding and receding, and Yonten did not. But where Yonten had walked as if the world could elevate his steps, Neto walked as if he could crush the world beneath his feet.

Neto, apparently, was responsible for making sure the twelve of us could walk with that same confidence.

He started the program by asking for a volunteer. What Maru didn't know when he offered to help was that he was going to spend the next thirty minutes getting the imprint of the cobbled platform imprinted on his flesh to teach us basic hand-to-hand combat.

Neto's 'hands-on' teaching style left Maru wincing and rubbing at his darkening skin was what reminded me of Yonten.

"Couple up, one with twelve, two with eleven… so on," he had instructed once he was done. We had all been assigned a numerical ranking in accordance with our skillset displayed. Usually, the numbers shifted after every phase of training, but because of the 'glass-shard debacle' as everyone so aptly put it, our numbers hadn't changed since we finished the trial.

I believe Kali was in eleventh, still, meaning she would be my partner. I groaned inwardly at the thought.

Her most redeeming quality was her sharp mind, whittled like a spear and twice as deadly. I could respect her for that. She seemed to surpass most people in strategy capability, myself included.

"What do you want to work on first?" I asked before she could start up a conversation.

Kali moved like a bobcat, with poise and silence, and straight shoulders that spoke in confidence. "I want to work on the throws," she said, making uncomfortably long eye contact.

I held back the urge to flinch at the intensity and nodded.

"Do you want to be the receiver?"

"I could use a demonstration," she said coyly.

Again, I nodded. I spread my legs, bent my knees, and held my fists in front of my face. I watched Kali shift her weight to her left foot, the one in front, then the right, in the back four times. Then she lunged forward, aiming for my right shoulder with her left hand. I pivoted to my left and grabbed her outstretched wrist, twisting it toward me and behind her. I balanced on my right foot and used my left to lodge between her feet, kicking my knee at the inside of her hers.

Kali crumpled to the ground and I spun my body about her arm to place my knee in the center of her back, still holding her wrist behind her. I heard a wince.

"Wow, Ma'at," she grunted. "This isn't how I imagined you holding me down."

My eyebrow twitched of its own volition; I quickly stopped it. Kali's innuendo sent an uncomfortable grating across my lower back. I stood slowly, dropping her arm. She pushed herself to her feet and shook out her body as if she had done something worthwhile.

Again, she lunged forward, placing a well-aimed punch to my sternum. I was grateful to Yonten for all those hours teaching me redirection because this time, when I pivoted, I grabbed the outside of her right arm, pulling her forward. I pushed on my left leg to jump and wrapped my right around the joint where Kali's hips met her leg. I pulled my leg inward and used my momentum to pull us both into a spiral. I wrapped my free arm around her neck in a head lock as I rolled us to the floor.

I released her and she slowly sat up, rubbing at her neck. "Gosh, go easy on a lady, will you?"

I pushed myself up as well. "Why do you handicap yourself like that?" I asked. "As if being a woman is all you are?" She needed to learn how to do it properly. And if she lacked ability in one regard, it was her responsibility to make up for it in another.

"Again?"

I nodded. I spread my legs again, ready to shift her about me this time. This time when she came at me, I pulled myself low in a squat, facing away. I grabbed her arm once more and pulled her forward, jamming my shoulder into the area her arm connected with her shoulder. I pushed up from the ground and hunched over, pulling her weight along with me.

Kali was not as heavy as Yonten had been. She went over me easily and laid flat against the stone flooring. Her olive skin was a stark contrast to the grey pieces.

It was one of the harder throws; A gust of air left her body. I let her arm go and stepped back.

"Ouch, that hurt. You should be nicer to me, you know," she chastised.

"Oh," I acknowledged. "I'll be more careful."

She hummed as she pushed herself up. "Oh, but I like it rough." She gave me a wink and blew a kiss.

It was like a cord snapping in me. Kali had not managed to stop a single one of my redirects or attempt one of her own, yet she was wasting both her time and mine.

My breath frosted in my lungs and I had to take a deep breath to keep the ice where it was supposed to be: locked up.

"Maybe if you spent less time flirting with me and more time practicing, you wouldn't be such a loser," I said coldly, too frustrated to think before I let out my thoughts.

I didn't move when Kali let her hand fly at my cheek; I deserved it for saying such a thing out of impatience.

I was prepared for the burning sting on the right side of my face. I was prepared to see her huff with anger. I was *not* prepared for the silence and the stares that came from the other ten, who have locked onto the spectacle we were creating.

Kali had a fire rampant in her eyes and her face was contorted with rage. She was now Medusa: all bite and bitterness. "Do not for a second think that I was not serious about my training," she warned with curt words.

My cheeks burned red from something other than the slap.

Kali pushed me with open hands on my chest. I fell to the ground.

She crouched down in front of me, making us level to one another. She poked my chest harshly as she whispered to me, "You listen here, Ma'at. You do not understand my motivations, and you have no authority to judge me until you do." Kali's eyes were harsher than I'd ever seen them, full of spite.

In that moment, I saw her, not for who she presented herself as, but what she was: A vast ocean of controlled chaos, knowing when to wane and when to capsize. For a brief moment, I wondered how someone would ever hide this part of themselves, how someone could bat their long lashes and rouge their heart shaped face as if that was all they were. In a moment, I felt my heart leap into my throat and my mouth go dry at the wonder of such a person.

She was right, to an extent. We all tried to live in ways that made existing easier; her personality was just the way she did that. Pride was stupid, but I still held it tightly with the rationale *You don't owe her an apology.*

I came to the realization that this needed to happen. She needed me to be rude to lose interest; I needed to see her snap to respect her.

She held her hand out, an olive branch for me to take. I took it, unflinching and unrelenting. She blinked rapidly, and her face returned to its normal, smug demeanor. Then she pushed herself up from the ground. I stood with her, hands still clasped.

"I think I am done training with you for today. I want to *practice* with someone closer in level." Her choice of words did not slip past me.

When I looked away from her, everyone seemed to snap their heads to look at the sky. It was obvious they had been watching us, but societal norms dictated they pretended they had not witnessed our spat.

"Sancus," Kali called out, moving on quickly. "I need someone to practice what Ma'at taught me; come here." She gestured with her hand.

Sancus was quick to start a jog in our direction from his spot with Iktomi. He shot me a, *"Sorry you got slapped, but thanks for getting slapped!"* look on his way. Puppy love, one would call it.

My fingers rubbed absently at my cheek of their own accord.

I walked over to Iktomi in his stead, more than happy take a moment to cool down. He stood with his arms crossed, watching the pair begin some blocking drills.

He looked different today. A kind of handsome that is rugged and unrefined, not the dopey slouch and pseudo-boredom, but a steady and easy confidence. His hair was a mess and he hadn't shaved his stubble yet. I thought about how unfair it was that he didn't need to put in any effort or take a shower to look pleasant.

"You were harsh," he said with a light lilt when I stood next to him, looking at Sancus and Kali from afar.

"I know."

I wondered if he and the others all thought less of me now. I suppose it didn't matter how they felt; I didn't *really* need anyone to like me. Still, embarrassment writhed in the pit of my stomach.

He humphed and nodded his head up in acknowledgement. "It needed to be said."

My head flicked up, searching his face for any form of sarcasm. There was none. Iktomi was rarely serious, but now he was. *And he thinks my actions are justified.*

It was nice to have someone back me up, even if I knew, deep down, I had overreacted. I really should have apologized. I wouldn't.

"I didn't know you were so interested in our love lives," I joked.

He let out a guffaw and finally looked down at me. He uncrossed his arms and clapped my left shoulder. "Only yours," he corrected. "You're so emotionally stunted that I can't look away. It's like watching a slow-motion train wreck." I wanted to argue I wasn't emotionally stunted, but that would have been a lie. I was self-aware enough to know that.

"Well, thanks for the stunning endorsement, senator."

Iktomi's hand fell off me in an instant. His laugh was pleasant, just as silky smooth as his normal voice and full enough that it echoed in waves around him.

I didn't know how to handle that reaction; I grabbed the brass band and spun it clockwise around my wrist.

Instead of saying anything else, I spread my legs and raised my fists to my face. It is time for us to move on, the motion stated. Iktomi was quick to follow my lead, but the smile never fell from his lips.

He nodded at me, acknowledgement.

I started with a turning kick to the head. He blocked with his left arm. He tried to twist my leg and me along with it, but I dropped to the floor and spun myself under him, making him focus on staying standing instead of getting me on my back. Iktomi moved forward quickly, faking a left punch and instead going for my right shoulder to twist. I barely snaked out of his grasp and went for the back of his knee. He folded, but instantly attempted a back-kick.

I could feel myself being watched again. I was sure the other ten had their eyes on us. I would have been watching, too, if I weren't on the inside of the fight.

Iktomi moved like mercury, I like a spinning leaf. We were so very different in our styles.

I fell into a squat and leaped up through the gap in his legs to wrap my arms around his middle. He rolled forward, leaving us both flat on the ground. I kicked myself around into another squat and leaped forward into a flying snap kick at Iktomi's face. He pushed me to the side with his right arm and punched me square in the nose as I fell.

I stumbled back a little. A blossom of pain erupted along the center of my face and my eyes began to water. I blinked to clear my vision, making a warm droplet trace down the side of my face. I smelled iron and tasted salt. I pulled my hands up tight to protect my face once more.

Iktomi didn't square his body to continue the fight. Instead, he let himself go slack. His face twitched, as if deciding what to do, and fell into a look of concern. He walked over to me quickly, his hands held palm out toward me. "Are you all right?" he yelled, a little too loudly for our proximity.

I blinked slowly and relaxed my own body, feeling the tension bleed out of the muscles. I felt fine. Yeah, it hurt like a bitch to get punched in the nose and I was still throbbing slightly, but it didn't feel broken, so I'd be fine.

"Yes," I answered.

He tilted his head to the sign, his brow furrowed in distress. I smirked and wiped my nose with the back of my sleeve. It pulled away red. I let my eyes bore into his stormy blue ones. Iktomi's mouth formed a little 'O' of shock.

I gave a crooked smile, one of two I permitted myself to give. I was fired up now.

"Let's raise the stakes with some weapons. I haven't had much practice with those yet."

I watched as the surprise faded into excitement. The usual cheerfulness returned as Iktomi exclaimed, "Yeah! I'll go grab them." He ran off to where the supplies were.

This match had made clear to me was that Iktomi was still leagues ahead of me. I had to try harder and dedicate more time to this. If I could not beat him, someone who was supposed to be at my beginner level, how could I ever hope to go after the assassins who hurt my family, the ones who had spent years learning to take a life?

Iktomi returned with two swords in hand.

I hated swords. They were large and impractical and difficult to manipulate. When I took one in my hand, it was heavy and felt awkward.

"You ready?" his question pulled me back from my thoughts. I gripped tight the item in one hand and spread my gait. I wasn't experienced in this, but looking at Iktomi, the way he stood, shoulders squared and hands drawn into slight tilt, I knew he was.

I felt my lips twitch and forced them down. *Good*, I thought, *kick my ass and make me better.*

I nodded once. I watched his lips twitch up in a smirk, as well. He didn't force his down. He stepped with a right lunge forward, slashing to the left. I raised my sword to the side. I was slow. The swords made a clunking sound and the scent of iron drifted up. Iktomi swept his back leg forward and shoved it between my own separated ones.

I sucked in a breath of air through my mouth. It tasted like sweat and disappointment.

His arm impacted my sternum, sending me stumbling back. The swords slid against each other, generating heat and noise. My weight shifted into my top, so I tightened my core and leaned forward. My jaw snapped shut of its own volition as I lunged forward, slashing upward.

I was sloppy. I could feel it when my footsteps faltered and I slashed again. I could feel it when Iktomi parried and elbowed my jaw. And I could feel it when I slashed down with both hands.

He moved like a river. It was like I was a passive observer through my own eyes, watching him dart in and out.

I know nothing of him, I thought as I followed my strike through. *He could be a bigger threat than I gave him credit for.*

I dropped my left foot to the floor and tightened my quad to push myself upright. I saw the glint of the metal in the sun before I registered it was there. I felt my pulse quicken and a dropping feeling in my stomach as I desperately tried to pull back faster. *I'm not going to make it,* my mind supplied, *I'm too slow.* A slice crossed my left brow a few seconds later. That was the second time I had left myself with no defense.

Inferiority dripped down my organs like tar.

My skin was slick, not from sweat, but from something much thicker. It saturated my eyebrow and dripped down the side of my face. Some drops fell into my eye, too, obscuring my vision. I shut my eye tightly to keep the blood out.

I could still keep going.

A kick to my sternum sent the ground to meet me. I jostled a little on the stone floor, knowing that I would be very sore when I woke up the next day. I winced.

"Oh, I nicked you!" Iktomi exclaimed, dropping his sword to his side. "That's the second time today. I'm so sorry." He extended a hand out for me to hoist myself up with.

I looked away and pushed myself up from the ground without help. My cheeks burned. They burned because he had hurt me twice, which implied that he held back. He held back and I still wasn't good enough to match his pace.

"Don't be," I grunted.

His brow furrowed in confusion.

I kept my breath steady as possible. "Never apologize for besting me."

Iktomi's face was contorted before relaxing. "I won't," he agreed slowly.

I looked away and wiped my bloody brow on my sleeve. It stung as if I was pulling the skin apart anew. Human flesh begins to permanently scar at .56 millimeters, with a standard deviation of .03 millimeters. The laceration felt deep, though I didn't know how deep. I hoped, if it did scar, it at least made me look a little older and a little cooler.

"I'm going to clean up," I mentioned absently. The thought of getting an infection still bothered me. I was used to avoiding anything that could lead to me using up my stores of antibiotics. Three and a half years of thinking in that way wasn't about to change because I now had stable access to healthcare.

I walked away from the others.

I heard footsteps running behind me before I saw Iktomi in the corner of my eye. I turned to look up at his profile. "I should help patch you up," he explained, "I'm the reason you're like that in the first place." He rubbed at the junction of his collar bone with the side of his thumb.

I looked to the ground in front of my feet. "You don't owe me anything."

"You're an idiot," he sighed, his shoulders and head drooping.

"Sometimes," I agreed, shoving my elbow into his side amicably.

He rubbed at his arm as we drew nearer the bathrooms.

"Sit on the sink counter," Iktomi told me as he began to rifle through the medicine cabinet behind one of the mirrors.

I sat on the leftmost sink counter, closest to the door in case I needed to dodge out of awkward conversation.

I watched him pull out a butterfly bandage and some antiseptic. My nose wrinkled reflexively when the scent hit my nose. It always burned my nose more than my skin. But when Iktomi pressed a cotton ball dipped in the liquid onto my skin, I felt the stinging prickle burn its way throughout the cut. I tried my hardest not to wince, but I felt my lip twitch slightly. I was a baby when it came to subtle pain. A broken arm was no big deal, but a paper cut was a fate worse than death.

Iktomi was too close for me to be comfortable, as he dabbed away at my brow. I could make out the sloping lines in his face and see the minute wrinkles that had begun their slow and steady march onto his face. He smelled like sweat and spring.

I came to the conclusion I didn't like being this close to him. If I could see his flaws, he was sure to see mine too.

He looked away from me and began to peel the sticky tabs off the bandage. He reached up and stuck the butterfly shaped bandage tight to keep my skin together. Iktomi's irises were visible. They had little dots of color that fluctuated throughout, making them look surreal.

"Good as new," he whispered, pulling away slightly.

"Thanks," I said. Then, unrelated and without pause, I mentioned that "We should trade."

He cocked his head to the side and raised one eyebrow, arms reinstating themselves across his chest in a closed off way. He was smiling again, the concentrated blank expression now gone. He thought I was joking.

Iktomi scoffed and looked off to the left before returning to me. "You can't run away because Kali hit you. Don't be childish," he chastised lightly, "and I like Sancus too much to give him up."

I shook my head. He had misunderstood. "No, I mean you and I should spar more frequently," I explained. "It doesn't do you or I any good to keep training with Sancus and Kali. We should spend half the time with them and half with one another."

Iktomi thought for a minute. I could tell he was thinking because he had this nervous tick where he switched which leg he was standing on. He bit his lower lip and opened his mouth. It closed unceremoniously.

Then he smirked.

Iktomi put his hands on either side of me and leaned forward into my personal space. "I'll do it if you do me a favor," he bartered, raising an eyebrow. He was baiting me.

Despite the sensation of entrapment, I asked, "What?"

"I haven't decided yet."

That pissed me off.

Lots of things pissed me off about Iktomi. I was pissed that he was so confident all the time. I was pissed off that he was charismatic. I was pissed off that he was leagues ahead of me with his talent and capability when I had the experience. I was pissed off that he seemed to be the better version of me. Mostly, I was pissed off that I really wasn't pissed off about any of this at all.

"One day, Iktomi," I warned, a smirk crawling into my cheek. "Don't forget about me; one day I'll kick your ass."

He chuckled, low and steady. "Looking forward to it," he responded with a shake of his head. He walked out of the bathroom quickly and quietly.

I stayed. I needed a shower and the bathroom was never empty.

Sancus was curled up in my chair. I supposed it wasn't mine in actuality, but it was my favorite chair. So, I sat on the floor next to him, reading a novel I had propped up on my knees. It wasn't a good book, but it wasn't bad enough to put it down either.

"I was thinking about going out to the town tomorrow," Sancus mentioned. I could hear the squawk of his charcoal tool across the pad of paper. I wondered what he would create this time. "You want to come with?"

I hummed and turned the page. "What are we going to do?"

"Walk around the market? Grab a couple drinks at the pub? I'd be willing to play a game of cards with stakes, too."

His response grabbed my attention. Cards? Stakes? Sancus had told me he followed a faith in which certain things were morally wrong, gambling being one of them. His God didn't like the idea of squandering money that could be better spent on the poor. "But I thought—"

I watched his head turn up from the page at me. He raised one of his eyebrows mockingly. "My God won't punish me for a little enjoyment every once in a while."

I nodded and looked down at the pages of my book again. The words blurred together. "Okay. That sounds nice," I agreed. I hadn't played cards in a while. I wondered what game we would find.

A shiver ran down my back. I tugged my legs up closer to me. I couldn't tell if it was the encroaching cold from the oncoming winter months or if someone was watching us. I knew we weren't through probation yet and that we were subject to monitoring in the meantime. I couldn't rule it out.

I heard the sound of footsteps approaching us, but I didn't look up from the book.

"Hey, Sancus," Diejiste called out from nearby. She sounded like a politician: Proud and confident. I admired her a lot, for the fact she was honest and open, unlike a politician. "Could you take my place in the game? I'm tired."

I looked up to her. She was standing in front of our chair, hands on her hips, stance spread shoulder length. In my mind, I bet she could have been an actress. She would have made a good super hero in a film. She looked the part, just plain enough to have a secret identity, just noticeable enough to have a distinctive heroic persona. Had the personality for it, too. All charisma and foolhardy effort.

"What game?"

"Chess."

I heard the leather of the chair squeak as he readjusted his position. "Not my game, but Ma'at will do it."

Nothing will ever compare to the immense betrayal I felt in that instant. My dearest friend, volunteering me for things I didn't want to do. My head snapped to him, mouth open in protest, but his beaming killed my argument in an instant. I was weak for that smile.

"Sorry, dude."

I very much doubted he was sorry.

I took a deep breath and closed my book before standing up. Diejiste clapped a firm hand on my shoulder, her way of saying thanks.

When I looked to the chess set, I wished I hadn't stood and let Diejiste clap my shoulder. Kali was sitting, regal as ever, on one of the stools that bordered the chess set.

I gulped. Things were still a little touchy with her. We hadn't really spoken since her slap earlier today. I didn't know what to say to her. I didn't before our spat, so I doubted the words would come to me now.

With an ever growing feeling of dread growing in my stomach, I made my way over to where she sat.

"Is it my turn or yours?" I asked as I sat, studying the board carefully. It had been some time since I played this game, but chess was like riding a bike in that you never really forgot how to play, you just weren't as fast after an absence.

"Yours."

I nodded and thought about which piece to move. The king was relatively isolated at this point, so I could stand to go on the offensive. I moved a bishop across the board to take a nearby pawn. The wooden piece was warmed from the proximity to the fire.

"You made a point earlier," I mused. I looked up to her fire-kissed eyes, but she was carefully studying the board, worrying her lip in thought. "I don't know anything about you."

She gave off a soft hum. She had heard me. I looked at her relaxed posture, slumped, yet still as stone. She wasn't going to say anything. I would have taken a punch to the face over this conversation. Nevertheless, I continued, "But I would like to."

Kali pursed her lips and trailed her fingers across the stool that held the chess board. Kali trailed that same hand up to push a loose strand of licorice hair behind her pierced ear. She picked up where Diejiste had left off, moving the knight up and over.

She said nothing as she looked to me. I swallowed. Her gaze was intense in the way that a slumbering serpent was. My eyes darted down to the board, looking where to place my pieces. I moved a pawn.

Her lips twitched at the corner, ever so slightly. "Chess is a funny game," she said. Her fingers danced atop the pieces, selecting which one she would move. This time, she went with a rook, moving it carefully across the board. "It tells you a lot about life."

I sucked in a breath of air. Being on speaking terms again was a good sign; I'd count that as a win.

I let my focus shift to her play. She left a pawn open. I smirked, and moved my queen to take it.

I looked back up to her, hoping to see panic in her face. Instead, I was met with a look of disappointment. It drew my eyes back down to the board. I saw what she had done. She had moved the rook into a place where it can take my king. But if I moved my knight to defend the king, it would take away the obstruction of her queen and my king would still be taken. I could not win.

I moved the knight to take the rook. She moved her queen to knock over my king. I stared at the board in befuddlement. Kali had beaten me in three moves.

"Sometimes your most valuable pawn is your rook," she advised. "Life gets easier if you know everyone is disposable." She turned her head to look at the barrage of books on the wall.

I stared at the board, not knowing what to say or how to react.

But I agreed with her. What she said made sense, in the most part. There were people in your life that were exceptions. Yonten was an exception. Sancus was becoming an exception. But she was right. I was using nearly everyone here for something, whether directly or indirectly.

Logically, I knew it was wrong that we thought that way.

Her voice was small and broken. "You don't have to believe it for it to be true."

I looked back up to her, watched as she stared through the chess board, and didn't have the courage to tell her I believed her.

I picked up the pieces on the side of the board and started setting them into their rightful places, all the pawns in a neat little row, all of the higher-ranking pieces in their carefully crafted order about the royal couple.

How many people must die so that the king may live? Did the king make an exception for the queen? Or would the queen always die to protect the crown? At least in chess, the answer was predetermined.

"You're right," I relented, tracing the outline of her face with my eyes, looking at the way she sat. Tired, was the word that came to mind. "I don't have to believe something for it to be true."

I didn't interject my belief that the converse was also factual: sometimes believing in something is often the very thing that makes it true. Us believing people were disposable was the very thought that allowed us to treat them as such.

I began placing her chess pieces back into their place. If I were the king in this analogy, how many would I let die to get what I wanted? I closed my eyes and took a deep breath that cracked my vertebrae.

I don't think I liked the answer I gave myself.

February 12, 2727

Belig

It wasn't hard to trace Abbadon's contacts to find the next party member.

I started with my region, looked into the transport records for the month of July, from the first to the fourteenth. Then I cross analyzed that list of people with a list of other places Abbadon Steward had shown up over the years. There were only three people with the name Abbadon Steward alive during the period, so I tracked those three. To verify which one was the right Abbadon, I looked into a total list of places each was and the unsolved murders that occurred during that time. From there, I found which one was the Abbadon I had killed and found lists of people in the cities he was in during the same times.

I cross analyzed those names, seemingly innumerable, with the names that were found in my region on July seventh. I found ten names.

Belig Kjalven was not exactly a man known for subtleties. He was cocky, arrogant, and self-obsessed. He was the kind of person who was strong and powerful, and would tell everyone in a ten-foot radius as much. I jumped to sign up for the first solo mission that cropped up in a nearby location.

A string of murders had begun occurring with regularity along the Ieracus Peninsula's southern tip. All of the victims were left with holes carved into their bodies on the forehead, in the middle of the clavicle, through the sternum, and through the gap between the tibia and fibula. The locals were calling the individual the 'Vole Killer' because of the resemblance the holes in the victims bore to the animal's.

The suit I was in was less stiff than the one that I had worn for my first mission. This one was meant for practicality, as I was imitating an International Investigator, an II. The identification they had me using looked fairly realistic. I wasn't disappointed in the slightest when they let me into the crime scene to observe the body.

"Not that I'm questioning your authority, but how is this an international issue?" a young woman with a short stature and long curly hair asked. Mun, as she went by, was the head investigator of the Vole Murders.

She leaned forward to look at the hole I was prodding around in with a beige stick. I caught a whiff of her perfume. Hibiscus.

I kept working, poking the stick further and feeling around the clotted blood to see if there were any remnants of the weapon inside. I felt nothing, but the hole narrowed toward the bottom in a messy fashion.

The tears of the skin almost looked like a large screw driver had been used to drill into the victim post-mortem. The beige stick stuck to the sides broken muscle and sinew.

"It's international because it has been reported on internationally," I said simply. It had been. All but two of the international news stations had aired a segment on it. "I'll be out of your hair when the murders stop."

I pulled the stick out and put it into an evidence bag. I pinched the blue wrist of my left glove and used the inside latex to peel off the right as well, tucking them inside each other. I stood up and Detective Mun stood with me. I had seven inches on her.

"I'd like to take a look at the case files for the others. Would you be willing to send them to me?" I asked. I always asked instead of demanded. People, I've found, are much more likely to assist someone who isn't throwing around commands.

She nodded quickly. Her stature was rigid and poised. Her face, hard and unflinching. "I'll have them delivered to you by our intern."

I faked a smile. It didn't reach my eyes. "I appreciate that. Thank you." I didn't need the files, but it was good that she thought I did.

The Vole wasn't my priority, anyway. Belig was.

As much as humans liked to believe their patterns were random, they weren't. The Vole Killer never hit the same town twice, but he always hit a less than ten minutes from the IS-29 freeway. This weekend, or next, the Vole Killer would strike at the Starlight Inn, with ninety-five percent certainty.

That night, I waited for him to walk through the door and peak into the window. I could tell it was the Vole Killer because of the icepick hanging off his waist and the lockpicking tools he was using on the room.

There was a teenage boy inside, probably waiting on his peers.

Why involve the kid? I thought, as I dropped from the roof. I heard a gasp as the Vole Killer heard me and turned around, dropping the tools.

"I was just checking the locks, I'm with maintenance," he lied with such practiced ease my skin crawled. Liars made me sick.

He couldn't see my face, so I didn't bother with my smirk. "James Morrows. Acandan male, age: thirty-four; height: five foot, eleven. Responsible for seven discovered bodies, plus four more undiscovered missing persons."

I saw his grip tighten on the tool in his hand. He didn't have a gun, then. Most of the time, the victims were found with bruises and lacerations to the head, evidence of battery before he tied them up and cut into them.

It wasn't hard for me to sweep his feet out and make him fall forward enough to grab the front of his shirt and push him toward the railing. Two stories wouldn't be enough to kill him, but the syringe of air that I pulled from my utility belt would be.

Morrow scrambled for purchase on the hand that held his shirt, surprised at the power shift. His face was contorted into a grimace and there was a trail of sweat running from his temple into his side burn. His hair was matted together in clumps.

"Look," he panted. His breath smelled like kale. "We can work something out. I don't know what you want, but I can get it for you. I don't take their things. Help yourself to any of the money or personal affects you want."

It was easy to ram the syringe into the space between his fingers and push the plunger, introducing just the right amount of air to cause a non-suspect embolism. It was easy to push him back enough for him to fall over the railing.

One life or a thousand, I was already a killer.

He moaned lowly when he hit the ground, but he didn't scream. He'd be struck by cardiac arrest momentarily.

I didn't stick around to watch. I jumped over the edge and swung onto the roof of a nearby car before sliding on my butt to the ground.

I hopped onto the moped I rented and popped the stand before starting the engine and zooming off. I didn't wear a helmet. I was reckless and high on the numbness that came with doing an unspeakable act.

The real reason I was in this city was a few miles away.

I had asked a favor of Amaethon to hack into his phone. I hadn't answered when she asked why I needed the information. She had just shrugged and did it anyway, saying something about how she checked up on old significant others, from time to time, too. I had let her think what she wanted.

His plans for tonight led me to an underground casino.

My grip tightened on the handles as I rounded a corner. The streets were empty. I had supposed a big city would never sleep, but the city wanted to prove me wrong with its neon red-lit vacancy.

The streets led to the parking lot of the bar with the hidden casino in the basement. I hoped the Kevlar jacket would fit in there. I left my utility belt on when I parked and dismounted. The black leather from the North Wind issued belts was much more at home on me than my personal brown set.

I kicked the stand down and dropped the keys into my front pouch.

Deep breaths, the voice in my head told me, much calmer than I was. I listened. The air smelled of sewer steam, piss, and half-used tobacco.

My jaw clenched. I walked inside.

I don't remember the way the door felt, but I remember how the inside of the red-lit bar smelled the same as the outside, but with the addition of human heat. My head swiveled around, looking at the bar pushed back in the far left, with the rows and rows of liquor and beer on tap, and the standing circular tables set up all about the room. There was a set of swinging doors on the wall to my left, with symbols indicating bathrooms; I walked straight toward them.

The leftmost bathroom was unlocked. I pushed the door in and locked it behind me. The lights hurt my eyes and highlighted all of the dust and fecal matter on the toilet. I stood in front of the mirror and looked at the scratched, reflective surface. My hair was longer than I remember, my collar bones more hollowed.

I reached into my pocket and pulled out two tubes, both black. I uncapped the first and rolled it out, smearing the bright red of lipstick onto my lips. I twisted the second cap off and rolled the dark oil of a tube onto my eyelashes.

Disgust soured my saliva and I looked away from the mirror.

I had to get Belig to leave with me. He would follow out a girl wearing lipstick, of that I was certain.

I dropped the two tubes into the trash can and left the bathroom, making my way to the dimly lit bar. Belig must have already made it to the casino portion.

The bartender was in his sixties and had the same facial structures as my dad once did: same shape of hooked nose, same arch to the brow. That was about where the similarities stopped. He was wearing a white button up and suspenders to keep his brown pants up, like an old-timey professional.

"I'll take a water, served in the glass you'd serve tequila in," I requested when he set down a Moscow Mule in front of another patron.

His dark eyes looked up to me. It was hard to tell if they were brown or black in this lighting. "An unusual order," he said. His accent confirmed he had come from my region.

I shrugged and forced a smirk. "Well, I'm hoping to run into someone here, but don't much like liquor," I explained, with a forced chuckle.

"Sure, I can't get you anything else?" he asked as he placed an embellished glass in front of me. My immediate thought was how sloppy the craftsmanship of the glass was.

"Can you make me a nine-oh-nine?" I asked, nonchalantly. I looked up to him without tilting my head.

I held my breath. That was what Belig had texted his buddy the passcode was, but I had a shaking suspicion it wouldn't work out for me. I had statistically bad luck.

The bartender gestured his head. "They serve that in the back," he said, voice low and scratchy. "Just head on into the kitchen and they'll set you up."

I looked where he nodded his head to see a set of doors, a bright light coming from inside.

I got up without thanking the bartender, the water glass still in my hand, and walked over to the set of doors. There was, indeed, a kitchen inside, but it had long-since closed, and there was not a chef in sight. There was another door to my right with 909 engraved into the wood.

I pushed the door in and saw a set of stairs heading down. I followed them, the wine carpet creating a cushion for my footfalls. The smell of cigars intensified as I got lower, and the smell of liquor lessened. I blinked to focus through the haze.

The lighting was the same, red, as if the bar hadn't been able to afford any actual lights and had to operate under LEDs. The room had a bunch of circular tables, raised high, with notches cut into them to hold playing chips.

It took me all of two seconds to find him. White male, thirty-seven, six feet and two inches, hair in dreadlocks, pulled back into a ponytail. His brow was thick and shaded his piercing blue eyes and high cheekbones. His jaw was rounded at the chin, but square on the corners, and his mouth was pulled into a frown. He hadn't changed since the picture taken five years ago for his passport.

I had sifted through ten years' worth of travel data. This was him. I was certain.

Lady Luck seemed to be on my side, for there was a seat right next to him. I worried my lip as I made my way to the empty seat. My vision narrowed into a tunnel.

The swivel stool squeaked as I rolled myself into it. "I'll buy a round," I said, pulling a hundred denarii piece from my breast pocket. That was the last of my leisure expenditures for the month.

The dealer took the piece and shoved it into her apron. Her short cut reminded me of Diejiste's, but her sour expression ruined the prospect of finding any other similarities between their looks. She handed me the chips.

I placed two dark blue ones in, to match everyone else. Cards were doled out in front of the five of us. The seat to the far right was empty.

Looking back, I couldn't make out what the others at the table looked like. I think it was because I was so focused in on Belig. I was focused on the way he tapped the cards softly against the table, how his back was straight near the top and curved near the bottom as a means of posture, how sometimes he would take a visibly deep breath that would cause his bones to crack.

I took a deep breath of my own before whispering to Belig, "I can't quite remember which is the better hand, a royal flush or a straight." It didn't matter to me which was higher, but it did matter how Belig would respond.

He smirked, without looking away from the table. "A flush is better," he replied. His voice was gruff and fit with the body structure he had. If I had to guess, his weight was over 210 pounds of solid muscle. "I suppose I should fold if you're asking that."

"Oh, not at all, I just wanted to get you to talk to me."

There was a moment of pause. I felt my heart skip a beat. *Please,* I thought, *please let him think I'm flirting. I need to get him alone.*

He hummed, deep in his chest. "How strange. I wanted you to talk to me, too."

"Interesting."

All five of the cards had been flipped over at this point. I had lost. I turned my own pair face down and pushed them along the table toward the center. The green felt of the table was soft in an irritating way. Similar to the tension of remembering the tune to a song, but none of the words.

The winning patron beside me swept up all of the tokens. I waited for the next hand to be delt. A puff of cigar wafted across the table. I suppressed the urge to cough. The smoke was no different than the smoke from the hookah that Yonten and I would see when we went to town, only less fragrant.

"You look too classy to be engaging in illicit activities," he mumbled.

"What part of me looks classy?" I quipped.

"It's how you present yourself."

I didn't care much for outward appearances on the regular. Hunaphu always said talking to me was like taking to a mirror: I would say what should be said, even if it wasn't pleasant to hear. Knowing that I had been successful enough in my acting to rein in that part of me, the abrasive part that even I didn't like, made me feel a little more secure.

"I see," I whispered with a quirk of my head toward him. "You're wrong though. I'm not classy. More like, I'm running away from being unclassy." I had a shit hand again.

I raised my bet. I'd bluff my way to victory. I kept raising until more and more people dropped out. Belig and I were the last. He raised his eyebrow at me and I gave him a crooked smirk. He folded.

Perhaps I would have some discretionary income after all.

I looked back to the dealer and placed my cards face down on the table. I didn't need anyone seeing that I had bluffed in case this game went longer than I wanted.

"What do you mean by that?"

"This world is full of broker-shady people who do terrible things to one another in order to make themselves feel better," I explained with a sigh, stacking up the chips I had won in the last round. I liked the soft-hued blue ones the best; they looked like Xbalanque's eyes. "I don't want to be one of those people."

Belig clicked his tongue against his perfectly straight teeth. His lips were thin and revealed them easily when he opened his jaw to take a sip of an amber drink from a glass identical to my own. "Sounds like you come from money. Money you're not proud of," he observed.

I shrugged.

I annexed into the game and the dealer passed me the first card in the set before doling out the rest of the circle. I raised to keep pace with the others, then knocked to pass. The first three cards were laid out for me to compare mine to. I had a two and an eight. I folded.

I took a deep breath, quietly, while Belig's focus was on something else. He heavily favored his right hand, to the point that his shoulder was hunched on that side subconsciously. I would assume the left was weaker.

Belig tilted his cards up, rechecking what he had, before placing down another coin. "Are you looking for confirmation you're not?" he asked.

I took another deep breath. "I'm looking for something tonight," I insinuated, taking a quick drink of my water, before placing the glass down on the table. "And it isn't a game of poker."

A bark of laughter echoed from Belig's chest. His piercing eyes looked deep into mine, not breaking eye contact for an instant. His hand to my knee. It was hot. Too hot.

I forced myself to smile.

I was reminded of a time not so long ago where I didn't have a choice in the matter of being touched, where something that left me broken and bruised almost happened. I felt like I would hurl thinking about that again, thinking about the moment I was in.

At least you caught him, the voice in my head reminded me. That was what I had wanted, after all. But as his fingers traced a burning line up my thigh, I had to fight away the desperate urge to throw a punch at his nose.

I swallowed hard and kept smiling. "Do you think I could persuade you to leave the game?" I asked instead, quirking my right eyebrow. I hoped my breath wasn't as shaky as I felt.

He didn't respond to me. Instead, he turned and threw his last hand on the table, face up. "I fold; cash me out," he instructed the dealer. The dealer did, writing a slip worth the value of denarii he had thrown into the game.

I pushed my own denarii to the player sitting next to me. "They're yours," I rushed, too anxious to do anything but stand up from the stool.

Belig stood with me. His hand immediately found mine.

It felt wrong, having his fingers in mine, tugging me out of the little underground casino and up the stairs and through the bar and into the biting two-in-the-morning air, leading me around the corner of the bar and into an alley.

When he pressed me into the wall and smashed his lips against mine, I felt dirty. When he touched me, I wasn't entirely sure I was in my own body. Still, one hand grabbed the lapel of his shirt while the other wormed its way into my utility belt to unlatch the clip that led to my knife.

I hadn't seen Xenon in two months. I didn't know where he was or what he was doing. And though this was a mission, all I could think was that it wasn't his hands on me or his knee pushing my legs apart or his lips pushing at my neck.

I needed to do this, I thought in way of explanation, trying to push back the guilt that came with someone using my body. *And I don't owe Xenon anything.*

Of course not, the voice agreed. *You don't love him.*

I pushed those thoughts down as my fingers wrapped around the red handle of the blade. One quick jab is all it would take. To the jugular. Then I could leave. And I could sleep.

I could finally sleep.

Belig went ram-rod straight against me. "Wait a minute," he mumbled, drawing his face away. His brow scrunched up and his mouth grew lines of disgust. "You're not…" *a girl.*

I swallowed. I had waited too long. I gripped the hilt of the knife more tightly and I swung upward, in a grazing punch. It cut through the pale flesh with ease, leaving a thin trail of crimson behind in its wake.

Belig let out a grunt and stumbled backward. He wiped at the line of red that traced from his right cheek up the swell of his nose with the back of his hand. Then, he smirked. "If you were just a convincing trap, then you wouldn't have tried to hurt me," he noted. "You would have asked if I still down to tumble."

I spread my legs and crouched at my knees, bringing my free right hand up to protect my face. *You got that right,* my stance answered.

"Well," he opened his arms with the bravado of a man, undefeated. "Do your worst."

The ice traveled through my core, spiraling outward in my veins before freezing the flesh around it, hardening up and solidifying. He would not get the best of me.

I threw the knife at him; he reached up to block it with his left hand. I tried to kick at the opening near his head that created with my foot, raising it up as high as I could.

It left me unbalanced. Belig grabbed ahold of my ankle and moved his head to the side enough to twist me until my right foot slid out from under me. My ankle stung from the snap, but not as much as the tarmac hurt when it scraped my face and the swells of my palms.

The air was sapped from my lungs like a tycoon snaps the hull of a ship. His boot was pressing into my spine before I could even move to pick myself up.

Find some way to overcome him. You have to kill him. If you don't, everything you've done will be for nothing. I tried to press down on the raw skin of my hands, clenching my stomach to try to force myself up under his weight. A grunt of air escaped me.

His foot shifted to the side slightly and the weight lightened, before he slammed it down with the fullness of his bodyweight.

There was a snap inside me, right where his foot pressed in so quickly. I gasped, a wheezing sound, as he lifted his foot and dug his heel in once more.

Fire laced my back, and warmth pooled as two more snaps echoed from within. I could hear my heartbeat speed up. My head swam and the dark and dirty ground that smelled of sewer and tobacco shifted around me.

I blinked rapidly, trying to make sense of what I was seeing. I couldn't. I needed more air. I couldn't *inhale*. My chest was sore and it was as if the lump in my throat was blocking my airway.

I barely heard Belig when he spoke to me. "I don't care who you are or why you want to kill me," he mused, as if he was bored.

I saw red as the ice curled me up in a violent blanket of glass shards.

My nails scraped across the ground emptily, grasping at nothing as specs of concrete muddled with my sweat. *I need to get up.* He was so close.

"I'll never let you kill me."

I'll never let you kill me, I snapped at him, my teeth grinding against themselves. *I don't lie. I'll never die by your hand.*

The pressure of his foot left me. His shoes made wet clicks on the morning concrete as he walked off.

Black dots swarmed at the side of my vision.

Get up, I screamed at my aching muscles. I clawed at the ground, dirt from the cracks filling the space beneath my finger nails.

My throat tickled, my diaphragm contracted involuntarily, and was coughing up a liquid that spilled onto my lips and down my chin. I wondered if it was mucus or blood or just plain spit.

It was hard to keep my eyes open. Each time I blinked, it took longer and longer to pry my eyelids open again. My field of vision got smaller and smaller, dwindling down into black as unconsciousness began its descent.

I wasn't naive enough to believe someone would save me.

I couldn't just lay and die. I hadn't kept my promise yet. I still had to keep my promise.

I promised.

I hoped the cold that it would coagulate some of that blood spilling out of me. I didn't think it worked like that. After all, the cold was just a thing I used to describe my anger. I wasn't one of those people who was gifted with an extraordinary power; the ice I described was simply how I viewed myself. Views would do very little to help me.

It hurt to breathe in, and my arms had stopped moving. I was made of lead, falling through the air at terminal velocity.

I heard a scream.

The metronome was steady. *Beep. Beep. Beep.* It quickened slightly. *Beep. Beep. Beep. Beep.* My eyes didn't want to open, but I forced them to, pulling at the groggy heaviness weighing down on my glabella.

The first thing I noticed was the stiffness in my right arm, how cold and immobile it was. The second was the press of plastic around my face, pushing cold air up into my nose. The ceiling was a gross beige, peeling and cracked, lit by the flickering fluorescent lights.

My left hand to tugged the uncomfortable, scratchy blanket that covered my legs, pulling it off of me. I clenched my stomach to sit up. A ripping pain, like dragging a rake over my lungs, forced a gasp from my mouth. *Beep beep beep beep beep beep.*

I blinked rapidly and moved my head from side to side. A seafoam curtain, a heart rate monitor, an IV pack. I heard the sound of footsteps rushing toward me, clacking against tiled linoleum. The curtain was pulled to the side, making a *shink* sound and a woman rushed in, wearing seafoam scrubs to match the curtains.

A doctor, my brain supplied, when I saw the comely woman tug on her lab coat. I must have called her away from her break. Her black hair was pulled back in a tight bun and rose tipped glasses framed her frantic eyes. She placed her hand gently on my shoulder.

"There, there," the doctor said. "Lay back for me, okay?"

I didn't want to lay back or do anything else she told me. I had only the frantic idea that I had to get up and go. I hadn't killed the one called Belig yet. I needed to go. I had to get on the road before the trail disappeared and I had to start all over again.

I opened my mouth to protest, but my voice was hoarse and came out in a breathy rasp of air. It occurred to me I was thirsty.

The doctor clicked her tongue at me and shook her head, pushing me back. I wanted to yell at her, but my throat wouldn't form the sounds.

"You're all right. Nothing's going to happen to you here."

That's the problem, I wanted to hiss.

She grabbed a clipboard from the side of the heart rate monitor and scribbled something onto it. I wanted to know what she was writing.

"Someone found you in an alley," she told me, thin lips pursed in focus. "If you were robbed, now that you're awake, you can file a police report."

I wasn't robbed, but she didn't need to know that.

"How long have I been here?" I finally choked out.

She looked away from the clipboard and smiled at me in a way meant to comfort. It didn't. "A little over two days. Should be two to four months before you're back to a hundred percent."

By the end of the four-month measure, it would have been five years since that day. Five years and I was still at square one. I hadn't accomplished a thing. I was weak and a failure and it shouldn't have been me who survived because I didn't have the power to do anything.

My throat grew sore and a lump nestled in the space between my spine and my mouth. I closed my eyes when pinpricks bit the surface of my left cornea.

I can't fix it. I had been self-centered and cowardly and incompetent and I had nothing to show for it, save a broken body.

For the first time in years, I wanted to cry.

Four months. How was I going to explain the extent of this injury to the North Winds? The target they sent me after was low profile and an airhead. This wouldn't have come from him. Nor could I give the excuse that I was mugged. It wouldn't be a petty criminal getting the better of me.

I would tell them the truth: an assassin had tried to kill me. I'd leave it at that and let them come to their own conclusions.

At least, I no longer had to justify why I wouldn't be going down to the pub with them.

I looked at the doctor. "When can I be released?"

She shrugged. "When can someone get here to pick you up?"

I closed my eyes again, frustrated. When I opened them, the unrelenting speckled ceiling panels greeted me. "No one is coming to pick me up."

She made a sound of acknowledgement. I heard the clipboard hit the plastic container on the side of the heart monitor. "Then you'll want to get comfortable," she told me quietly. "We aren't releasing you for at three more days. You had a lot of internal blood loss."

I had felt two of my ribs break completely, with the potential of a third. They must have punctured something.

She sighed and turned away from me. Then, she stopped, her fingers touching that off-green curtain. She spoke to me like she was breaking my heart, "You almost died, kid."

She didn't need to talk in that way to me. My heart had already broken. It had been broken since the day I buried Jace.

The doctor left in much the same way as when she came: without hesitation. I was left to myself again, the sound of that beeping filling my ears. *Beep. Beep. Beep.*

I didn't feel like I had almost died. I never feared death. What I feared was the suffering of living without capability, that it may befall me inescapably. I was not ready to die with my failures looming over me. I still had things to do before I joined my family in the dirt.

I stared at the ceiling, all of the fissures and the uneven pieces that made up the speckled firmament of the hospital room. I blinked until my vision was no longer blurry.

I was not fated to die here. Not yet.

Six months later, I killed Belig. That time, he was the one who had his lungs punctured by his own ribs. That time, I didn't leave him for dead like he did me.

That time, I threw a knife at an unwelcome voyeur without looking, hissing "I have no quarrel with you." That time, I cut through his skin without spilling my own bile. That time, I finished the job.

I told Belig something when I first spoke with him: The world is full of broker-shady people who do terrible things to one another in order to make themselves feel better. I told him I didn't want to be one of those people.

But I was becoming one.

January 31, 2726

Hunaphu

It had taken some time for the North Winds to mold us into the perfect soldiers for their crusade. We had been here six months, and the cloying scent of spring had begun to settle in the air. I loved spring in theory, but it always came as a reminder of how much time I had wasted so far.

Summer was just a hair away. It would be four years, soon.

I took solace in the fact that we were almost done. Just another six months, and all twelve of us would be fully vetted, under less scrutiny. That was when I would start my true crusade. Frost laced my lungs.

Good. Let the ice freeze with renewed vigor. You will need that rage, that resolve.

Sometimes it was hard to tell if that voice in my head was my own or someone else's because sometimes it felt like something I would say to myself and other times it felt like something that I needed to say to myself, but would never be able to articulate.

We had passed through the hard skills portion and moved onto the soft skills portion. This time we got to choose our own partners for the matchup: Sancus and I readily chose one another with well-aimed, not-too-hard punches to the gut that stole the wind from our chests.

"Tell me when it gets hard to breathe," I announced quietly, pushing into his solar plexus. Sancus fought to push a wince off his face. The goal was to force the area down, to compact the skin into a bundle on the sensitive area. It got easier to do with practice. I had learned this a while ago, in a little clearing with sky blue trees and lemon-yellow sand.

I watched Sancus's chest stutter in its movement. My head darted to look at the twitch in his thick eyebrows, an indicator of the amount of pain he was in. The left quivered slightly at the crest. He wasn't going to say anything. He was going to bear it because he still saw himself as the weakest link.

It wasn't true any more. Sancus had grown his skills an incredible amount in recent months. He was an excellent sparring partner and had the lean musculature required to pull off a number of feats that many of us were physically incapable of.

A frown tugged at my cheeks. I wished he could have more confidence. If only Sancus could see himself the way the rest of us did, the way I did.

I knew my work was good, so I released my push on his skin.

"Your turn," I told him as I set myself down to lay on the ground. When we were the bodies, we laid down like we were about to experience acupuncture. It wasn't as gentle as acupuncture and it certainly wasn't as relaxing.

Sancus pushed himself up in my peripheral. I watched his calloused fingers pick up the yellowed pamphlet. "I swear," he mumbled, "it's like we're at a bad all-inclusive sometimes."

I smirked. "I could go for a few free drinks. An all-inclusive wouldn't be bad."

He nodded, intense eyes still studying the paper carefully. "I'm going for the gumline," he said. I closed my eyes. There was a *thwap* sound of paper hitting a flat surface and there was only a brief second before I felt pressure on the soft spot behind my ear.

I didn't wince, pain was not a new feeling that warranted reaction. I did open my eyes, because no matter how much pain I had experienced, every time I felt vulnerable, I flew into attack mode. An unfortunate side effect of life.

Sancus's shirt hung off him loosely, the beige cloth revealing dark skin. I tried to look away. It wasn't kind to look down a friend's clothing, but a thin, raised white line caught my attention. It ran from his clavicle down to his ribs on the opposite side. There was a break in the center where the sternum should have been. The North Wind brand connected the two edges together. Immediately, my brain ran through the list of times I had seen him shirtless. Was it recent? How could I not have noticed it?

"Sancus, is your scar new?" I asked him. The pressure on my left ear relented and he leaned back.

Immediately, his hands fly to clutch at himself all over, a fanaticism and energy that he usually donned pulling through. "Which one?" he asked. "I think I got a couple since getting here."

I knew what he meant. A scar through my eyebrow (which Iktomi kept apologizing for, unnecessarily), one on my ankle (which had been my own fault for dropping a weight on it that took off a hunk of skin), and one on my lower back (from a rouge thrown knife, courtesy of Amaethon).

I pushed myself up to a sitting position and batted his flitting hands to the side. I pointed at the mark that just barely peeked out of his shirt. "This one."

I watched calmness overtake his emotions once the mark was identified. In the rare moments that he was calm, Sancus wore a soft and slow smile instead of the brilliant one; there was ease in his breath, a steady slouch in his posture.

"Oh," he responded, touching it with his fingers. "No, that's an old one."

I hummed in response, letting him know I had heard him.

"You missed it, didn't you?" he asked in an accusatory way.

"Oh, I absolutely did," I admitted with a light tone.

He flicked my forehead, probably leaving a red mark behind. "Dude, you need to start being more observant." Sancus scrunched his nose and his freckles bunched up in the folds of his skin. "Stupid people get killed quickly."

I let myself give a crooked smirk as I dragged my knee up to rest my elbow on it. "You act like I don't have a brain knocking around in here." I tapped my head with my knuckles. "I do… It just happens to be off most of the time."

He laughed, light and airy, throwing his head back. His laugh was a contagious one; I always had to fight to keep my own laughter down. I had to remember to keep my face plain here, with these strangers who would throw me to the wolves in a moment.

Sancus may be an exception. I *felt* as if I could trust him, but feelings often muddled reality, and I could not take the chance that Sancus was not an exception. I couldn't share my desires with him, or the emotions that revealed them. Not now; not yet.

In a flash, he darted his fingers forward, falling right into the spot above the center of my clavicle.

I spluttered, coughing and gasping for breath and fall over to my side, leaning on my forearm for support. He had squished my esophagus and made it hard for me to get air. I could feel my eyes bugging out.

"Obviously, your brain is still off," Sancus mumbled. The sound of crinkling paper hit the air. "Okay, suprasternal notch, check." I heard the smugness in his accented voice and it was *really* hard to be mad at him.

When I had gotten control of my breathing, I stated, with all of the confidence and none of the intention of keeping my word, "You've just started a war, buddy."

I sat up straight and let myself kneel forward. I pushed on his shoulder until Sancus was lying on the ground once more. "So how did you get it?" I asked, looking over the places we hadn't touched yet.

"Instep," I warned before pushing into the inner ankle.

"My brother gave it to me."

I knew I had just opened up a new door that I wasn't really ready to peek into. Asking about his scars was an unspoken contract allowing him to ask about mine. The raised lines beneath the bandaged left arm burned with phantom attention.

I hummed at him to acknowledge I had heard what he said.

"On your stomach, I want to try some of the back ones," he instructed. I listened. The floor smelled of dust and stale air.

"Internal saphenous nerve." I felt the pressure sear into the back of my leg, right on the hamstring.

"It's called internal. Move to the right," I instructed.

This time, the pressure felt hollow. I could feel my muscle quiver beneath his fingers. It felt rough and cold on my cheek. I didn't get up when the pressure was relieved. I heard the crinkle of paper once more and knew I had made the right decision. This time, I felt a pressure in my shoulder. Hollow and aching. Sancus had gotten that one right on the first try.

I felt his sigh more than heard it. It tickled the skin of my exposed arm. "It was the only way for him to prove his loyalty to the Alahooɫ, a warring faction he wanted to join. The girl he loved joined them when the civil war broke out. He wanted to follow."

My access to technology was stunted in the tribe and we didn't learn about current affairs until the end of primary school in my region. On top of that, the information I garnered from radios I had sometimes heard at markets was varied, and sometimes not even in the common tongue. I had no idea of the accuracy of my information.

Maybe I should pick up a book that hasn't been sitting in a mountain for the past millennium.

I felt a press on my lower back; this one was wrong, too. "Left and up," I corrected.

It was his turn to hum.

"Apparently family means nothing to a man who stands to gain power and love," he said, almost sadly.

I didn't know what to say about that. Deep down, maybe Sancus's brother really thought he was making the right decision by betraying Sancus. I don't know if I could have ever done that. I would have never been able to harm Jace, not for the world.

"You know that saying? 'War takes and it takes and you get nothing in return?' Civil wars are worse than that. They don't just take what you have, they take what you can give, too."

I didn't know what he meant by that. I never figured it out for myself and I was too much of a coward to ask him.

I was left without words to give my friend. A part of me felt like repressing all of my sorrow for years prevented me from having empathy now. I never felt as inhuman as I did when I couldn't let Sancus know I was there, that I would listen if he wanted to talk, that life is shit and that I'd do everything I could to make it easier on him.

The pain receded.

I said nothing about war and nothing about family. I said nothing to dull the bitter sorrow. Instead, I asked, "Which ones haven't we covered?"

"I've never seen him look like that before," Kali says in a hushed tone. She leaned forward across the table, as if closing the distance would be more discreet.

Nyami Nyami placed his arm on the back of his chair and swung to look around at Iktomi, effectively ruining the covert feeling of the discussion. Kali smacked him on the arm that rested on the table. He jumped and looked away again. He stuck his tongue out at Kali; she returned the favor.

I smiled at their interaction, before quickly forcing my lips to curl back down.

I, too, took a peek over my shoulder at Iktomi, albeit more furtively than my adjacent counterpart. He was alone, hunched over the book that had a listing of all of the human pressure points on a diagram, sitting in the brown chair I favored.

I saw the frustration, the worry, etched in lines across his face. It was barren of the happiness it usually showed.

Frankly, I thought he was naturally skilled. It was nice to know that he, too, needed to learn and practice to improve. I hadn't been watching him at practice. I really hadn't been paying attention to anyone but Sancus, who, at that moment, sat on the other side of the table, socializing with the twins and Nakkrah.

I turned back to the group. I didn't have anything to say, so I took another bite of the stew. I got a potato chunk this time.

Amaethon cleared her throat and brought our attention to her. I looked up. "He seems like the kind of guy who didn't fail a lot growing up." She pushed a lock of red hair behind her ear nervously. "Like, he must have had super strict parents who thought that imperfections weren't an option, you know?" Amaethon continued.

She blinked a lot, I noticed, when attention was on her. Normally, her brown eyes were calm, but when she had attention pulled her way, she scrunched up her mousy nose and batted her eyelashes a lot.

Nyami Nyami nodded slowly and hummed. "Can't be easy being number one in the trial, demeanor, and martial arts, only to lose out on the human physiology portion."

It was not easy to take the plunge from the number one position; I had been quick to climb to his spot for this unit. In the end it was my fault he was like this. The other three at the table were kind enough not to say as such.

I sighed and looked down at my plate. The other three changed topics, but I was no longer privy to their discussion. I wasn't hungry any more. I used the wooden fork to push the thick stew around my plate, forming a wreath. I hadn't done that in a long time. I had taken every bite of food I could, stored it in my stomach in case I didn't eat the next day.

The only reason I was so good at this portion was because malnutrition in my early teens stunted my growth and Yonten had wanted to teach my ways to bring down a bigger opponent.

I should be happy that I was now number one, that I had been able to so easily best the best. But I knew it was a pyrrhic victory. If Iktomi was no longer the best, then I gained nothing by being better than he; he was no longer an accurate gauge for my skills.

My left eyebrow twitched and I scowled at the food.

Serves him right. Iktomi always thought he was better than us. He came in cocky and happy-go-lucky and joked around all the time, like this was some game to him. Why shouldn't he suffer being less than perfect for once? Why shouldn't he learn what it meant to be average.

I huffed out in frustration, silently damning the ebbing sense of obligation. Then I pushed my hands against the table and stood, turned about face, and made a straight path toward Iktomi. He looked up at me when I came to stand in front of him.

"With me. Don't argue," I commanded.

I turned back around and headed for the exit that led to fresh air. I walked quickly and without looking back. If he didn't follow me, that was his loss.

I pushed open the door and walked into the hallway. I led through the tunnels and shafts as well as I could to get us out onto the outdoor platforms. I could hear his feet echoing, now, against the stone walls.

When we got to the outside platform, I turned to angle toward Iktomi and crossed my arms. I closed my eyes and hoped desperately that a vein wasn't popping in frustration.

I opened my eyes as Iktomi drew to a stop in front of me. He waited for me to say something, but I didn't feel like talking just yet. Or maybe I couldn't articulate what I wanted to do.

He pushed his lips out and arched his brows, asking a silent question. I still didn't respond. "Did you pull me out here just to look at me or—"

"Can it," I cut him off. "You're struggling with the pressure points, aren't you?" I tapped my foot.

He pulled a hand to rub at the back of his neck. His eyes fell to the ground. His face grew quite solemn in that instant, and despite my anger, I felt that same sense of obligation I felt earlier.

"Yeah," he admitted.

The scowl fell from my face.

Ainsley, you are a fool. A fool who doesn't know when to stop. I uncrossed my arms and walked close. I grabbed his wrist in my right hand and turned again to pull him with me.

"You paid me a kindness once," I reasoned. When he had fixed my brow. "I can do the same."

When I reached the bench with a chip in the side, I let go of his wrist and laid down on top of it. He looked confused as he stood over me. "We'll start at the basics," I told him. "Do you know where the ulnar nerve is?"

His face cleared of confusion and turned to focus. He looked down at my body and kneeled next to me.

I looked up at the sky. It was a dark night and I could see the milky way clearly.

Two finger pads pressed against my left arm, at the area right below the inner elbow, leaning toward my body. His fingers were calloused and cold. I held back a shiver at the feeling of someone that wasn't Sancus touching me.

The only time Yonten had ever touched me was when he was giving me a new bruise.

Iktomi had found the spot without fail. The studying was good for something. I nodded. "Good, now press it."

"Wait. I could hurt you," he objected, the worried expression marring his handsome face once again. "You trust me?"

I closed my eyes and inhaled. The air smelled differently at night. It smelled like purity and safety, crisp and biting. "You haven't given me any reason to distrust you yet. Why should I?"

Iktomi wasn't meant to answer my question and I wasn't meant to hear any reason he could come up with.

His fingers drilled into my muscle and tendon slowly, the pain rising with his action, but it wasn't the same kind of hollow pain I should feel; it was more of a sore pain, like he thought of muscle as glass he could break rather than a braided rope he should part.

I reached over with my right hand and adjusted Iktomi's own. I moved the thumb into a position where it would apply pressure on the tip and the rest of the finger could wrap around my arm to give him stability in his motion.

"Try again, like that," I said.

Iktomi listened. This time, as he pressed into my flesh, I did feel the hollow pain I was intended to. A pain that made me want to fidget and buckle. I kept my breathing as controlled as possible, my chest rising and falling every two seconds. In and out.

I opened my eyes and let myself look at him, the person I compared myself to, as I taught him how to beat me once again. "You got it," were the only words I felt capable of saying.

Iktomi's head snapped to look me in the eyes, his eyes wide. His fingers loosened and the pain went away. He looked back to my arm and I could see the outline of his Greek nose against the bright night sky behind him. He let out a puff of a laugh, and a surprised smile crossed his face, like he hadn't believed he could do it

My lips twitched up in a smile on the left side of my face. I fought to make my face still. It was dark, I argued, Iktomi wouldn't see it.

"Want to try again?" I asked.

He nodded his head eagerly.

I let my gaze drift back to the sky. "The common peroneal nerve. Find it." He did.

"I'll still beat you," I warned, without bite, if only to let him know... something. Something I couldn't articulate, but burned the inside of my skin. Something that made me want to grab the collar of his dumb white button up and ram my forehead into his. Something that made me want to ask him why he always looked at the fire poker as if it had done him a disservice. I wanted to let him know something that was both aggressive and vulnerable, friendly and antagonistic. Something. For some reason, my mind saw Iktomi and his immense skill as my goal post, the ticket to being good enough to keep pace with the assassins I was after. Something. "Don't forget it."

His eyes flashed with a different something than mine and his jaw fell slack. In a moment, he pushed those expressions away. "I won't."

We went practicing for another two hours. I would name a sensitive spot on my body, Iktomi would find it. If he couldn't find it, I would tell him the location. Then, I would tell him to press down. When he needed adjustment, as he frequently did, I would fix his positioning and tell him to try again. He didn't stop reacting in that overjoyed way.

At no point did it even occur to me that I would wake up the next day feeling heavy all over, sore from having my body poked and prodded at. The need to have a proper rival took precedence over any physical handicap that the activity may have caused.

When we were done with the impromptu lesson, we headed inside. I immediately turned to Sancus and Kali, who were sitting together by the coffee table, laughing about some joke Sancus had made.

"Where are the twins?" I asked, knowing that they had been sitting with Sancus just before I left.

"Xbalanque went to medical. He cut his finger open on a knife and needed stitches," Sancus supplied.

I shook my head. I didn't think Xbalanque was ever a fully healthy person. As soon as one injury of his healed, another one seemed to pop up.

I looked up to see Kali pointing over her bony shoulder at the entrance to the bathroom. "Hunaphu went in there a little while ago. Hasn't come out."

I nodded again.

I walked over to the bathroom, seeing the bright white lights on the inside echoing out into the dimmer room we were in. I peeked my head inside. None of the showers were running. The sinks with the porcelain bowls had no one before them.

I realized why when I heard the sound of choking. I looked at the ground and saw Hunaphu's legs and black sneakers poking out from under one of the stalls. They stood in stark contrast to the grey tiled floor.

I took one step toward her, then another, listening as the sound of choking stopped and the sound of flushing started.

I peeked into the crack in the stall and saw her body, hunched over the bowl. Her long black hair was tied in a braid, a feeble attempt to keep it away from the toilet. Her body convulsed and she wretched into the toilet again, that same choking sound coming out of her throat, deep in the recesses of her esophagus and trachea.

The smell of bile made my nose crinkle involuntarily, an acidic, pungent smell nothing like the food Hunaphu had eaten. It grossed me out, the smell, the concept. Humans were disgusting.

Leave her here, my mind advised, *She's as old as you were when you left home; she can take care of herself.*

I found myself kneeling at the side of the porcelain bowl instead, placing a shaky hand to a shakier back. Hunaphu's yellow shirt was thin and bunched when I touched it. It was warmed to the temperature of her skin and damp with what was likely sweat.

She flinched under my fingertips; she hadn't heard me come in.

"I'm here," I informed her, rubbing her back slightly. I couldn't settle her stomach and I couldn't sooth her ills. Being there was all I could do.

She lifted her head from the bowl and propped it in the crook of her arm, resting on the seat. I watched Hunaphu blink water from hooded eyes. A droplet rolled down her nose and plopped into the toilet.

"Xbalan?" she asked in a daze.

I shook my head. "He was asked to go see Asclepius sometime after you excused yourself." He would have come running if he knew.

I watched her throat contract as she swallowed. Hunaphu's brow furrowed. "Can we keep this between us?" she asked. "I don't like being seen as weak, even if it is just food poisoning."

Silently, I wondered if it really was food poisoning, or if she had sampled some of the liquor that had been left on the table. I nodded anyway.

Hunaphu smiled at me, a gesture of gratitude, but it was faint and weak. Her lip quivered and she shut her eyes tightly again, before flipping her body to heave into the bowl once more.

Delicately, I pulled back the tendrils of her frizzy black hair, gathering it so that it stayed clear of her face.

She coughed a little and saliva dripped off that quivering lip into the bowl. *Vile,* I thought as I rubbed Hunaphu's back, hoping to coax out the rest of the vomit.

It came.

For twenty minutes, I watched her heave the entirety of her meal out of her stomach. And when she had finished throwing up food, she dry heaved for a while, choking on her own contracting throat. The others had the decency to stay away if they had to use the bathroom.

I helped Hunaphu to her feet when she decided she was ready. "Do you want to go to bed now?" I asked her, letting my right hand fall from her back and my left slip out of her grasp.

She wrinkled her nose. "I want to take a shower," she countered.

I nodded. I stood to walk away, to give her some privacy and find Xbalanque, if I could, but an insistent tug at my shirt stopped me. "Stay so no one comes in." She didn't look at me.

I was taken back to a day years ago, when a girl much smaller than her held to the fabric of my shorts as tightly, a girl with emerald hair and a busted lip.

I couldn't say no.

I pulled Hunaphu's hand off of me in the same way I pulled Yaya's hand off so long ago. "I'll grab you a change of clothes." *I'll be gone for only a moment.*

It was her turn to nod. I left the bathroom in a hurry. I made my way across the common area, with some of the night owls still up. Nyami Nyami, Kali, Sancus, Diejiste, and Iktomi were still awake. I was content to dart past them into a room that wasn't mine. I looked for the gold-plated name *Hunaphu,* scratched onto the foot of the bed and reached under the proper one to grab a change of clothes.

I heard the constant stream of water on tile in the middle shower. I set the clothes on the bench just outside the trio of showers. I hoped Hunaphu would see them before she stepped back into her soiled ones. Soon, I heard hacking once more, another bout of dry heaving.

She didn't seem drunk, didn't have the glassed over gaze that people have when liquored up. She must have gotten the one piece of food that wasn't good, since no one else was throwing up.

"I'll wait outside the door," I shouted, just loud enough for her to hear me over the sound of running water.

"Okay," she panted, out of breath from the heaving.

I sat on the floor, my back pressed to the side of a book shelf and my outstretched foot pressed to the doorless doorway of the bathroom.

I pulled up a free knee to prop my elbow on. My eyes scanned the room, but nothing registered in my head.

I shook my head at everyone who tried to use the bathroom for the next half hour, watching as people slowly left for sleep. My fingers absently twisted the brass band in slow circles around my wrist while I waited.

She came out with her hair dry and a smudge of toothpaste on her clean shirt. I almost smiled at that, as I looked up at her. She was almost fifteen, but she looked like a little kid just then.

"Xbalan?" she asked again.

I shook my head. He hadn't returned from the medical branch.

She shuffled her feet and went to sit on the couch near the fire. I leaned onto my hand and pushed myself up to follow her.

"Do you need anything else?" I asked as I drew closer. Iktomi left the common area, too.

"Can you—" she cut off. She wasn't looking at me, she was looking through me. "Can we cuddle? Touch makes me feel better."

I nodded and sat next to her on the couch. She slowly inched over to my side and leaned her head on my shoulder. I wrapped my arm around her shoulder and applied firm pressure on her arm.

Diejiste's stool scraped the floor at the chess table she sat at, running different configurations of the board over and over to memorize different possibilities. She didn't do strategy, couldn't think more than two steps ahead, but her memory was a steel trap.

Soon, like everyone else, Diejieste propped up the pieces in their rightful places and departed the common room.

"You and Xbalan feel the same," Hunaphu whispered, as if she had been waiting until we were alone to speak.

"How do we feel?"

"You feel like the fresh bread smells." Any child who goes hungry for a time understands what that means. It means one whole day where you don't have to ask if the pangs in your stomach will finally kill you off. It means an end to the suffering, however brief.

I leaned my head on top of hers gently, just to let her know I had heard what she had said. I propped my feet up on the table, my bright red sneakers a stark contrast to the deep brown of the table.

It was quiet. The only sounds were the crackling of logs, the shift of padded fabric beneath us, and the sound of two breaths, one steady and low, the other ragged and sharp.

"If I had been born with an older sibling, I would have wanted them to be like you," Hunaphu mentioned against my shirt, nosing her head to the side to block out the soft light of the fire. She said it like a secret only meant for her ears, mine having been an unfortunate voyeur.

I held her a little more tightly. She was too big, far too big to be striving for physical contact from someone. But when I held her, I was able to imagine holding Jace. I saw, not only her small, dark hand clutching at the rim of my shirt, but also the pale one of my brother, with the little scar on his right middle finger he had gotten by playing with the broken latch of a rabbit cage.

"Did you have younger siblings?" I asked her.

Her hair tickled my arm as she shook her head. "I don't know," she admitted. "Did you have siblings?"

"Yeah," I responded, looking off into the fire, remembering a totally different fire that I never actually saw. "One brother."

I had a sibling. A little boy who once left sunflowers on the window sills of every village elder every single Saturday morning, without fail. A little boy, who swore up and down that he could burp the whole Nepsilu alphabet, even though he only ever got to *ka'ash*. A little boy who was too young to meet death, yet was old enough to suffer it regardless.

My vision got hazy and my throat went sore. I blinked and swallowed carefully, and thought of letting the ice grow a little bit, fanning out enough to bring me back and ground me to the world I was in now.

I had already done my crying; my tears had mingled with the crimson rivers of my blood in the dry dirt of my village. Crying wasn't a luxury I allowed myself any more.

"Do you know where he is now?" Her voice was raspy and raw.

When Hunaphu asked me that question, I didn't know what to think.

A long time ago, I would have said that he was in the sky, with the Sun God. He was holding one of her many hands, reliving his happiest moments. But after I saw how he had left black marks on my white flesh as I carried him around, trying to keep him with me for just a little longer, after I saw Jace tossed into a hole in the ground, and covered by shovel after painstaking shovel of dirt, I couldn't answer her question with a yes. Even though Jace's corpse was in that hole, probably only bones by now, I didn't believe there was a soul that was somewhere else. The sad part was, I don't think I believed he was just a body either. He was stuck somewhere in between life and death, suffering alone.

Slowly, over time, beliefs fizzled out of me, burning embers slowly eroding to ash, one after the next. If there was a God out there, their negligence had lost them my respect.

I closed my eyes and took a carefully measured breath before I spoke. "No, Huna," I said quietly as possible, "I don't know where he is."

I held her a little tighter, and she never got up to go to bed.

Eventually, Hunaphu's even breathing could be heard, indicating she had fallen asleep. I was a little too warm from the fire, a little too uncomfortable with her pressed to me.

Selfishly, I refused to wake her. I was trying to make up for all of the years I missed out on with Jace, years that would never happen.

"Farrah," I whispered the name of the forgotten Psoe Nespul, quiet enough it wouldn't disturb Hunaphu, before I let my mind go blank.

I didn't sleep restfully that night, but deep within the vestiges of a hollowed-out mountain, with the scent of a used leather chair and a snapping fire, I found a way to feel normal again, like I had Jace with me.

September 3, 2727

Yssir

Yssir didn't have a last name. She was orphaned before infantile amnesia could fade away and did not remember her family name.

I wished I could say that I knew just by observing her that she had helped butcher my tribe. Sight, alone, did not immediately instill me with a gut's intuition of that.

Sight, alone, gave me the impression of normalcy. She was an assassin by trade, yes, and every move she made was intentional, but not a single one of her actions had the heavy-set pressure of a murderer. Maybe she had lifted the weight for so long that it was as natural as breathing.

She was a woman with an expressionless face, of which her plain features were not easily distinguishable. Still, Yssir was distinctive in that she always seemed to be looking at something off in the distance; even when she looked directly at someone like she was looking through them.

She liked to hike at five in the morning, before the sun had crested the hills. It was hard to follow her like this, when there was no one else to provide cover and the sound of cracking twigs and tumbling rocks were created by my boots and the earth. I needed to stay far enough she wouldn't notice me, close enough that I wouldn't lose her.

Unfortunately for me, I could tell by the pinch of her gait and the hunch in her shoulders that she knew I was behind her, it wasn't like I was invisible. It became a question of whether or not she knew I was trying to kill her.

It was chilly outside. The kind of chill that sets in with the steady roll of an autumnal fog, all-encompassing and reaching down to the bones, coming back out in visible whisps of breath. It was the smell of crisp moisture sticking to the remnants of a dried-up leaf, crunching underfoot in the padding of cold soil.

I took a deep breath and sped my pace, feet sinking into the earth a little with each step. As I drew closer to her back, I could make out coloration and texture. Her hair was dark brown, almost black, thin and straight. Her skin was dark olive and worn with the toughness of sun exposure and faded scars. She had a wiry build, tall and broad, but skinny like a tarp.

The body will never go where the mind has not been. My left hand wrapped around the line of rope hanging off my hip, pulling it from its clip. I imagined how I would use it, getting close enough to just strangle her, pull the line over the top of her head, spin, and use my shoulder as leverage to bring her to the ground. I could imagine the heat of her body on my back, the feeling of all of her muscles tensing before she became dead weight.

She was within distance. I could smell the lingering perfume on her: sweet cream and coffee.

I pulled the rope tightly between two hands and thrust my arms forward, throwing it over her neck. In accordance with the mind of a trained assassin, she was able to react quicker than I was able to act. I was pulled over her shoulder and thrown forward.

My eyes clenched shut of their own accord and my body tensed without my consent. Breath left me as tenderness scorched the sinews of my back, vibrating my brain inside my skull. If I hadn't already received irreparable brain damage, Yssir had given it to me. My lungs shuddered with the phantom pain of broken ribs.

I forced my eyes open when I heard a click. A glint of silver was pulled from Yssir's leather belt, hidden beneath the lose folds of her shirt. She pulled back the hammer as the frame was leaving her makeshift holster.

I pressed my palms flat to the ground and curled my core so that my foot would raise. The metal felt hot as my ankle collided with it, knocking it out of her hands. *Boom.* It discharged, dirt specks flying up into the air and falling onto my skin. I rolled forward and spun back to face her once more, open palms up.

I thrust my hand forward, into her clavicle, knocking her two paces back. She raised her own hands in fists and hunched her shoulders, taking on the stance of a boxer.

A strand of hair fell loose from her tied back ponytail. She didn't look mad. Or upset. Or surprised. She had nothing on her face but for that strand of hair and a splatter of light brown freckles across her nose.

Rather than wait for her to make the first move, the cold chill jolted me forward, right hand aiming straight for her nose. She deflected with the back of her wrist.

Yssir didn't waste any unnecessary movement. When I moved my knee to her ribs, she stepped back and brought her elbow down on my femur. When I snap kicked from that raised knee, she moved forward and struck my stomach with a closed fist.

I was wide and erratic, my brain knew that, but my body was reluctant to listen to what my brain was saying. For all the fact that we could have been evenly matched, same height and likely similar weights, she was calm, while a crimson frost obscured my view and muddied my movements.

Hand to hand, parry to parry, we exchanged blows like poor lovers, caught up in arrogant and unhealthy passion. With each movement of her feet, every shuffle of her balance, she bore that same unreadable expression, with slack lips parted just enough to suck in cold air.

Fuck this! I dropped down and pushed forward, lodging my shoulder into her sternum. She coughed and sucked in air. I didn't look up to see her reactions, my eyes were trained on the knee I jammed between her legs.

She fell back onto the ground, arms still up to protect her face. I stepped forward. Yssir rolled onto her side and swept her leg underneath me. It caught my left ankle. I stumbled back and looked down just in time to see a heel colliding with my own sternum.

I skidded across the dirt, the sharp sting of rocks shredding my forearms through the cloth covering. I grunted, my throat seizing up around an imaginary lump.

A twig snapped under Yssir's foot as she stomped toward me, all power and purpose. Her movements were calculated again, calm. She lifted her outer shirt and pulled out another gun placing her index finger on the frame over the trigger guard.

I moved my palms to the ground once more, to push myself up. The sharp edge of a rock cut through my hand and the blood made me slip. My face hit the dirt.

I rolled onto my back and scrambled away from the encroaching form of Yssir, pushing my heels into the dirt. My fingers clawed at the earth, pulling it up beneath my nails. The gravel pieces entwined with my flesh where my palms were raw.

Tke vikja. *Not yet.* I could not have come this far just to die in the dirt like scum. My lungs had just finished healing.

Her face showed no signs of anger when she raised the barrel of her pistol to my face. I realized, with the thrum of my pulse in my ears, that indifference was more frightening than anger. The hard-set lines of Yssir's mouth and brow and the dark, lightless eyes were more dangerous than any emotion could be. Yssir didn't have a single emotion left inside her.

The hollow, circular center of that barrel seemed endless, though it was smaller than a denarius coin. The gunmetal gray wrapped around that infinite chasm in a cool embrace, giving the timely warning that the trigger had not yet been pulled, that the recoil had not yet shaken the gun.

My elbow buckled and my hand slid from beneath me. *This is how I die,* I thought, *with no one to hear me scream.* My skin tore away my elbow with a burning sensation. Something cool and smooth brushed against the tip of my middle finger. It wasn't rough enough to be a rock.

The missing pistol, a voice that did not belong to me echoed in my mind. *Grab it.*

I slid my hand back further and wrapped around the wooden hilt of the gun. Without thinking, my thumb forced down the hammer as I swung the gun around to my front. My other hand flew up to wrap around my first and pull the trigger.

My back hit the ground with the startling jolt of the pistol and the loud crack that accompanied it.

The splash of droplets speckled my face, hot and cold at once. The wet taste of copper lingered on my lips like the kiss of a lover. I sucked in a breath, I hadn't realized I was holding it.

Yssir didn't pull her own trigger. I didn't give her the chance to.

My thumb pulled down the hammer once more and my forefinger pulled the trigger again. And again. And again. And again. Then, on the sixth time, the revolver clicked when I tried to pull the trigger, emptied.

Yssir was still standing, holding her pistol in her dangling left arm. Her face was still immobile, the tender lines of her low cheekbones existing without even a twitch. Her eyes fluttered shut. And she crumpled, five deep red flowers blossoming across her torso.

She was limp when she hit the ground, a collapsed heap of human, her arms and legs twisted at awkward angles.

I let out a shaky huff and pulled the gun down. I pressed it into the earth and released it. It had left the skin of my hand chapped and raw, a blister forming in the junction of my forefinger and thumb, but I was still the one in the better condition.

I pushed myself up and crawled over to Yssir's corpse, slowly leaking red into her blouse. If she wasn't dead, she was in shock. The crawling crimson should have been a familiar sight to me, but it seemed surreal.

I stopped looking at the messy body and pulled out my knife.

I set to work on her right hand first, methodically, as I had with Abbadon and Belig. Sawing through skin and muscle sinews had become much easier, a well-practiced skill. Then, the left; it came off just as easily as the right. The head always took the longest, detaching from the corpse in a series of slices. There was so much blood that leaked from the neck. It stained my hands and made the knife slip every time.

This could have been me, I thought. But it *wasn't* me. Instead, that little voice in my head reached out, telling me about the gun.

It wasn't the voice I normally heard. It wasn't one that I was familiar with, but I knew it was the voice Jace would have had, if he had still been alive. It had none of the childish pitch Jace had in his life, but it was his, of that I was certain. My brother had reached out to me, I was sure of it. Ik ves ovrai dves Arrakaul dves Psoe, *by the grace of the Sun God,* Jace had saved me.

When I had finished dismantling the head, mens rea, and the hands, actus rea, I placed my hands in the cold, damp earth and began pulling it toward me in heaps. I was going to bury the body. The whole didn't have to be deep. After all, I wanted someone to find it. I wanted Yssir's body to be on TV screens across the globe. I wanted her to serve as a warning to the others, others who may not have seen the broadcasts of Abbadon and Belig, that I was coming.

I dug, quickly, and with painstaking breaths that cooled in my chest and crystallized in air.

It occurred to be that out of three intended victims I had almost died three times. I felt the gnawing inadequacy eating a hole through my stomach, pressing at the base of skull in an insistent and slimy cadence. I swallowed thickly, hoping to push away atelophobia for a moment. It stayed, telling me over and over that I was useless and that, no matter how good I had gotten, I was playing the catch-up game, that I would *always* be playing the catch-up game.

With shaky familiarity, the image of Xenon popped into my head. It was the same thing, just with new people. Again, I was faced with being second-best, just underachieving enough to be the first loser.

I didn't want to feel that any more.

When the hole was big enough, I rolled Yssir's body inside of it, pushing the dirt atop of her, filling the space between her legs, the gaps between her arms and torso. I patted the dark dirt down, making a mound out of the moist dirt.

The sun was beginning to crest the horizon, drenching the world in liquid tangerine. I reached for the limp hands and placed them on top of her buried body, laying the fingers of her right hand over those of her left in a cross stitch. Then I grabbed her head. It was still sticky on the bottom, and the short tips of her hair were wet and crusted together with the stickiness of blood. I laid the head behind the hands, facing at me.

When my breath evened, I realized, clinically, I could count another down, scratch her name from the list. Abbadon, Belig, Yssir. Almost half way.

I felt nothing inside me, save for the ice that creaked and fractured and refroze endlessly. Slowly, it ebbed and melted, sated, for the time being.

I wouldn't lose next time. I had a divine mandate: Att tjai ik att fjai. *An eye for an eye.*

I pushed myself up from the ground. The damp soil stuck to the clothing on my knees. I looked around me, trying to orient my body, to clear the fog in my mind and *think*.

I came from the east. I had to follow the rising sun to get back. There was a stream there. I could wash off the dirt and the blood and wait for my adrenaline to clear out.

I cast one downward look back at Yssir. Her face as expressionless as ever, thin lips pressed together in a relaxed way.

Then I pulled myself forward, to that blinding light, through the brambles of arching roots, I pulled myself forward, dragging my adrenaline-filled, shaking body, until I reached the stream that was deep enough to wet the skin of my knees when I stood.

I didn't use the foot bridge as I had earlier. I waded into the cold water, feeling it numb my skin when I sunk down. The water passed my shoulders. Red and brown danced downstream in the translucent water around me and I knew the freezing water was a better alternative than going back into town.

My hands scrubbed at the clothes hanging tight to my body, trying to wash away the impurities. The smack of cold collided with my cheeks when I pushed my head under. My fingers rubbed at my face, trying to get the speckled red that had dried in itchy droplets off.

It wasn't particularly cold outside the water, but it wasn't particularly warm, either. Drying could have taken anywhere from one to four hours. My mind was blank the whole time, as I lay in the white pebbled creekside, watching the billowing and dulled green from the not yet dying canopy above me.

My heart tried to match its pace to the shaking rhythm of the trees.

When the last remnants of moisture left me, I pulled the light blue overshirt out of my utility belt and threw it on over my long sleeve shirt before pushing up the black sleeves to show my forearms. I bandaged my left arm. I didn't have clean overpants to cover my suit.

The trek to town was short.

Just don't be the weirdest one here, I instructed myself. *They only notice the weirdest one.*

And no one did notice me, in spite of the tight clinging pants and combat boots. I could easily dip in and out of the midday crowds and make my way back to the bridge I had stashed my false identification cards in.

My movements were fluid, my shoulders turning and my feet barely gracing the ground.

Steel balls chained to my wrists yanked me back to earth in a heartbeat.

He had grown a little older. Still clean shaven, I didn't think he could even grow a beard. His monolid eyes were still just as dark and intense, and the little scar that raced through the straight eyebrow over his left one was just as prominent against his tan skin. His jaw was a little more angular now, his nose a little straighter. He still had the same cheeks and the same lips, but now the two weren't pulled up in the smile that forced his eyes to crinkle in the corners.

I swallowed hard. Had my throat always been this dry?

Lee looked like he had seen a ghost. To an extent, he had. My name was written in the death book as *deceased, 06/01/2723.* I had checked.

It was almost as if I was seeing a ghost, too. A ghost in red clothing, still wearing the matching ear piercing we had gotten in our cartilage at the spring festival seven years ago. He was a visage of the past that I had cast aside.

The thing about casting humans aside, is they tend to do what they want, not what we want them to.

"Hey," I choked out, my voice a little unsteady, "been a while."

"Do—" a woman trailed off. "Do you two know each other?"

I hadn't noticed her before. I was too focused on Lee. She was dark, with light hair and eyes. She had a medium build and soft features, like her face had been made from painstaking hours of a sculptor's fingers gliding, feather-light, across stone, until all of the harshness of rock had been eroded away by gentle love.

My eyes flickered to him again. There was shock on his face. It was a shock filled with anger and pain and the accusation *You let me think you were dead.*

Lee flinched a little closer to the woman at his left. Her arm tensed. I followed that tension down. Their hands were entwined. Matching tattoos adorned the back of those hands. A black square, with olive branches looped in a wreath around it.

It wasn't only confusion on Lee's face. There was shame there, too, shame he had a new life I wasn't a part of. Survivor's guilt.

If Lee was still the person I grew up with, there were a thousand things I could think of him saying to me in that silence. He would say that the time we had spent in our youth was still vital to him, to who he had become. He would tell me that he had spent a year dealing with the loss of me and that he still had days where he couldn't move from grief. He would tell me he shed so many tears, not even Josephine and Emil could chase them away. He would tell me that he was sorry because if he knew I was still alive, things would have been different.

He didn't need think any of those things. Where we were now was not a reflection of his choices, but of my own. I had made peace with reality years ago, contented myself with being a scratched-out face in the photo of their past.

Despite the discomfort in my stomach, I smiled at the woman beside him. "We were friends," I explained. That was what we were, once. It was all we would ever be.

"Do you want to go ahead without me?" Lee asked her. Her round, lavender eyes tracked him; his didn't leave me. "I want to catch up for a little while."

Suddenly, the smell of copper that clung to me like cheap perfume wafted up. I prayed no red marked my clothing or stained my skin. I prayed that he couldn't smell the scent of blood.

Ia, tke kvenpe supitt meriv att yttig. *Please, don't let him know I'm a murderer.* I wanted, at the least, to keep the monster I had become away from Lee.

She pulled away from him and walked past me. Frankly, I wasn't paying her much mind. Lee turned around and walked toward a park bench, implicitly telling me to follow. I did.

He sat down all the way to the left side and swung his arm over the back of the bench. His head tilted up exasperatedly at the sky, his eyes shut.

I was grasping at straws. I bet he was, too. What do you say to someone you thought was dead?

So, I tried for something. "You picked a good one... She's gentle," I commented, hoping it was enough. They did seem like a good fit, the opposites-attract couple of the wild and the consistent. Though, Lee didn't seem as wild as he once was. I remembered him with constantly messy hair and flaming eyes. But that day, his hair was combed away from his face and his eyes were tired. "What's her name?" I asked.

"Why did you leave?" he asked in turn, ignoring my question.

I took in a sharp inhale and rocked up onto my toes before sitting down on the bench, too. We were seated too far to be friends, too close to be strangers.

I pressed my palms together. They were sticky. I felt flushed.

"There wasn't any reason to stay," I offered.

"Bullshit!" he hissed, a little too loudly and a little too harshly to not turn heads.

I pressed my lips together. They were shaking. I kept my eyes fixed on my lap, on the left seam of my black pants. I couldn't look at him. "We were—we were there. We should have been a reason to stay..." He trailed off, as if something was left unsaid. I didn't push it; I wouldn't like what he had to say.

I looked at him; I regretted it instantly. He looked how Yonten looked when he talked about his daughter. It was a look of mourning, brows drawn together, lips shut, but jaw unlocked, eyes empty, staring at a future that never was.

An uneasy guilt slithered inside my gut when Lee whispered, "I should have been a reason for you to stay," his voice broken and tired. *That* was what I hadn't wanted to hear

For you, he had said. Disappointment made its home, hot in the hollow of my throat. In my frustration, I let the ice inside me grow. It tingled against my nerves and swaddled my muscles.

I could look away now. I looked to the grassy field in front of us, some kids playing with a can. It gave me something to focus on, that sound of clanging metal and the occasional scent of dirt and grass.

"Fine. Then, I had more reasons to go than there were to stay," I noted, no bite in my hurtful words.

It was the truth, but some truths are better off kept to oneself. Some things I said because I didn't understand how they would hurt people. I said that because I *knew* it would hurt him. Somehow, I thought that hurting him would make me hurt less.

"You've become a cold person, Ains," Lee murmured.

I shrugged. I was being cold. There was no argument to be made. "I know." If only he knew how cold.

I watched a kid kick the can and run away, darting behind trees and bushes, picnickers and large dogs. They were playing a game. I was sure I played it before. Maybe with the man sitting next to me. I didn't remember the rules, if I had ever played it. I bit my bottom lip in frustration and dug my nails into the backs of my hands.

"You could have been happy. We could have helped you—I don't know. You should have stayed."

"Maybe."

I could have.

I was grateful for all of the people I had met, for Sancus and Xenon and Hunaphu and Xbalanque meant the world to me. But if I had stayed, they *wouldn't* mean the world to me. Lee and Josephine and Emil would. Lee, someone who once had meant so much to me, now meant little more than the barkeep I paid last night for information.

The worst part was, I wasn't even sad about that.

"Are you going to tell them?" I asked. "That I'm still alive?"

"No," Lee shook his head. I watched his slicked back hair fall loose as he ran a shaky hand through it. Why was it shaking? "They don't need to know you didn't care enough to say goodbye."

His words hit like a slap. Worse than a slap, really. A slap stung for a moment and disappeared. His words sunk into my chest like tar, pushing me deeper into murky depths. I opened my mouth to say something in response, to give out some semblance of excuse, but I didn't have one.

I closed my mouth and folded my hands tight, knowing I was

objectively in the wrong. I had messed up.

"You were..." Lee trailed off. He clenched his eyes shut tightly and I could have sworn his eyelashes were shinier than usual. "You were my everything." His voice hitched on the word 'everything'.

Lee didn't have much growing up. He was an only child and his parents neglected him for constant business trips. To a boy who knew the periodic table more thoroughly than he knew his blood, I had been the closest thing to a family he had.

And I had left him with nothing. I couldn't expect forgiveness for that.

Lee pushed himself up from the bench, with a humph of air. He didn't look at me.

I would have given anything to see his eyes, but he was cold. He was cold in the way someone was to an asshole who wasn't worth their time. I wasn't worth his time any more.

"You know, you're dead to the world," Lee said, barely audible over the clatter and chatter of the busy park. "Now, you're dead to me, too."

Then he left.

His shaking hand hadn't been fear, it had been anger. Intense, hot anger that burned like a metal brand.

As I watched Lee walk away, I felt like I was looking back in time. It wasn't really him I was looking at, but myself, as I had been when I was almost fifteen: quick to laugh and giving to others instead of using them for what I needed.

I wondered when the outcome became more important to me than my values. Did it happen when I lost my tribe? When I found out I could take justice for them? When I met Yonten? When I finally became a God?

In the end, it didn't matter when it had happened, because it *did*.

Losing oneself is a bit like forgetting a passage from your favorite novel. It leaves slowly, straying further and further, crossing your thoughts less and less frequently until one day is the last day you think of it. It goes forgotten for years. Then, when you read it again, it comes rushing back that you had been missing a once important thing. It's a little sad, because no matter how much you repeat the passage, or try to become yourself again, it's always just a cheap imitation of what it once was, it's always missing something.

I was missing something and it shattered some part of my life.

I had spent enough time around glass to know that when it shatters, it cannot be fixed. There are too many dangerous shards and the fissures will always mar the transparency of the surface. I could not fix what I had broken; I had to live with that knowledge for the rest of my life.

For the first time in many years, with five deaths staining my hands, I felt regret for the choices I made. These choices took away who I had been. Knowing I'd lost who I was, if I could go back, would I make another decision?

I closed my eyes and tilted my head up toward the mid-day sun, peaking momentarily through the overcast sky. It was a comfort to me to do this, to feel the Sun God warm on my skin, drinking her in. I sighed out softly to myself.

Even knowing I lost who I was forever, if I could go back, I would make those same choices.

March 18, 2726

Nakkrah

Breakfast that morning was meatballs and rice, with some swirled pastry dessert. There was never any breakfast food. It was like they were serving us last night's leftovers, though we always had a different dinner the night prior.

I pushed my fork into the balls and cut them up so I could mix them into the rice to make it appear as if I had eaten. Turning down food would have been unheard of for me this time last year.

Sancus and the twins had enjoyed their food enough to grab a second serving.

Although Sancus had always held a healthy body weight, the twins had been scrawny when they first arrived. As soon as the two had stable nutrients, their height shot up. Though, Hunaphu still had an inch or two on Xbalanque.

I pushed another one of my whole meatballs onto Hunaphu's plate.

She looked up at me. "Are you sure?" she asked, her mouth full of food. She asked like there wasn't plenty to go around.

I nodded at her. I noticed she had a bit of brown sauce on her face. "Your cheek," I mentioned as I pointed toward the mirrored spot on my own face.

"Oh!" she exclaimed, wiping it off with her napkin. Her cheeks did not darken with embarrassment; she wasn't the type of person to be embarrassed over something as insignificant as food on her face. "Thank you."

I nodded again.

"No fair!" Sancus interjected from across the table. "How come you tell them when they have food on their face, but not me? You let me walk around for an hour with crumbs on my lips two weeks ago."

I leaned forward onto my elbows. "It's funny you think they were only there for an hour." I shot him a crooked grin before leaning back in my chair, balancing on the last two pegs.

"Dude, everyone saw me like that. It was so embarrassing." Sancus pushed his fingertips through the roots of his hair with a forlorn expression on his face.

I scoff. "There are so many things you *should* be embarrassed about and you choose that?" I jived lightly.

Sancus's eyebrow twitched and his face went deadpan. "If you don't shut up, I'm going to throw a muffin at your head," he warned. Apparently, he didn't find me as humorous as I found myself.

I looked at the table. There were no muffins in sight. The only vaguely pastry-like thing was a swirled cinnamon bread. I let out a sarcastic gasp. "Bro, bro. What do you mean?" I asked, feigning confusion. "They're cinnamon rolls, bro; we don't have any muffins," I patronizingly explained.

I was rewarded for my sarcasm with Sancus grabbing a cinnamon roll, fast as a marlin, and chucking it with a sideways spiral at me as hard as he could.

An undignified squawk left my throat without my consent as the bread flew past my uselessly raised hands and hit my left cheek. My eyes snapped shut. It fell down onto my lap. I opened my eyes. I felt a sticky residue on my cheek that I tried to rub off with the back of my wrist, only resulting in making me sticky in two places instead of one.

"Yuck," I complained, picking up the roll and putting it back on the table.

Sancus wore a cocky smirk of victory. "I told you."

That was fair. He did tell me. Still, I stuck my tongue out at him in retaliation.

The door to the common area swung open, and we were greeted by Ifri, one of the senior educators. He held a stack of papers under his arm and his shoulders were hunched with the weight of them.

Maybe it wasn't just the papers that made him slump. His eyes had dark circles under them and his clothes were wrinkled in the way clothes get when you've slept in them and haven't changed out of them yet. I could practically see the stench of alcohol coming off him, even though I couldn't actually smell him. I let myself believe he had stayed up late at the Aces Pub that we all frequented.

Ifri looked like he was special forces in the past. He stood at the godly height of seven feet tall and looked like he would win a fight against a brick wall. His arms were cut with jagged kinds of scars that looked like they had been made from ropes. He had the most well-defined jawline I had ever seen.

"All right, everyone line up," he yelled, a little too loudly for the small room. He winced at his own voice. Yep, certainly hung-over.

He transferred the folders under his arm into his hand and smacked them against his open palm, looking at all of us, lined up like obedient dogs. "Missions," he explained in a single word.

A few gasps and flinches came from the group. We all knew the day was coming, but we didn't know exactly when.

I looked to Sancus from the other end of the line. He stood with his shoulders pushed back and his legs spread far enough to make him look like a soldier in a Roman armada. He looked at me out of the corner of his almond eyes and flashed a smile. Partner acquired.

Ifri shook his head and flipped the paper over, revealing the next in the stack that was attached by a black clip. "You'll pair up with the number closest to your own ranking. One with two, three with four, so on and so forth. I'll pass out your info packets now."

I felt my chest collapse upon itself, as the sneaky smile fell away from Sancus.

I looked up to Iktomi, staring straight ahead and extending his hand to grab the packet that Ifri was handing us, sealed in a yellowed envelope with a red tie. He pulled it toward himself and began working at the knot.

Iktomi tugged out a few papers on that were inside. There were false identification files, reservation information, and information on our target. "I'm kind of nervous," Iktomi said. "I've never stopped contract fraud before."

He extended half of the papers for me to look through. I took them. They smelled like the information had just been printed; the ink was still fresh and stuck slightly to the back of the previous pages. "Have you stopped other types of fraud before?" I asked, as I read through the documents.

I saw him shake his head out of the corner of my eye. "I guess not," he replied. "I'm also excited. We get to go to the Camaeris Region. I've heard it's lovely." His cheeks were pink as he looked over flight plans. I never thought I could see an adult make that face, the one of high expectations and bewilderment.

I readily focused my attention back on the papers in front of me. It wasn't a vacation.

When I finished, I looked up to seek Sancus out. He was standing over his own packet with Kali. When he looked up and made eye contact with me, he smiled and nodded his head slyly. I could hear his voice in my head: *This time, Ma'at. This time I'll make Kali fall for me.* A hopeless romantic.

I looked away. I couldn't make eye contact with him when he acted like that.

Kali wasn't awful. After the day she smacked me, I started to enjoy her a little more, with her quick wit and cunning. And though I knew Kali would never look at Sancus in the way he looked at her, he still craved Kali in the way a junkie craved drugs, hooked on her dopamine drip.

I handed the papers back to Iktomi.

"Done already?" He took them and shoved them back into the folder. He was biting his lip, peeling off the chapped skin with his teeth. He claimed he was nervous, but I had never seen him wear it before.

"Yes," I stated. Hypertension pulsed in my skull. "You aren't?"

He chuckled, that silky, low chuckle that seemed reserved, like he was holding something back, like he didn't want me to know what he was thinking. He rubbed the back of his neck. "It's just pretty amazing how quickly you read."

My face warmed and I found it difficult to look at him any longer. A weird pit of discomfort made a home in my stomach.

I waved my hand. "Don't forget, this mission is my chance to prove I'm better than you," I told him, looking away. "My reading speed isn't what you should be worried about."

He laughed, this time uninhibited. The laugh was genuine.

He looked down at the folder and fiddled with a corner of it, creasing the paper. "Don't forget about me, either. I'm still ten times more competent." It was a declaration of war, but he looked happy. I don't think he even noticed he was smiling.

"I won't." I smirked.

A weird, high-pitched sound come from his throat.

My eyebrow twitched up in confusion.

Iktomi grabbed my shoulders and turned me to face him. Then he raised his fingers to my cheeks and pinched them like a grandma would.

"You little shit, you have no right to be that cocky," he grunted without malice. I could imagine my skin reddening from the rough treatment. I tried to pull away and he let go easily, but flicked my nose on the way out.

"Little? You're only three years older than me."

His face drooped. "I was referring to the fact that you're only five-seven."

My hypertension came back at a blinding speed. I made a silent promise to put something smelly in his pillow case later.

"I'm five-eight, dude," I argued under my breath. "Just finish your reading and we can discuss it tomorrow morning."

I turned around the room, searching for Sancus or the twins. All three were occupied in their case materials. I frowned. Even Nyami Nyami was preoccupied. Hunaphu was separated from her partner. I searched the room for him, asking myself why he wasn't with her.

When I saw Nakkrah, engrossed in his own paper, sitting on the red arm chair, I realized why he wasn't with Hunaphu. He was a loner. Friendly, but never stuck around for long. He probably excused himself under the guise of wanting to sit down.

He had a peculiar look on his face, a dazed look. I've never been one to ignore my curiosity. I walked over to him, careful to stay out of his peripheral until the second I leaned onto the arm of the chair. He held the mission slip in his hand, looking at it as if it were something precious.

"There's no invisible ink," I joked, leaning a little closer to him. He smelled like a camp fire.

The right corner of his lips twitched and Nakkrah nodded. "I guess I just can't believe the day has finally come," he admitted. His eyes never left the yellow paper.

I leaned a little closer and let our shoulders bump together. It was meant to be a gesture of camaraderie. He bumped me back.

"Are you nervous?" I asked.

When Nakkrah shook his head, a strand of carefully waxed hair fell out. He raked his fingers along his scalp, pushing it back into place to rejoin the rest of the brown sculpture.

"Then why are you looking at it like that?" I asked, gesturing to the paper with my left hand.

I heard him inhale sharply. It was a soft sound, a baby's sigh. "I just can't believe I finally get to do what I came here for."

I blinked. "You came here for this?" I made sure my face was neutral when I heard the surprise evident in my voice.

Nakkrah nodded slowly. He turned to look at me, but when our eyes met, his eyes grew wide and he looked back down at the paper quickly. His cheeks darkened. The realization hit me that *Oh, he's shy.* I thought he was just reserved and preferred the company of himself to others, but shyness was responsible for his limited interactions. *Cute,* I thought. *Like a little kid.*

"Yeah, I'm not like everyone else here," he elaborated. "You all have such sad lives and came here with limited choices. I'm just the normal guy." I didn't think I would have used the word normal to describe him.

"Normal?" I pried.

Nakkrah nodded again. "Yeah, normal. I came from a happy family; all six of us are alive and healthy."

I watched him reach inside his shirt. There was a chain around his neck with a rectangular locket. He pulled it over his head, handing it to me. I took it in my hands. The metal was warm from his skin. I felt the heavy burn of the string around my own neck, the pendant hitting my sternum, as I looked at his chain.

I undid the clasp. There was a photo of a family of five and their dog standing in front of a water fountain. I noticed he included the shaggy, white shepherd in his count of family members. Nakkrah was the eldest, and looked just like his father. Strong jawlines, button noses. The brother and mom looked similar, too, with bright lemon hair and delicate features. The youngest, Nakkrah's kid sister, looked like the mother with the father's coloring. All of them had the same stunning sapphire eyes.

I closed the locket and handed it back when I felt I had stared too long. "Why would you leave them?" I tried very hard to keep the judgement from my voice. I would give anything to have my family back, and Nakkrah had given his up willingly for a life of servitude. I swallowed down that lump that prickled my throat, tried to force back the anger that clinked the metal chains inside me.

"Even though my life was perfect, there are so many lives out there that are not."

My body tensed. Instead of analyzing what he meant, and getting the meaning wrong, I waited. I waited with my nails biting crescents into my palms, anticipation becoming physical marks on my palms.

"I had the option to make a difference, to help make the world a little different." His voice was soft, as if he were mumbling to himself. He was speaking to the very depths of his desire, to his core, where sat a burning flame instead of an icy spiral. "Why shouldn't I try to make that difference?"

You will condemn yourself to monstrosity to be the salvation of others, I thought. "What can you give in pursuit of that goal?" is what I asked instead.

"Protection," he stated, bluntly, with a determination in his voice. "It is the one thing I can give to them."

I wondered why he wouldn't, then, have joined a police force in his hometown, he could have protected people in a better way than he did now. Nakkrah would have been better off if he had chosen to become an investigator, a protector that didn't need to do the dirty work from the shadows.

I bit my tongue lightly to hold back the thoughts threatening to spill from my mouth. The thoughts articulated we don't save people or protect them, not really. They had already been victimized by the time we were dispatched.

I watched as Nakkrah clicked his heels together. His legs were long enough to reach the ground, but he didn't let them, choosing instead to swing his feet out and in, and occasionally click his heels together.

"Why do you think we protect people?" I finally asked, deciding to use the word he did. It could be seen as me wanting to know why he came here, rather than me doubting the function of the North Wind.

A dark look clouded over his sapphire eyes, erasing the vestiges of light that crept into the corners. "Sometimes, people have hands that move without intent," he explained. "Purposeless hands often cause more harm than good." The rest of what he thought didn't need to be said: He would kill those people he spoke of, because he valued their lives less than those of the people they would harm. The innocent, in his mind, were more valuable than the guilty.

As if I needed it said more explicitly, Nakkrah clarified: "Some people need to die so that others have the opportunity to live."

I swallowed. It was a very black and white perspective, no doubt about that, but I was a fond believer that the world was black and white. In a way, his goal was more noble than my own.

"You'll get your wish," I acquiesced. My fingers clenched and unclenched on my knees.

I clapped him on the shoulder, squeezed the defined muscle firmly, and let my hand fall away. I walked away, leaving Nakkrah to look at the paper in that awestruck way. I didn't rejoin the others, talking over their mission slips, setting up their secure laptops with Hephaestus. I walked past them and pushed the door open, falling back out into the soft, stuffy light of the outside world.

I winced at the intrusion. It was delayed, like I had missed the sharp dusk for a moment. I took in a deep breath, feeling my core compact in upon itself. I couldn't get enough air. It didn't taste right. It felt like my lungs were squeezing wrong.

I ignored it, like everything I didn't want to deal with.

My feet made clicking noises against the stone flooring as I led myself to the overlook, the area we had our martial arts training, right above the waterfall, right next to a small cascade of rocks that I could find some semblance of seclusion in.

I needed to stare out at the trees, turned an unnatural violet color, lit with the glow of hundreds of lazy floating lights with wings, and let my mind wander in the balmy summer twilight.

The rocks near the edge felt spongy and jagged underneath my hands. They bit through my skin in a flurry of gentle kisses, leaving patches of red to remind me of their existence. I kept going because I needed to be alone for at least a little while, away from the man who willingly gave up his family because I knew I had no right to begrudge him that... Yet, I did.

I sat in a little crevice, one where all of the light seeped in, keeping the shadows far and away. I hugged my knees to my chest, making myself small. I felt small. I don't think I could have articulated into words why I felt so small next to Nakkrah's soft heart and steadfast will.

I was a thief, yes, but I had never stolen something as precious as a life. Maybe, if I had any semblance of courage, any sliver of character that he had, I would have ended up as someone else, even just someone at all, instead of a tool. Nakkrah had chosen this life, but I could have just as easily have chosen a path that didn't make me a murderer. Courage would be choosing to prioritize what I wanted when my existence screamed with the need to devote itself to justice.

It was a strange feeling, to dread something, know it will be a permanent regret, and still intend to do it anyway. It feels a little like the second before pain hits, the moment right before the searing dulls the senses. It is a moment of unease and adrenaline and fear, of being aware of everything.

I clenched my fists, felt the sting of the raw skin catching against itself in a jagged slide. I had promised myself that I wouldn't be consumed by fear again, but that promise was a hard one to keep.

I rest my head on my knees, letting my gaze drift back into focus on the horizon. The sky broke in an array of shapes and colors, an endless expression of the infinite beyond I could never hold. It was an explosion, violently ripping its way through the clouds, illuminating them in sparks of fulgurant and bloody color.

It occurred to me then how much I looked to the sky to ease my tensions. It was associated with my god, but she could give me nothing. Why did I still look to her for comfort?

I remembered a story my grandfather told me years ago. He said that the sky has seen more of the world than any of us small minded humans could understand. The sky has watched countless people and civilizations born and die, rise and crumble to dust. The sky has seen us for what we are, wretched beings, and knows us more intimately than we can ever know ourselves.

Maybe that was why I looked to the sky so desperately. I was calling out, yelling *Can you see who I have become?* It wasn't a call for pity, nor a call for a solution. I took comfort in knowing that the sky could see every raw inch of who I was, wretchedness and all, and that it didn't change despite this.

Man created masterpieces and engineered worlds in front of this sky. Humans were desperate to grasp time by the throat and etch our stories into the heavens, screaming that *we will make monuments that transcend our lifetimes.* What did it say about me that the monument I was building would be built on the corpses created by my hand?

The feeling of eyes on me made a shiver trace down my neck. I sensed no ill intent. My shoulders relaxed and a harsher than usual exhale left my nose, as if I had been holding in my breath.

I heard the footsteps approaching; there was no attempt made to silence them. When they stopped next to me, I looked to the owner. Iktomi.

He shrugged. "I came looking," was all he said, before sitting down next to me to watch the sun set.

I hummed in acknowledgement.

Although I could have reached out and touched him, it was like there was an infinity of distance between us, a chasm that couldn't ever be filled. What a thing it is, to have someone right next to you, and still feel alone.

I looked back to the valley below, content with the unreachable presence beside me.

I admired Nakkrah for his ability to go forward without regret, but that day, in the silence of the early summer's sun, my heart beat a little steadier knowing I'd wouldn't become a murderer alone.

March 20, 2726–March 23, 2726

Iktomi

The suits were stiff and itchy. Money was a powerful attractor and we were made to look like we had a lot of it.

I grabbed a few tiny food items on a plate. They were round and their brackwater smell made my nose crinkle in disgust. I held the plate out to Iktomi.

He took the plate and laughed at me. "You haven't been to one of these before, have you?"

I shook my head. "Absolutely not," I informed. "I was too busy trying not to starve."

He hummed. It wasn't a judgmental hum, nor was it a shocked hum. It was one of acknowledgement, as if I had just confirmed information he already knew.

His hair was slicked back. I should have done the same to mine. It would have looked more professional.

"People who come to these things usually starve themselves on purpose," he informed. "Think it makes them look nicer."

My stomach churned. For a whole year, before Yonten had found me, I had to worry about what I could and couldn't get my hands on. There were more than a few winter nights where I struggled with the cramps of hunger because my traps hadn't caught anything that day.

Reina Vazquez walked in like she owned the place. She was a benefactor of the charity hosting this event, so she was here to mingle. If she had to launder and steal money from the poor, at least she was incentivized to give back to the community.

Her hair was pinned up into a curled bun, displaying a thin neck and dainty shoulders. She was the epitome of class and beauty, looking like a business tycoon with her all-black dress and the old-money pearls dripping down the elegant slopes of her long neck. I recognized her for the shade of her coloring. All browns. She looked like warm honey tea on an overcast morning.

I nudged Iktomi's shoe with my own. I watched his head move slowly up and down, a barely there nod.

As much as it irked me, Iktomi outranked me. I had to defer to him for tactical issues.

So, we waited. We made idle small talk while our focus was on Reina, instead of the conversation.

"Come on," Iktomi told me, setting the plate down on a nearby table. He began a quick paced stride to Reina.

She was grabbing a glass of champagne when we approached from the side. Her lips were the color of black cherries.

"Excuse me," he said, timidly. So, Antonio Frost was bashful... much unlike Iktomi. "Are you... Reina Vazquez?"

She looked up. Her eyebrows raise in acknowledgement. "I am," she spoke with a voice like butter. I watched her take a sip of her wine. She had a ring on her finger, an indicator she was married. Her spouse didn't attend parties with her. Possible reasons why ran through my head, but they weren't important enough to divert my attention to.

Iktomi leaned over to me and whispered loud enough for her to hear, "I told you it was her." I smiled and nodded. It made my cheeks hurt. It felt forced and fake; I hoped it didn't look that way.

"We were just taking a look at some of your properties. We're looking to buy a lot for our business to expand overseas." It should have been concerning how natural Iktomi was at this, but I also knew that he didn't need more than one attempt to pass our demeanor training.

"Oh!" she exclaimed. In that moment, I was certain my fake smile must have looked it, because hers did. "Well, what is your business? Perhaps I can help you find a suitable fit."

I took a step forward, but Iktomi continued instead. "We run a distillery. We are trying to expand into foreign markets and noticed this region is a big importer of scotch. We wanted to try our hand here," he explained our fake situation.

Reina tilted her head a lot when she spoke. She also moved her hands a lot, not in creative movements, but back and forth. Typically, this would make us trust her. I understood now why she would have been such a successful con-woman. "I have a wide variety of properties, how large was the area you were hoping for? Would you like a building on it, or would you like to start from scratch?"

She said she *had* them, as if they belonged to her. What she did was control the properties, selling off the assets owned by other people. Small vocational tribes, like my own was, who had no legal aid to represent them and ensure their assets were protected.

My stomach churned.

I kept forcing that fake smile. "Do you have somewhere that would be easy to vertically integrate?" I asked.

Iktomi reached into the breast pocket of his suit and pulled out a falsified business card. It linked to a website for Rakifani scotch and had been backdated. Her gloved fingers looked slim and delicate when she took the card to examine.

Her eyes squinted. *Poor vision,* I mentally catalogued.

In the corner of my eye, I noticed a few people laughing over a champagne flute. It was so normal, so unlike anything I had seen. None of the people here, not the servers, nor the heirs, not the business owners, knew what Iktomi and I would do.

"It would be great if you could show us some places. We want to get started as soon as possible," Iktomi charmed with the shy smile he seemed to have mastered in the past five minutes, a smile where he looked past dark eyelashes and hunched his shoulders like a teen asking their sweetheart to dance.

I watched Reina flush. "It — it would be my pleasure," she stammered.

"All right," Iktomi responded. "Please email us a time and location to meet you. We will keep looking around in the meantime." My stomach clenched in a different way: Admiration. He put the pressure on her to get back to us soon, so we didn't find a better option.

He gently put his hand on my elbow. We turned and walked away. The seed was planted.

We got an email later that night.

"Are we actually going to sign the contract?" I asked.

Iktomi shook his head, looking down at the blueprint of her house. It was large, even by billionaire standards. It was ostentatious, as if even the washer and dryer needed separate rooms.

"Look here," he indicated, pointing at the blueprint, then to the city map. I leaned over his shoulder to look where he was pointing. My nose crinkled involuntarily in discomfort. "It leads out to Avenida Pessoa, which is a mile from here." It did not escape my notice he did not answer my question.

"It's not like we have much of a choice," I informed him. "She has security cameras on the building. She only disables the front gate." If we tried to leave in a different way, local law enforcement would have our faces plastered up around town the next day and we wouldn't be able to leave. Vasquez only disabled the entrance cameras as a means to establish plausible deniability in the case her fraud was discovered.

Iktomi leaned back and crossed his arms over his chest. A small scowl pressed itself into his face. He looked much older than twenty-two in these moments, when he was thinking. Maybe everyone looked old to me because I felt like a child playing the game of being an adult.

"We don't have many shadows to hide in on our way out. And we should erase any presence of ourselves being here," he mused.

I thought for a moment. "Should we?" I asked.

Iktomi tilted his head back to look up at me. "What do you mean?" he questioned.

I fought back a scoff of amusement. "Well, I just think that it would be worse if people saw us with her at the party earlier and then didn't see evidence of us being here," I explained.

I didn't think the people who killed my tribe hid themselves. No, contrary. They probably joined the region at different times, left at different times, and made themselves seen. They would have created an alibi that was vague enough to allude to the possibility of innocence.

I swallowed the memories threatening to drown me.

He nodded his head. "Maybe," he trailed off. I could see the gears turning in his head. Iktomi turned to me with a bright smile. "Then, we should leave out the front doors!" he exclaimed. "We just have to hide our faces from the camera, well placed hats to hide from here, here, and here." He pointed at the blueprints where the cameras would show.

I nodded resolutely. "There aren't that many. We can show up in casual dress. It's hot enough that we can get away with baseball caps, if we reply to her email that we will need walking shoes."

I took a step backward and turned, walking over to the desk where the laptop was propped up. I sat down and pressed the button to power it on.

"Ma'at," Iktomi called to grab my attention.

I hummed and looked over my shoulder at him. He looked like a bride at her wedding, something different from his normal look. His eyes may have crinkled more, his lips may have been pulled back further, or his head may have tilted when his shoulders raised. This time, his smile seemed warm instead of cold; it seemed human. "You're really something."

I turned back to the computer quickly and began drafting the email. "You should go to bed," I changed the subject. "We'll be up late tomorrow."

"How soon can we sign the contracts?" I asked, trying to sound as eager as possible. We had spent the whole day looking at plots of dirt. Five, to be exact. We had her meet us at the one furthest from her house and zig zagged to the one closest, asking questions that wouldn't impact us.

Reina had a charming personality. "We can sign them right now," she answered. "My house is not far from here." Though she genuinely looked as if she were trying to help us, her charms were fraudulent.

She started walking and we followed. My feet were swollen from walking in the heat all day.

"Do you two have families back home?" Reina asked over her shoulder, trying to make conversation.

Iktomi was the one to talk first: "Yes, I have a lovely wife and two dogs," he lied.

She laughed. "What, no kids?" When she laughed, I wanted to laugh, too.

"I think we're a little young for that," he expanded the lie. "She's still working on her doctorate and the economy is a little too volatile to chance work without it."

"And you?" she asked me.

"No family," I said. "I haven't met anyone I want to start a family with yet." I didn't mention that I wasn't looking. I wouldn't look until I had crushed the man in white's skull beneath my boot.

"Ah, then there is no one to nag you about chores," she laughed, raising a freshly manicured hand to cover her mouth.

I laughed, too, a hollow, empty sound. "Thankfully, not," I responded.

She didn't ask about any further relatives. After the war, it was common courtesy to avoid prying too hard into what living relatives remained. Though that was more than two-hundred years ago, the tradition had stuck.

She led us to a gated home, with one of those driveways that pulls in a circle in front of the house, around a fountain. It was a large unit, three stories high, white and royal blue. It looked like a castle.

I gulped.

She let us into the front. It did not escape my eyes how she tapped the gold circlet on her wrist twice. That was her disabling the cameras. If she turned them back on with that bracelet, we'd have to use it to disable them a second time.

Inside the home was just as nice. It was filled with velvet and mahogany furniture, with light pillars of quartz and high arching windows. There were red hallway rugs on the floor that felt like stepping in pliant moss. I had always thought my family well off, with our many glass cups and the chandelier that hung in the living area. I was so wrong. We had lived in squalor compared to the luxury Vasquez enjoyed daily.

I suddenly felt as if I had sullied her floor by walking on it.

The stairs echoed under our feet. "You have a lovely home," I told her as we ascended. "Your daughter must have had fun growing up here."

"Ah, she did," Reina agreed. "Sadly, she doesn't run around like she once did. Too old for that, now." There was a lilt of longing in her tone, as if she had watched the years slip past without her consent.

I understood that regret. I felt it when I looked back to all the times I had opted to study instead of being with my family. What did those hours of studying do for me now? Nothing. I was a dropout and the memories that would have meant so much to me didn't exist.

We walked past hanging paintings and tapestries of painted nature that adorned those high walls of hers. Until she led us into a room with a desk in the center, a window behind it. The room was illuminated by the setting sun.

"I'll just have you sign these," she said. "Do you need to look them over? You have three days after signing to cancel the contract without penalty." She pulled the files from a manilla folder and handed them over to me.

"I don't mind signing now," I said to her. "Frost?" I looked at Iktomi, pretending I didn't think he'd have the same answer.

"I'll sign now and read later, too. No point in delaying the inevitable when we found the right spot," he agreed.

Vasquez gave a slick smile and handed over a pen with a flick of her wrist. Iktomi took the pen in his hand. Where her nails were sharp, his were blunt. Where her finders were slender, his were thick. Their hands were opposites in every way. He signed the paper, I signed the paper, and she signed the paper, all with very, very different hands.

She took the files over to a machine in the corner that started whirring. "Just need to make you a copy," she sang, trilling out the last word. The machine made a whirring noise as it spit out page after page of the contract. Finally, the machine stopped and she gathered all the loose papers together.

As she straightened her back, ready to hand us our copies of the files, Iktomi made his way closer. I watched as his fingers flipped out a butterfly knife, the silver glinting in the light of the lamp.

He didn't need to do more than grab her around the waist with one arm and press the metal to her neck with the other. The papers slipped from her grasp and fluttered down to the floor. She gasped.

Iktomi spoke in an unintelligible whisper, probably demanding she stay quiet. Vasquez nodded quickly. I walked over to her desk and sat down in the leather chair. The computer was unlocked.

I pulled open a web browser and clicked the link in the favorites bar to take me to her business's archival data. The site was green and grey and poorly designed. It wasn't hard to find the financial panel. I skimmed over the skewed books. There were two tabs, one for books that had been cooked and one for actual accounting data.

They were surprisingly quiet when I searched through the tabs, analyzing what we actually came here for. Numbers made sense. Numbers couldn't lie the way Vasquez could.

I pulled up the bank websites Vasquez belonged to. Six, total. "Passwords for your banks?" I asked, without looking up from the screen.

There was a moment of silence before I heard a gasp. "Six Neptunia four five nine one." Her voice quivered, but she did not stutter.

I tasted blood in my mouth. "Which one?" I asked.

Another gasp. I look up. Iktomi had traded the knife for holding her head in a locked position. It gave him greater range to move and made her feel more pressured. "All of them," she stated. "All of them, I swear."

I logged into all six accounts. I had memorized the number of the bank account we were intended to transfer her wealth into. *821727365-932*. The keys were light when I pressed them down. My hands shook with adrenaline. I hoped that she couldn't tell, and in spite of myself, I desperately hoped Iktomi couldn't tell either.

All of Reina Vasquez's wealth gone in an instant. Everything she had taken in her lifetime, pooled in some other offshore, untraceable account. It would be returned to the people she had taken it from, in proportion. It wasn't repayment, but it was *something*.

I logged out of all of the accounts, cleared her web cache, and shut down the computer. "Time to go," I said, looking up from the screen after confirming the transfer had gone through. The money was gone. The only assets Vasquez still owned were the physical objects in the house we stood in.

Iktomi had dragged them both farther back, but I could see Vasquez clearly, as if she were right in front of my eyes. Her breathing was ragged and her chest heaved with each second. Hyperventilation. Her brown eyes searched for an escape, darting around the room like a mosquito in summer. Her jaw was clenched and her face was screwed up in an unpleasant way.

Iktomi nodded, but he didn't let go of the head lock around Vasquez's delicate throat.

I saw him thinking, the gears turning in the shadow of his furrowed brow.

"Did you hear me?" I asked, trying to pull him back from where he was lost in thought. The mission objective was accomplished. We could leave.

He looked up at me, his eyes desperately scanning my face, like he was asking my permission.

Then, his face went blank, eyes obstructed by the relaxed shadow of resolution. Iktomi nodded. "Yeah, I heard you." His voice was still like decay.

I heard the crunch before I registered the movement of that neck to the side, at an impossible ninety-degree angle. His arms slipped from around her and Vasquez's body crumpled to the floor.

Where it lay, head twisted grotesquely, limbs strewn about without care, front down to the red carpet, I felt a sickening deja-vu. I had felt the same way when I found my mom's body twisted unnaturally. Knowing that we did to this woman what someone had done to my mom, knowing Vasquez's daughter would see her in the same twisted manner carved my lungs to bits.

The wave of nausea hit me like lightning streaks the sky,

instantaneously and intensely. I pushed the feeling down with a swallow of souring saliva.

"Why?" I asked, careful to keep my voice as steady as possible and my face still as stone. "We got the codes; we made the transfer." *We didn't need to,* was left unsaid.

Iktomi's shoulders were tense, like he was feeling attacked, even if there was no one in the room to attack him. It was the stance an animal takes when they feel threatened, when they will have to defend themselves. He viewed my question as a verbal assault.

His head tilted up and he turned away from me, shielding himself from my imagined onslaught. "She would have done it again."

It left a pit in my stomach, the ice cracking and breaking and returning back to its lazy curl around my heart, dormant for a while longer, because Iktomi was right. She *would* have done it again. Our job was to make sure she couldn't and we succeeded.

So why did it feel like I had failed? Why did I feel that shiver of shame tracing it's cold route along the inside of my skin?

"We should go," he noted. I walked around the desk and started toward the exit, watching his back as we made our way through the too big house, a house that was built from the concentrated suffering of others.

I watched him walk out of the front door into the night air. He seemed fluid as he moved, and content to get back to our room quickly, without detection. We wouldn't be stopped. There was no blood on Iktomi's clothes. There was no blood on mine.

But there was an invisible crimson, staining our hands and dripping from our fingertips.

The humidity in the twilight air settled on me like dust settles in a valley. I rubbed at the annoying beads of sweat that had quickly made little pools in the cervices of my collarbone. I pushed my sleeves up as far as they could go, wondering how I had ever gotten through the day in a wrist-length shirt.

"I see them a lot," Iktomi said quietly, a ghost of a whisper, barely drifting through the balmy breeze. "When you change, I mean."

I blinked. "What?" I asked a little too snappily.

"Not that I watch you change or anything," he added quickly. His cheeks visibly darkened and his hand flew up to rub at the back of his neck. "But we are roommates and you don't sleep in your bandages any more."

"Oh," I responded, a little kinder, looking down to my left arm. He meant my scars. I had taken off my bandages because they would have drawn attention to my clothes. I didn't think anyone would have noticed in this low-light area.

I held my arm out to him, giving him a better look. "They're a burial rite. One for everyone I've lost."

His cold fingers made me flinch when they touched the scar on my pulse point. I felt slimy as he touched the next one down, then the next...

"Sixty-three," I announced, pulling my arm back. I still don't know why I told him that then, told him something so personal I hadn't even shared it with Sancus. My best guess is that the adrenaline had blurred the lines of what mattered and my lips fell loose.

I didn't tell him that I had lost people that were still alive, too, that the reason they weren't marked was because it would curse them. Maybe someone had marked me on their arm. Maybe Lee had been willing to take on that tradition to say goodbye to me.

"Sorry," Iktomi told me after the chirping of crickets dragged on for too long.

I looked up to his face, half shrouded by the rim of his cap. I could only see his clenched jaw clearly.

I reached to the brass band that dangled on my wrist and spun it around counterclockwise. "Iktomi, don't apologize for things you can't control. It doesn't do any good," I cautioned numbly. Pity wouldn't bring them back.

He looked toward his feet and his shoulders slumped. "Xenon," he mumbled, letting his hand fall away from his neck.

"Huh?"

"My name," he clarified quickly. "My real one, anyway."

One of the rules of the North Wind was that the people we were disappeared when we were named. To say our birth name was one of the nine sins punishable by death. Not turning Xenon in for breaking this rule was another.

I should have been cross with him for putting me in that position.

"Ainsley," I said instead. The name felt heavy and soiled on my tongue, *wrong* somehow.

Xenon didn't cease his movement, nor did he make any discernable expression of recognition. "It suits you," was the only indication I had that my words were heard. Then, after a few minutes of silence, he said, "Thanks for sharing."

I curled my hand into a fist and punched his arm lightly. "Don't think because we had a heart to heart I'm going soft. Don't forget me; I'm your competition."

He looked up to me, his lips tilted crookedly to the left. "Yeah, well, don't forget about me either."

I scoffed. "Like I could, attention-whore."

And it should have been hard talking to him after watching him snap a woman's neck like a twig. My stomach should have felt queasy standing that close to someone who must have killed before to have such a practiced ease of movement.

It wasn't hard and my stomach wasn't queasy. I didn't want to think too hard on why that was.

A cold grip on my wrist stopped me from proceeding down the gas-lit street with a dirt road and empty sidewalks.

"You're so hard to deal with," Xenon formed, a dramatic change from moments ago. "You're so standoffish, like people are in your favor or they're a chore. And you try hard, too. So hard you make everyone else look like a slacker."

His face screwed up and his eyes shut in frustration. Xenon's grip on my arm tightened. "I hate that you fade into the background so easily, but somehow still manage to keep space in my mind."

I tugged my arm a bit, but Xenon's fist held on tighter. The warm breeze blew a strand of hair across his cheek, making him look crazed and disheveled. "It doesn't make sense," he said. He opened his eyes and stared daggers into me. "None at all."

Then his lips were on mine. A brief touch, fueled by anger, a whisper of feeling before he was pulling away and storming ahead, foraging on without me.

I was shocked, certainly, as I watched his receding figure, caught up in the paralysis that came with his guttural confession of interest. More than shock, nausea clawed up my throat and scratched down my back. The nausea was there because I knew Xenon was paying attention to me.

He was smart. He'd figure out I didn't join the North Wind for a fresh start. It was only a matter of time before he recognized I was out for blood.

Jace, I thought, *I think the noose around my throat just tightened.*

December 7, 2727

Kobe

This time was different.

This time, when I was in the area Kobé Deauxhomme called home, I had a tail on me.

Sancus sat with me, holding fried cheese street food in his hand. He always seemed to be snacking on junk food when he could get his hands on it. A few crumbs had landed on his cheek, right below the singular dimple on the left side of his face.

He was here for help me with a woman who went by the moniker Siren. Siren ran a human trafficking ring, stretching the expanse of three regions. Siren had a little girl and a husband, neither of whom knew what she did for a living.

Siren was a white female, late thirties, with a medium build. She was a short woman, only about five feet tall, with long tendrils of blond stretching from the crown of her head to her waist. She had a circular face and a pointy nose, resembling a child or a mouse.

Her eyes were dark. I can't remember their color.

"She looks happy," Sancus said.

I hunched over and leaned my arms on my knees. The park bench was cold and hard under me. "Most people in her line of work are, when they make it to her status." The status of someone who no longer has to do the dirty work.

Sancus hummed and took another bite out of the cheese. It made the quiet crunch that only fried food can make.

The air smelled of oil and mulled wine. Autumn had come and gone and winter had begun to seep into the world, crisping the grass with white, crystalline spirals and settling deep into our bones. The first snow had not yet fallen, but the ghosting of goosebumps on my skin signaled its imminent arrival.

"Do you think she'll be enough?" I asked, keeping an eye on her back.

Her husband and her sat on a strewn-out blanket in front of us, huddled together, and very much in love. The way their fingers laced together between them sent a lance through my chest.

I hoped Sancus answered yes, that only one family had to be destroyed today.

"No." Because, of course not; things were never that simple.

I nodded. "The board meets at eight. None are combat-trained."

It was his turn to hum. The soothing sound assuaged the pressure in my chest. "Then," he mused, "it will be pretty quick."

I pushed myself to stand. The cold air hit my back and sent an unpleasant tingle down my spine.

"I threw a tracker in her purse," I informed him. "We don't need to tail her. It's functional."

Sancus rose to meet me. It was weird seeing him in a winter coat, dark blue with fur lined insides. I was so used to the airy beige and vibrant orange he favored in his simple cottons. But it was better for him to fit in with the local colors and safer for him to retain his body heat.

"Then we go."

The Sancus who was my friend was a different man than the Sancus I worked with.

I had seen a little of the working Sancus during the O-Blow case. He had proven then, as he proved once again during the Siren case, that he embodied the three C's: Cold, calculating, and competent. He was quick and methodical, the way a practiced pickpocket was.

We took a room in the hotel across from the conference center. We stripped off our coats and slacks, leaving only the fitted uniform and gear. The time was seven forty-five.

Watching through binoculars as everyone got there was the hardest part. We both felt like we would miss something, our shoulders pinched and our hearts in our throats. It was silent. We watched as Siren's underlings trickled in, one after the next. The table was filled by seven fifty-seven.

It was then that Sancus broke the silence. "How long do you think this will take them?" *How long do you think we will have?*

"Maybe an hour," I surmised.

Sancus moved to ready the ropes.

I walked to the window we had cracked open.

One can remove the sealant on a window with a tiny bit of caulk remover and a putty knife. After that, all that's left is to rig the ropes to an immovable object, something that could bear weight.

The suction cups we used had a better name than 'plungers' but they looked so much like toilet plunger heads to me, that I could never remember their actual name. Sancus was the one who shot them from the crossbow; he had better aim than I did.

I was sure Siren heard the plunk on the window of her boardroom. I was certain she and her goons could hear the shredding sound as Sancus and I zipped across the building divide. And I was positive she knew the glass was going to shatter before my hand closed around the back of her neck.

I pushed her face forward into the table. I got a good look at that face. There was fear there.

Meanwhile, Sancus was shooting out tranquilizers. *Fwip, fwip, fwip, fwip, fwip, fwip.* It took thirty seconds for the tranquilizers to kick in. Two of the men tried to bolt. The others attempted to rush at Sancus. Their blows were weak and they were quick to collapse. Sancus put them flat on their backs.

"Siren," I projected with all of the authority I could muster. "We're here because of your crimes against children and adults."

I pulled a knife from my belt and lined it up with her neck, pressing the blade against the C4 and C5 vertebrae existed, right where the skin was soft.

"Please, no," she pleaded. Her voice was sultry and charismatic. Uncharacteristic for her child-like appearance. "Let me go. I'll do anything. Is it money you want? I have money. Please, let me go!"

Milky droplets clung to the table, spreading across the mahogany in randomized patterns. She struggled, her arms fighting for freedom, her legs squirming and kicking out. I pressed my chest into her back to keep her still.

It didn't irk me to know I would kill her. After Abbadon, it was easy. After Belig, easier. Now, I could compare it to making a peanut butter and jelly sandwich: second-nature.

If Siren stepped down, someone else would pick up her human trafficking trade. We had multiple units taking out her operatives in other locations. We had to cut off all of the hydra's heads at once, that was the only way to ensure a stop of operations.

My tongue tasted sour.

Siren fell still, her body going lax against my own. She spoke only two words: "Let go."

A hazy fog settled over me, dimming the lights and dulling the colors. My gaze drifted to something far, far away, like I was dreaming.

I let go. I told my hands to grab back on, but they only hung limp at my sides.

Panic spread across my back and my heart beat rapidly beneath my skin. I couldn't move. Still, that dream-like fog stayed, preventing my adrenaline from converting to movement.

"Ma'at?" Sancus asked. I couldn't even respond.

I had heard about people like Siren, the ones who the radiation hadn't killed off. Some, like Siren, could make use of their genetic mutations. Some, like Siren, were the true, the ones parents whispered about to keep delinquent children in line.

"Step back." My feet moved without my consent.

She stood to full height. For a brief moment, I could see her confidence as manicured nails adjusted the hem of her dress. Then, she fell to the ground, a knife lodged in her throat, right above the juncture of her clavicle.

It took a while for the gurgling to stop. When it did, the fog drifted away and I was able to relax fully. The squelch was intimate. The sticky substance matted her hair and made her skin slippery.

Sancus and I held brief eye contact before we set to work on the others in the room.

Sancus knelt down to the one beside him. He began to mumble in a language I didn't speak, his lilted voice coming out more elegantly than normal. It was his prayer.

My tribe's elder had been fond of quoting a historical warlord: *Just as the hand has five fingers, each to do its bidding, God has given humans many religions to serve.* Sancus was still serving his god in the ways he could.

I moved to him and placed my hand on his shoulders. "Will you pray if I kill?" I asked. *Let me shoulder the burden on your faith.*

Sancus nodded and shut his chocolate eyes. I slid the knife into the same spot on the first man. I didn't want Sancus to touch them. The second. I knew the day we met for the second time that I would let myself burn for Sancus. The third. I would be the one to take the blood, the guilt, the sin.

The fourth. Because Sancus deserved more than that weight. The fifth. I'd burn in a thousand pyres so he wouldn't have to touch a candle's flame. The Sixth.

I wiped the blade on the suit lapel of the sixth man. The black fabric showed no signs of moisture on its dark surface.

The words I didn't understand stopped coming. I looked to him, dressed all in the black operational attire we wore, his own equipment hanging off his waist. He pushed himself from the ground, his shoulders sagging. I was relieved to see that look on his face, the one that always calmed me down, saying *it's over* in wordless whispers.

"Buy me a beer?" he asked.

I inhaled. "No, not tonight," I responded. "I need some time to myself." Time to kill the man that was in the same city as us.

His smile fell from his cheeks and confusion wrinkled his nose. "Oh, that's cool," he lied. "I'll see you back at the inn?" There was a tinge of unspoken concern that hung in the air with his question.

I nodded.

I walked to the window we had smashed through and drew the cable rope from my hip. I looped it and slung it out the opening, onto the roof of the building adjacent to ours. Sancus could take the original rope.

I jumped. The familiar weightlessness hit me as I slammed into the force of the air. I leapt again, to a shorter building, then a lamp-post. My heels fell a little too harshly into cement as I met the alley ungracefully.

I pulled my rope in and attached it to my belt once more.

On went the pale green over-shirt and the khaki shorts stored as spares in my utility belt. It made me fit in slightly more, though I no longer had a coat to wear.

I surveyed my surroundings. I was on Third and Vine. Five streets North and seven East would take me to Kobe, who would be having his afternoon coffee in *The Chilly Roaster*. He would leave half an hour to sunset. I held my hand to the West. Six fingers. I had an hour before Kobe would depart.

I started, stair-stepping my way through the city streets. I remembered, without a doubt, that there was a bookstore across the street with a rooftop lounge area that peered right into the tall glass windows that faced the South and the East. I would have approximately twenty-five seconds to get down the stairs before Kobe took a turn that led out of my view.

When the temperatures dropped around me, my vision pulling deeper into a tunnel, memory helped me to avoid the panic I felt when I watched Kobe go east from that rooftop view.

I pulled my arms into myself to conserve heat. My breath spiraled in the air and obscured my vision, but I could still see Kobe. Dark hair and eyes. Looked to be either the same ethnic category as either my dad or Diejiste, but it was hard to pin. He wore a black coat and white pants.

I watched him round his way into a small bed and breakfast, the kind with mismatching sheets and newlyweds who couldn't afford a better city for their honeymoon. I entered through a different door. The one in the back. I saw the tips of those white pants go up the stairs, past what I could see. I climbed with him, placing my feet down softly as I could.

Kobe had a wiry frame and seemed to be the type of man who would have gone into the arts rather than assassinations. He must have had many tricks hidden in his palms; I made a mental note to stay away from them.

I counted the steps he took above me. *One, two, three, four, five. Creak.* Left side. First or second door. I finally let myself enter floor two. It was the first door, right near the stairs. I would have to be cautious about noise.

I pulled two pins from their spot on the collar of my shirt and bent one straight. I wedged it into the door, feeling for the gaps in the rungs of the lock. Clink, clink, the sound of steel brushing up against brass. When I heard the telltale plunk of the first pin hitting the back of the lock, I forced the other pin into the same opening, alongside its sister. The second pin was turned slowly, very slowly, to ease the sound of the latch coming undone.

I opened the door quickly and stepped inside.

A force slammed into the junction between my shoulder and my chest. A sharp wheeze tore its way through my throat as fist bundled itself in my shirt, pulling me forward. A blotch of skin invaded my vision. Pain bloomed across my cheekbones and liquid spilled from both my lip and my nose.

I shoved my hand out and clocked Kobe on the trachea. He wheezed a coughing, dry heave. I threw my open hands up against his right shoulder and bicep, blocking a punch. My hands fell flat on his back, fingers pointed down, and I pulled his shoulder forward. I drove my knee into his stomach once, twice.

He swept my left leg and shoved me over. He was tall and he towered over me as he sent a well-aimed kick to my groin. I gasped.

A blur of white and black entered my vision and my eyes were watering again as fresh pain erupted from my nose. The next kick went into my eye, forcing it shut for the foreseeable future.

I grabbed for his ankle and tugged it up with all of the might I still had in me. Kobe stumbled backward. It shouldn't have been enough to take him out of the running.

A familiar grunt echoed inside the room. A mop of dark hair with light tips bobbed as a third person threw themselves on top of Kobe and began to pound into his head with a something. It looked like a wooden door stop.

I saw Kobe's legs twitch under the black cloth clothing Sancus wore. I pushed myself to a sitting position. All I could think was *I was supposed to protect him from this.*

Two more thumps of the rounded edge of the wooden wedge. Sancus's back heaved as he sat panting on top of a motionless body. I couldn't even tell what Kobe looked like any more. The image of his head, smashed to a bloody pulp was what stuck with me.

Sancus cast the stop to the side. It clattered against the wooden floor. He staggered to his feet and looked over his shoulder at me. His lips were parted and he took in shaky breaths. He didn't seem to be asking me what I was doing or why he had to step in; his eyes were vacant.

I licked my lips. They were wet and salty with blood. My eyes darted across Sancus's face, trying to read it. His skin had crimson specks on it, mixing with the dark spots across his cheeks and nose.

I pushed myself to stand. He looked at me, dark eyes gaining sharp post-adrenaline definition. "You looked like you could use some help," he shrugged, his left cheek pulling up into a half smile. His tone was jovial and light for the situation, seemingly ignoring what he had just done.

Our training had changed him, *hardened* him.

I smirked at him and cocked my head to the side. "I didn't want your help, nor did I ask for it," I retorted quickly. My throat felt scratchy and my arm would be out of commission for a day or two, but my own adrenaline kept me from investing too much attention to their pain. The swelling on my eye may stay for the better half of the week.

I was lucky Sancus had ignored my request to be alone; if he had gone to the inn's tavern... I decided not to dwell on that.

"Ma'at, how can you be simultaneously the smartest and the stupidest person I know?" he asked with a shake of his head and a shark exhale.

I shrugged at him, "They say stupid is contagious."

His face dropped to a blank slate. "Hah, hah," he deadpanned.

"You know, it's common to thank people who saved your life." He raised his palms and swayed them side to side in mockery when he continued, *"Oh, Sancus, I appreciate you putting yourself at risk so that I don't end up dead because of my shady back-door murders."*

"They aren't backdoor murders," I was quick to defend. "I'll explain on our way out."

I walked towards him quietly. The leasing office had been paid for two more months. By the time the body was found, Sancus and I would be gone. It would be quite hard for the local investigators to find the culprit when the victim couldn't be identified. This time, I didn't cut off the hands or neck. It wouldn't send the same message as it did when the bodies were recognizable.

He wiped his arm off on the towel hanging off the bedpost as he mumbled his prayer once more. I wiped my bloody nose off on my sleeve.

We walked out to the street quietly, and with our gazes downtrodden.

It was snowing lightly outside, the first snow of the year. The town was quiet and only a few adults moved about in the night, headed with a destination in mind. Sancus and I linked arms, to appear as if we were in a relationship.

Our feet made barely noticeable clacks against the cobbled ground. "You going to explain?" His question was hushed and it barely reached my ears, stifled by the still winter air.

I sighed and my breath turned to a small cloud in the sky. "He hurt those I cared deeply for," I told him. He hummed in acknowledgement. I had to be careful with my words.

"I thought we were supposed to cast aside our pasts."

"I haven't made it that far, yet."

"When will you?"

"Five more."

"Christ, Ma'at," he chuckled, the concern he expressed earlier in the day returning with the slightest hint of desperation. "You are playing a dangerous game. We aren't supposed to work in self-interest." Worry seeped his words like coffee stains satin.

I clenched my jaw and scowled at the ground. "Will you tell them and save yourself? I wouldn't blame you." My words were monotone and icy. It would hurt me if he answered yes, but a part of me was hoping he'd act in his own self-interest, for once.

"Actually, I'm going to help you."

My breath caught in my lungs and I turned to watch his face. From the angle, I could see the scar on his lower right jaw that he had received from Nyami Nyami during training. I could not make sense of the swell in my chest and the uneasiness that crawled along my back.

I scoffed and faced the ground again. My stomach sank in anticipation.

He squeezed his arm tight against mine, reassuring me that he didn't intend to take back his words. "You don't make illogical choices." It was his explanation to make sense of my actions.

But he was wrong.

The logical choice to make would have been made years ago. After burying my family, the logical next step would be to inform the local enforcers of what happened, give information on the crime, and leave it to them. The logical action to take would be to talk to a grief specialist and create a new normal. The logical choice would have been to spend the remainder of my days playing music, running through summer-dry brush, and being happy. No decision I made since that day had been logical.

I didn't have the heart to tell Sancus all this. He believed I had my reasons and he was right, but I would be lying to myself if I said they were rational.

Not for the first time, I asked myself why Sancus was so good to me. Why had he chosen me to share his compassions with? I wasn't like him. I did not brighten a room with my laughter and I didn't help old ladies cross the street in my spare time. Still, he had chosen to devote himself to me.

We walked in silence the rest of the way to the tavern. I did not want to mar our friendship with the foul weight of a half-truth when I wasn't ready to give full ones yet. Instead, I would wait until I had another name, another location, and I would ask him if he intended to keep his promise.

He would say yes when the time came. Sancus and I were similar for one reason, alone: we kept our word. I used to admire that in him. In that moment, it just made breathing hard.

The tavern was still lively by the time we made it back. A soft yellow glow emanated from the windows, and raucous laughter seeped through the cracks in the walls.

I pulled open the cast iron handle felt the heat hit me with a bite that stung my cheeks and made them feel colder. I looked down as I walked inside, wiping off my face with my dark sleeve. When I looked up, I froze.

"Oh, look who came to see you," Sancus said with a nudge to my arm and a gesture to the bar. From the inflection in his tone, he was as surprised as I.

I hadn't seen Xenon in a year, really. We wrote each other, but that was the extent of our contact. I think, when it came down to it, anything else felt forced. We were both caught up in knowing it wasn't sustainable and wanting to hang on anyway.

That bitter acknowledgement left a sour taste in my mouth when he smiled and waved as if it had only been a day since our last meeting, a sourness caused by a fraudulent 'welcome home'.

Sancus knew me too well not to notice the stiffness of my shoulders and the stillness of my body. He coughed once and clapped me on my arm, "I'll leave you to it, then." He was quick to disappear to the back of the room.

I forced myself to take that first step. Then another. Then another, until I reached the bar and sat down on a stool next to him, smelling the familiar scent of the sea: salt and ozone.

I swallowed thickly. "Been a while."

"Yeah," he said in that silk voice, "it sure has." There was a silence then, as he signaled the bartender to grab us two steins. "I thought about you. Every day."

Suddenly, that bitter taste left me, vanishing like the snow flurries on warm skin. I didn't have any right to be mad. "Why visit now?" I asked. "You could have stuck around between missions long enough to say hello."

"I actually didn't come to say hello," he admitted. His shoulders hunched like a child who had just been caught lying.

The bartender clicked two steins on the mahogany countertop. Xenon threw down two denarii and wrapped a hand around the stein closest to him. It was a deep amber color. He didn't drink from it. He was nervous.

Xenon had been a great actor on cases; he never was in his personal life. I guess, when it came down to it, I wasn't either.

"Then what did you come for?" I questioned, grabbing my own stein and taking a sip. I tried to keep disappointment from slipping into my tone.

"I heard a rumor," he started. "It's been traveling around for a while now."

"I'm willing to bet it's a rumor about me."

He scoffed. "An avenging angel has been taking out members of a group of assassins called the Rabum Giru."

I clutched the handle of my beer tightly and brought it to my lips. I stared straight through the back of the glass mug, at the bar lined with multicolored bottles in no particular order. I could feel his eyes trained on me as I lowered the glass slowly to the table.

I didn't like the concept that there was information circulating about me. That meant the Rabum Giru would know I was coming, and potentially, what I was capable of. My jaw tightened up and I felt the strong urge to scratch at my palm with my nails. I forced myself to relax.

It didn't mean a death sentence to have a rumor about me. I could cut my hair; I could wear colored contacts. In addition, I had a partner. Since Sancus agreed to join me, I wouldn't raise as much suspicion. The human subconscious wouldn't associate a pair as a threat when looking out for one person.

It wasn't over. I still had the upper hand.

"Why is this my problem?" I asked, trying to sound as bored as possible, as if the rumor wasn't about me. "If angels exist, it sounds like the assassins are getting some divine payback."

Xenon's hand flew to my bicep and squeezed, a little too hard to be comfortable. From the corner of my eye, I saw Sancus tense up in his chair. I locked eyes with Sancus and slowly moved my head from side to side. *I'm fine.*

"This isn't a fucking game," Xenon whispered angrily when my eyes shifted to his. The cobalt rings were dark with flames I hadn't seen in them before. "These people are dangerous."

I swallowed, cold starting from where his fingers were pressing purple marks into my skin. He was worried; I was angry.

"So am I," I argued, unflinching and indifferent. "You lost your right to comment on my life when you disappeared from it."

I was glad for the encroaching cold that clawed up its throat. I didn't want to allow myself to see value his words, to see value in him. When it came down to it, I was still what I was all those years ago: a vessel. At the end of the day, I would do nothing more than get justice for others. That was my function, my purpose, my reason for being. Xenon wasn't a piece that fit into that puzzle.

His brows knotted together and his mouth scrunched up. His grip on my arm released and he no longer seemed able to maintain eye contact. He looked hurt.

"You're right," he said. "I'm sorry."

For some reason, that was worse. The ice inside got so cold it burst. I saw red and heard my blood rushing in my ears. "You're sorry?" I breathed out.

I lunged forward and grabbed the collar of his shirt, pulling him off his chair. I tugged him to the back of the pub, into the foyer that held the stairs that lead to the rooms. I slammed his back into the wall as hard as I could. If Sancus saw, he was smart enough to stay where he was.

I heard a wheeze leave his mouth and my fist tightened in the stiff white collar of his shirt. "You don't get to be sorry," I snapped, my voice low and wobbly with anger. "You left me, *not* the other way around."

He didn't move, he just stood there with that sad expression on his face, looking like he was about to cry.

I didn't even think about the expression I was wearing. It didn't matter. What mattered was expelling the red cold that I felt in the most effective way possible.

"You tricked me. You told me that we could be happy, but you turned tail at the first opportunity. You're a liar and a hypocrite and a coward." My face was inches from his and I wanted to close the distance and shatter his teeth with my forehead.

"I didn't want to hurt you," his voice broke. "I'm not a good man."

I took a slow breath. "You don't get to decide that," I snarled through my teeth.

It seemed like ages we stood in that hallway, trying not to be the first to look away, our heavy breathing a cacophony of rushed puffs. Finally, his head turned down. *I know,* the action said.

"Are you going to stop?" he inquired in a small voice.

"You know the answer to that," I spit, my rage finally sated, as I released his collar. It was spotted with crimson. My right palm was wet and slick where my nails had pierced my skin through the fabric. "I'll make sure they never hurt anyone again."

His hand was too cold as it touched the skin of my hand, reaching for the pinky. I was colder; I pulled away.

"There's nothing I can do to change your mind?" he asked.

"I'm going to kill them," I blurted. My own voice was rough and hushed. It was the first time I had explicitly admitted what I was doing out loud, the first time I had verbalized the horrible things I had been doing, the things I intended to do.

My body tensed up as the sound of squelching blood from my clenched hands made its way to my ears.

Still, I didn't regret saying it. *Let Xenon think the worst of me.* I knew Xenon would never betray me, no matter what I did to him. It was evident in the way he looked at me, like he would steal the sun and stars from the heavens if only I asked.

It was a dreadful power to hold over him. It was a horrible thing that I took advantage of. It was a tragic thing that I wouldn't extend him the same courtesy.

I inhaled, slow and deep. The air still smelled of stale beer and body heat.

"Every last one of those bastards who killed my tribe," I continued, further incriminating myself, further tightening the noose around my throat. Everyone who touched any of the sixty-two people who had made up my life. Everyone who had dared to mutilate the bodies of the kids not even old enough to hit puberty. Everyone who took a breath from my mother and father. Everyone who played a part in taking away Jace, *my* Jace, who had matching bracelets with me because he thought they would make us look like a superhero team. I'd kill them all if it obliterated every piece of me until I was nothing.

Despite the feeling of getting locked in a cage, I was made of hubris. That hubris laced through my clenched jaw and unfocused eyes.

I tapped my finger pads against the leg of my pants, still damp with iron and snow. "I'll get my family justice." A promise, an oath, the only reason I was still *breathing.*

I heard a light cracking and felt a pressure on my left shoulder. A sigh. "It won't make you happy," Xenon whispered, his voice barely audible.

I don't think it reached me. It didn't melt the cold away; it didn't ease the tension in my shoulders. It sat there, heavy, a weight bearing on me. The worst part of what Xenon had said to me wasn't how it made me feel, but that I, without lying, replied, "I don't care."

The creaking sound of cold metal filled my ears, even if it was warm inside, and there was no metal in the old inn.

I felt cold when his fingers latched onto my own. I felt cold when he took me to my room and pressed me to the door to kiss me. I felt cold when he pulled me on top of him and began to take off his clothes.

I was always angry. I was angry because I cared far more about my dead family than the man willing to give me everything. And I was angry because my anger would always overpower my ability to care for others.

I would spend my whole angry life chasing ghosts.

May 10, 2726

Nyami Nyami

I loved quiet mornings. I liked the slow awakening to the sound of whispered breaths, the blinking away of blurred vision, feeling the ghost prickles of goosebumps blooming across my arms and legs as I stepped into the cold air. I liked steaming, black coffee, bitter enough to stop me from dozing back off as I stared ahead, still half dreaming.

That morning, I did not like any of those things. The silence was deafening, the cold too heated, and the coffee too sweet. More than any of that, the crushing weight of expectations loomed overhead, forcing down, like mustard gas settling in a trench.

I didn't pass any looks to Sancus, Kali, or Xenon as I left the room. Sitting on the chair I had come to think of as 'mine' didn't feel right, so I sat at the hard, wooden dining table chair instead.

One of the shinshi was setting the table, laying out the silverware by the plates and forks. Bobcat nodded in acknowledgement of me.

I watched her unblemished fingertips grab at a white porcelain mug and fill it with coffee and push it toward me, a small kindness.

My hands wrapped around the mug, its warmth searing my palm. I raised my fingertips to my chin and extended my arm toward her at the elbow. *Thank you,* I signed.

She smiled with only her lips and bowed her head. She was no different than the other shinshi, who walked the halls without tongues. She couldn't respond verbally. She brought her upturned palm toward her center, then moved her arm outward at her elbow. *You're welcome.*

How cruel of them, a voice echoed, *to give those who fail training the option to die or become a slave. That, really, is no choice at all.*

Bobcat bowed once and left the room quietly, as if she had never been there at all.

I pushed the coffee mug Bobcat filled away from me, the scent now making my stomach churn.

Everyone had made it back from their missions safely. Some were injured. Xbalanque had a busted brow, from hitting his head on a table during his mission. He had joked that maybe we would have matching scars now. I was thankful that was the worst he had gotten, since he always seemed to sport a new bump or bruise every time I saw him.

It wasn't long before I heard a shuffling from behind me. It came from furthest away from the dining table. My room. A soft and muted crackle, the sound of blanket being dragged across wooden floors. Xenon. He plopped down in the chair next to me. His shoulders were sagging and the blanket was pulled up over his head like a cowl. His eyes weren't even open.

"Morning," I greeted quietly.

My silence was for nothing, because when he scraped the chair he sat on against the floor to bring it closer to mine, I was fairly certain he had started an avalanche... On the other side of the world. I winced at the noise.

"Oops." He didn't seem very sorry.

I propped my elbow on the table and leaned my head on my hand, looking forward at the door.

Xenon leaned his head on my shoulder. The blanket was warm.

"Today, politics?" I asked, knowing the answer.

He simply hummed, too tired to formulate proper words. I felt him turn his head so his forehead was on my shoulder.

It was an odd sensation, having a shadow. Xenon and Diejiste slowly incorporated themselves with Sancus, Hunaphu, Xbalanque, and myself. We became a coven of six, rather than four.

Xenon always seemed be just in reach now, unless it was just me and Sancus. When I asked him why he left Sancus and I alone, but no one else, he shrugged and said, "You need your alone time with your best friend. If you don't want me around with the others, feel free to say so." I never did. Hunaphu loved him and he was slowly winning Xbalanque over, so I had no qualms.

I didn't like his subtle touches. His hand reaching for mine under the desks during our politics lectures, the hanging over my shoulders when he was 'tired' after training so hard, the constant requests to sit so close he was almost on top of me, the current press of his forehead into my shoulder. It was suffocating, a reminder that he was always watching, pulling on the noose a little more.

Still, I said nothing. I kept justifying my inaction by telling myself I could use him and this small sacrifice was the cost.

I needed him to care for me enough to not betray me, to keep my secret when the day came that he figured it out. Because he would. There was no way I could keep it hidden forever under such an attentive gaze.

Perhaps it was a little twisted, what I was doing to him, but I tried not to let it get to me. It wouldn't be the first time I was responsible for ruining someone.

I turned my head to whisper against his hair. It seemed like the actions I would take if I cared for him. "Do you want me to pour you a coffee?"

He shook his head. "No; I want a hug."

"So, a coffee with cream and two sugars, then?"

A small grumble. I picked up his head and lay it on the table. Xenon didn't protest in the slightest. I pushed up from the table and walked to the area with the coffee pot.

The acidic smell of burning beans filled my nose as the hot liquid hit the inside of the porcelain mug. The coffee rippled outward as I plopped the two sugars in and topped it off with a milky white liquid. I didn't bother to stir it before I pushed it across the table to him.

Xenon blindly grabbed at it, spilling a little of the brownish liquid over the edge of the mug. His face scrunched up when he brought the mug to his lips. Ah, not enough cream then... or maybe sugars. Xenon did not like bitter things.

Before I could ask if he needed another, Amaethon threw open the door that led to the external corridor. She was covered in a thin layer of sweat. *Morning run.*

"Good morning!" she called out cheerfully. She was energetic, even in the early dawn. I liked that about her.

Xenon picked now to open his eyes and give her a disgruntled look.

"Coffee?" I asked over my shoulder.

"Oh, yes. Black, please."

I handed her the mug and watched as she tossed her head back to suck it down in one gulp. I winced as she poured herself a second serving. Her energy might have come from the obscene amounts of caffeine she consumed.

Nakkrah stumbled into the room next, wobbly on his feet and sagging from side to side. He didn't say anything, but sat down and started immediately helping himself to the bread, slathering an obscene amount of butter onto a pre-toasted piece.

The others slowly trickled in, waking to the sounds of multiple alarm clocks going off at once.

Kali shot me a smirk as she sat down at the table. I didn't want to decipher what it meant; I had a feeling I wouldn't like what I learned.

I pulled my hand out of Xenon's.

"Good morning, my peppery pal," Sancus yawned as he sat down in the chair I was standing in front of.

"Peppery?" I questioned.

"Because you're pleasant, but only in small doses."

"Wise," I respond sarcastically.

He shoved a whole chapatti into his mouth. "Don't choke," Xbalanque advised, handing Sancus a glass of water.

It hit me how much we all acted like school kids sometimes. Yeah, we were adults by all accounts, but times like this made me appreciate how we had made a family in one another, in the broken childhood dreams and the shattered remnants of hope we carried with us like worn umbrellas. We were all still kids, trying to raise one another in the absence of any real parents.

Only the important things make it into a book; the things that the author thinks are required to tell the story. How much of the day to day, the things I value the most, are left out, burned from the record of time? If my life were a book, would this moment make it inside? Was this moment important enough in the story to be told? I thought it was. I would never know.

I'd stop seeing Xenon pull all the blankets from the bed and Amaethon drink five servings of coffee and Nakkrah's odd eating habits. The thought that I may forget hurt. The thought that the rest of them would, too, hurt far worse.

My eye twitched. Xenon was tugging on my fingers in an instant, roused from his position at the table. *What was wrong?* He was asking with his silent gesture and his speckled gaze.

I didn't answer him.

When I ruffled Hunaphu's morning bed head, I tried to memorize the feeling a little more than usual, even the sharp sting of her batting my hand away.

"The Enesich region is segmented into two different portions, vehemently opposed to one another for secular beliefs," Mergen projected. He stood at the front of the room on a podium of oak and black paint. He wore the same dark black and silver robes every other instructor wore, ones that swallowed him in darkness.

Though the content he had put together was quite detailed, Mergen was not a good lecturer. He lacked emotion in his voice and rarely looked up from his notes and he only interacted with us when it was time to pass out papers or someone asked a question.

His neck was hunched at an odd angle, rather than his eyes turning downward. "Although once unified under a common school of thought, the east and the west have become staunchly divided among perspectives."

His gingerbread fingers ruffled through a folder for a set of pictures. He took the glossy notes out and handed the set to Diejiste. She took them in shaky hands. She had a slight tremor of the left wrist due to a childhood injury, though she had never elaborated on what that injury was.

"The West believes in the power of nature to influence the individual," he scratched at the raised pink scars lining the collar of his neck. "The first picture details their perspectives. You can see highlighted a silhouette of a person before a great tree. The tree acts as a light of wisdom and a beacon for humankind." The picture was in Amaethon's hands now. I had no idea what was on it.

I scratched at the wooden desk of the lecture-hall with my left middle finger. My foot was bouncing my leg without consent. I couldn't sit still while waiting for that picture to slowly wrap around in front of me, where I could peer over Sancus's shoulder and look at it.

He sat directly in front of me. We sat in order of our ranking, and sadly, Sancus hadn't managed to climb that high because of the entrance exam. He was sitting at sixth. It, to my great pleasure, *did* make whispering dumb things under my breath easier. Each time the lectures got too boring, I'd try to make him laugh; I was only successful about eighteen percent of the time.

I scratched a little harder at the wood and took a deep breath. I felt a light tap against the toe of my right sneaker.

Xenon didn't look at me, but I could tell he was keenly aware of my gaze on him. The tap to my toe was a silent question. *What's up?* I looked back away and was more careful to keep the anxious movement to a minimum.

"The second exhibit is a piece of art from the East. If you'll examine it closely, you will see a rigor in the image, where man is the central focus, rather than nature. He bends it to his will and nature succumbs."

The first exhibit was slipped into Sancus's fingers. I leaned forward in my chair to see what Mergen was speaking about.

There was, indeed, a person below a gargantuan tree of lime foliage. The picture was done in linear perspective, the focal point being just slightly beyond the outer rim of the page. It was drawn as if the environment was encapsulating the person, not only within the twisting vines of the tree, but also within the stumbling shrubbery, the crawling moss, and the skittering critters that the artist incorporated into the shadows, meant to look hidden.

I leaned back and looked to the front again.

"The reason the West have a more naturalistic perspective can be linked back to the torrential and devastating weather they had immediately after the war," Mergen droned on. "The dramatic changes to their landscape altered previously established norms."

"Didn't those same landscape changes happen to the East as well?" Kali asked. She leaned forward onto crossed elbows. She had her hair tied up and pinned in place with a pen.

"They did," Mergen answered. He crossed his own arms in imitation and leaned up against the wall. "Anyone know why it turned out differently?"

There was a silence in the room. Xenon whispered, just under his breath. "Don't you know the answer? Get out of your moody delinquent attitude and give us a help."

I wasn't good at whispering. I sprawled on the corner of my paper. *I don't know much about this.*

He reached over and scribbled back in a messy cursive script, *Why not?*

I actually never finished primary school. I stopped going when I was fourteen.

He shifted sideways to read my chicken scratch. There was a moment where I waited, holding my breath before he had a response. *What??? How is that possible???????* he scribbled again. The corners of my lips twitched up at his unnecessary punctuation.

I taught myself what I needed, nothing more. I didn't elaborate and he didn't ask me to clarify.

That was fine. The second exhibit was handed to Sancus and I leaned forward to look at the other work again. This one indicated a flat perspective without dimension. There was a line of people, passing goods to the next person in line, while accepting things from the person on their right.

"Because the West didn't have Teia Kian."

If Mergen was expecting any kind of reaction, we didn't give it. He looked disappointed in us, rubbing the bridge of his nose and shutting his droopy and tired eyes. "The Kian Clan, led by Teia, spent all their personal wealth to establish a system that provided survival crops to those in need after the devastation."

It was growing hard to keep my eyes open. History had been one of my worst subjects in school. Actually, I did poorly in most subjects. If I didn't like the material and had no interest, I didn't perform well. I excelled in music. Everything else, I was overwhelmingly average in.

Mergen tapped his podium with the tips of his fingers. That was odd. I used the pads of my fingers to tap. "The success of their philanthropy instated an enduring State based off of that same intent and formed a sort of non-religious religion around it." That was... actually interesting.

"In lots of books we see the struggle of human versus nature. Most of the time nature is seen to be the stronger of the two," Mergen explained. "This is seen in West Enesich texts, certainly. But humankind is seen as superior in Eastern texts."

"According to the current scion of the Kian family, 'The world is chaos; humans were born to tame it.'"

The papers were passed to me. I looked at them a little more closely. I liked the Western one more. It was more visually appealing. However, I think I related to the Eastern picture more. We just didn't live in the kind of world that was ruled by natural disaster any more.

Xenon pointed at the Eastern exhibit and I held it closer to him. "What do you think it says?" he asked. I hadn't noticed it was writing. It looked like it was just part of the background and I hadn't given it a second thought.

I shrugged.

I liked the way their writing looked. It was smooth and fluid, like someone had been trying to create a painting when they were making it.

My native tongue, by extension, was slanted and rushed when written out, like a suicide note would have looked.

"Remember, currently, the situation between the two realms is peace, but it is fragile and has broken multiple times in the past."

"The last time was less than ten years ago, right?" Maru asked. His voice sounded like a snowstorm: deafening and loud in a way that left you gasping for air and holding your breath to keep the cold out.

"Nine, by next month," Mergen supplemented. "And the conflict only lasted a week, but it completely decimated the border towns. Less than five percent of border citizens survived the warfare."

"Why did it start?" Hunaphu asked, taking the pen she balanced on her nose down.

Mergen shrugged. "Both sides have different records. West claims easterners kidnapped a political figure's kid. East claims that the West was burning their reserves."

"But why do they fight over something like this? It seems they were not fighting over the same thing. How do we not know who was right?" Diejiste pronounced her "th" sounds as a "t" when she spoke.

Mergen stood up straight again. "Well, since it was such a short turnaround, records had been scrubbed before international authorities could get there and verify. Grain houses *were* burned. A political figure's daughter *did* go missing. It's anyone's guess what really started it and it wouldn't matter what did start it anyways."

"What does that mean?" Sancus asked.

"It means, wars kill more people than can be justified. There is no right side in a war. They are both in the wrong." Mergen's black eyes stared into the ceiling, looking dazed. "That's why we exist. We are the shadow hands that keep order. You'll all learn that in time."

That's very self-aggrandizing, I thought. What was it that made us killing people different than a country killing people in a war? Ours was just more discreet. Self-aggrandizing would only delude us into believing we were to men what men were to animals: beyond the food chain.

Who do those Gods worship? a voice in my head asked. *Who is it that they answer to if no one holds them accountable?*

A chill settled in then, encroaching slowly on me and crawling across my skin and wrapping my limbs in a dry chill.

I thought of Xbalanque and Hunaphu and Sancus as my new family. As my gaze drifted over the tops of their heads, I realized that I would do everything in my power to ensure their right to live a prosperous life. I would die for them and I would kill for them. *I would start a war over them.*

I propped my head against my hand. My cheek was warm and my head was heavy. Perhaps that was love? Or was it blind devotion? Was there even a difference? No matter the rationale, I would still be a murderer, just like a politician who lost their daughter.

Yes, I still intended to disappear, but if a certain three asked, I would drop everything. That may have made me stupid. I hoped I'd never have to choose between my family and my old one. Either way, I'd forsake the ones I loved.

"I'm going to drop the play with you kids," Mergen groaned, pulling a hand down the left side of his face. "I don't feel up to talking more today, so why don't we table this and move on tomorrow?"

A resounding mumble of agreement broke out in front of me.

"Great. Bye." Mergen slipped his hands into the folds of his robe and strutted out the door quickly, leaving his notes behind in a scattered pile on the podium.

The mumble of agreement turned into easy chatter as everyone gathered their things and started to leave. I leaned back in my chair and stretched my arms above my head. The steady release of tension pushed the breath from my lungs and made me feel at ease.

I pushed myself up from the chair and walked to the bookshelf in the front of the room. My finger ran along the varying edges of the books there, pulling out the one I was looking for: A translation book. The last time I used one of these, I was in a different city, chasing a lead I didn't know existed. That was the day I learned of the North Wind and how they could turn me into the avenger my people needed.

New Alexandria, the city where Elonqua gave me my coin, seemed so far away.

I blinked quickly and began leafing through the pages as I returned to my seat.

"Still up for sparring with us?" Xbalanque asked when I made it back to the cluster of people.

I nodded. "Yeah. Can I join you three in, like, five minutes or so? If I'm not there, you can hunt me down or something," I joked.

No one laughed. In their defense, it wasn't funny.

"Sounds good," Sancus agreed. "Come on, guys. Let's go warm up." The three left the room in a swarm. Poor Xbalanque hadn't hit his last growth spurt yet, and his head bobbed shorter than the others.

I picked up the second picture from the space between Xenon and me and drew it closer. I squinted at the small sprawl, a series of loops and swirl from a new age language I had yet to learn. The writing was important to the East Enesich region. Yet it meant nothing to me, a flurry of text on a page that I should memorize for future reference.

I felt a squeezing on my right little finger. My eyes darted up to catch Xenon's. They were dark, shadows cast upon them by a contorted brow. "I promised Diejiste I'd help her with weights." It seemed odd to me that he was telling me this instead of just going.

I gave a nod. "Have fun."

I saw his jaw clench before he drew away, jerkily, and moved swiftly to the door. He didn't look back. He was so stiff when we parted now, like he was worried I was going to be attacked when he left.

I turned back to the page in front of me, flipping through the book of translatable symbols, trying to determine their origin and meaning. *Is it kaiatothh or tsikae?*

"*Tsuihan ikkanaie ona nokkana ii ya shotitah ut.*" Nyami Nyami's deep words echoed in the near empty room. He sat next to me, but had not moved to look at the book I had, nor the paper I had scribbled possible solutions on. His aquiline nose poked firmly into the pages of his own book, with a red leather cover. "It means, 'One firm voice leaves a choir in its wake.'"

"I didn't know you were a polyglot," I mumbled under my breath, amusement evident in my tone.

Nyami Nyami didn't chuckle. No, I doubt he was even capable of laughter. What he did do was lift his shoulders up and down in a hearty jiggle.

He caught my gaze. "I like being able to communicate," he explained.

I blinked. Nyami Nyami wasn't exactly someone who was fond of explaining what was on his mind, or talking at all. He rarely opened up, and if he did, it was with Hunaphu, who had a way of getting even the most disciplined of spies to spill their secrets.

He thumbed at the corner of his paper nervously, folding it in a series of straight lines, back and forth. "After I divorced my wife, I realized lots of those problems could have been avoided if I knew what she was saying."

"I see," I mumbled, awkwardness creeping up on me.

"It isn't something to be sorry about, it's just something that happened." Nyami Nyami clarified quickly, "Things do happen, but they can only hurt us if we let them.

Nyami Nyami was surprisingly wise. Thousands of words could spill from others, but I valued the ones that dripped from his downturned ones more thoroughly. He was twenty-five, had a good six years on me. Six years was, apparently, enough of a difference to give someone the wisdom to say shit for that.

"So, I started to learn," he elaborated. "Figured that if I could communicate with others—Well, if I could communicate with others, maybe I'd be able to listen a little better, too."

"Oh," I said again. My lips tingled and I bit them. I was certainly being insensitive when I asked, "Do you know where she is now? Your wife."

Nyami Nyami did the jostling, soundless chuckle once more and I felt a little less like a jerk. "Last I heard, she was seeing someone new. I hope he is better to her than I was."

I nodded. Maybe it didn't mean much to him, but I thought Nyami Nyami was too kind already. Then again, he may have been a different person than he was before.

Briefly, my mind drifted to Lee, back home. I hoped he had found someone who was better to him than I was. Someone who didn't drop off the face of the earth and fake their own death. Emil and Josephine had each other. He had been alone.

"Do you think she'd want you back if you proved you could listen?"

He smiled softly and shook his head. "Even if she would, I wouldn't take her."

"You wouldn't?"

He shook his head again, this time more resolutely. Not a single strand of his spiked hair was displaced. I noticed now his face showed no signs of resentment or bitterness.

"We're different people than we were when we met. Why would we try to force ourselves to love someone who no longer exists just because they bear the same face of a past lover?"

I looked at my hands. My fists were shaking. What would Josephine, Emil, and Lee say if they met me now? Would they still be friends with the person I had become? Would they try to force themselves to be in the name of the friendship we once had?

"Are you—"

"Ma'at!" I heard a call from out in the hallway. My head spun around to look at the doorway. Footsteps were fast approaching.

"Looks like someone needs you," Nyami Nyami informed me. I nodded and pushed myself to stand, walking out to the hallway.

I made one last look to Nyami Nyami, sitting in the top row of the lecture room, with yellow desks, beige walls, and a huge chalkboard stretching the front, all lit archaic candle and cast-iron chandeliers. He was staring at that chalkboard, at the green with white smudges all across it.

I don't think he was looking at that board, pinned to the light stone wall with iron nails. I think, his black eyes were looking at his wife and her new lover. I think, he was seeing the pair happy. And I think he was smiling because it was the kind of life he wanted for her.

I don't know what I was starting to ask him, but it felt too much like a betrayal to ask anything more. A betrayal of silence or a betrayal of memory, I couldn't be certain.

My fingers dug into the oaken doorframe and a splinter wedged its way into the tip of my middle finger. It stung, but the pain was grounding. It was the kind of pain that kept the clenching of my core at bay.

My core clenched because I was reminded of home and the people I would have, at a time, given everything for. I didn't even know if I could feel that for them any more, that unconditional agape that overflowed from Nyami Nyami's fingers, numbing him with a soft lilac hue. I didn't believe I was capable of that.

I never thought too hard on love. Not in the rushed kisses I took as a teen, not in the slower ones I was learning to take now. I must have been missing a fundamental part of the equation. I wasn't giving to Xenon what Nyami Nyami had given, was giving, to his former wife.

My chest felt like it was collapsing in upon itself, imploding in dust and smoke and I felt cold in a way I had never felt cold before. This time, the ice expanded for a reason that wasn't anger. It was expanding, freezing up my joints and my heart, encasing them in an artic shell.

It hurt me physically to move and I could hear the steady creak of the ice as it fractured, rather than melted. It made the sound a child makes when it's hungry. It made the sound an animal makes when its foot is stuck in a trap.

I headed after the three voices calling out my name.

Xenon didn't taste like what I think he was supposed to taste like; he didn't taste like home. Instead, he tasted like unrealistic expectations. The hardest thing I had to do to that day was tell myself I couldn't force him to be what I wanted by simply being good to him. It was a joke: one that Nyami Nyami was privy to, I didn't understand, and Xenon was the subject of.

For now, Xenon was a tool to me.

And because of what he could have been for someone else, someone a little less fucked up than me, that made me profoundly sad.

December 8, 2727

Abran

Waking up was instantaneous, with the sound of glass clinking on oak softly rousing me.

"You're never with me when I wake up," I rasped. He had a habit of leaving. I was fond of that habit.

I threw my arm over my eyes in an effort to block out the sun for a moment longer. The floorboards creaked and I realized I was prolonging the inevitable.

I pushed myself up and moved to sit with my feet on the ground. Xenon stood at the mirror, brushing his hair. His stupid hair that he seemed to put so much effort into. I hunched over and turned my gaze to the floor. Wood was easier to look at than him.

"What changed?" I requested.

Footfalls made their way to me. I didn't move my gaze from the floor. He grabbed my chin softly and tilted my head to look at him. His hands always felt like the moon to me: cold and distant, even in their proximity.

"I wanted to try once more to change your mind," he whispered, like he feared starting another fight with me again. When I found the courage to look up, his eyes looked stormy and chaotic and desolate. His lips were drawn up in a sad smile, one that was obviously forced. His thumb stroked a cold line down my right cheek.

I pushed his hand away from my face, fleeing the miniscule comfort it offered.

"I keep my promises," I argued. I'm sure I was the one who seemed cold to him now. I was unrelenting, a tornado running its path of destruction. I drew my face tight in a scowl.

He sighed. "I know you do," his voice was dejected and defeated. "That's why I love you."

I inhaled sharply. My eyes combed his face for any sign he was teasing me. I found nothing. No jovial tune. No crooked smirk.

I wanted to love him back. I wanted to love him so fully and completely that it stained me and ruined me and made me into a shell of a person, capable only of devotion. I couldn't do that. A part of me believed I never would.

"But I can't," he continued. "I can't watch you go down this path, Ains." He knelt to the ground in front of me. His hand reached toward my own that hung from my knee. He squeezed it gently, but didn't return his gaze to my own.

The tightness in my shoulders released, replaced by a tightness in my stomach. He sighed again. "I can't watch you die going after these people. Even if you survive, you won't be Ainsley any more, I know it." He refused to look up at me, lost in his own world that was our two hands, likely the last time they would ever meet.

"I—" *don't know what to say.* He was right; I wouldn't be Ainsley any more. I'd be a hypocrite and a killer. But I knew those things long ago; my mind hadn't changed.

He scoffed in a soft way, as if he knew how this conversation would go. He looked back up to me, faking a smile again. "I want to remember you as my savior," he confessed. I knew what he was really trying to say. He wouldn't see me as that if I kept hunting the assassins down, if I became what I hunted. He didn't want to stick around to watch the process.

"I'm not naïve. I know what role I play in this story," I retorted. "I'm the villain. Villains can't be saviors; don't delude yourself." I'd be the villain. I'd perjure myself as much as I needed to. My promise came before my salvation.

"You aren't the villain in this story," he said, a ghost of a whisper. The words were meant for himself, I could tell. I believed it was a plea to remember me the way he wanted, instead of with all of the flawed cracks and splinters.

He looked like he had something else to say to me, but couldn't find the words. I knew what he needed to say.

No tears welled in my eyes, no pain filled my chest, no lump grew in my throat. I was numb in the way that a phantom limb is numb. "So, this is where you leave me," I said for him. If I couldn't love him, at least I could speak for him.

Xenon nodded, short and curt, and gripped my hand tightly once more before standing to full height. He wrapped his arms around me, a cold embrace meant to be a comfort one last time. It wasn't comforting.

I didn't lift my arms to return the favor.

His hand stroked my head softly, cold fingers threading through sleep-messed strands. "I want you to be happy," Xenon wished tenderly. "I hope you can let go of the past and find that."

What would he know of your happiness? An angry voice hissed. *If he loved you, he would know this is the only way for you to get closure, for you to seize justice, for you to achieve happiness.*

He pulled away from me and put his hands on my shoulders. It was a soft touch, too light to be the full weight of relaxation. He was holding back, treating me like I would break; perhaps I would.

One piece of me said, *You won't. You won't allow yourself to break before you're done crossing every name off that list of yours.* Another part of me was pleading, *please don't leave. I'll stop when it's done. I want to be happy and love you back. Don't leave me alone again.*

It must have been my pride that stopped me from speaking; I didn't want to watch myself become the person who needed someone else in order to be okay.

He leaned over and pressed a kiss to the top of my head.

Stay, that second part of me wanted to plead when the pressure left. Nothing came out.

"You won't like what you find at the end of the road." His hands dropped to his sides. "Goodbye, Ainsley."

"Don't forget me?" One last request. One moment of weakness. *Stain me into your heart, even if it kills you,* I thought selfishly. I wanted to be important to someone, even if that person didn't fit into my life.

"Don't forget *me*," he responded. I smiled a little at that small acknowledgement of how important we could have been to one another, if things had been different.

"Take care of yourself, Xenon."

He placed his hand on my cheek once more, for a brief moment, too brief. Then he turned away from me, walking toward the door. He didn't look back when he opened it or before he shut it.

It occurred to me that it would have only taken one phrase to change his mind and make him stay. All I had to do was tell him, "I love you, too."

I didn't say those words because they were a gross perversion of reality. No matter how much I hoped it was true, I knew it would be a disservice to us both to pretend. So, I didn't pretend.

I had always thought Xenon's personality was like the tides, adaptive and reflective. I was wrong. He was much more like the moon. His glow was soft and mellow and he represented how far man could reach.

But the thing about the tides is that we can only really see a small, surface part of them. We only ever see the waves and the seafoam.

I pushed myself to stand and walked over to the mirror that Xenon had been at a moment before. I took myself in. It wasn't a good sight: the sight of a ghost.

My fingers found the strands of my hair and gave a gentle tug. It had grown again, past my shoulders.

I looked around the ground for my utility belt. I saw the thing in a heap by the foot of the bed. I walked over to the belt and riffled through it for a familiar lacquer hilt. I pulled the knife from its holster and walked back over to the mirror to look at myself once more.

I'd change everything.

I held the blade in my right hand and grabbed my hair with my left. I started to cut. Strand after strand fell to the floor, messy white bunches falling soundlessly.

I could start with the hair. I could find henna at the market to dye my hair black. I could color my face with powder and I could change my eyes with contacts. I would try to look like my father, like a barrage of browns and honeys.

I set the knife down on the counter and took one last good look at my face. I didn't need the reminders of who Ainsley had been anyway. Ma'at was enough to keep my promise.

Sancus was sitting at a round table for two with his bags packed when I came down.

"Let's scoot," I said as I dropped my duffel on the floor next to him.

Sancus looked up at me. His brows knit together and his mouth fell open a bit as he leaned back with his hands up. Then he closed his mouth and eyes and clapped a hand on my shoulder. "It's okay, boo, there are other men."

I shrugged his hand off my shoulder. "It wasn't because of him, jackass," I argued. "Iktomi told me that there was a rumor about me. I didn't want to be distinctive."

Sancus pushed himself up from the table. "And you thought spray tan was the solution?" he inquired. "You're a moron." The teasing made the tension in my shoulders dispel.

I smirked. "Takes one to know one."

"So," Sancus transitioned, leaning a little forward to bounce on his toes. "Where to next?"

My head shifted to the side. "What do you mean?"

"Well, who's next on your list?" he asked. "Now that I know why you take so much time to get back, we should just check another one off, say we're traveling or something."

"Abran," I answered. "His name is Abran Dayan."

Sancus made a soothing humming noise, deep in his chest. He looked through me as he pushed me to the side to move toward the back of the inn, where the computer was probably located. I saw him lean over the counter to whisper to the lady who stood there.

His hand flew up to rub at the back of his head and he gave her that bright smile that was never far. His eyes crinkled in the corners so much they were almost shut.

A dusting of rose danced across her nose. She smiled and was all too happy to gesture with her hand to wave him behind the bar. He turned back briefly and shot me a thumbs up.

I waited for fifteen minutes before Sancus peeked his head out of the falling curtains that hid the staff-only section of the inn. His shoulders were slumped and he gave of the distinct impression of a kicked puppy. "This guy's virtually a ghost, Ma'at," he pouted. "I couldn't find him anywhere."

I wrapped an arm around his neck and pulled him in tight enough to cause him to splutter.

Sancus reminded me of a copper penny that had been heated in the sun. The color of summer days and a harp's sound. He was always so warm. I wanted to soak in that warmth, feel it nip at my chilly fingertips.

"That's fine," I said before I pushed him away. Sancus raised his left eyebrow in question. I smirked at him and placed a confident hand on my hip. "I happen to be great at ghost hunting."

I tugged on Sancus's sleeve, pinching the skin tight black fabric between my thumb and forefinger. He stopped and looked to where my head was pointed.

It was a home like one of those in the old-time scary movies. A mansion on top of a hill with a cast iron gate guarding it. I was sure it looked much nicer in the spring's daylight, when all of the viridity could be seen. At night, with the first snow of winter behind us, it looked like the home of a widowed Count, who spent his days looking sadly out the window.

Spindly and bare trees lined the stairs leading up to the front porch, and dead sprouted forlornly through the other areas. I could see the makings of fruit trees and rose bushes, without any blossoms on them.

The house was high and arching, with too many gables to count and dark colored shingles cascading down. The windows were lined with bright red curtains, that matched the color of the grandiose double doors out front.

I pushed the cast iron gate open. It wasn't locked. Sancus and I looked at each other.

People who have nothing to fear don't lock their doors. Abran Dayan was either incredibly complacent or incredibly dangerous.

We began the trek up to the main doors the way a child rides a bike for the first time: with trepidation and excitement. Sancus and I shared one mind in these moments. That's why were the ideal team.

The front door was unlocked, too, and lead into an atrium with a hanging chandelier and dual staircases stretching to the top floor. I could not escape the thought that a mansion as big as this should have more people there, servants or staff of a sort.

Sancus and I moved to the top of the stairs. We should start from the top back of the house and work our way down. It was only three stories above ground. I couldn't tell if there was a basement or not.

Rooms are cleared much like one reads: from left to right. The only difference is when clearing rooms, there is always someone watching your back and looking out toward the other angles to ensure both of you make it home.

The top was empty, not just devoid of people. There was nothing in the rooms. No furniture, no dust. But for the curtains hanging up near the windows, deep crimson and heavy, there were rooms filled only with the light *tuk tuk* of our footsteps on wooden floors.

The second floor was much the same.

The first floor, at least had some signs of life. A bed was pressed to the center of a wall in the far back of the house. The fridge had some left overs in little paper takeout boxes. But what furniture there was, there was only enough for one, and it was always placed in a distinctive way that indicated no one actually used the space.

The house had the scent of a house that was lived in. The slight tang of musk and skin.

I opened the door to the pantry. That, too, was empty, save for a single packet of crackers, stored right on the center of the shelf at my eye level.

"Damn it," I mumbled. I felt the urge to hit something. My fingers gripped tightly on the aluminum handle of the pantry door. "Fuck!" I shouted and slammed the door shut.

It clanged loudly, echoing throughout the empty mansion. Underneath the echo, I heard a clacking sound. *Clawble warble claark.* I opened the pantry door again and looked inside the small area. Nothing could have made that sound. I balled my hand tight into a fist and reached forward. I lightly rapped my knuckles once on the back wall, between the shelfing.

A hollow sound answered me.

I opened my fist and let the pads of my fingers brush over the stucco of the wall. The hollow wall fell back with ease, swinging forward silently to reveal a darkened staircase. The steps looked different than the rest of the house. While a fine wooden flooring made up the entirety of the mansion, carpet made up the steps. The walls, too, were draped in those same crimson curtains that barred the light from entering through the windows.

Sancus flinched in my peripheral. I turned to face him. "They do this in theaters," he whispered, his eyes trained down the dark staircase. "It stops noise from echoing."

Great, I thought, *Secret murder tunnel.*

I took a first step down, then a second.

The smell of mold hit me first as I rounded the corner. Next was the smell of copper. Old blood, dried up and stained into the beige carpeting, and new blood, iron dripping slowly down a dark flash of skin.

Abran looked just like his identification photo, save for a few more wrinkles worn into his skin. He had that peppered beard and brilliant green eyes. His nose was large at the bone and shrunken into his upper lip at the tip.

Abran's body curled protectively over the top of a smaller body. It wasn't protective in the way a parent protects their young. It was protective in the way a predator guards his kill. In Abran's brilliant eyes, there was bloodlust, blowing his pupils wide.

"Help!" the boy screamed. His small hand reached out. It was covered in a pale dust that had made his skin dirty. The dust clung to him so desperately, not because of sweat, but because of the coppery liquid that flowed from the lines where his skin had been peeled away from his muscle.

Tears streaked the pale dust, leaving dark, muddy trails on his face. "Help me!" It was the worst sound I had ever heard.

I reached for my rope and watched Sancus lurch next to me.

Abran whispered, "Don't move," in the calmest voice I'd ever heard.

Sancus and I froze. Abran looked down at the boy beneath him and pressed his knee into the boy's chest. The boy hacked and Abran lowered a gunmetal knife to the boy's flesh.

The sound that tore through the air was like a chain forcing its way through sheet metal. My eyes widened and my pulse thrummed in my ears. I felt hot. Too hot.

Ai'ier. Meriv to'or rekc kveptești, vikja bviiste zi'ir ai'ier. *Stop. I'll do anything, just make it stop.*

My face felt *hot*.

A piece of flesh, walnut on one side and maroon on the other was peeled away from sinews of muscle. It was tossed to the ground, like it was nothing more than yesterday's paper.

The boy was kicking his feet, screaming that chain-metal sound as loud as he could. His black eyes reached out to Sancus and me. "Why won't you help me!"

Sarret to'or ytiie. *Because you'll die.* Abran would kill him if we took another step. He would kill the boy if we didn't. The boy was dead either way. And there was nothing we could do but stand there like two idiots, clutching at useless tools.

Abran grabbed ahold of the little boy's hair and yanked him up into the air. A yelp exited his mouth. Abran pressed a knife to the pulsing jugular, holding him from behind so that we could see the threat.

"Don't!" I yelled. I could hear the panic in my voice. I wasn't supposed to show emotions, but thousands of them were splayed across my face, across my demeanor. They were uncontrollable because I wasn't seeing the little boy with teary eyes and shoes too big for his feet; I was seeing Jace.

Sancus tensed up beside me. "Let the kid go," he said calmly.

"You know," Abran mused. "Most of us are in this for money." A drop of red trickled down the boy's neck and into the ratty collar of his shirt. The little boy's nails raked across Abran's arms, trying to force it away. I watched the red lines raise without a single pained reaction from Abran.

My hand clenched tighter around the rope, cutting little ribbons into my palm.

"Not me," he continued. "I couldn't give a rat's ass about money."

"Then what do you want?" I asked through gritted teeth, a little more controlled than previously. "I'll make it happen."

Abran chuckled lowly. His blade dropped from the boy's neck as he laughed hysterically. Sancus and I both flinched and jolted forward. The laughing cut abruptly and the blade was back at the kid's throat. The message was clear: *Not a step closer.*

We froze. I looked at Sancus from the corner of my eye. A bead of sweat rolled down his temple.

My eyes shot back to the kid. "I want exactly this. I want to hurt people."

My breath caught in my throat as it hit me that the kid in front of me was going to die either way.

Jace! I cried inside my head. *I'll figure it out this time!*

My heart thrummed rapidly. I didn't feel the usual cold steadiness I felt when dealing with these people. Instead, I felt too hot in my skin, the overwhelming desire to hurl, shaky hands and wobbly knees.

Abran removed the knife from the boy's neck and moved it down. With a flick of the wrist, the boy began to scream hysterically. His finger rolled to the ground in front of us.

How dare you? I screamed. My jaw hurt. *Stay away from my brother!*

The knife was brought back up to the boy's neck. "I want to hear the pain in their voices and," he paused and inhaled deeply, "smell the fear in their sweat."

He looked into my eyes directly, then Sancus's.

"That is the greatest feeling in the world."

Abran sliced backward and dropped the boy. The boy didn't even have time to scream. He crumpled to the floor and red spewed from his throat, stretching up into the air. My windpipe closed up.

"You bastard," I seethed. The cold encased my every appendage, racing up my veins and turning my eyes hard in their sockets.

There was nothing to stop me and Sancus then, and we surged forward with reckless abandon.

I threw out my rope and it wrapped around Abran's left leg. I wrapped the rope around my arm once and yanked it back. Abran tumbled to the ground. Sancus was on Abran in an instant; he swung his arm down, a knife in hand, at Abran's head. Abran shifted his head to the side. I heard a squelch, but couldn't see where the knife had landed.

Soon, Sancus was on his back, Abran leaning over him, forcing a knife down at Sancus's throat. It was the same knife that had gotten the boy. Sancus held Abran's arm away from him, but he was working against gravity.

I lunged forward, pulling my scimitar from my thigh's sheath. I almost never used it, but it felt normal in my hand.

I contracted my left bicep and swung down on Abran's back, cutting through the dark fabric and through the tawny skin underneath. Dark red seeped from the gash. It was the same color as the little boy's had been.

Bile rose in my throat.

I brought my left leg up and kicked at Abran's hip, shoving him off of Sancus. He landed with his stomach facing the sky. I shuffled my left foot forward and stepped on his wrist with my right. The knife clattered on the ground. I dropped my left knee to the center of his sternum and dug in with all the weight I could muster.

I heard a cracking noise. My scimitar quickly found his neck. I could see Sancus stand from the corner of my eye. I didn't pay him any mind.

"Do you even care when they die?" I asked. A drop of my sweat slid down the tip of my nose and plopped onto his face, spreading through the heavy wrinkle on his brow.

Abran was still smiling like he had just had the best meal in his life. I could feel his pulse echoing beneath the sole of my foot. He was high on the adrenaline boost of what he had done. It made me feel colder, yet.

His lips parted. "No," he said. "All those people were games. They just lost, that's all."

"You're psychotic," Sancus exclaimed, parroting my thoughts.

Abran wheezed a shaky inhale. "And?"

My eyes squeezed shut for a moment before I forced them to open up, to lock down on Abran's own.

My blood dripped from my palms down the curved slope of the blade. I pressed down with both hands, slowly forcing my way through the skin of his neck, through the muscle of the esophagus, to the back of the spine, where I sawed back and forth until the head was removed.

I felt the sting of a blade scraping against the bone in my hand. I ignored it. I cut off the hands, easier work than the head. Then I pushed myself up to stand.

I put the blade away in my holster and sniffled. "Let's go," I said. I could feel Abran's blood seeping into the dark fabric of my clothes.

I started walking down the darkened hallway.

"Wait," Sancus interjected, three fingers wrapped gently around my wrist. My throat closed up. It was hard to breathe. My vision grew blurry.

The way Sancus looked at me felt so nice that it hurt. It was the look that said he was *there*.

A soft tug of his lips and an upward tilt of his brows. I wondered if he still saw me beneath all of the dyes I had stained myself with. *Does he still see me?*

He pulled my hand up and looked at it. Without a word, he pulled out the first aid kid we had in our utility belt. Sancus laced the needle and thread through the cut on my hand with such practice I wondered if he had ever been a doctor. He tied the gauze around my palm with such gentle care, I wondered if he had ever been a father. I knew the answers to these thoughts were no, but I couldn't help to picture him in a different life, one where his future was much more peaceful.

What a fucked-up thing the world was to have led him here instead.

When I looked up to his face, flashes of red spewed from his neck, splattering the world around us. I sucked in a breath.

Then, it was gone. I forced my gaze away. I couldn't look at Sancus and see that, phantom flashes of a reality that didn't happen, but very well could have.

We walked out of the house and began the descent into the town below. I was quiet. Sancus was, too. A single street lamp glowed yellow at the cast iron gate. We picked up our bags from the bushes inside the property and stood directly below it, waiting for a taxi to drive by the main strip.

Sancus tapped my shoulder. When I looked to him, he immediately looked at his toes. "You have a little blood," he said. He scuffed the sole of his right shoe on the ground and then shifted his weight thrice between his legs. "On the left cheek," he elaborated.

I looked down at my toes, too, and furiously scrubbed at my cheek with the back of my wrist. "Thanks," I mumbled. I gave Sancus a quick one over. "You're clean."

"Thanks," he mumbled back.

A taxi pulled to a stop in front of us. "Can you take us to Nai'Seip?" Sancus asked the driver.

"Of course," came the reply.

My hand found the cool metal of the door and tugged it open. I crawled into the back seat. Sancus fell in behind me.

I pressed my lips into my fingers and turned my head to look out the taxi window. Numbness overtook me. I was still just as useless as I always had been. I could do nothing to protect the person in front of me. It was the same every time. I brought shame upon my tribe and shame upon those I cared for. I couldn't protect anyone. I couldn't even protect one child when I had a partner.

Sancus placed a hand on my shoulder. It felt heavy and warm and it was everything I needed. "Ma'at, there's nothing you could have—"

"Don't touch me," I bit lowly.

I didn't look at him. I didn't want to see the pain in his eyes. But mostly, I didn't want to see the blood spewing from the side of his throat again.

The rest of the trip back we spent in silence. I'm sure Sancus was thinking of me. That's the kind of man he was.

I was thinking about the sickening dripping noise of blood as it hit the ground from a spurting human fountain. *Shiuhh,* it sounded.

It snowed again on our way home. The snow seemed to follow us all the way back. It fell in white little flurries to the ground, obscuring our visibility.

I hated that color. The color white. White was the color of death, the pallor of a corpse, a mark of lost opportunity and regret. It was the color of scorching hot light, that burned and blinded. It was the color I associated with myself. And if I were being honest, maybe the only reason I hated the color white was because I actually hated myself.

I wasn't even a person any more. I was a monster, worthless beyond all measure. Maybe that's what happens to everyone eventually: we just all eventually get sick of ourselves, wretched things that we can't escape.

I trudged my way up the mountain and into the cave, down the stone hallways that always seemed too cold, and into the room we lived in.

Xbalanque and Hunaphu sat by the fire, smiling and chatting. I didn't hear what they were saying. I saw flashes of blood drip onto the couch below them, staining the leather. I saw them spasm and go limp against the couch. I saw the light leave their eyes and their chests stop moving.

I dropped my bag and ran over to the pair of them, dropping on my knees in front of them and pulling them into my arms, desperate to feel the heat of the living on them.

Hunaphu's hand shook on my back. I must have startled her. Xbalanque didn't react.

"Ma'at, what's wrong?" she asked. Her voice sounded sore.

My eyes squeezed shut and I pulled them both a little closer. Xbalanque's hand lifted to my back as well. He had grown taller than me, had shot up like a sprout. "Come on, dude," he complained. "What's with the new look?"

I didn't answer. I didn't let go.

I had already lost one younger sibling. Watching the little boy with blood spurting from his jugular had told me that I wasn't prepared to lose another.

Hunaphu and Xbalanque weren't related to me by blood. Neither was Sancus. Still, the thought of losing any of them left a gaping chasm inside me that I didn't know how to fill.

I didn't know how to explain to the twins that I had seen them die today. Nor did I know how to tell them that I wouldn't sleep easy for weeks picturing it.

All I could do was hold them in my arms and say, "It's been a long day."

June 30, 2726

Diejiste

I saw a woman clutching the corpse of a young boy in her arms. She wept, but no tears left her eyes. She had tattoos around her arms. A straight line around her biceps, with snaking lines coming out of that circle toward her elbows. A small circle also graced her forehead, with snaking lines coming out to form the symbol of our people. This woman was our Grand Crafter.

The Grand Crafter pulled herself to the field. She fell to her knees and pleaded with the sun, "Save the village; go into hiding long enough for the crops to collect midnight dew." She took a blade and slit her wrists, letting the blood leak into the soil. The blood looked black on the baren, dry dirt.

The sun asked the Grand Crafter to bring the remaining villagers to her, so that she may see her children one last time before she left. The sun didn't say this, but I heard the words like an echo in my head. The Grand Crafter must have heard it, too.

The Grand Crafter brought the survivors to the field to see the sun. The sun blessed all of her children with her light, endowing a piece of herself to each human so that they may see in the days without her before she plunged the village into shadows.

The world was dark for twenty-eight days. In the days of darkness, the crops grew and water quenched the thirst of the tribe. Her children had changed in her absence. Skin like parchment, hair whiter than snow, eyes of gold metal. They look like me, *I thought.* I look like her.

The sun smiled. She asked the people if they would make works that could share the beauty of her light with the world. The village, indebted to their sun, obliged. They captured the light in their hands and created scintillating dancers that breathed marigold and transformed heat.

I inhaled a sharp gasp and threw myself forward quickly. It was just a dream, a memory of an imagined story. It wasn't even a scary dream, but it still left my heart racing, struggling to calm itself. I grabbed at the white tank top I wore. It was slightly damp to the touch, another physiological symptom of a dream.

I pushed myself up from the bed and began to dress. It was early, but I had no desire to sleep any more.

It had been like this since the mission. Endless dreaming.

Mostly it was the man in white. I didn't mind that dream so much. That memory in particular, filled with the most powerful raw emotion I have ever felt, was still the one thing I held onto. My life since that day was bland, a continuance of days stretching forever because I knew I would never feel to the extent I did then. I lived my life knowing I'd feel that rush again when I met him again; I craved it like an addict.

I walked into the common area and found my chair. It wasn't really mine, but I always used it when given the choice. It was my favorite, with its faded brown leather and studs to keep that fabric stretched in place. It felt soft and warm when I curled into it, since it was closest to the fire.

I stared at the fire's flames flickering in nimble patterns.

I recalled that day from so long ago, the somehow untouched glass sculpture of the sun in the center of our village with viscous black liquid leaking downhill on the dirt beneath it, the unmarked graves, the burn of my palm's broken blisters, the dripping blood on my forearm from a dull blade slicing open my skin sixty-two times, the numbness I felt in that moment.

Blood, my mind had told me when my blood dripped off my fingers and turned the orange dirt below a sickening black, an unwelcome stranger in my skull. *That black liquid you saw was their blood.*

A cold chill licked up my spine.

The clock above the fireplace read four twenty-three in the morning. I sighed to myself. Another lonely night spent staring at the wall and hoping for sleep. If I really wanted something to do, I could help myself to a book or go to the balcony to watch the sunrise, but the I reasoned that the company provided by the fire was fine.

The floorboards creaked behind me. The sound was faint, but long, signaling someone moderately average in size, but good at creeping: Xbalanque, then.

"You're up early," I noted, not removing my eyes from their fixed location on glowing flames.

"I heard your gasp," he responded.

"Then what took you so long?"

I didn't get a verbal response, but he came to sit on the arm of my chair. He could have chosen a different chair.

He was silent for a minute. Finally, a sigh, "What did you dream of?"

How did I begin to tell someone about how a perfectly unscary dream made me shake? How could I explain it reminded me of the opportunities I would never have and how everything had fallen apart?

I thought about growing up to watch Jace marry Illya, like he had promised me he would. I would have perfected playing the viola and told my parents I got into the Philharmonic; they would have been so happy for me that they wouldn't have cared that I didn't want to be a glazier. I would have spent more time with Emil and Josephine and Lee, causing trouble until we had to stop the younger generation from causing that same trouble.

Any dreams of home caught my brain up in that melancholy process. Melancholy was a quicker intoxication than rum.

Xbalanque's hand touched my shoulder, gently requesting a response. It was gone in a second.

"Home," I breathed, not knowing how to elaborate.

"Scoot over, jerk," was the response I got instead.

I did as I was told and moved to the right side of the chair as far as I could, allowing my feet to fall to the ground. Xbalanque sat down in the actual seat and threw his legs over mine, trapping me within. He leaned to his right to fall against the chair, closing his eyes.

He was really close.

I didn't know if he expected me to hold him. It felt wrong for him to do so, not like Hunaphu, who was always casually touching someone. He wasn't tenderhearted and I could count the number of times I'd seen him smile instead of scowl. I clasped my hands together in my lap, nails biting into the skin between my knuckles.

"Did I ever tell you about my mom?" his calm voice startled me from my thoughts. It was still in the slightly-cracking stage that happened before puberty had fully set in.

I shook my head.

His scowl dropped off his face. My chest felt tight. "I only knew her for a while; really, I can only remember bits and pieces of a year with her. When I was four, she died," he told me. Then, we had both lost our mothers.

"I don't feel sorry for her," he said bluntly, "Dad was a real piece of work and she was better off without him, even if that meant she was dead."

That was where we differed. My dad was a great man, who gave me his everything, even when he suspected I was not his child.

"Sometimes I wonder what would have happened if she hadn't fallen into the water and been hit by the boat's propellor," he confessed. "I wonder if she would have stopped dad from raping me. I wonder if I ever would have met Hunaphu. And I wonder who I would have become if she had finished raising me."

Sorrow and anger welled in my chest and the scent of iron drifted up into my note. The sting on the backs of my hands came only after I realized. I made myself bleed. "What happened to him?" I asked. "Your father. Did he die, too?" If I ever met Xbalanque's father, I'd kill him myself.

Xbalanque shifted beside me. "I killed him. With a fire poker. I hit him with the handle to get him off me and kept hitting his head until I couldn't distinguish between blood and brain and skull sticking to the carpet." His voice didn't quiver at all when he spoke, like it was a far-off film he was narrating.

During demeanor training, I had learned he killed someone. That night by the fire, I finally learned whom.

"I see."

It was quiet for a moment. "But I always wonder," he continued. "How would things be different? Would it be better?"

I swallowed hard and forcefully. "Does it help?" I asked him, refusing to look at him again. "Does it make things easier for you to spend time wondering?" My voice was raspier than usual, heavy with the remnants of sleep and with the tumultuous feelings I was never equipped to handle.

He chuckled. His voice was hollow and even. It was always hollow and even, pinched at the edges and mellow, like wind could drift through him and he would make the breeze his own. "I don't think making things easier is really the point."

My lips twitched upward without my consent. He was right. I didn't think of the possibilities because it made things easier for me. I thought about it because it was a way to remember the people I care about.

"You know, kid, you're pretty wise for a fifteen-year-old."

Xbalanque's eyes were still closed, but his brow twitched when he smirked. "So help me, I will push you out of this chair, you soggy loaf of bread," he threatened emptily.

I poked Xbalanque's relaxed stomach. "I want to be offended by your comment, but you have the most creative insults," I rationalized.

Xbalanque hummed in affirmation. His head hadn't moved from its rest on the back of the chair. He must have been awfully tired; Xbalanque was the lightest sleeper out of all of us.

"Do you want to go back to bed?" I asked, hoping he wouldn't expect me to carry him. I was able to amass quite a bit of muscle in my times, but he was almost as big as me, now, having bulked up quite a bit in the past two months. It would be a struggle to get him into his top bunk.

Xbalanque's head moved against my shoulder and his left hand curled into his waist. "Not really. I'll stay."

I didn't say anything back.

Allowing me to stay close while he tried to doze off, I realized, was a subconscious admittance that Xbalanque didn't think I would hurt him like his dad had.

My fingers pushed his hair out of his eyes to look at his pointed nose and soft jawline in curiosity. He still looked like a child. He was a child, I supposed.

I wanted to make sure he wasn't ever hurt again. If his mother could no longer protect him, I wanted to. *I won't let anyone do what he did to you again,* I pledged. *Not as long as I breathe.*

I knew it would be a waste of my time to get attached. I was playing a game Xbalanque wasn't a piece in. I still intended to defect. He would still be issued orders to kill me on sight. It was illogical to let myself become invested.

But I was.

I turned to look back at the fire. Xbalanque stirred for a moment, but returned to sleep soon enough.

Why do I enjoy things that can burn me?

Humans were an interesting breed, I was beginning to find. Although we were all unique, we were surprisingly similar in everything.

For instance, all humans could be made mad, even sociopaths. We all express it differently. For instance, I was made mad by people who seem to turn serious matters into a joke. One needed to know when was a proper time to be serious, in my opinion.

On the other hand, it made Hunaphu see red when someone would hurt an animal needlessly. The last time we had gone into town, I had seen her break a boy's nose over a kicked cat. Xbalanque had to hold her back from doing worse.

Anger was something we were told to prey on. Because anger made mankind a slave to their desires. If you want something, get someone angry, while retaining your own sense of logic. That was why Yonten had always told me to keep my desires close.

Dolos was a rigid woman, with dark hair pinned tight to her skull by a series of shiny brown clips. She seemed to never be angry. Probably because she had learned enough about it to no longer fall victim to outbursts. As she had started today with, "Anger is not a primary emotion. It stems from something else."

I thought she was full of it. I had anger in spades. I saw red when I thought back on my past, felt the ice prickle cold enough to freeze over my muscles, the rushing blood in my veins, and even lift to chill my skin. I hadn't felt much since that day. But anger? That I could feel. Anger *was* primary for me.

Anger was the only thing I took comfort in, convoluted as that sounded.

"One of the ways to use this feeling to your advantage is to confuse someone. Make contrasting statements, containing an underhanded compliment. Can someone give us an example?"

I wasn't surprised when Maru came up with a comment on the matter, "It's amazing how you can really sell the whole idea of a trash bag as a fashion piece." I smirked a little and leaned back in my chair. Maru's sarcasm was unparalleled.

Even Dolos's lips twitched a little toward her high cheekbones. "Yes," she remarked, "that would certainly be a way to affect certain individuals."

She turned toward the chalk board at the front of the room and began the slow and steady scratch of white on green. FRUSTRATION, EGO, SHAME, BETRAYAL, FEAR, she wrote, in a line down the board.

She leaned up against the board. "Top to bottom: least to most effective," she said, sternly. Her posture indicated indifference, her voice importance. All the lecturers seemed like they didn't even want to be teaching.

"To truly get someone mad, get them to fear an outcome. Not to the point they are paralyzed, but just before. When tension is high and adrenaline kicks in. What do people fear? Well, most fears can be linked to death, but not always. Above all else, humans fear uncertainty. Uncertainty maximizes adrenal output."

Dolos used the word humans, like she was not one of them. Like we were of another world, studying the lifeforms on this one. What a convoluted perspective to have. A chilling reminder of the words *Who do the god's worship?* echoed in my skull.

She rapped the board next to the front letter of *EGO* twice with the knuckle of her left index finger. Her shoulders hunched, then slouched. "You can use these tactics, but they're a little rudimentary, so they'll primarily work with those who have low emotional intelligence."

I felt a sickening feeling in the pit of my stomach, a gnawing sensation eating through me. I was standing before I could think. "But Sir, it's ethically wrong to manipulate others in such a way." My voice didn't sound as monotone as usual, and I heard the desperation in what I was saying.

I took in a steadying breath to even out that quiver in my throat.

"Is it not also ethically wrong to deceive and kill others?" Dolos quipped. Her eyebrow quirked in question. "Both of which you have already done, Ma'at."

No, I thought. *I never laid a hand on Vasquez. And not once did I lie. Xenon did all that for me.* I didn't dare say this out loud.

A louder voice in my head thought *That's fine, if that's how you want to justify your innocence.*

"Sir," I acknowledged her again as I sat down.

I was, after all, an accomplice. Was I morally under the obligation to correct Xenon's deception and to stop the snapping of Vasquez's frail neck?

My lower lip began to taste coppery between my teeth. I sat back down.

Dolos walked herself forward slowly, hands behind her back. She was stocky, I could tell from the motion, unshakable in both body and mind. Stiff, stubborn. "You all would do well to remember that the conventional rules of morality do not apply to us," she articulated, calmly.

Her voice was like a sprouting tree, slow, steady, strong. "We do things for the greater good. The end result, creating the greatest good for the greatest number of people, *always* justifies the means."

Her sangria eyes met each of ours, slowly, deliberately. When she got to mine, she stopped for a little longer, lingering ever so slightly. "We don't have the luxury to think on morality." *You don't have the luxury to think on morality,* she meant.

We don't have the luxury to think on morality, the voice inside me agreed.

I swallowed and blinked before tilting my chin down and up in recognition once more. Her eyes moved on to Xenon beside me and I was left with a startling sensation of having just been a lectured child, scorned by a parent's disappointment, shame making the back of my neck hot.

My embarrassment prevented me from listening to the rest of the lecture that day.

I should have kept my trap shut.

Her hand was soft on my back, warm, guiding me to keep my spine erect as I lifted upward. It strained the rhomboid major muscles, but I think that was the point. I couldn't believe Diejiste lifted weights this heavy regularly... She could kick my ass if it came down to pure strength alone.

"Thank you."

Instead of smiling, like she usually did, she looked away. An angry pink that matched her short hair stained her cheeks. "I don't like that," she announced bluntly.

"Like what?" I thought aloud.

When she looked at me, her eyes didn't have any light in them. "You say thanks like you've never been given help and it breaks my heart." Her arched eyebrows twitched and her full lips were pulled down in a scowl.

The slow, uneasy creep of guilt weighed on my shoulders. I looked down at my toes. I *had* been given help. More than I ever would have thought.

So many people had helped mold me to the person I was. And I didn't like that person, not by a long shot. That person was weak and broken and still working through things, a mess that pretended to have their shit together. But I could *see* myself *becoming* someone worth liking. One day, I wouldn't go to bed hating myself.

I looked up to her. She was still mad, seeping anger out in waves. It wasn't an anger directed at me; I could tell. Besides, anger wasn't a primary emotion, as we learned. Anger stems from something else.

I released the weights. They clanged against the padded floor. "Wanna tell me why the way I say thank you irks you? Or am I going to get some practical experience today?" I inquired.

She fidgeted. Her cinnamon skin wrinkled around the neck when she forced her shoulder in. It was a topic she wasn't comfortable with.

"I didn't grow up with much back home. You say thank you the way I once did," Diejiste said, while she bent to lift her own bar. Her knees bent and she hoisted herself upward. She lifted three times and dropped it. "I don't like reminders of that time."

I didn't say thank you when she moved to place her hand on my back when I leaned over. The weights on the side clinked against the metal bar. I felt the strain throughout, from my back into my calves. Three lifts. One, two, three.

"Where is home?" I asked.

"Ziblah Airah."

That wasn't too awful far from where Xenon and I had carried out our last mission. As far as I was aware, there was extremely high-income inequality in that area. The top one percent garnered more than half of all the wealth in the region. The rest of the country seemed to live off of scraps.

I would be willing to bet what little wealth I had on the notion that Diejiste had not been part of that top one present. What had she looked like when she lived there? Was she covered in scrapes and bruises, skinny and gaunt like a palm? My eyes flicked to the jagged scar on her wrist.

Most of us here had one thing in common: Hunger. It wasn't plain to see to those who had never experienced it, but to those of us who had, it was obvious.

Hunger was evident in the little things: Eating when we weren't hungry because we still feared another meal wouldn't come. Rationing was more subtle, but unanimous. We rationed everything. How little of an antibiotic could we take for it to still be effective? How little covers could we use so that when the winter did come, we wouldn't be shivering and have to buy another? We rationed because it felt like a little control when we couldn't even control our own survival. I could easily determine the eight of us who suffered these ills.

I had seen Diejiste ration her bandages around her wrists when she set herself up for boxing, even though those could be reused and she didn't have to pay for them.

"I don't like reminders of home, either," I added, thinking back to my dream and how it left me without solace and without rest. So much so that a fifteen-year-old boy had to provide me with comfort.

She laughed. It was dry and brittle. Usually, Diejiste smelled like warm cloth, but that dry and brittle voice made me associate her smell with desert sand, a scorching dry that chaffed my skin and blinded me with mirages. It turned her smell to an insurmountable obstacle, rather than a comforting return.

"Shit upbringing?" she asked.

I shook my head. "No," I replied. "Great upbringing. Shit circumstances. You?"

She smiled spitefully; it didn't light her eyes. "Shit upbringing and circumstances."

I hummed.

I could imagine a little girl with a shock of pink hair and bright green eyes being happy before she understood she didn't have any reason to be. I watched as her cinnamon skin slowly got darker and darker with dirt because there was limited water and they had to use it to drink. I witnessed her cut off her hair so that she could dress as a little boy so that the old men who did terrible things to little girls would pass over her for a little while longer. I saw her grow up and decide she had enough of waiting for death to come for her and left in the dead of night to seek a better option.

Of course, I had no way to know if this was the life Diejiste had led. And in the end, it didn't really matter if it played out in real life like it did in my head. It wouldn't change the fact that we were all just a little messed up, a little flawed, a little rough around the edges.

"Yeah, anyway, just don't do it again," she mumbled, adjusting her shirt.

I smirked. "I won't."

This time, when she held her hand on my back, I didn't say thank you. Instead, I made a joke about how they could pay for a multitude of fake credentials, but not a sound absorbing mat for our weights.

I think we were both content with letting the conversation die out. Sometimes it was just easier to pretend the past didn't happen than to try to make peace with it before you're ready.

It was nice to know I wasn't the only one chasing whispers of regret.

March 24, 2728

Maile

I didn't do much more than lay in bed for two weeks, waiting until I felt like I did my first year on the road: Hungry. Then, I could push away all those thoughts about the little boy and focus on the pain of hunger.

Sancus would crack lame jokes at my back to try to pull me out of it. He would drag me to shower. And finally, when I had moped for two weeks, he yanked the covers off of me and said in a very stern voice, "Pull yourself together."

I turned over to watch Sancus leave the room in a very un-Sancus like fashion. I had never seen that look to him. That look wasn't often on him, the set of disappointment where his shoulders connected stiffly to his neck. His fists clenched and his arms rigid. It was the first time Sancus had ever truly been angry with me.

I pulled myself out of bed and tugged my overclothes on. My knees were wobbly; I dragged myself to the common area.

Sancus was alone, sketching in a notebook with unlined pages. This time, he was sketching Amaethon. In the sketch, she sat with her arms clasped in her lap, looking out the window. There were delicate sloping lines in her neck, leading gracefully to her pronounced clavicle. She appeared to be looking out at something that made her happy, by the indication of an upturned brow and amused quirk of her lips. On the paper, she wasn't in a wheelchair. She was just sitting, the same way she used to, with her ankles crossed.

"Hey," I tried. "I'm better now." I said it like those words actually would fix everything, like I'd stop fixating on the flash of red that tinted the air and made my vision run rancid.

Sancus looked up from his drawing and flipped the charcoal in circles around his fingers. The tips of his fingers were sabled from the drawing tool.

"I'm better now," I repeated, more confidently.

He didn't say anything.

"I have a request," I stated. My fingers tightened around empty space.

Sancus leaned to the side and placed his parchment and charcoal tools on the table. They didn't touch, or the dark of the tool would've bled onto his art. He set them down so delicately, like they were dried flowers, ready to crumple at the slightest pinch. He looked up at me, waiting.

Some days, Sancus's silence would diffuse in the air around him like tea leaves cloud hot water. *What?* his silence asked.

"Can I ask for your help once more?" I asked, tightening my shoulders and my jaw. Atelephobia creept up on me again, taunting *You'll never be able to succeed alone,* in my ear.

Amusement crossed the planes of his face. "I already told you it was a team effort now," he said, like I had messed up a simple math problem.

My lower back loosened, tension easing away slowly. The air was dry; I closed my eyes. He did that so easily: kept his word.

"Her name is Maile," my voice hung flat in the empty room that should echo. "Maile Aguillard. She lives in Bosquet de l'Ouest."

Giving myself a name and a place was easy. I should've done that two weeks ago.

Really, I had no ties to that boy. The overwhelming melancholy had not been about him. It had been about Jace. I couldn't do much other than replay and replay the image of a burnt corpse, lighter in my arms that had been the day prior. I imagined that little boy's last thoughts were similar to my baby brother's. I could do nothing for Jace then and I could do nothing for that boy now.

I'd spent too much time being numb, wasting precious time trying that I could have channeled somewhere else. I didn't want to be numb any more.

"What do you know about her?" he asked me.

I shrugged, even though I knew a lot. I knew her favorite restaurants, her current permanent address, the way she took her coffee... But nothing of intelligence value.

As far as I knew, she grew up in a well-adjusted household and had clean psychology records. She kept no social data, not even an email, but regularly associated with multiple unrelated peer groups.

"Then, I guess we're going to Basquet de l'Ouest," he said, pushing himself to stand. He walked past me, into our empty room.

I heard him mumble, "I can't wait to try their specialty cheeses... I goddamn love cheeses."

I fought back a smile at the sound of words not meant for me.

For Sancus and I, our next goal was knowing what party Maile was showing up to and getting ourselves an invite to it.

I saw the owner of the house, a girl with dark skin and dyed blond hair. She wore a pressed sweater vest and a set of wide frame glasses. She was the preppy girl next door every person dreamed of having at least once.

I nudged Sancus with my elbow. "Yeah, yeah, I'm on duty, right?"

I nodded. I had had my fill of flirting to last a lifetime. I think the fact that I had just gotten dumped made him willing to pick up the slack for me. *Thanks, Xenon.*

I watched Sancus walk backward toward the girl and stick his hand in the air like he was waving goodbye to someone. I flicked my sunglasses down over my nose and watched from the corner of my eye as Sancus strategically tripped over the girl and knocked the binder out from its spot under her arm. He fell on his butt and looked up with feigned sheepishness.

He picked up the binder and handed it back to her. Her wine-colored lips quirked up in a smile when he rubbed the back of his neck nervously. They were talking, words I didn't hear, and when she laughed at something he said, she threw her head back and her cheeks stained with color.

They talked for a moment before the girl reached into her book bag and fished out a pen. Her fingers wrapped around Sancus's wrist and she pulled his arm out to write on it. When she was done, she slipped the pen back into her bag and waved with her fingers as she walked away. Sancus waved, too.

He made his way back over to me, the joyful scrunch of his nose not falling off his face. "Enjoy yourself?" I asked with a smirk.

His cheeks darkened.

"We got an invite!" he exclaimed in lieu of an answer, holding out his arm, with an address scrawled onto it.

"Good job."

"You're going to need some new clothes."

I tilted my head, looking down at myself. "What's wrong with my clothes?" I shifted my weight from my right foot to my left, seeing if the new position would reveal to me what he was seeing. Nothing, just the plain black underclothes and my loose-fitting shorts and shirt.

Sancus put his index finger in the center of my clavicle and flicked up, hitting the tip of my nose. I rubbed the itching skin the flick left behind with the pads of my fingers. "What's wrong is that they're the same clothes you wore when you first came to Asgard," he explained. "These are rich university kids. You're not going to fit in."

I dropped the burner phone onto my thigh and shook my head in exasperation. "You're supposed to be my best friend. Why are you insulting me?"

"It's because I'm your best friend that I am insulting you."

"You ever been to a college party?" I asked, quickly switching subjects.

He shook his head. "No. You?"

"Nope," I grunted.

"This will be fun," he mumbled sarcastically.

Despite his reticence, I think Sancus fit right in with the crowd. He messed with all the students like he was one. I watched as he played beer pong with the other kids. His aim was excellent, so he and his partner rarely had to drink before the round was over.

I surveyed the room from my perch on the arm of the sofa once more. They were about 150 people at the house. Most here had forgotten their outer layers in the effort of showing off their assets. If Maile was still young enough to get an invite here, she couldn't have been much older than me when she was first introduced via proxy to me.

I sat close enough to a group to pretend I cared about what they said. Really, my focus was on the front door and the sliding glass back door, both of which I could view from my location.

I had tied my overshirt around my waist, to obscure the knife I had strapped to my inner thigh. It left my arms exposed, my gloves only covering the skin up to my wrists. My shoulders felt vulnerable without the heat of a fight on them.

I took a drink of the denarius beer. It tasted like piss. I finished the cup.

The guy next to me let out a slight guffaw. "Want some more?"

I smirked and responded, "Not a chance. You've got shit beer."

He was wearing only his over shirt, contrary to the rest of the flock in here. His teeth were pearly white, but left incisor overlapped its neighbor slightly. He was quite plain and gave me the distinct impression of spring humidity. There was something charming about his slightly too big ears and his dopey smile.

"I'm Ben," he informed me.

"Ma'at."

"What do you study?"

"Does it matter?"

The front door opened and Maile stepped in. She had the same look as her passport photo, a mixture of caramel and obsidian, with lips that looked like she was keeping a secret. She looked happy.

Imaginary ice marched a calculated warpath across my skin.

"I need friends, so, yeah, it matters," Ben said, but I was no longer paying him any mind.

"Literature," I responded resolutely. My eyes followed Maile's form as it gracefully floated across the room, socializing with groups along the way for no more than five minutes. She grabbed a cup and poured herself a glass from the keg.

I had already chosen my weapon. I tasted it remnants in my mouth now. Peanuts. Maile was severely allergic. Anaphylaxis was a powerful ally, and more importantly, a clean one.

I had never seen myself as one to use poison. To me, it seemed underhanded. I wanted to feel the full weight of killing someone, instead of letting a chemical compound do the work for me. I was able to use this poison because it married the cleanliness of poison with the ability to tell Maile it was me who had done this to her.

"Woah," I pretended to be amazed. "Who is she?"

Ben's eyes trailed to where mine stayed, fixed on a girl who looked just a little too old to still be a student.

I looked her up and down. Late twenties. Definitely too old to be here.

"Maile?" he asked. "Girl with a scar on her elbow?"

I nodded.

"Dude, give up now. She only dates guys with biceps bigger than her head," he announced. Then, quieter, he mumbled, "I know."

I clapped a hand on his shoulder and rose a suggestive eyebrow at him. "Good thing I'm not looking for a date."

Ben's face contorted confusion, then he smiled like he was a part of a secret joke. "She likes music," he advised slyly.

"Thanks, man," I said, pushing myself off the couch.

As I walked towards the kitchen, Sancus and I locked eyes. His eyes darted down to my hand. *Stand by,* I signed at him. He went back to his game, an amor tight hunch heavy on his shoulders.

"Excuse me," I said as I approached her. Maile's dark eyes found my own curiously. "You're Biacaran, right?" I asked, in a tongue I hadn't used since my father passed.

Her lips spread to a slow smile. "I am," she responded in the same tongue. "I so rarely meet a fellow countryman so far from home."

I smiled at her, all fake, all nausea inducing.

"Me either. I'm Ma'at," I told her.

"Maile." I already knew that.

"Do you like music, Maile?" I asked, already knowing how she would answer. The puzzle pieces were clicking into place, one after the next, slowly creating a picture.

"I love it. I go to concerts all the time."

I ran through the mental database. Her credit and purchases. I remembered seeing a purchase for two concerts by the same band. "Do you listen to Night Drives?" I asked. "They're newer."

"They're my favorite band!"

"Have you seen them live?" I asked.

"Yes. They're amazing."

I thought so the only song I could remember by them. "Did they play *Forever* when you saw them?"

A smug expression crossed her face and she held up her hand in a peace sign. "They played that song at both concerts I went to."

"So tight!" I exclaimed.

"You're fun," she said. "Let me know if you ever want to go to a concert together."

"You're fun, too," I articulated, carefully trailing my words. Then, calculated, I continued, "Let me know if you ever wanna date."

I closed my hand over my mouth and forced my face to heat up. Blushing was a lot easier when it was intentional. "Oh, my gosh," I mumbled through my fingers. "I've been drinking." I had been, two cups of the grossest beer I'd ever had.

She blinked and threw her head back. Her long hair fell like silk over her shoulders. Her voice sounded like grating sheet metal when she laughed.

I looked at her body. Skinny, too skinny. No muscle definition. Did I have the wrong person? Has she retired?

I assuaged my intrusive thoughts with the notion that if it resulted in a fight, I wouldn't need help. Her proximity indicated that she didn't have any sneaking suspicion that may lead to a fight, but it would be naïve of me to believe that this assassin was without any tricks up her sleeve.

"It's a little loud here; do you want to go somewhere quieter?"

She gasped and pushed up my chest playfully. "My, my, are you flirting with me?"

I raised one eyebrow up and gave her my best crooked smirk. "Depends... Is it working?"

She studied me then, with pursed lips and an expectant hand on her hip. After six seconds, she pressed her front against mine and her hands found my shoulder and neck. "Follow me," her breath whispered across my skin.

I was covered in thick slime, dirty where her skin touched my own. My saliva soured on my tongue. When her fingers laced through mine, my skin felt like it would melt from the bone. I wanted to pull away and smash the clear bottle on the table across the apex of her skull. Instead, I forced myself to squeeze her hand and follow her to the stairs.

Again, Sancus and I met eyes. *Marked door,* I signed. His chin shifted a little, a barely there movement to acknowledge. He saw. I quickly signed the number ten to give him a time reference.

I followed her up the carpeted stairs. My hand reached to the underside of my shirt pulling the charcoal nub I had hid in between my belt and my skin; charcoal because it was easier to remove than marker.

Maile rapped her fingers on a closed door and leaned her head to the crack. She deemed it empty, and turned the gold painted knob.

The room was plain — full of shades of white and black. Everything had a place, from the meticulously placed pillows, to the carefully stacked textbooks.

Maile let go of my hand and her fingers danced up my shoulders into the back of my neck again. My skin crawled. She gave me the same sensations Belig had. Only, this time, I didn't feel like a cheater.

"This is a one-time thing," she whispered, her lips barely brushing against my own. "Don't fall in love with me."

Vomit threatened to burst out of me. I swallowed it down.

I lifted my hand to her cheek and ran my thumb across her lower lip, red and puffy.

"I don't intend to," I articulated. There's no way I could love someone who had hurt my family. What I felt for her was a waterfall of disgust and anger. It crashed over me, becoming shards that pierced my bone and left me bloody and sore in a way no one could see.

"Don't fall in love with me," I said back.

A pain shot through my lungs when I said that, stealing air from me. Change *love* to *forget*, and that was what I had last said to Xenon. Okay, so maybe I did feel a little like a cheater.

I closed the distance between us and kissed her. I pulled her body closer to my own and she gasped. I took that opportunity to shove my tongue in her mouth. She sucked on it, unaware of the substance on it, buried beneath the tangy taste of liquor.

I wanted to vomit. The taste of her, the smell, the feeling... all of it was disgusting. How could I do these things with someone I hated? My skin *crawled*.

Maile had severe allergies. It wasn't exact science, but I could expect a reaction about twenty minutes. Twenty minutes is all I had to endure.

Twenty minutes as I pushed her back onto the bed and leaned over her. Twenty minutes as I told her, "Let's go slowly." Twenty minutes as I felt her body against my own, eating away at me more and more every second.

It was the easy way, that was what I told myself when I planned this. Now, in the middle of it, I knew I had made a mistake, but I was already in too deep to back out.

Welcome relief came over me when she pushed me away and commanded, "Stop."

I pulled back and wiped my mouth on the back of my wrist. "What's wrong?" I asked, fighting to keep the relief off my face. Whether it was relief it worked or relief I no longer had to touch her, I couldn't be certain. Maybe it was relief that the symptom of breathlessness meant I had gotten the right person.

"I can't feel my tongue," she advised.

"What?" I asked.

"Have you eaten peanuts?" she slurred, looking frantically around the room. There was no EpiPen here that could save her.

Instead of answering her question, I pulled her to a sitting position and checked her face. Flush skin. She was panting hard. Too hard for it to just be from our earlier actions.

"I was," I admitted dully, examining her with the clinical gaze of a medic. "You're allergic; I wanted to make it look like an accident."

"What?" she gasped. Recognition crossed her face. Then, her pretty, arched brows contorted in anger.

Her hand smacked my own away and she pulled up her fist. She forced her arm forward to punch my face, but she was too exerted to land the hit. I caught her fist in my hand and squeeze tightly. Sweat made the skin damp.

I leaned in close to her. "June first, Twenty-seven-twenty-three. Does that day mean anything to you?"

Her eyes widened. "You are," she wheezed, unable to finish her sentence. Her skin was beginning to have a sickly pallor. "Not one of them." *Why do you care?* Was left unasked.

Her statement was the only confirmation of identity that I needed. I reached my right index finger to my eye and brushed it across the surface of my cornea. The contact I had placed there pulled away from the surface readily.

I hoped she felt fear when she saw my eye. I hoped she grew cold when I leaned into her ear. I hoped she wished she had never taken my baby brother from me when she heard my indifferent voice whisper, "I am."

I watched her skin turn blue and her eyes roll back in her skull as her wind pipe closed up. *Three more,* I thought as I watched.

It only takes five minutes to be brain dead after lack of oxygen. Five minutes and I would only have three more.

I sat on the floor and pulled my knees up to my chest, waiting for those five minutes to be over so I could set to work on her hands and head. I watched the top the clock tick steadily.

My eyes traced down the shape of Maile's limp body, twitching every so often as the last of her neurons fired. The music from downstairs pounded tonelessly against the walls, sometimes syncing with a twitch.

After the second minute, the twitching stopped. The body turned a sickly color.

I couldn't look at her for the last few minutes. I stared at the space between my knees, counting down, looking at all the little microfibers in the carpet. I was certain that the smell of day-old flesh was my imagination.

I shut my eyes.

One, two, three, four, five, six, seven, eight, nine, ten, eleven, twelve. One, two, three, four, five, six, seven, eight, nine, ten, eleven, twenty-four....

After enough time had passed that I was certain she was dead, I pushed myself up and walked over to the bed. I felt bad for the kid who lived here. Not only would the room be a crime scene for a period of time, but that fluffy looking comforter would be ruined, if they ever got it back from evidence.

I pulled the knife from my inner thigh, where it had been concealed, not hidden, by the shirt tied around my hips. She should've felt it when her knee was pressing between my legs.

This time, the blade was not serrated. It was harder to slice through the bone under her flesh when I reached her wrist.

I pulled her shirt up over the top of her head. Her head lowered to the side and the tongue lolled out. I wrapped the maroon article around her right wrist, skin peeled to the bone. My hands wrapped around either side of her wrist. *Crack,* sounded in the air when I forced my thumbs up and together. The sound of bone snapping was muffled by the shirt. I unwrapped the shirt and continue to slice of the skin. Give away from the forearm more easily.

When I moved to the other hand, I snapped the bone first, separating forearm from the metacarpals. I was thrown back to the younger years, with Yonten. He had yelled at me for breaking this part of a man's hand. I was grateful he could not see me now, as I sliced over and over, through still warm skin.

The neck took the longest, but Sancus was watching for me. I had signed the number ten. He was probably on the stairs, monitoring the entry of people upstairs. I did it practically, methodically, with the ease and someone who done it before.

I wiped the bloody knife on my black undershirt when I was done. It slipped easily into my holster again.

I moved to the door and place my knuckles against it tap, tap, tap, tap, tunk, tap, tap, tunk, tap, tap, I lightly drilled into the wooden door. *Safe?*

A moment of silence, before the white frame sounded back at me tunk, tap, tunk, tunk, tap, tap, tap, tap. *Yes.*

I pushed open the door. My eyes met Sancus's own. His brows were knit with concern. He looked over my shoulder and his body tensed.

I think, when he had seen me dismantle Abran, he thought the man deserved it. To Sancus, Maile was just a PhD student. He hadn't seen what she had done and he didn't correlate the violence with her hands.

He looked away.

"Where have we been?" he asked. Our cover story.

I shrugged. "They never care. No one ever asks if you don't come back with an injury."

He swallowed and turned. Revulsion has a way of showing itself and it was never more obvious than it was in the atypical distance Sancus stood from me. I saw it in the tension along his spine and throughout his broad shoulders. I saw it in the way he held himself as we faked smiles and left the house.

"I checked crime statistics in the area and most is petty theft. It'd be wise for us to avoid this town for a few years. Wait until the hype has died down," I angled our conversation, looking at the dark tarmac ground.

Sancus scoffed.

"What's so funny?" I asked him in response, searching his face for any indicator.

Sancus shook his right hand at me, brushing it off. "Nothing, just a phrase that was common in my village. Being wise is for people who started believing that logic was more valuable than happiness."

"Is it?"

"I still don't know."

I looked down at the beds of my fingernails, dark with the sticky scarlet I hadn't been able to completely wipe off on my clothes. When had I gotten so good at ignoring the slick on my skin? The smell of tawny copper in my nose?

I couldn't seem to remember.

The common room was quiet when we returned. There were only three people absent. Xbalanque, Hunaphu, and Xenon. That was to be expected. Xenon made himself scarce and Xbalanque and Hunaphu were a matched set; if one was missing, so was the other.

Kali stood up and walked over to us first. "Sancus, you're needed in medical," she advised. "Something about a chemical test for that case we worked a few weeks ago."

Sancus dropped his bag and spluttered. "For fucks sake, why?"

Kali shrugged and raked her fingers through her dark hair. "I don't know. My blood came back clean, so it's probably nothing to worry about."

I bent over and picked up the straps of Sancus's bag. When I moved to stand, an exhale of air left me. It was so heavy it strained my lower back. We were only gone for two days—how much did he pack?

I shrugged and lifted the bag to my shoulder. "I'll put it away for you," I informed him.

He nodded and left the room.

Kali turned to me and placed a hand on her hip. "And you're needed in the weight room."

I stared at her blankly.

She rolled her eyes, their heavy coating of mascara weighing her lashes down. "Xbalanque came looking for you an Sancus a while ago."

I nodded. "I'll go find him," I said.

I walked past her into our shared room with the eternally empty bed. I know what the rest of us were doing, but what missions did the highest rank get? How much harder could they be that he was never around.

Maybe he died, a voice in my head whispered. *He died knowing you didn't love him enough to leave with him.*

I threw one bag carelessly on my bed, and heaved the other up on the bed across from my own.

I needed a shower and I needed a sleep. A meal would be nice, too, my stomach informed me.

I forced my tired legs to move away from the quarters and down the beach-colored halls with dancing orange lights.

The weight room smelled a little too much like feet and sweat. The padded mats were always a little less than new, and the metal bars always echoed a little too loudly when dropped. That was why I found Xbalanque so easily, those loud echoes as he finished a set of weighted squats, his thighs shaking from exertion.

"Hey," I said to him, grabbing his attention. His shock blonde fluff of hair was plastered to his forehead with sweat, having lost any remnants of a cotton ball long before I had arrived.

"Sancus is at medical now. He can't be here yet," I advised.

Xbalanque didn't answer. His eyes barely grazed over me before he looked back ahead to the wall. His lips pressed in a line and his face was screwed up. It didn't look like his usual strained face. Something was wrong.

My gut burned. "Where's Hunaphu?" I asked, leaning up against the weight machine. I tucked my hands into the crooks of my arms.

Xbalanque finished one last squat and released the bar from his shoulders onto the stand. He crossed his arms atop the bar and rested his chin on his forearm. The sweat beaded on his brow. His breath came in puffs.

His face was blank as he looked at me. "No one told you, then. Good, I wanted you to hear from me." His voice was small, quiet, fragile.

My stomach seized in a noose of barbed wire. "Told me what?"

Xbalanque rubbed his face. The black gloves looked like shadows on him, blending without form. "She's dead."

It seemed like air could knock me over and rain could erode me away. It was as if a thousand little needles, made their homes within my organs, creating warmth in small rivers of crimson. It felt like it did when I thought about Jace.

"Who?" I asked. I would steal their breath from their lungs.

Xbalanque shook his head. His eyes were gazing though me at some far off being I couldn't see.

"Cancer."

I blinked, slowly. Suddenly, many things seem to add up. The throwing up in the bathroom, the sickly color of her skin, the days she was too tired to leave bed, the migraines, the shaky hand that clutched at my shirt two weeks ago.

Cancer.

"Cancer," I repeated, nodding like it made any semblance of sense to me, even though it didn't. My arms dropped limp at my sides and my eyes fell to the floor. Suddenly, the tiles and the mats that made up the training room were very interesting, the harsh lines giving me something to focus on.

I couldn't say anything else.

There's a feeling of emptiness you get when someone you care for dies. An emptiness like hunger, only nauseating your mind as well as your body. All you can think is *She was only sixteen* and *I wish it were me* and *Why?* Nothing dulls that sensation. It stays with you.

Some days are better than others, I've found. Some days I barely felt empty at all; I was distracted by my new family and by the task at hand. Some days are worse than others. Some days, old memories danced in danced to the song of despondency that washed over me in waves, one after the next.

I had already been through those feelings once. I was still going through it.

The wrappings felt heavy on my left arm, hiding a litany of pink lines. I'd add another mark to it soon. One for Hunaphu.

"I stole so many pills for her from the medbay and she got treated and she was getting fed and she was in the best physical condition. So why didn't she get *better*?"

Xbalanque was so 'accident prone' to steal painkillers. Hunaphu couldn't tell people she had cancer because they would have turned her away from the program for being unfit. She would have had to wait to be a full member to go through chemotherapy; they wouldn't be able to kick her out, then.

Turned out, Xbalanque was a great liar when it came to protecting someone else.

My jaw clenched. She may have survived if she had started treatments a year ago. If not survived, maybe she would have had a little bit more time.

I pressed the palm of my hand gently into Xbalanque's shoulder and tugged him into my arms, feeling his weight sag against me.

"It's not fair," he mumbled, voice muted against the cloth of my clothes. Xbalanque's hands were shaking as they bunched my shirt into tight fists. My arms rose of my own accord, one to fall in his mop of hair and the other to pull him closer by the shoulders.

I wanted to force back everything he must be feeling in that moment, the incredible grief and loss he must have. I could do nothing.

I held him tighter, feeling his warmth seeping into me and a moist patch form on my left shoulder where his face was pressed. I blinked back blurriness clouding my vision. One of us had to be all right.

Xbalanque sucked in a quiet gasp. "She didn't want me to say anything and I didn't and now she's gone." His words were frail. "If I had said something, if I had told someone, she may have gotten help." The sentiment *she may not be dead* hung heavy in the air between us.

He felt guilty because he thought he could do something and didn't. It was how I felt when I thought back to the day when I hid like a coward behind that barrel, a barrel that should have hidden my brother instead of me. It didn't matter if he couldn't do anything to stop cancer, it didn't matter if I would have died with everyone else that day. That feeling eats away what makes you human.

Though I had no right to say anything, I felt compelled to tell him, "Nothing would be different if you had."

He froze, before his hands clenched tighter. "But maybe," his voice broke half way through the last word.

"No," I cut him off. "You did everything you could for her."

I had no idea of her motives, but if I were Hunaphu, I wouldn't have come here for treatment. I would have come here so that when I died, Xbalanque wouldn't be alone.

Silent sobs wracked Xbalanque's body.

They may not have been blood, but blood means little in this world. They were more than blood.

I dropped my head into his neck, hoping to share his grief, take some of it onto myself.

He shook, all over. A full body shaking that felt too chaotic in the too empty training room. "It's not fair," he mouthed against me. I don't think I heard it, not really, but I knew that was what he said because I was thinking the same thing; I had thought that same thing, no matter how much time passed.

"She was just a kid," he said, his voice cracking, despite the whisper. "We're kids."

He was right. They were just children, barely pushing sixteen, cast into a world of disorder and violence. Life hadn't been kind to them.

I moved my hand in a circular motion on his back, trying to smooth the wrinkles on his shirt and the wrinkles on his heart.

We all have scars. Right now, Xbalanque was bleeding. His wound would become a scar. He just needed to pierce his skin with a thin needle and pull a black thread tight enough to stop the bleeding.

"You're right," I said instead of everything else that I wanted to say, instead of letting the chaotic thoughts of my own grief run ramped. "Sometimes I forget you're a kid."

The wave of pain washed over me. My throat swelled, my vision blurred, and my lip quivered. I felt the overwhelming urge to scream, to push over the weights stand, to punch the wall until the scars on my knuckles split open again. Hunaphu losing her life was unfair, but Xbalanque being left behind was *worse* because he had to deal with everything that came after. It was *always* worse for those who remain.

He was just a kid.

I heard a sniffle in my ear; it brought me back. I took a shaky breath in and tried my hardest to keep my breath in a steady tempo. I let the face I wore slip. My eyebrows knit together and my mouth screwed up and my eyes clenched shut tight. It was the most expression I had shown in a long time. My voice still wavered when I whispered, "You meant so much to Hunaphu, Xbalanque. You were her family."

"You—" He shook. "You were, too. You were, too."

I felt the water leak out of the side of my eyes. *Just this once,* I thought. *I need to mourn her.*

I wish I could do something, to mend the cracks in us that were about to implode. Instead, all I could do was rub circles in Xbalanque's back and let his tears wet my shirt and mine wet his.

"She was better than us," I mumbled; I mumbled this not to provide comfort, but because it was true. She was better than us because she always found the bright side of things. She was better than us because she made the room seem a little homier. Hunaphu was better than us because even after she knew she was dying, her first thought was to find a home for Xbalanque.

He was like me. He was calculating and dark and a husk of a person. I wanted better for him than I had become, but I couldn't help but think Hunaphu was his Jace. All I could do was be a useless shoulder for him.

"Gautami," Xbalanque whined, letting out another rush of tears when he rubbed his head against my shoulder. "Her real name was Gautami."

I let out a puff of air, the closest thing I could get to a laugh. My rubbing turned into a pat briefly, before returning to its original action.

"It suits her," I stated.

I pictured her in my head, with the name Gautami instead of Hunaphu. It seemed more natural. He nodded into my shoulder, agreeing with me.

"Did Gautami want the best for you?" I asked after a moment.

There was a pause for a moment, Xbalanque working through the question in his head. "Of course." His hand splayed out on my back, flat instead of in a tight ball.

I hummed. "Will you give her the best, then?"

This time, there was no hesitation. "Of course."

"Good."

It would be hard to move on. There was a Gautami sized hole in our lives, one that was ominously empty and bare.

Loving someone who is sick is a little bit like drowning. You struggle against the water, clawing upward desperately toward the light, but you keep sinking further and further away. You keep trying, even as cold fire scorches your lungs, fighting to reach the surface. The sick twist is that there is no surface to reach. Admitting that is making the decision to inhale the water, to let that icy water burn your lungs.

As my fingers clutched at the raised outline of the sun on his left shoulder, I knew Xbalanque was making the conscious decision to inhale.

September 18, 2726

Aruna

Humans were so incredibly resilient. Our bodies would mend broken bones, give us superhuman strength, and allow us to create previously unimagined things. Yet, add a small amount of cyanide and we were vulnerable as a bee in rain. Thus, was the duality of man.

$C_{21}H_{22}N_2O_2$—Strychnine. A poison derived from seeds. The seeds that produce the compound aren't typically strong enough to kill alone. The shell is too hard to relinquish the toxins within the digestive process. Once crushed, however, an adult can be killed with as few as thirty milligrams, pure.

I was making that lethal, crystalline powder now.

They gave us wooden bowls, with a wooden crusher that was flat on the end. Grind it up as finely as possible, we were instructed. We needed to know how to crush it because it was dangerous to keep pre-ground strychnine with us. We could too easily ingest it, as a colorless, odorless compound.

This substance, I thought, would make a great tool, but it was a coward's tool, one that meant you wouldn't feel the full burden of a kill. I hoped I would never have to use it.

"I feel like a chef," Hunaphu remarked. "I actually really loved to bake." Loved. Past-tense. She looked a little pale. Flourescent lighting was not a good look on her.

"Well, it's not food, so be careful… I guess you already know that," I teased. She nodded anyway, like she was taking the advice to heart, and adjusted the safety goggles on her face. The strap was too big for her and the heavy equipment threatened to slip down her convex nose.

I understood why we needed goggles, but they were a handicap that obscured my vision and gave me blind spots. They turned my perception to a hazy fog and left me anxious.

"My dad and I used to bake all kinds of pastries. He was a

professional," she noted with a ditsy voice. I watched her carefully press the seeds, as to not let any of the contents jerk upward. She pulled up the blue surgical mask to make sure it was secure.

"I'm sure he didn't mind," I thought aloud. "I certainly don't mind when you 'help' with the cleaning." I made air quotes with my fingers when I said the word help.

Hunaphu put the crushing tool down on the counter and looked at me with straight brows and pressed lips. "Hah, hah," she deadpanned.

She picked up the handle and began pressing on the seeds again. They were slowly becoming more and more fine. I turned to work on my own.

They crackled when they were forced between the two wooden objects. The sound drove a shiver across my spine.

That was the sound of mortality. I should get used to hearing it.

"I think about poisons a lot," Aruna said from beside me. Her brown bangs were too short to tie back with a band and too long to stay out of her face. "Definitely not the same as baking," she added bitterly.

Hunaphu looked at Aruna, flabbergasted that she would have anything to say about it. "They're absolutely the same thing! You put things in a bowl and mix."

Aruna's mouth scrunched up in a scowl. Displeasure was apparent in her demeanor and she radiated the silent intent to argue in every harsh grind of her hand. It was clear she disagreed strongly.

"Hunaphu, let's leave it," I whispered. She grumbled at me, but didn't say anything more.

I looked at Aruna's back, turned to us and rigid. I wouldn't compare Aruna in that instant to a wall, but rather a statue. She gave off the impression of unrelenting stone, an unbreakable expression carved into her face and into her posture.

I sped my pace to match Aruna's. I ground and sifted like her, testing my poison on the rats in time with her. I watched them lowly falter and stop moving silently, next to her.

Then I left with her.

I held my notes in my hand, skimming them without really reading or retaining any of the information. The paper irritated my too dry hands.

As I flipped another page, I asked, "Want to explain why you went off on Hunaphu, or do you want me to keep thinking you're an asshole who is mean to little girls for no reason?"

She humphed, turning around to squint at me. She seemed irritated to have to acknowledge my presence at all. Her light hazel eyes were dark with anger. "Respectfully, it's none of your business; I don't have to tell you shit."

I shrugged at her. "You don't," I acknowledged. *But I'll hold a grudge against you for a long time.* I was really good at holding those. I didn't share that last tid-bit of information because it didn't need to be said.

She sighed. Her shoulders slumped and she turned to lean up against the uneven, sandy colored bricks that made up the walls.

She ran a hand across her face. Her fingers were slightly crooked and her nails were no longer than the tips of her fingers. Her hand dropped limply to her side.

"My son died from poison," she admitted. Her eyes looked glassy. Her honey voice didn't break, but it was scratchy and weak, in the way only a grieving mother's could be.

Aruna was young. Not a single wrinkle had yet graced her cinnamon face. Not a single strand of gray burst through her chocolate hair. To know someone a year my senior had been a parent sent chills down my spine. It must have been hard to lose a child when you, yourself, were still one.

And by all the stars in the sky, she still was just a kid, carrying the weight of a dead child in her arms every day.

"How old was he?" I asked. I couldn't bring myself to say sorry, because I wasn't, really. And neither pity, nor apologies would bring the kid back. Just like pity and apologies couldn't bring Jace back.

"Not even three."

Aruna was twenty. She came here a year ago. At the latest, she had given birth when she was seventeen.

"I tried my best to raise him well," she said. "Dropped out of school, got a job as a tailor, moved us to a town where I could lie about my age and call myself a widow so he wouldn't be branded a bastard."

I hated this part. Hearing all the tragic things that humanized everyone. It made them people in my mind, instead of just figures. I wanted so desperately to keep them as simple figures, people I could throw away.

"A fucking corporation, with enough lawyers and money to make the problem disappear," she fumed quietly, despondently, bitingly. "They poured their chemicals into the water and he wasn't big enough to push them out of his body. Pele was too little."

She looked down at her hands. They were clasped, squeezing an imaginary infant's hand. Her eyes shut, wanting to block out the light and the memory.

"North Winds took out the execs," she said. "I owe them my life for getting my baby justice. It was my duty to come here."

"Must have been hard," I commented. I felt like slamming my head into a wall, screaming at the top of my lungs, killing every last bastard who had anything to do with the death of my brother.

I couldn't even imagine the feelings she had had for her little boy. Did they resolve with the deaths of those executives? If they did resolve, Aruna was more mature than I. I was certain I would still feel that frigid hatred long after my mission was complete.

"So, you were mad because the poison reminded you of Pele?" I asked.

She nodded, her bow lips stretched tight. "I'll never use poison to kill, not when I don't know where it will end up."

I let out a deep breath, my heart sagging. I closed my eyes now, too. *Duty,* she had said. We were bound by the same thing, albeit for different reasons and with different outcomes.

Just when I found a way to demonize her for being snippy, I find out there was some relatable reason for her actions. It sure takes effort to hate people.

I looked back down to the papers in my hands and flipped another page, turning my gaze toward it again.

"Hungry?" I asked, as if there was nothing wrong. "They finish baking fresh bread at four every day."

She opened her eyes and I saw a smirk on her face from the corner of my eye. "I could eat," she replied, as she pushed herself off of the wall.

I'd always admire that part of Aruna. The part that could feel intensely one moment and quell those feelings on command. It was more logical like that, with far less room for error.

Jace, I thought, *I can't be like her. I can't isolate and make myself logical.*

I clenched my fist as we walked toward the kitchen, hoping to steal some food before dinner.

The North Wind worked in the line of prevention, not punishment. The executives had been killed because they would have still threatened others by existing. The people who eradicated my tribe were still alive because they weren't likely to decimate another population.

Aruna had been fortunate to have justice served to her, handed to her by people who made it their business to right the wrongs of this world, playing judge, jury, and executioner in the name of prosperity.

I didn't have that fortune. I had to take justice with my own hands, pry it from the world with all the strength I had because that was the only option. It was the only way I could give purpose and meaning to my survival.

I made a silent promise, not for the first time, not for the last. *Nothing will stop me from getting you justice.*

"I don't think that counts," Xbalanque mumbled, staring at his lap. His mouth was scrunched up and his eyebrows furrowed in confusion. He was perched on the right arm of the couch, birdlike and calm.

Sancus scoffed and threw up his hand with open fingers. He sat with his back against the other arm of the chair, his legs extended on the couch toward Xbalanque. His brow, too was furrowed, more from frustration than anything else. "I'm telling you, the library is cursed. I've seen way too many books mysteriously fall off of shelves." Sancus looked to me, desperately. "Tell him, Ma'at. You're always in there with me."

I shook my head. "I have to side with Xbalanque on this one, man. It doesn't mean there's a ghost just because weird things have happened," I explained with a shrug. "Sorry."

Sancus's shoulders fell and he slumped forward, his brows twitching up in disappointment. "Come on, man, back me up here."

"I'll back you up," Xenon commented. "I get the heebie-jeebies in there." Xenon was cross legged on the floor, leaning on the pillar of my chair.

Hunaphu shook her head. "Iktomi, the 'heebie-jeebies' are not a good enough reason to believe in a haunting or a curse."

Xenon just shrugged. "I trust my gut," he argued.

"Even though I don't think this place is haunted, I can't wait to get out again," I mentioned. The four of them turned their heads to me. Shadows from the fire skittered across their skin. "I'm getting a little bit of cabin fever in this glorified cave."

"We haven't really had time to get out," Sancus noted, crossing his arms. I noticed, with a tinge of jealousy, that his triceps had grown. "Between now being responsible for our own physical training and having to study all of the new material we're learning, it's not like we've had time to go out much. I can't remember the last time I went down to Aces."

The pub at the nearest town. We used to go there after training all the time when we were only doing physicals. Our bodies were too weak to keep practicing, so the only thing to do was try to fill the time. Aces became the place for that.

Xenon propped his elbow on the coffee table in front of him and leaned his head into his hand. "Well, after our next trial, I'm sure it will seem like we have all the time in the world."

Right. We were almost at the finish line.

It seemed like only a few weeks ago we had been arriving at Asgard. Without realizing it, my body had been acting in a fight or flight mode for almost a whole year.

Xbalanque's hands found a prop in front of him to lean on. I watched Hunaphu unconsciously mirror him as she mentioned, "I sure would like to visit a theme park when we finally get a break." His eyes darted up to the ceiling as if he was looking up at a roller coaster.

"That sounds fun," I responded, looking at Xbalanque and then Hunaphu, in turn. "I'll take you two, if you'd like, on me."

Xbalanque didn't smile much, but when he did, was a soft kind of luminance, like gentle beams of moonlight through the window.

I never took him to that theme park. We never got to eat cotton candy and ride roller coasters and play each other in game booths. I never earned that smile of gratitude.

Sancus spun so his feet were planted on the maroon rug that covered the wooden planks of the floor. "Does that offer apply to me?" he questioned, pointing a relaxed finger at his face.

I tossed the pillow behind my back at him. He caught it one handed and gave a crooked smirk as he set it behind his own back. "Not a chance. You still owe me for all the bar tabs."

"Is there no love among friends?"

"Not for a theme park."

He chuckled, deep and mellow. "That's fair," he acquiesced, throwing his hand up in the air flippantly.

After a beat of silence, the weight of the day hit me. I was no longer in the mood for small talk. "Well, I'm done for the night," I announced. "See you all in the morning."

"Dream of a world where you pamper me," Sancus chided.

"Yeah, yeah," I mumbled with a wave of my hand.

Hunaphu stood up, with me. "I'm calling it, too," she noted. "Goodnight." She walked away, waving a hand over her shoulder.

A chorus of "night" came from those who remained sitting.

"Yeah, see you guys tomorrow morning," Xbalanque added as he moved to exit as well.

Kali's soft snores echoed in our room when I reached it. I pulled my overshirt off and began to unlace my shoes before I realized that I left my notes in the common room. I rubbed a hand over my face before trudging back into the hallway to collect them.

I stopped behind the ledge when I heard Xenon speaking.

"I like it. It's new."

Sancus scoffed. It was the first time I had ever heard a sound like that come out of his mouth. He sounded aggressive and cold. For some reason, I thought that his typical amber scent would be different in that moment, cloying.

I pressed my body closer into the shadows made by the wall, hoping they'd envelop me a little more, hoping they would hide my voyeurism. My fingers tapped the broken watch face on my wrist, trying to ease the sensation of listening to words not meant for me. My father would have chastised me.

"I can tell by that scoff that you think I'm full of shit."

"I don't trust you," Sancus bit. "Not as far as I can throw you and I can't throw people very far."

I had never heard Sancus angry. He was always so well composed. My stomach twisted with the sensation of worry. *What did I miss?*

My fingers moved from the watch face to the broken necklace pendant. My mom would have known how to stop a fight before it even started, with her easy political charm.

"You're scared," Xenon observed after a while, his voice silver, even in its astonishment. "You're scared I'll hurt Ma'at."

"I know you, Iktomi," Sancus warned. "You're not a good guy. No matter how hard you pretend to be."

Xenon took in a deep breath and let out a controlled counter-claim: "I learned my lesson in hurting people." He sounded almost tired.

"What do you mean by that?"

"What do you want me to say?" Xenon finally snapped. I could imagine that cocky demeanor slipping from his face like spilled porridge. "Do you want me to say that my mom tried to forage me into the perfect weapon by any means necessary? That she tried to do the same to my father and that it broke him because he wasn't made of the same metal I was? Do you want me to say it made me a better man to have my father leave me with my abusive mother and that's why I'll make the perfect lover?"

I tasted blood.

I didn't know much about Xenon's past. I didn't like asking about his because I didn't want him to turn around and ask about mine. Still, I should have known about his parents by now.

"I want you to say you don't regret who you are now," Sancus's calm voice pierced through the heated hair, like an air conditioning vent kicking on in humidity. "Ma'at doesn't need any more baggage to carry."

Guilt settled in me.

"For the most part, I like who I am now," Xenon explained, voice less turbulent than it had been a moment prior. "And even if I didn't, I would never make that anyone's problem but my own."

I heard the couch fabric shift and watched as the dancing light and shadows scurried in new directions across the floor.

"Good," Sancus said. His footsteps fell on the floor three times. "I don't care how incredible you are, if that changes…" he trailed off.

My heart pulsed in my ears. "Ma'at is my — my family now," Sancus started again, trying to articulate his thoughts in his second language. I could tell he was mad because it was harder for me to speak the common tongue when I was mad. I backtracked and stuttered and rephrased, too.

He paused again and I heard him inhale sharply. "If your issues become Ma'at's issues, I will kill you myself."

My heartbeat thundered in my skull.

An unhappy chuckle came from Xenon. "I believe you."

July 12, 2728

Tatsu

Asgard was never quiet. Only, on the day of the trial, it was.

It left a gnawing sensation in me, that quiet I walked into. The air was dense, stagnant and stuffy in the same kind of hushed way a child with neglectful parents plays.

"What happened?" I asked Kali as I set my bag down on the floor near my bed. At first, I thought Gautami's death had finally hit her.

I saw Kali flinch from the corner of my eye, like she has been too absorbed in her own mind to notice I had come home. Her shoulders shrunk in and her neck lowered until her face was obscured behind a curtain of black. She didn't answer me, but I heard a small wheeze echo from the hollow of her throat, the kind that came when someone had forgotten to breathe.

I looked back to my bed. The sheets looked too firmly pressed. "You never stop talking," I stated, bluntly. "Why are you choosing now to be quiet?" I was sure I kept my voice even, despite the indignation festering below my collarbone.

I heard her bed creak as she moved. "Aruna is going to be killed," Kali rushed, like the words scorched her tongue.

It was my turn to flinch. Underneath the shock was the easing into heart-pulsing, stomach-clenching panic. The tightening of my muscles and the rushing blood in my ears served as physical reminders of my own situation.

Aruna would be killed because she had broken one of the rules. I had almost certainly broken more.

Imaginary walls began to enclose me.

My throat was dry and itchy when I swallowed. I couldn't do much but look at the cherry blanket and the cream sheets and choke out a stifled, "When?"

A sigh. I'd never perceived Kali to be frail. Weak, yes, but never frail.

The Kali that was carried on that sigh was a paper doll left out in the rain.

"There's a moratorium on jobs. Once everyone gets back, we'll be called to witness." *Witness,* like it was some sort of public event.

How long would that moratorium last? A day? A week? More? What was Aruna thinking now? Did she know they would kill her or was someone waiting by the entrance to take her into custody upon her return?

We, a voice reminded me. *Does she know that* we *will kill her?*

Where had she messed up to get caught? Would I fall for the same thing? I didn't have the luxury to lose my life. Not yet. Every stiff, leaded breath I took was another reminder I existed in enemy territory and that I had to be cautious if I intended to keep my promise to my family.

I placed my right toes on the back of my left sneaker and pulled my left knee up and out of the shoe. I did the same to the other side. I left my socks on this time as I laid down on top of my bed.

The air was cold. It felt right to subject myself to it.

"I see."

It was six days.

I didn't know there were so many people in the North Wind. Hundreds of us gathered in an amphitheater deep under the mountain, so deep that the air smelled more strongly of bones than it did rock.

Aruna's stocky form kneeled at the low center of the unit, her hands bound in cuffs before her, attached to a metal loop embedded in the ground. A thin layer of sweat and dirt muddied her skin in streaks and her chocolate waves were stringy and black with grease near the roots. She didn't look up, but if she did, I was certain her eyes would be bloodshot and puffy from exhaustion and dehydration.

"Aruna," the voice boomed in the cavern. It shook me to my bones, echoing in my hollows. *Aruna* could have easily been replaced with *Ma'at.*

"You stand accused of abandonment," the person continued. I couldn't see their face. It was hidden behind a white mask with no form, protruding from a cloud of white robes. "How do you plead?"

The air was curdled with anticipation. Beside me, Xenon grabbed my fist for comfort. I tugged my hand away. I didn't have to see him flinch to know he did, the metaphorical slap a painful reminder that we were strangers again.

Aruna looked up. Her eyes were, indeed, puffy and bloodshot, but the hazel colored iris appeared lucid. The purple discoloration and the awkward shape to her usually Greek nose made me want to wince. I bit down on the tip of my tongue to focus on that pain instead, tasting the raw skin and copper in my mouth.

She smiled, soft and tender, looking past us, at something far past the underground amphitheater. "Guilty; I forfeit the right to a trial."

There was a pause. Another of the twelve spoke in a hushed tone I could barely make out, "Are you certain?"

Aruna nodded slowly. Her, I could hear clearly, as if she were right next to my ear as she said, "No trial, but I'd like to say something before you take my life."

You idiot, my mind supplied, as if she could hear me, *you'll die. Ask for a trial; a trial gives you a chance, if only a slim one.*

"That is fine," another of the twelve said slowly.

Millions of thoughts slammed against the walls of my skull, but there were no words coherent enough to articulate.

Aruna had a warm voice. It sounded like a marshmallow whose tip had caught on fire, sugary and exciting, in a slow kind of way. Now when she spoke, it was raspy with dehydration, but I smelled a phantom a camp fire.

"I have come to think of this place as home. I am grateful to all of Asgard for that, at the least," she said. I was trapped, hanging onto every word that she projected.

"Homes can be lonely," she reflected. "She stopped my loneliness."

My heart skipped a beat. Aruna had deserted for a person? I had almost done that, not too long ago. As if to notify me he had had the same thought, Xenon grabbed my sleeve. This time, I didn't tug away.

"I don't want to live in a world where I can't slowly piece together the rest of who she is, and learn to love every portion of her," she explained.

I understood. Aruna had found a kid who reminded her enough of Pele that she could care for them. It was likely the North Wind killed that girl, same as they did to Yonten's daughter. Without a proper goodbye, this was a mother's last words to her child.

Did my mom say a silent, lonely goodbye like this when she passed? Did her voice sound as simultaneously warm and lonely as Aruna's did?

My chest collapsed in on itself. No one around me could see it collapsing. I didn't move an inch. All the same, debris flew about the cavity of my rib cage, and not even the effort of all of the ice I had could hold the pieces in place.

My throat was dry and swallowing was difficult. I knew loving people was a curse. It ruined Yonten, it ruined Aruna, and it would ruin me, too.

Not once, I noted, did Aruna meet my gaze. Not once did she meet anyone's. I wondered if she said the only goodbye she had to the air, hoping a whisper of it would be carried to the little girl she spoke of, wherever that little girl was.

One of the twelve placed a gentle hand on the back of her head, easing it down. She yielded without resistance, a sign of trust.

Look where misguided trust got her.

The axe was sharp as it was placed on her nape, hair parted to reveal a hunk of her tan skin. I thought I saw a bead of blood slip down the blade's edge, but it may have been my imagination.

"Aruna, you have turned your back on the North Wind and the penalty is death," a figure boomed. It was Charon. He brought the axe high and sliced down.

The thing about being a murderer is that you never miss a waiting target. I didn't look away, nor did I wince. No, I was too desensitized to the messy chopped meat of a human neck at this point. The cut wasn't gruesome as mine usually turned out.

Aruna's rolling head caused a few gasps. I couldn't tell if it was painless; her face wasn't visible from my vantage.

I debated, for a moment, if I should mark another notch on my arm or add another token around the chain on my neck for her. Then I remembered Aruna hated religion and 'baubles'. Perhaps not, then.

"A reminder," was all the fourth needed to say before everyone began to file out. A scapegoat to remind us all that the unit is stronger than the individual, that the North Wind is inescapable.

I wanted to protest that sentiment with the example of Yonten.

But I hadn't heard from Yonten in a while; no messages had been left at The Aces Pub for 'Bahadur' another pseudonym of mine. A piece of me thought that by saying Yonten was fine, I would soon learn he wasn't.

That was naïve of me. Things would happen regardless of what I would say.

That night, food remained uneaten, games unplayed, and thoughts unspoken. That night was quiet, but it was far from idyllic.

The bar was classy and old. It played blues music from a gramophone and the air was filled with the smoke of expensive cigars. I recognized the tune playing as "Juke."

I made a straight path through the dimly lit relic of the past to the corner seat at the bar, with a line of sight to the whole room open.

I wouldn't have been able to picture Tatsu in my mind, but she was distinctly recognizable in person for how plain she looked, despite the fiery hair that was very obviously dyed, as if she were trying to draw in attention. Strange, for an assassin. Perhaps her face, neither handsome nor hideous, left her wanting.

She hunched over one of the outer booths, playing cards with three other people. She had a glass of clear liquid I was certain wasn't water.

"What can I get you, sugar?" a syrupy voice asked me. My gaze trailed lazily over to the owner. She was a stout woman with broad shoulders and an even broader belly. She was classy through her many years, all dark eyes and big lips with high cheekbones and cascading curls.

I leaned forward in my barstool, balancing my weight on my toes. "It depends," I responded, "Do you only serve food and drink or do you sell whispers, too?"

A look of understanding crossed her face and she pulled the pen and paper she kept for orders from her stained, orange apron. The woman slid it across the counter to me. She wanted to know how much I was willing to pay, and what I was paying for.

I pulled a 100 denarii bill from my wallet and slid it between the folds of the pages before picking up the blue ink pen from the table and scribbling on the paper, More with each answer. Woman with red hair: What do you know?

I slid the pad of paper back to her and watched as her eyes raked back and forth across the page. She looked around the bar until she found who I was talking about.

She turned around and grabbed a pitcher of water and a glass. I watched as the water sloshed from one container to the other, then watched as some of the clear water slipped over the lip of the glass as it slid across the shined oak counter into my palm. I grabbed the glass with my left hand to keep my right open for sleight of hand.

The woman leaned close with a rag and wiped the counter free of the water that had spilled. She spoke in a hushed tone, "She comes in almost every week night. Gambling addiction is almost worse than her drinking habits."

It wasn't water I saw in Tatsu's short glass. Her addictions made her predictable. *Desire is weakness.*

I nodded as the bartender pulled the 100 denarii bill out and slid it into her pocket. She pushed the pad back to me.

"Is she local?" I asked as I slyly showed the woman another 100 denarii bill and tucked it between the folds. I didn't slide the pad back. Frequent movement would draw too much attention. We were far enough we couldn't be heard, but not far enough to avoid being seen.

The woman wiped at the now clean counter, more from nerves than necessity. "I think so, but she leaves on frequent business trips. When I try to ask what she does, her answers are… inconsistent." The phrase *answers are inconsistent* was indicative of someone who works in assassination and isn't smart enough to come up with a cover story.

This bartender was an amazing source.

I had one last question: "Do you know where she lives?"

The woman's brow drew tight in the way I associated with an ethical dilemma. Shadows kept across her face. Her eyes turned down to the pad.

I shot the bartender a crooked grin and shoved two 100 denarii bills this time. Older women liked that grin, I found, and extra cash never hurt anyone.

"Miss," I probed.

Her cheeks turned a darker shade of brown, I couldn't tell if it was from shame or attention, and she looked at the table.

She pushed down the flames of shame on her cheeks, then leaned forward. "Fairly certain that doll lives up in the complex on Fifteenth and Vine," she said.

I nodded and took a five-hundred-denarii piece from my wallet. "For your time," I stated. *For your silence,* I meant.

Her jaw clenched as she drew back the pad, now 800 denarii heavier. I saw the guilt in her eyes, but she seemed to value the money more than the information she had just sold.

A thousand candles were the source of light in her home, making the few shadows there flicker with opulence. Her hair seemed to whirl about with the flames, wrapping red tendrils around invisible floating rods.

It was mesmerizing in a way I couldn't explain. She wrapped me in her complicated warmth with every calloused finger tracing the page of her book and swaddled me in longing with every scratch on the side of her too elongated nose. Tatsu was a light and I was a moth drawn in.

I wasn't naive enough to believe good and bad weren't arbitrary terms, but I knew enough to state Tatsu would use that charisma to benefit herself at the expense of others. I'd be damned if I let her do that. Not again. Not to another family.

My hands wound tighter on the hilt of the staff. I inhaled deeply, brisk air that smelled like pressed corn filling my lungs. The tension pulled at my flesh in an all too familiar way.

This was familiar.

My eyes fell shut and my mind went blank. My anger grew hard like a stone in my core, spreading through my chest and my stomach and my arms and legs until it reached my phalanges. It creaked and groaned when I moved, but relented easily to my will.

My eyelids blinked open and I saw through the hazy white of my eyelashes that she hadn't moved.

I took a deep breath and let the tension push my shoulders up and then down. Then, I put my left hand on the smooth concrete and pulled my legs into a crouch. I'd have to crash through the window on a cold night like this, when the pipes were brittle from the weather.

I stood to full height, pressed back on my right leg and crossed my arms in front of my face. The mask should guard against glass, but it was better to be safe.

I pushed forward, and three steps later, I was flying through the air into the frail glass window, feet first, like a long jumper.

I managed to land upright.

I reached my right hand out and grabbed that fake red hair. It threaded around my gloves like rushing water. I yanked and pulled her over the back of the couch. She fell easily to the floor, looking stunned.

"Get up," I spat, taking out my rage on her because I couldn't take it out on anyone else.

She scrambled to her feet. "Get the hell out of my house," she whispered. "Or so help me, I will make your last moments a lesson in modern torture."

Maybe it was the fact that I was so close, yet so far from reaching my goals. Maybe it was because I was tired and a bit hungry. Whatever the reason, I was quick to backhand her across the face.

The strike rang in the air, a red mark of my knuckles and back of my hand printed across her skin.

There was a moment of silence before she screamed, guttural and discordant. I didn't like how it sounded. Her head snapped back toward me.

"You insect!" she shouted. Her eyes burst into flames and her hair rose up from her shoulders like snakes from a den. She grabbed my wrist but her hold was soft.

I understood why the instant scorching flames molded my pores together, causing my flesh to boil and graft in blinding, white agony. I had forgotten what my scream sounded like until it ripped through my throat.

My body reacted first, swinging the staff into her head and knocking her to the side. I heard a grunt and a thud as she fell to the ground.

She was one of the humans who could bend reality, like Siren. I understood her lack of fear in that moment. Because she controlled and summoned the flames at will, she thought herself untouchable. For the most part, she was right. I could not make contact with her skin, for my own would bubble and blacken. Tatsu's ability was dangerous.

I wasn't thinking about that. Another thought came upon me, crashing down with such force it sapped the air from my lungs.

"He was my—" My voice broke helplessly. My mind throbbed, pictures of a little boy with a little beauty mark on his palm flashing in front of me. "He was just a child."

My eyes darted down to the burn on my right wrist and back to Tatsu. I didn't see her lying on the ground, I saw six blackened lumps, vaguely shaped like humans. I saw my dad and I saw Jace.

She pushed herself from the ground, orange flames licking up the sides of her hands. She didn't seem to care I had said anything.

My chest collapsed in on itself, a metaphysical weight that was more painful than the burn she had just put on me. As I stared into her uncaring, flaming eyes, my throat grew sore in a new way. My hands shook. *She doesn't care.*

Ice may melt from heat, but my ice was permafrost.

I clenched my jaw together. I wrapped both hands around the staff and tightened my core. "They were kids," I repeated, my voice low and surprisingly even. Her eyebrows twitched in recognition; she heard me.

I ran forward. Her flames grew. No frontal assault would land. I pushed hard on my left foot, pushing myself into a rightward jump. My right foot collided with the beige wall. From my new height of two feet taller, I pushed down toward her. Tatsu's head barely turned by the time I tightened my biceps and swung at her head once more.

A guttural scream came from her mouth. The flames blinked out for a moment.

I hadn't hit hard enough. If I had snapped her neck, she wouldn't have screamed.

Three black husks were children, the ones that lay mottled and converted to coal. Tatsu killed my dad and my brother and four others and I would be a liar if I said that knowledge wasn't affecting me, running horrendous images through my head and sullying my work and my focus.

It wasn't just my tribe who I thought of. Now, I had lost another child. Hunaphu, Gautami. She, like Jace, was taken too young from me, before I could say goodbye.

I bit the inside of my cheek to hold the tears back.

I couldn't even say that was the end of my list of people I lost. I had said goodbye to Lee for a second time. Xenon called it quits. I had watched Aruna be beheaded. I hadn't heard from Yonten in months. People were leaving faster than they were coming and I could do nothing to stop it.

I knew it wasn't Tatsu's fault. I knew that she was only responsible for Milo and Jace. But I also knew I was really angry and really confused and really ready to hit someone.

I pushed myself backward, trying to create as much distance as I could. I wouldn't let someone like this, a person who can kill children without remorse, burn me.

My blood curdled at the thought Tatsu would suffer the world her existence when Jace and Gautami never even got the chance to live.

Tatsu let out a laugh, it started slow and quiet, jiggling her shoulders up and down, and rose to loud and cackling as she threw her head back. The flames burst from her skin more intensely now. She looked like a mad woman possessed. She was the devil.

I never saw the flames reach beyond the scope of her body. I did not believe she was able to extend them beyond a certain distance, which would explain why she leveled no attacks until she had made contact with my right wrist.

My right wrist throbbed in protest. I thrummed my fingers against the warm metal of the staff. The mark was only skin deep. No lasting nerve damage had yet occurred.

She didn't seem to have much tactical experience, I presumed, since she began a run straight toward me, both arms outstretched. She would go for my throat.

There were a number of ways for me to proceed. I could go for an attack from the side again, meeting her from a higher vantage. I could dodge to the left, because she favored her right, and attack the spine.

I didn't do either of those.

"You took my baby brother from me!" I screamed.

My legs dropped from beneath me when she was close enough and I pushed my right leg out and pulled it back in a sweeping motion. Tatsu met the ground with a thud and a dramatic convulsion of her body. I used the centripetal force of my sweep to pull my body up to full height. I shuffled that same foot forward and brought my left up, only to slam it down right onto Tatsu's chest, just right of center.

I felt a cracking beneath my weight. Good. Even if I didn't kill her, she would die from the ribs puncturing her lungs.

She wheezed. I watched her face contort in pain as the flames vanished. She tried to summon them to my foot. It scorched my ankle, the pain momentarily stealing my vision, but I pressed down on her chest harder.

More cracking. She let the fire go and focused on her breathing, gasping in and out from thin, chapped lips.

"You—" she wheezed. She was pathetic like this. Tatsu had thought herself invincible because of her ability, but I was more than happy to teach her people can't win wars with a single battalion.

"Who are — are you?"

Right, she couldn't see my face.

I pulled the ski mask over the top of my head. The air felt cooler entering my lungs without it. My hair flopped into my eyes slightly, but mostly held in place with the moisture of my sweat. I didn't think she would recognize me, not with the contacts and the dyes, but everyone deserves to know the face of their executioner.

I tightened my ten fingers about the staff, feeling the rub of metal on the skin. "I'll make it quick," I informed her.

As I raised the staff above my head, ready to force the end into her eye socket, I had to ask myself why I paid her mercy instead of letting her slowly choke on her own blood, instead of peeling the skin from her muscle like Abran had done to that little boy. My hands were still shaking with rage and I wanted nothing more than to give her tenfold what pain she had imparted on Jace.

I took in a deep breath, my shoulders rising and falling, before I pushed the pole down hard through her dark brown eye. It squelched and resisted slightly. Her body stopped shaking beneath my foot. I stepped off her.

I took inventory of my injuries. A busted lip, though I wasn't sure how it got there, still bleeding when I touched my middle finger to it. My ankle, first degree burn. My wrist, second degree burn. I sighed; what a hassle.

I collapsed the staff before putting it back on my utility belt, in the little clasp I had made for it. I'd have to clean the tool of brain matter before it rusted.

I pulled out the knife instead. It was a bummer she had burned my dominant hand's wrist. Now that the adrenaline high had left me for the comfortable feeling of an after-fight surrealism, I could feel the pain distinctly. I winced as I set to work curing off her hands. Every jostle of my hand from side to side as I sliced through muscle made the scorching sensation rise up again.

"Be at peace, Milo, Jace," I grunted as I start the next hand. "The guilty's hands won't harm another."

It struck me as off that I was accustomed to butchering a body, that it didn't faze me when her olive throat was bloodied by my work. That was easy, too. A voice advised, *Now you've crossed the threshold. You're a monster, like her.*

I ignored that voice in favor of reaching out to talk to my mom. "Amani," I called, saying her name so she could hear me from the beyond. "I don't know who did it to you, but I've only got two left."

I licked my lips. I was thirsty.

A gaping chasm washed over me, an empty feeling of drowning. My throat swelled and my eyes blurred. My lip quivered. I shut my eyes and clenched my fists and jaw.

I could get justice for my tribe and family, sure, but I could get no justice for Gautami. After all this time, still, no one could kill cancer.

I was alone, nothing but a dismantled corpse to keep my company. The wave pushed again, forcing me under the water, whipping me around and throwing me against rough sand.

I was fighting, pulling myself up, trying desperately to push against the ground, to rise against the current, but I could do nothing as my lungs grew tighter and my heart rate spread up.

I let it crash into me.

My knees shook and I lowered myself using Tatsu's couch. The ground was cold through my clothing. I wrapped my arms about myself, pulling and scratching at my skin, hoping that some semblance of pain could bring me back.

My face felt wet.

It occurred to me that I never really mourned my family. I was too busy burying them. I was too busy surviving. I was too busy looking for justice. It seemed to me that the final straw in the grieving process was knowing I couldn't save Gautami, just like I couldn't save Jace. It was like I was trying to force water into a glass that was already full. The leakage slipped out along the edges.

"Vekja rois ikajjis oia," I whispered to the empty air. *They were just kids.* I could hear how my voice sounded, like a shattered window. It was unfair. It was unfair Jace died screaming in pain and that he never grew up and that I never got to know who he became.

I crunched over and leaned my head into my knees. The ground smelled like dust and blood. I had gotten used to those smells, become accustomed to them. It was something else that left the jarring smell stinging my nose. It was the smell of salt.

It was the wet-dry scent that overwhelmed my senses. It was the smell that told me that I was supposed to be like this, wretched and weak and without a single person in my life. It was the scent that told me the only thing I truly had was the *memory* of my dead brother. I never had *him.* He died before I could.

Oh, the salty smell was coming from my eyes.

I screamed and cried in a pathetic heap until my throat was shredded and my eyes were bloodshot.

November 20, 2726

Maru

He was a museum owner. He owned a grand total of thirty-seven museums, all of which were the legitimate front for his illegitimate continental drug trade of a dangerous psychedelic: Orange Blossom.

Orange Blossom, more commonly referred to as O-Blow, produced an extremely intense euphoria lasting approximately twenty minutes. The drug destroyed dopamine and serotonin brain receptors, meaning the only way to experience that same elation was to take the drug again.

Recently, it had been seen more and more regularly among teens, meaning Audius was expanding his territory. Which is how the four of us found ourselves in his museum in Ifari, on a tour group through the modern Mapaanian cultural exhibit.

This time, we did get to pick our partners for the last trial mission we would do. Sancus and I, of course, chose one another. Xbalanque and Hunaphu teamed up. Xenon and Diejiste. Nakkrah and Nyami Nyami; surprisingly, since neither of them talked much and I couldn't imagine either carrying the conversation (though the more I thought about it, the more I believed that to be the exact reason why they chose one another). Amaethon and Aruna. Kali and Maru.

The real nasty trick was when they paired us up with another team. Sancus and I were grouped with Kali and Maru.

Kali clung to Maru's hand tightly. I knew it was an act, we had discussed it before-hand. They would be a young couple and Sancus and I would be a separate pair here for a school project so that we could split easily.

Since this was a history museum and not a sciences museum, there would likely only be one or two labs in the building.

I coughed into my elbow twice, trying to get Kali and Maru's attention. They looked over at Sancus and I. I nodded at another brick corridor that branched off from the main area.

If the map in my head was correct, that one would lead us to an area of the museum that sat right on top of the sewers. It was one of the more probable locations, out of the corridors we had already checked, since it had a means to traffic unsavory goods without arousing unnecessary attention.

Kali gave a wink and signaled *Understood* with her free hand. She had dressed down for today, electing to put her hair up in a low bun and wear a dark blue baseball cap. Maru was pretending he was still listening to the tour, but I watched his hand flinch in Kali's.

I nudged Sancus and we slowed our pace until we were at the back, pretending to be fascinated with a ceremonial mask from a small tribe in Ancaad. When no one was looking, we slipped into the corridor.

"Unmarked room?" I suggested.

"Likely," Sancus responded.

We ran down the hall as silently and quickly as we could, attempting to limit our time away from the tour group and still maintain discretion. Despite having a heavier weight, Sancus actually ran more silently than I. As he checked in all the rooms, I marveled at his precision.

I smiled to myself. I remembered when he could barely hold a knife properly.

"This one," he announced, peeking into the vertical rectangular window on a door. Sancus opened the door and poked his head through the crack. "It's empty."

"Then let's take a look." The room didn't look anything like the museum outside.

Outside, there were high red and orange brick arches that held up skeletons on strings for us to look up at. There were mosaic floors and sand-colored stone borders around exhibits of stuffed animal hides and fake shrubbery.

Inside this room, it was sterile, white, with tiled floors and bleached walls. There was lab equipment, in shiny stainless steel, and plenty of white napkins. The all too fluorescent lights gave me a slight headache with their brightness. I pulled my olive cap closer over my eyes.

"Hey, check this," Sancus called out, gesturing with his hands. Next to him was a live boiler, a milky white substance inside of it, heating up. He wasn't looking at that, though. He was looking at a piece of paper with a molecular compound on it.

$C_{12}H_{17}N_2O_4P$. "Psilocybin," I remarked, surprised. "That's the stuff that makes mushrooms hallucinogens."

"There shouldn't be any need for a compound like this in a history museum." We had found our evidence.

The creaking sound of a door echoed in the room. Sancus and I leapt toward the door and spun around just in time to see a man with glasses too big for his face enter. It smelled like he was eating a tuna fish sandwich, which he held in his slightly trembling left hand. *Childhood injury?*

He moved his hand and it flinched again. *Possibly. Could be nerves.*

I leaned my hand against the nearest table, as if I had done nothing wrong. I hadn't really, but getting caught always made me feel like I had committed ten felonies and kidnapped a free-range goat.

"What the hell are you kids doing here?" A man projected across the space. His face was partially obscured by a blue medical mask and he wore a painfully white lab coat. Sweat beaded on his brow and marked his underarms.

I pushed up against Sancus's arm, silently urging him to say something. Partially because he was more confident than I, partially because I didn't want to lie, and partially because I needed a distraction. The beige fabric of his t-shirt felt thin beneath my forearm.

Sancus took a step forward, hands open in front of him. His eyes were warm, but I could see the irises shaking in the way they did when his mind was churning out possible courses of action. He was quick to say, "Sorry, we were looking for a bathroom and got distracted. What are you guys working on? Are you carbon dating?"

The chatty airhead... I could work with that.

"If you are dating some artifacts, would you be able to answer questions for us?" I asked.

The man turned a little red in the face, but his shoulders relaxed and his knees straightened a bit. "Why do you need to know about carbon dating?"

"A school project," Sancus answered cheerfully, gesticulating wildly. "We're PhD candidates for anthropology! I want to work in a museum as a curator one day, actually." While the man looked at Sancus, I drew a sticky tab from my pocket and pressed it to the rim of the table I leaned on, just inside lip of the overhang. It would go without notice for a while. *Thank you, Hephaestus.*

The man nodded. "We're pretty busy here," he explained. "You'll have to research the old-fashioned way." In other words, he wanted us gone.

I grabbed Sancus's sleeve and pulled down on it slightly. "Thanks anyway." I didn't wait for a response; I tugged Sancus with me back to the outside. I kept pulling him until I found a bathroom in the red brick building that was empty. I popped us both inside and handed him one of my earbuds.

The crackling and dim voices of the room echoed out. "I told him it was bad security," someone said. "We can't just expect people not to wander in. It's a museum. Curious people come here."

"Yeah, well, they were just dumb kids. They didn't get anything."

A groan. "Yeah, well, if dumb kids can find us, then so can the Feds, moron. I gotta call up Audius about this; I better have this taken care of by tomorrow."

"He'll hate that. He has his anniversary tonight."

"Yeah, well, he can skip it. This could get us all thrown in the slammer for a long time. It's more important than an anniversary. He'll just have to spend the night in his office."

I looked up to Sancus. He was looking at me, with a crooked smile on his lips and a twinkle in his eyes that wasn't from the bright yellow lights. He was happy. And I was happy, too, because it meant we could confirm Audius Welsch as the head of the O-Blow Trade.

There wasn't much planning for this case. I suggested that we split the teams up differently, to give us experience with alternate individuals. Everyone agreed.

I had also suggested it to give Sancus some time away from worrying about what Kali and Maru were up to. His clouded mind hindered our work, and I was selfishly motivated to give my friend a better chance. I didn't tell anyone that.

Maru was surprisingly easy to work with. As I sent the hand signal for *target, window, five,* he immediately nodded and dropped his rope near there. He didn't fight and he trusted me.

His hands were nimble, and quick, too, as he fastened the notch to himself, and lowered himself toward the window. Since I was on the ground, looking up at the red and orange brick building, I would have to climb up on the end of the rope he left for me.

I was thankful for the black gloves they had us wear, the ones that covered every inch of our hands and protected my skin from abrasion as I pulled myself up the rope. My arms would hurt tomorrow.

"Ready?" Maru confirmed when I reached him. His eyes were fixed inside the room.

Welsch sat with his back to us, at an oaken desk with a swivel chair. His room was well lit, and showcased a couch and a few chairs. There were bookshelves that went up higher than he could reach and probably hosted a compendium on artifacts the museum specialized in. He was on the phone, most likely trying to broker a deal for a new building to run operations out of.

I nodded. Then I realized Maru wasn't looking at me and said, "Ready," aloud.

Maru grabbed ahold of the rope between us and pulled it away from the window. When it began to swing back, he pushed off the wall with his legs.

I pushed my feet out, colliding into the window. It shattered around me, creating a cocoon of shards. As soon as my feet hit the ground, I grabbed my knife from my belt and flicked it open.

Welsch gasped as I grabbed his hair and pulled his head back, pressing the blade to his jugular. His hair was dark and wiry, and only filled the bottom half of his head. He was on the trimmer side, with the body shape of a runner. His nose was narrow and dainty.

I noticed the photo of his family on the desk: a wife and two kids that looked around the same age. That gave us leverage.

I loathed that had been my first thought when I saw the photo.

"Keep talking like normal," I whispered into his ear.

I could hear him gulp, but he kept talking. I didn't hear the words; my brain tuned them out as unimportant. After a while, Maru blinked at me. It was the only part of his face I could see through the mask. I knew he wanted me to end the call. "Wrap it up," I whispered.

Welsch nodded slowly. "Look, just fix it," he said. "We can hash out the details on Monday." He removed the phone from his ear and placed it on the receiver.

There was a moment of silence, before he opened his mouth. "Whatever they're paying you," he said in a deep timber, "I will double it."

I took the knife off his neck and leaned back. I kept it out.

"We aren't getting paid," Maru commented, "we're something of good Samaritans, really concerned about the state of your business."

Welsch kept a calm face.

"Well, my museums are doing just fine, tha—"

Maru interrupted Welsch by clapping a gloved hand to his shoulder. His eyes crinkled shut, an indication of a smile. I could tell it was a false smile by the pinch between his brows. The way his fingers flexed around Welsch's shoulder and the way his shoulders raised and core tightened only further confirmed my suspicion.

"Let's cut the bullshit, why don't we?" It was like a switch had flipped. Maru reminded me in that moment of a sadistic school bully.

I walked around the desk to face Welsch. "We know you started the O-Blow trade," I told him. "We want it gone." I didn't leave any room for argument in my words.

Welsch's face contorted in confusion, before his mouth fell apart in realization. I could see barely-there stubble, shadowing his jaw.

Then, he smirked, as if he had everything figured out. It made my blood freeze over in my veins. What did he have to be confident about? Why were his shoulders relaxed?

My fingers twitched, wanting to curl into themselves and ram their knuckles across his cheekbone. I didn't. I stood there, still as a mountain, and let Maru do the work. Trust. I had to trust him, because he was closer now.

"If you kill me, the trade won't stop."

Maru laughed, a curt and sarcastic laugh. "Look," Maru drawled, "I ain't a bad guy. I won't kill *you* if you don't make a call to the lead scientist."

There was a pause. I didn't realize my breath was locked in a bubble in my throat until now. I took a controlled exhale. I had to trust in Maru's process.

"But it would be a shame if you lost your little girl and little boy." Maru had seen the picture, too. "Your daughter looks so much like you. And your son has the same curly, colored locks as your wife. Such a happy family. We wouldn't want anything to disrupt that, would we?"

Maru was a great guy. I had seen him lay bird feed out for the birds that sat on the archway rails. I had seen him use his off time between missions to assist at a home for folks with dementia. Now, it was a different man that wore his face.

I had seen glimpses of it before. Maru shut off who he was when he was working. It was like a split personality that he controlled. An 'adaptive personality' one might call it. The man I saw now was not the violet eyed man with the birthmark shaped like a chameleon on the left side of his rib cage, who still stuck q-tips into his lips and pretended he was a vampire. This was the vampire, who had cut his fangs off to masquerade as a man.

And I had no doubt he would draw blood if necessary.

I hoped, to a god I had forsaken, that he wouldn't lay a finger on Welsch's kids. The girl with the curly brown hair or the boy with aurora borealis locks that had their likeness in a frame on the desk. If Maru did try to make a move against either one, I didn't know what I would do, not when I knew it would be right to save them, but still held onto the idea I would be saying goodbye to the resources that would help me play the game of justice.

"You're sick," Welsch spat. Still, he sat down and started to dial up the lead scientist responsible for the drug.

I heard the phone ring dimly as Welsch held it up to his ear. A garbled grumble came from the other end, though I couldn't make out what it was saying.

"It's me. Sorry to call you so late, man," Welsch said. His voice didn't waver. He was surprisingly good under pressure.

"Look, the Feds showed up at my home the other night, asking if we had seen any of O-Blow in my neighborhood." So, he was good at lying, too. I stood rooted to the spot as I watched Welsch think about the best way to spin a tale believable enough that it got us what we wanted and kept his family safe.

A muffled garble. "No, man, we can't just move locations this time." His fingers scratched at the wood of the table. "We have to scrap everything. Maybe now is a good time to get out. Quit while we're ahead."

The words were still indistinguishable, but louder and more rushed this time. Welsch's lower left eyelid twitched. Stress, fatigue, frustration. His fingers stopped scratching and tightened into a fist.

I walked around the room, my eyes looking up to Maru. His skin nearly blended in with the dark oak of the bookcase he was near. I could see the whites of his eyes and the stunning violet irises, chalked with lines of indigo, dark around the rims. There was no light in them, but there was a message: *I'm losing my patience.*

Maru didn't have to give me a verbal cue or a hand signal for me to get the message.

"Just get rid of it," Welsch sighed. "I will pay you the amount owed for you to stop. Whatever you think is fair. I—" Then, his voice shook. "I don't want to be locked up, have my kids spend Fathers' Day alone, leave my wife nothing because all of our assets were seized. I—"

Welsch's voice broke and he looked up at me, intuitively noticing I was the compromised one. "I don't want my kids growing up without a father." He wasn't talking to the person on the phone any more. He was talking to me, trying to toy with my emotions.

I was grateful for the masks we wore.

Unlike Maru, I could not separate work and personal life into two people within me. What I could do was let the ice roll over me when I thought back to the fact that this man let hundreds of kids overdose on a substance he made.

Another garbled sound from the phone. "Five bill, fine. Yes, I'll pay it." He turned on his computer with a touch and began typing.

Maru leaned over his shoulder, and peeked onto the screen. The blue lit energy registered across the gloss of his eyes. They crinkled a little at the corners.

He nodded softly after a while, just a tilt of the chin, confirming that there had been a transfer of funds. I leaned up against the wall and crossed my arms in front of my chest. I wondered if I looked calm and collected.

Welsch turned off the computer. "Did you get it?" he asked the man on the phone.

"Good." He slammed the phone onto the receiver.

He heaved a stressed-out sigh and ground his teeth with an irritated twist of thick lips. "It's over," he said, pointing a look at Maru filled with bloodlust.

"We're gonna need the name of the man you just called," I said, just loud enough for him to hear me. It wasn't for collateral. We needed to confirm Sancus and Kali had the right guy, the one who kept the formula that would die with him.

He mumbled under his breath.

"Speak clearly," I instructed. My voice was almost as cold as I felt.

"Zeke Andrapaji."

I hummed and pulled out the burner from my belt, before texting the Caesar's cypher version of that name. *Chnh Dqgudsdml.* I'd need to crush the phone and throw it into the river later.

I looked up at Maru and tapped twice with two fingers on my forearm. *Message sent.* He nodded slightly again.

"Pleasure doing business," Maru said. I could imagine the smirk on his lips as he said it, the deranged alter ego popping out to admire its handiwork.

His hand clapped Welsch's shoulder and he squeezed.

I felt a churning in the pit of my intestines, making me feel like I was witnessing something I shouldn't.

"Yeah, yeah," the man said. "You got what you wanted, just don't touch my kids."

Everyone was the hero in their own story. In Maru's story, he was valiantly stopping the spread of O-Blow, saving countless lives. In Welsch's life, he was protecting his children at any cost. Both thought they were in the right.

What about people like me? The ones who thought we were in the wrong, but acting anyway?

But you have to. You want justice for Jace, right? The voice reminded me. *Killing all these people is a small sacrifice to make for achieving that goal. You're owed sixty-two lives, after all.*

Maru stood to full height and walked toward me, toward the exit of the room. "Ah, don't worry about them for now," he said with a shrug. "We won't touch 'em."

Welsch slumped in his chair, the moonlight coming through the window glinting off his partially bald head.

"But," Maru continued, voice calm and calculating, "we'll keep an eye out. If supply doesn't dry up in a month, we'll be back." Maru left the door with a wave of his hand, walking out toward the outside, like he hadn't just issued a threat.

I followed out.

I could practically hear Welsch turn red when he yelled, "I'll tell the authorities about you. The both of you will get locked up."

This time, I was the one who spoke, tired of the self-righteous attitude and the flippant attempt to manipulate us. "Go ahead. You won't be able to find us without our faces… and you'd have to explain why we were here. Sounds like a bad mix, to me."

I looked over my shoulder, saw his fists clenched and a sneer on his face.

"Good luck with your legitimate business dealings, Mr. Welsch." I shut the oak door behind me.

Maru and I walked in silence through the museum halls. We were intended to meet with Kali and Sancus in the museum, near the aquatic exhibit, the only one that hosted live animals and was more for children observers than for adults. It was one of the best exhibits in the museum, in my opinion, because it was always simultaneously lit and dark. Maru and I walked through tunnels that held water above our heads and watched the water breathers swim around us.

Maru looked up at them with a forlorn expression, like he had missed them and couldn't quite remember why.

"They're beautiful," I commented, watching a particularly colorful fish swim along the side of the tunnel. It didn't seem to be aware of our presence.

Maru pulled the mask under his chin and it bunched around his neck. "They are."

He didn't move, so neither did I. I just kept watching as angelfish, clownfish, tigersharks, and other aquatic animals swam about the cerulean water, casting shadows across the rolling waves of light that cascaded randomly across our bodies.

"I like looking at beautiful things," he said. "I didn't use to, but I grew up and started to realize there's beauty in simplicity and all that junk."

I smirked. "Eloquent."

He chuckled. "It makes me feel calm after something like that."

I paused. "Split personalities?" I asked, unable to keep the curiosity from my tone.

"I don't think so. He only comes out when I'm doing certain things. He doesn't compel me to do them, it's like he's a part of me and I'm watching him through a theater. I think I developed him to…" Maru trailed off and his tongue darted out to wet his lips. "Well, what we do isn't easy." He said it like it explained everything. In some ways it did.

I looked at Maru, at the patterns cast by the shifting water on his carob skin, reflecting in his amethyst eyes, and hoped to understand him a little better. It was hard, because I didn't have any basis for that understanding. He had two parts that made him whole, whereas I had forced myself to become one thing, alone, until all the pieces that weren't useful were pushed out and abandoned.

"It seems like there is never any meaning to what we do. We call ourselves gods, as if we carry out divine purpose, but if there is no end goal, nothing in sight, then there is no purpose," he mumbled in Greek. I didn't believe it was said for me, so I pretended I didn't hear him.

The sound of footsteps didn't startle me. I'd recognize the sound of Sancus approaching from anywhere.

Kali and him bore the same clothes that we did, but in lieu of empty hands, theirs had bottles of clear liquid. Kali hoisted the one she held above her head. "Post-mission celebration?" she asked.

Maru smirked and walked over to meet them. Without a word, he took the offered bottle and took a huge swig. I winced at the sight of his Adam's apple bobbing. I hated the burn of liquor. I decided to decline whatever bottle was offered to me.

"What of Zeke?" I asked.

Sancus looked at me. His lips were dark from the alcohol. "We couldn't let someone who knew how to produce that substance stick around," he said. *We killed him,* he meant.

I nodded. At the very least, I was glad that they both made it back all right. I don't know what I would have done if Sancus had gotten hurt, fully knowing that I allowed putting him with Kali.

I had mixed feelings about that she-devil. I held a grudging respect for her standing up for herself. However, I hated how she showed off her beauty like that was all she was. She was more than beautiful. She was lethal, too, and whenever I looked at her, a part of me died believing she let that piece of her slumber.

"I'm glad you both are safe," I said, honestly.

Kali's lips were dark and her cheeks were flushed red. "I'm just glad I got to pretend to be someone else for a day. It sure is tiring being me."

Maru threw his arm around her shoulders. His eyes crinkled when he smiled. "Ah, don't say that," he teased. "I really enjoyed having you dote on me."

She threw her head back and laughed. "It wasn't all an act," Kali said slyly. Her hand traced up Maru's jaw and she was pulling him into a kiss, right in front of me and Sancus.

I wanted Kali to be happy. I wanted Maru to be happy, too. But I would condemn both of them to a life of suffering if it meant that Sancus didn't have to feel what I knew he was feeling now: rejection, heartbreak, worthlessness.

In that moment, I felt hatred for Kali and Maru in a way I had only ever held toward a particular group of people, personified by the man in white.

I looked at the ground, guiltily.

Sancus's fingers flexed tighter around the neck of his bottle and his jaw clenched. "I'm gonna head back to sleep," Sancus lied, quietly. I don't even think they could tell he was lying. "I'll see you guys back at the room."

Sancus walked off into the dark of the museum. His shoulders were hunched and his head was low. I saw his arm raise. He was drinking more of the liquor.

I looked back to Maru and Kali, who couldn't care less that I was still there, giggling and whispering to one another like a couple of teenagers.

"I'll head out, too." Maru and Kali could be happy together if they wanted to, but I didn't want to see another second of it.

I trailed after Sancus, far enough away to escape his notice. His head wasn't in the right space to notice me. Nonetheless, his body pressed forward, pulling itself up flight after flight of stairs on the classically styled building.

Sancus sat on the roof with a resounding clash of hollow metal as it bounced under his weight. He took another swig of the liquor and looked out at the city below. His legs were splayed and his left hand propped his body up from behind.

His eyes were unfocused.

"Hey," I said, coming to sit down with him.

"Hey."

Sancus didn't say anything else, so we sat in silence for a moment, until he pushed the bottle to me.

I took a deep drink. It burned as it traced the line of my throat and made me wince. It left a lingering numbness on my lower lip when I finished. The taste of liquor. It was harsh and it muddled my mind. But Sancus liked it well enough and the thought occurred to me he may have needed to be numb.

I extended the bottle back to him and watched him immediately bring it to his lips. His head tilted back and his almond eyes screwed shut when he took more in. The Adam's apple on his neck bobbed once, twice, three times before he pulled the it away with a sharp exhale of air.

"She's just never going to see me the way I see her, is she?" he asked.

The clouds framed his head like a halo, spreading out in their blue hued wisps in a flurry of sorrow. He looked like a painting tonight. He looked like one of those sketches that he drew of the woman he spoke about.

I wanted to tell Sancus a great many things in that moment. I wanted to tell him he was the most incredible person I knew. I wanted to sing praises to his upbeat attitude and his endless, unwarranted faith in human goodness. I wanted to argue Kali was not worthy of his light and that there was a woman out there who was and who would give as much as she took. Those things couldn't be put into words in the way I wanted, not without skewing the meaning.

"No," was what I said instead. It was the only way I knew how to answer.

Sancus chuckled, shrill and whiny. It was a sharp contrast to his deep and melodic voice. It was sad and desperate. Almost as broken as the cracked voice that whispered, "Why can't we just be normal?" Sancus's fingers shook around his bottle and his jaw clenched and unclenched. "Why are we so desperate to choose the thing that hurts us? Why are we so *broken?*" He said the word with disdain, like it was a roach he held over a toilet.

"Being broken means that we can put ourselves back together the way we want," I offered with a slight shake of my head and a shrug of my shoulders. "Can't do that if we stay assembled the way we were when we were born."

I knew he needed to hear some distraction, so I searched my mind desperately for a topic that Sancus would enjoy. "Hey," I tried, "do you think one of the stars out there has a planet with two people sitting on a roof talking about love and drinking bootleg hooch together, like us?"

I watched his shoulders tense and he turned his head to me. His freckles were barely visible in the dark. That was a shame; I loved his freckles.

"Maybe," he mumbled. Sancus pressed a hand to his cheek, a gesture he did to sap the heat into his fingers when he felt hot. The alcohol must have settled in. "I don't see why not."

I smirked at him and drew my leg up to myself to prop my elbow on it, my chest open to him. "You think we could take 'em in a fight?" I asked.

This time when he chuckled, it was genuine, albeit weak. He had this crooked smile, where he raised one eyebrow. When his face bore that expression, I knew he was going to be okay and felt an airiness in my breathing. "We're sitting on the roof of a world culture museum, and your first thought about other worlds is if we can win in a fight against two people who are also on a roof?"

"It is a legitimate question, Sancus," I joked.

He threw his head back when he laughed. He looked up at the sky, as if trying to spot out those people who would be our competition. I looked away, toward the city below. There were people walking quickly to try to catch the slick white train before its doors slid shut. There were hardly any cars.

"I think we could," Sancus mused.

"But what if they were also from some secret society, but theirs was, like, way better than ours?"

"Then, we would just, we would just have to outwit them." I saw his hand from the corner of my left eye. It found its way to mess my hair. I batted it away without malice. "Though I don't much like our chances. You're an idiot."

I felt warm inside. Calling me an idiot was a sure-fire sign that Sancus was all right. It felt nice when he touched me like that. He was barely six months older than I, but sometimes he really felt like an older brother. It was silly, I had come out here to provide Sancus comfort, but he was the one bringing it to me.

"Your only respite from being brain dead is strategy," he continued.

"Shut up," I told him without any bite.

In the world below our rooftop tryst, the chatter of late-night business folk filled the air. They weren't aware of us, of how easily we could hurt them. They were all too fragile. I wondered if that's how the people who killed my tribe thought of us.

The thought made me sick.

"Hey, can I ask you something?" Sancus requested.

I nodded my head. I had zoned out and had found I didn't want to zone back in to look at him. I was tired. It was draining to go on these missions, down to the core. It was more tiring, still, to deal with the aftermath.

"Why do you like Iktomi?"

My gaze immediately refocused. Liked him? I could barely stand Xenon. At the same time, I did *really* like being with him. The answer was complicated. "I don't... not really," I said honestly.

I thought back to the day I overheard Sancus and Iktomi arguing in the common room. I think that was the day I stopped thinking of Xenon as a tool. Now, I couldn't tell what he was to me, but I could admit to Sancus, "I like how he makes me feel."

"How does he make you feel?"

I shrugged. *He makes me feel like my existence isn't worthless.* "He makes me feel wanted." I couldn't answer articulately, but I could get close.

Sancus scoffed from beside me. "Frankly, I am offended that you like him instead of me."

I'm sure that if I were not so committed to hiding my facial expressions, I would have shot Sancus the biggest look of offense I could muster. "Sancus, bro, you are into *girls.*"

He laughed again. "Yeah," he said, "but still."

I closed my eyes and took a deep breath in. The air smelled more purely in the night.

"He's in love with you, you know," Sancus said, under his breath.

I did know. I knew and I took advantage of it because I could do so with impunity. Maybe that made me worse than Kali, who only showed interest in those she wanted to love.

I scoffed and held my right hand out. He didn't do anything, so I looked over at him. I studied his face carefully. The slope of his roman nose, the curve of his lips, the slant of his eyes and brows.

I nudged him with my outstretched elbow and moved my hand up and down again. "Pass the hooch," I said, "I'm going to need a good buzz going before I talk about feelings."

I realized why they had sent us on two-person team ups for now. It's not only so that we can learn from each other and protect each other. It's also so we can pick up the pieces afterward, all the shattered bits of humanity that we lose during the mission.

The liquor tasted a little sweeter when I took my next sip.

We returned to the mountain tired and sore, slumping against each other in the common room.

"God, my neck feels awful," Sancus complained, rubbing it with his fingers.

"Then ice it," Kali drawled out quickly. I'm sure the slight flinch Sancus made didn't escape any of our notice. Still, no one said anything.

It's for the best, I thought. Sancus would finally be able to get over her. It was a fresh wound, prickling and itching where metaphorical skin mended itself together, but it would heal and the skin there would be tougher than it was before.

I dropped my pack on the oaken floor, and it made a resounding thunk. Sancus wasn't the only one who was sore. I ached all over. A lack of sleep did that, made you more in tune with the strain put on your body.

The internal door swung open; a panting Aruna hunched over. Her forehead beaded with sweat and her eyes were wide below a knitted brow.

"It's Amaethon," she said, in a rushed tone.

We all knew that tone. Then we stood, ignored our aching bodies, and ran behind Aruna, through endless curving beige hallways with black sconces and dusty scents. We all knew that tone. She threw open the doors to the med bay and we clambered inside, into the clean room that smelled like antiseptic and stainless steel. We all knew that tone. There was a steady metronome of beeps as we all drew closer to the feet peeking out from a white blanket with blue lines, partially obscured by a seafoam curtain.

We all knew that tone.

Kali gasped and threw her arms around Maru's shoulders, burying her face in his neck. He rubbed her back in small circles, mumbling words I didn't care to focus on now. Sancus stood closer to me, silently requesting companionship; I moved to let our shoulders touch. Aruna moved to hold a pale, freckled hand, hanging limp off the side of the cot. Hunaphu and Xbalanque stood beside her, hands linked and shaking. Quiet tears tracked down Hunaphu's face, running red where it mixed with blood coming from an open wound on her lip.

Amaethon looked like an herb branch, left out too long to dry. Tubes hooked up to her to help her breathe, and wires and needles stuck into her arms and tucked under the blankets to where we couldn't see. Her nose was blue and her posture looked twisted under the sheets.

I turned to Haoma, who was checking her vitals and jotting down little notes. She didn't say anything.

I swallowed, my heart heavy in my throat. I was careful to keep my face steady and my voice steadier. "Will she live?"

She didn't look it. All battered and bruised, it looked like the steady beep of the machines she was hooked to were the only things to keep her alive.

Haoma looked up from her notes. Her face was blank.

Because they don't care, I realized, *we are the pawns they play with. We are expendable.* It made me go cold. My fingers curled into my palm and pressed crescent moon marks into my skin.

Haoma looked back down and continued writing.

I always knew I was mortal. I knew I was playing a dangerous game and that I was always a breath away from losing. I thought if I were smart, if I were skilled, I could crawl past, surviving and staving off death for just another moment.

Looking at Amaethon, twisted and covered in aquilegia flowers made of flesh, I realized I was far more mortal than I gave myself credit for. One wrong move, and I could break, just like Amaethon did, and I could lose everything.

Was I ready to die? Was I ready to lose everything in the pursuit of justice? Those questions made me want to scream because I didn't like how I'd answer them. I didn't like that I would give my body, blood, and spirit if it meant killing the people who took my brother from me.

I doubt Amaethon even had the chance to ask those questions.

"If she lives," Haoma's monotone voice sounded in the room, "she will never walk again."

December 10, 2726

Amatheon

Most of the scars on my body were made by my own hand. Even the first scar on my left arm I had given myself when I was too young to know how my blood would make the knife skip on my skin. Only six were not of my own volition.

When I had received my first burn scar, purposely inflicted for the sake of identification, I had felt true pain. It festered and bubbled and permanently glued together the pores of my skin in a raised pink line with twelve equidistant notches along the inner edge.

This time, we got to pick how our skin would be marked, what would go within the clock face. I chose a feather, a symbol of the God I was named for. Ma'at weighed a feather against a person's spirit. If their spirit was the lighter, they could pass on to the afterlife; if their spirit was heavier, they faced eternal penalty.

Xbalanque and Hunaphu had chosen a sun and a moon, because it represented one another. They got their brands. Their clasped hands, one pale and one dark, shook as the hot irons were pressed into their skin, on their left and right shoulder respectively.

Hunaphu's lip quivered and Xbalanque's brow furrowed. I watched as their cores tightened under their clothes, trying to bite back the pain.

Red stained my vision.

Sancus's hand grabbed at my elbow.

My foot had slipped forward. I stepped back, ashamed of my impulsiveness.

It seemed surreal as a gel and bandage was pressed over their skin and as the next members were called up. A shield was pressed to Nakkrah's sternum. A lion's profile pressed to Kali's right hip. A circle on Diejiste's lower right back. The Rosetta Stone on Nyami Nyami's throat, right where his clavicle met. A koi fish on Maru's forearm. A dual edged sword on Aruna's calf. A flower on the base of Amaethon's spine. Sancus got a pen pressed into the scar his brother gave him.

As for myself, the searing pain laced my skin, slowly forming a point and ridges of a feather. My jaw clenched and I fought to keep my eyes open, to stare at the beige stone floor in front of me. I tasted metal, like the sculpted stick had bled through my skin to find my tongue. It felt like thousands of tiny pinpricks, shredding apart the sinews of my skin instantaneously.

I thought to Jace, imagined how he would have gone through this pain, felt it all over his body on the day he died. What a horrible way to die.

I liked to imagine if it were him here instead of me, he would bring his head up to meet the eyes of the twelve. He'd blow hot air through his nose, a tranquil bull, and give a cocky grin to those who cared to look. Without saying a word, he would ask *Is that all?*

He'd look a lot like my father, I think. Strong jawline with a sharp nose. He'd have grown up a little, not only in how he looked, but also how he handled things. I wondered if he would handle the whole genocide thing the same way I did.

Probably not. He always had his own way of going about things.

I pushed those thoughts away. They hurt more than my shoulder did.

The pressure of the iron left me, but the pain wasn't in the iron, it was in my skin. The hot was inside me, crawling like bugs chittering over a fallen log, scrambling to cover as much ground as possible. I couldn't even feel the shape of the feather that I had requested.

Then, it was gone and I took in a breath I didn't know I was holding. I tasted blood, coppery and faint and my skin throbbed a dull thrum.

My hand found purchase on the cool beige floor and my stomach tensed as I pushed myself to the balls of my feet and then stood. I joined the others back in the line.

"Iktomi," was called out and Xenon stepped forward. The last of us. As I watched him kneel, I realized, with a prickling feeling of guilt that I was still envious of him.

I knew better than anyone how many hours I put in, how long Yonten used me as a punching bag, how many days and months I worked to get to where I was. To someone else, it may have looked easy, but I had used every breath for years to forage myself into the person I became.

I should have known better than to judge someone for being a natural genius.

But I did. Because Xenon seemed to breeze through things the way someone breezes through brushing their teeth: like it was a chore. I knew he worked hard. I knew he was trying. And I knew that I envied him for being better than me, regardless.

It was a fine line between admiration and envy. The fact that we had been seeing one another just blurred that line further. His flaws had become more apparent, and in spite of them, he continued to grow. That growth was cause enough for envy.

They pressed the hot iron to the skin in front of his heart and removed it, the shape of a little flame, rising in delicate wisps, left behind. Then he stood up, much more quickly than I had and rejoined us.

"Congratulations. You are now all official members of the North Wind. It is your duty to protect those who would worship us," Pluto said. I could see a glint in his eye; something akin to approval.

With that, the ceremony was over and a chatter burst from everyone.

"How does it feel?" Xenon asked in a whisper, leaning into my side.

"Hurts like a bitch," I grumbled. There were more practical ways to identify ourselves. Ink would have functioned just as well as body mutilation. I had enough scars without a brand; we all did.

My right hand reached for the wrapping I kept on my left forearm. I had always been self-conscious of them, scared of someone asking me about them.

Xenon rammed his shoulder into me. "Stop being so moody. You aren't a fifty-year old man on a dating show."

His hand brushed against the back of my own, trying to get my attention with its icy itch. I was the one who linked us together. I didn't entwine our fingers. It was easier to let go that way.

"Hey, do you think we will get assigned together again?" I asked. "I think we did a good job." And I wanted something stable. I was incredibly selfish for loving what Xenon could give me instead of loving him.

He tugged at our hand and took a step. I followed him to the side of the room.

I noticed Sancus wasn't with Kali this time. He was chatting it up with Nakkrah instead. My heart leapt. It was good for him. Better to squash unrequited love than to let it fester, rotting like flowers in balmy summer heat.

Sancus seemed happy. A little glint in his eyes indicated either pride or elation. Most likely, it was both. His nose was all scrunched, like a caricature, and his freckles were darker than usual. I wanted to catalogue that happiness forever, filed away in a make-believe storage cabinet for him to pull out later.

When we stopped, Xenon turned to me. His dark brow was scrunched up in concern, like he had something weighing on him.

"What's wrong?" I asked.

Xenon had been content to live as a fixture in my life, happy with the little bits of attention I could give, soaking it up like water. And though he was expressive, he had never looked like the drawn lips of frustration, the pinched eyes of sorrow, and the red cheeks of shame that he was now.

He took an inhale, his shoulders seizing up momentarily. "We won't do another mission together," he told me in a rush, his voice low.

I blinked once. "You don't know that," I said. I felt my eyebrow twitch in surprise and made an effort to straighten my face.

"I elected to only do solo missions from here on out."

The surprise hit me like a wave crashes against the shore line, all at once. I didn't even know that was an option for us.

I knew that they liked having partners to provide backup and administer emergency medical services, but I didn't need those things. I had taught myself to stitch my flesh together and I could ignore pain.

"I may just ask for the same thing," I mumbled, looking at the floor.

I didn't have time to speak again before Xbalanque and Hunaphu joined us, jostling one another like puppies.

"Congrats, guys," Xenon said as they drew into earshot.

Xbalanque didn't smile that much. In fact, he was pretty grumpy all the time unless he was causing mischief with his partner in crime. But the newly lit up face suited him well.

He took in a sharp breath before talking. "I can't believe it's over," he mumbled. "Maybe now I'll stop getting hurt. I'm convinced it was bad luck because I'm a beginner."

I raised my free hand to his fluffy hair to mess it up and push his head a little. "I'm pretty sure beginners are supposed to be lucky, not unlucky. You get hurt because you're clumsy," I argued. He pushed my hand away with scrunched up cheeks.

"Do you two want to do something right now?" Hunaphu asked, tucking a spare strand of wiry black hair behind her shoulder. She, too, was sporting a wild expression. One that twisted the tip of her nose in a series of fine lines.

Xenon turned toward the pair more fully. "What did you have in mind?" he asked, with a forward tilt of his head.

"Well, we want to play one last game of capture the flag," Hunaphu explained. "Yeah, we're supposed to be mature now and focus on what lies ahead, but this may be our last chance for a while, since everyone is about to go their separate ways."

A hot stone slid up and down in my throat. Fatigue hit me.

"I'm a little drained," I told her, placing my left hand on her elbow. "But Iktomi will play with you guys."

I looked up to him. His hair was tied up to keep it out of his face. His dark eyes searched my face. He was worried. I gave him a squeeze on his hand, a silent *later*.

He looked to the pair. "Yeah, I'll play. Let's go find Nyami Nyami, too."

Xenon dropped my hand and followed them off. My hand felt warmer as soon as his cold skin left it. But my body seemed to want that coolness, drawn to it as if it were water in a desert.

I leaned up against the wall and tilted my skull back against it. I was tired.

I heard the squeaking of tires. "Hey, Amaethon," I said.

She looked battered, but it wasn't what we could see that was the problem. A fractured spine, paralyzing both her legs. Honestly, I sometimes had to remind myself she had been injured. Most of the time, it just looked like she was sitting

Her hair was pulled up into her normal high ponytail, only today it looked more polished. "You looked like you were moping and I wanted to join you. It's been a shit week for me." She pursed her lips and propped her head up on her fist.

I crossed my arms and offered a raised eyebrow. "No kidding," I scoffed with a small head tilt and a small quirk of my lips.

She thought about for a little bit, scratching at the purple swell of her nose.

Apparently, she had jumped at the target and pushed them through a window because they were about to shoot a gun. Guns were an expensive rarity now, since gunpowder was in such short supply. It was unlikely that the target would have had a gun.

But they did. And they saw it fit to aim the trigger at Aruna. Amaethon probably didn't even think about what she was doing when she jumped and condemned herself to this life. She was just that kind of person, selfless, the kind movies were made about and memoirs were written for.

For every selfless hero, there's a Kryptonite lying in wait. I'd bet that Aruna would spend the rest of her life blaming herself for what happened to Amaethon.

She hummed, finally. "Yeah, but can't we host meetings somewhere else? It smells like burning skin in here and it's hard to breathe."

It was. The air was thick with our sweat from the burns and the relief of finally being full-members. I tighten my core and stand to full height. "Do you want me to take you outside?" I asked.

"Please." She nodded, spinning one of her wheels to swivel the wheelchair so that her back was toward me.

She wore a cropped white shirt that cut off before her arms and covered her neck and chest fully. It was tight fitting, not loose, like much of the other clothing around us. I supposed that was because it would be easier to brand her back if she didn't need to leave her chair.

It was crazy how much forethought she had to have, now. I felt a pang of pity, but I didn't say anything. My pity wouldn't change anything, and knowing Amaethon, she wouldn't want it, either.

I noticed the little tattoo she now had, the puffy pink skin marking her up forever. "It's beautiful," I said, as I gripped the handles of the wheelchair.

The burn was peeling, but I could tell detail had been put into the design, a spiral of interlocking pointed petals growing outward, in layers, like a never-ending flower that could only be seen through the outline of the circle.

She hummed. "Thank you."

"Why that?" I asked.

"A spiral means resilience," she stated, plainly. So, it was a spiral, not a flower.

I pushed her along the open-air balcony until we could only hear the dull thrum from inside the walls of the mountain. The air was chilly as it hit me, and there was a sense of living through a fog that made it hard to breathe.

The air smelled like snow, though it wouldn't be winter for a month. Snow and uncertainty.

"He said he would train me to be the next Hephaestus," she stated. "Take the mantle when he leaves."

She wasn't looking at me. She was looking at the dark night, at the ground below us. I wonder if she could smell the mist from the waterfall as strongly as I could, or if her seated position prevented her. I wonder if she could feel the occasional droplet on her freckled cheeks.

She looked down at her lap, clutching her hands together. "I guess I should be happy to ascend to the twelve without even really earning it. Most people here die before they can get that chance."

I placed my hand on her shoulder the way a soldier would put his hand on his comrade. "You should be," I told her. She tensed beneath me.

I understood what Amaethon was feeling. Helpless. She felt like a waste of space because she could do nothing any more and she would spend the rest of her life like that. She had spent so long trying to work herself into a warrior, only to have it ripped from her grasp at the very last moment. She hadn't even gotten a year. Her future must have seemed as broken as her body.

"But you're allowed to be sad, too," I stated, just as bluntly. "You are allowed to mourn what could have been." I certainly did.

Amaethon wasn't a pretty girl, by my standards. Her nose was a little too small and her teeth were a little too large. But when I looked at her, and saw tracts of tears leak silently from her red eyes, rimmed with orange, clumped lashes, I thought she was the most incredible thing I had ever seen. It was quietly tragic how she seemed to look most like a painting when she was sad.

A sniff broke her silent sorrows. She rubbed the back of her right hand against her face, trying to hide the tears. I looked away, trying to give her a bit of privacy. My chest clenched.

A tittle came from her. Her voice sounded out, scratchy instead of modulated. "I guess I've reached the 'sadness' part of grieving."

I sat down on the bench carved into the granite arch, facing toward Amaethon. "Ah, you're way ahead of me. I'm still in 'anger.'" It wasn't a lie, but I passed it off as a joke. My back felt cold against the stone.

Then, her voice broke from the brittle cadence and turned vibrant once more as she let out a guffaw. This time, when I looked at her, I saw relief slashed into the drawn brow and the pulled lips. Even though she looked like a statue when she cried, I much preferred this Amaethon.

"Yeah," she sighed, looking down to her lap, a soft smile marking her features. "I guess I am."

I don't know what compelled me to reach my hand out and grab hers. It was warm and soft and freckled, just like the rest of her. My fingers slotted into the area between her thumb and fingers and my thumb traced her knuckles.

I'm here, I hoped she understood. I couldn't do much. I wasn't a renowned doctor and I couldn't magically trade places with her. But I could stay. I was good at that.

She placed her free hand atop my own, rooting it in place. Her way of telling me something I couldn't understand.

But you won't stay, will you? A voice in my head asked rhetorically. *You still plan to leave. Now that you finished up training, you're onto your own killing spree, starting with the man in white. And when you finish, you'll leave and Amaethon will be alone.*

Guilt hit me, eating away at me as she held on a little tighter. Yeah, I'd leave; then who would hold her hand?

I couldn't look at her anymore, so I looked at our hands, calloused on the palms.

Hands were such delicate things. They cramped when we spent too much time trying to work with small tools and our nails were so weak that they would often crack and cause us pain. Hands were also powerful things. They could crush the sleeves on walnuts between them and they could pry apart hermetically sealed jars.

Hands always looked different. Some were meatier, some were narrower. Some had long fingers, others wide wrists. Different lines traced down our palms. But all hands, regardless of how they looked, were made with the function of reaching out to others.

A sniff. She was the first to let go, to bring her hands to her face and wipe the wet tracts from blotchy and red cheeks.

She gave me one last smile. It was too forced, a little bit too kind. Amaethon wanted the smile to be real, to force her to feel inside what she was pretending to outside. "Someone's looking for you."

"Would you like me to take you inside?" I asked.

She shook her head and looked away at the valley below. "No, I think

I'll stay here just a while longer. It's peaceful."

Cameras never captured everything. There is always pollen from a wishing puff or a particular beam of sunlight that blurs your vision that you can't quite keep in the photo. Those tiny imperfections are actually what makes the experience meaningful. My eyes saw a lot, but they were still just a lens that a camera focuses through. I had no idea what Amaethon was thinking. I couldn't see it.

But Amaethon was watching our backs from behind, getting told that she could never do what we did. That had to hurt like a bitch, there was no way it was peaceful.

"Don't stay out too late," I advised over my shoulder as I walked over to our shadow.

I guess their game had ended.

"Can we talk?" Xenon asked.

I nodded. He started walking off and I followed.

Despite being the one to ask if we could talk, Xenon wasn't saying a thing. He didn't seem to want to look at me and his knuckles were pale in a clenched grip.

I was tired of waiting.

My gaze was trained on my hands as my fingers traveled up and down one another. "Didn't we make a good team? We could again." I tried to keep my hope from my voice, from my face, from my body language. I had to force myself to look at him.

"I—" He stopped. It was like the words caught in his throat, strangling him. I could see it written in the twisting of his features. "I just can't work with you. I'm sorry. Let's talk about something else."

A nail wedged into my forehead. I wondered if maybe I was just dead weight, still so far behind that it would just hold him back.

A pang in my chest forced my gaze away.

My head tilted back, looking at the sky as if it could provide me with some semblance of wisdom that I didn't know I needed. Looking past the brambles of the leafless tree, I could see only indifferent lights, twinkling through the midnight blue hue that made up the heavens. The cloudless night would offer me nothing.

"I—" he started, then he stopped. He looked at the ground and his brow furrowed, like he was trying to find something that had fallen. "This life— I wanted—I wanted it for a long time, but then I didn't. I mean, now I don't." He was fumbling over his words. Xenon was normally such a smooth orator.

A snort of amusement pushed past my lips. "That wasn't very eloquent," I teased, bumping his shoulder with my own. It was a bid at humor, a feeble attempt to lighten the mood. His head snapped to mine, disgruntled that I had interrupted his nervous tirade. I grinned and raised my eyebrows; I would do it again if need be.

His face softened. Xenon sighed and his shoulders sagged. "Now I just want to stay with you. I think, if we try, we could disappear… forever. You're already legally dead. I haven't had a paper trail to me for years. We could do it, if we tried."

A million thoughts danced around my head: the logistics of creating fake identities, the actions we would need to take to make sure the North Winds never found us, the means by which we could live. Xenon and I could be the home with a blue door that smelled of bread and grass and took in kids with nowhere else to go. And my core ached with something akin to longing because Xenon was right. We *could* do it. And I wanted to. I wanted to be a place that stopped someone else from being like me.

I must have been quiet for a while, because I felt a tug on my hand. My sight drifted to him, meeting his hopeful eyes. I was called to view those little spots again, the ones that made up the pigment in his eyes. They made the tsunami-colored eyes look fake. But then again, my eyes looked fake too.

His gaze darted down and up again. His eyelids obscured those eyes and he leaned in. The kiss was barely there, just a brush of skin against my own, just enough for me to know what it was: a plea.

His hand held the back of my neck and he didn't pull away. His forehead pressed against my own, cold and soothing

"Please," he whispered, lips brushing against my own as he spoke. His normally silky voice had cracked a little. It sounded broken in a way I had never heard before.

I had never really known what it felt like to glue myself together. When my family was killed, I hadn't given myself the opportunity to break apart. I had wrapped my body in a string tightly enough that I could put them to rest, then I hadn't taken the string away. I had left it tied around me because I didn't have the luxury to break.

Everyone had slowly plucked away at the thinly woven string and tore it out fiber by fiber. I had put myself together in the time it took for the string to snap. Watching Xenon, a man I admired and envied, shattering before me, I realized that I could love him back. If I had more time, if I wasn't so stubborn...

My free hand reached to hold the back of his neck. It was the only thing I could think to do. Xenon was the strongest human I knew, physically and mentally, and he was breaking in my grasp. Seeing him break, made me break, too.

Never in my life had I felt the pang in my chest hit with enough intensity to halt my breath. Never in my life had the lump in my throat grown so thick that I could not even swallow. Never in my life had my body felt so tense that it seemed it would implode upon itself. Never in my life had the searing pain tore its way through every inch of me, down to every molecule.

I felt this way because I was the only one that could stop his hurting. I felt this way because, no matter how much I wanted to pull that hurt away, I wouldn't. That was the worst feeling in the world. Worse than grief, worse than anger. I could do something about it; I held that power. But in every world, in every universe, in every circumstance I could ever live in, I never would. It was far more important to me that I keep my promise to my people than anything else.

I pulled him into a hug. I had made many bad decisions in my life, but I had never regretted a single one of them. They lead me where I needed to be. Now, I did have a regret. I regretted that I hadn't known Xenon before I made the promise to my family. I regretted I wasn't good enough to push aside the past and look to the future. I regretted that I still didn't love him enough to pick him over the dead.

Xenon's hands gripped my t-shirt tightly, tugging them into fists. I could feel his hands shaking, moving the fabric in a way the winter wind didn't. His shaking meant he understood. I was glad. I didn't think I had the strength to say 'no' outright.

"I'm sorry," he mouthed against my neck, as if he were the problem.

Xenon smelled of salt water and spring, he sounded like silk and air, he felt like lessened burdens. I was walking away from that.

"It's not forever," I said. I didn't know who I was saying that for.

April 15, 2729

Concord

Jack swiped his two-denarii tip off the counter and followed with a rag in his other hand. "Gonna put my kid through school," he mumbled.

"Oh, sorry," I teased, "college educated bastards are the worst."

Jack gave me this half-smirk huff he made when he was mildly amused, even as he warned me to, "Shut up."

As if remembering something important, his face twitched momentarily. He reached into his pocket and he pulled out an envelope. "This came for you," he informed me, tossing it onto the counter ahead of me. An envelope with a chicken scratch sprawl, addressed to a Bahadur.

I knew, even before I opened the envelope, what it would be. My fingers were steady as I tore back the sticky part of the envelope. It serrated slightly left of center and I had to jam my thumb in to pull through the rest of the ridge.

The envelope was heavy, so I tipped it over. A silver key fell out, attached to a paper tab with a hand-written address. I pulled out and unfolded the paper that had stayed stuck in the envelope.

There were just two sentences: Everything of mine, I leave to you. Cast aside your hatred.

Straight to the point, even in his final thoughts. I usually burned the letters, so there was nothing that could link the pair of us, but I didn't want to burn this one. It was the last piece of him I had.

Yonten was dead.

I clutched the paper tightly in my hand, looking at the words again and again. It was just like him. Few words, never more than necessary. A two sentence will and testament that was equally efficient and nagging. I couldn't bring myself to burn this letter.

I didn't feel like crying or screaming; I had done enough of that already. Instead, I gave Jack a curt thanks as I tucked the letter away inside my shirt.

I pushed away from the bar with the intent of finding Sancus.

Concord was next on the list. It wouldn't make me feel better to kill him, but it would make a great distraction from the sinking pit of grief that slicked the insides of my lungs.

The town Concord had holed up in was the kind of town with less than five thousand people, where everyone knew everyone and outsiders were met with distrust.

The people here looked like they were from a fairy-tale with their varying shades of pastel blue flesh. I thought that this may be the influence of radiation, or of an underlying consistent ingesting of silver-nitrate.

I crossed the dirt street, mucking dark soil onto my light pants. It sunk into the fabric easily enough and I noted it would be a bitch and a half to clean.

The visitor center really shouldn't have been called that. It was a shack with rotting wood. Trifold flyers with 'Explore historic Chizur' splashed across the front sat in little plastic containers dangling off a wall. A few pictures of the town were hung up in the walls, edited to be grainy and monochrome. No one manned the desk.

"Hello," Sancus called out, rapping his knuckles against the pillar of the entryway. "Anyone in?"

A clatter sounded beside me. On impulse, I reached for my knife and my head snapped around.

There was a young woman there. She had been so quiet, blending almost mutely into the background without my notice, which was quite a rare occurrence. She gave me the distinct impression of someone who would become an accessory to someone else's life, fading easily into sepia toned wallpaper as if she belonged nowhere else.

There was a book on the ground, an atlas with a crimson cover. I bent over to pick it up. A sturdy, blue worker's hand reached over to pick it up as well. "Thank you," said the girl as I handed the book to her completely.

I looked to the bearer of the hand. "No proble—" the word fell limp on my tongue. "—em."

My throat tasted like sand.

Though I knew we held no relation, she was the spitting image of my mother on her wedding day. She had a round face, with a pointed chin, almost delicate looking. Her brows were straight and her nose had a little ridge right where glasses would rest. She had full lips that were enclosed by smile lines worn into her jaw. Her hooded eyes were rimmed dark with heavy lashes. If she were fair instead of dark, I wouldn't be able to tell a difference.

The girl cocked her head to the side. "Is something wrong?" she inquired pleasantly.

"No," I choked out. "You just look awfully familiar."

She smiled. "I get that a lot. Just one of those faces."

Sancus nudged me. His eyes indicated *Dude, you're being weird.* He was right, but I couldn't push past the mysterious specter that haunted me, a reminder of all my shortcomings, the *one* person I had yet to get justice for.

"Sorry, my friend here is a moron. Can you help us?" Sancus asked.

She chuckled good naturedly. "What is it you need?" Her voice resembled stones tumbling atop one another.

"We're looking for Concord Kemran. He moved here three years ago."

She looked down at her computer and began to type. "He's our foster mom's brother. She died recently and we want to give him what she left to him," Sancus lied easily. Sancus made everything look easy.

Her blue skin matched the color of the screen she squinted at. "Ah, yes, I know him. He only comes into town for food."

My eyes wandered around the room.

A shut in. Those were the easiest people to off: The ones who weren't expected, the ones with no connections, the ones who could just disappear. No one would miss him.

I heard a piece of paper rustle and the scratch of a pen. Her body was hunched over, dark hair obscuring her movement. Her eyesight must have been horrible to require that close of a look. She stood back to full height and extended the paper in hand.

Sancus took it and looked it over.

"I marked where we are and where he is," she said. "It's not to scale, but keep traveling west."

I nodded. "Thank you," I articulated, looking at her fully.

Mom, I thought. *Mom, I'm almost there. Just two more.* I wished, briefly, that I could tell that to my real mom, the one whose brain matter stained the floor of our home.

Her lips turned down and her eyebrows knit together. "Why do you say it like that?" she asked.

My body seized. There had been a crack in my armor. I was getting sloppy.

I forced myself to slump and said, "Thank you for your time," with a fake smile. I left without answering her question.

Sancus followed me out. We walked west.

The weather outside that day was foggy, dimming light and watering our lungs. My eyelids fluttered, getting harder and harder to keep open as we trudged along.

As we crossed outside the town borders, we began to peel back the outer layers of our clothes, leaving behind only the black underthings and our utility belts.

Utility belts were commonly filled with money, precious objects, and communication devices. Ours were filled with weapons and a cyanide tablet.

"What exactly are we looking for?" Sancus asked. "Will it be a murder mansion like the first time?"

I shook my head. "I don't know. I couldn't dig up much about this guy. Only the town of residency." It wasn't my fault that he was an outcast.

Still, it was an uneasy wandering, keeping eyes out ahead, as well as to the side. I was glad for Sancus being there, in that unfamiliar environment, the sounds of all kind of unintroduced things sending shivers down my spine.

"Sancus?" I asked as my foot sank into the ground. I pulled it out with a squelch.

My sneakers weren't waterproof. I had forgone the black boots that were a part of the uniform, replacing them with the worn red sneakers I had before I joined the North Wind. When I thought about it, I realized I was probably trying to hold on to a piece of who I was before the mess I was in.

He hummed from behind me. I heard his footstep lightly compress on a rock with a tap, avoiding where my own foot had sunk into the ground.

"What do you think it means to be a good person?" Over the hundreds of times we had been alone, I never had the inclination to ask him that question. But in that moment, the desire sat stagnant in the air.

A breathy chuckle came from behind me and I could vividly imagine him raising his left brow and giving a crooked smile as he said, "I think the meaning is different for everyone. To me, it's helping as many people as I can. To another, it's about making a life for their kid."

I hummed. I should have known he wouldn't give a straightforward answer. He was never good at that.

Piercing through the fog was a dim burst of muted yellow: Light. I pivoted and headed for it, believing it must be the house of Concord, the hermit. Ice rushed through me, hardening.

That ice blinded me to what was really present. I knew that, but my muscles tensing, my blood thrumming, and my heartbeat rushing always made me *feel* unbeatable.

I needed to feel that way. I craved it like an addict craves heroin. Nothing could beat the high that came with knowing I was one step closer to my goal.

As we drew closer, the lines that contained that light became more distinctive. Rotting wood, turned gray from the moisture exposure, was held in place a shaking sheet roof. The windows were cracking around the edges, white putty peeling from its place of binding. If there had been any wind, I was almost certain the place would have blown over.

"And you?" I heard suddenly.

I didn't look to Sancus. I was too busy looking in front of us, looking for any exits more than just the door and the two windows. It looked too small for another door, but maybe a window on the backside.

"What do you think makes someone a good person?"

Humans are imperfect. Years ago, I told Belig that people do horrible things at the expense of others to numb the pain of existing. They cheat those called friends and lie to those they claim to love. Everyone is capable of atrocities. That's why 'being human' is used to excuse making mistakes. Our existence is the ultimate sin. *I am the ultimate sin.*

"In all honesty," I said lowly, "I don't really believe there are good people."

I still couldn't look at him. If I did, I would tell him he was the exception. He has always been the exception.

There was a beat of silence. "You're a massive buzz kill."

With all the seriousness gone, I could bring myself to look at him. "Had to go out the way I came in, right?"

Sancus nodded at me. "Yeah," he mumbled. He was smiling, but I had never seen a more heartbroken face, the worry lines so fine they seemed painted.

I don't remember what I thought, when I saw him looking at me like that, but I remember the feeling: Longing, wanting to say something to him that I didn't quite know how to. Him, trying to find the words he wanted to say back. We were both at a loss, grasping for the right sounds. We ended up looking away without saying a thing.

Sancus and I walked into the hut's opening with our shoulders hunched and our guards up. It was a one-room shack, with a fire to keep it warm. Silhouetted against that warm, enticing fire, was a figure in a rocking chair, looking into the burning embers.

Concord was not the same as his identification photo, at first glance. He was gaunter, with deep inset eyes and wrinkled skin. His hair and nails had grown long from poor maintenance and his skin had gone pale from lack of sunlight. I wondered how often he left this foggy marsh.

I clutched my knife tighter. "Concord," I projected, loud enough to be heard inside the wooden house. "Concord of the Rabum Giru." I didn't need to be very loud; my voice carried across the soporific air like it was meant to take up space.

His chair rocked forward and creaked softly. It sat on a fluffy rug and had a meager pillow under his bottom to provide cushioning.

The entire room seemed like it was on the verge of poverty: a stained twin mattress had only one ratty and torn blanket; an iron furnace with one plate and food crusted bowl and a few sparse utensils; plenty of cans, unopened and empty, alike, piled up high in the corner of the room. How anyone could live like that baffled me.

His voice sounded like the voice of Charon, the partitioner of death. It bore no malice, but sent chills up my spine all the same. From the corner of my eye, I watched Sancus recoil at the sound as he said, "I am Concord, no longer of the Rabum Giru."

I raised my free hand to my left eye and plucked out the contact in it. I flicked it on the floor. I didn't need it any more. I plucked the other one from my right eye and did the same. I pulled down the mask that covered the lower half of my face, too.

Cautiously, I crept into Concord's view. He made no movement, showed no signs that he noticed me. His pale brown hair was faded, like a puzzle left too long in the sun. I was careful to stay out of arm's reach, but my skin did not crawl to alert me of oncoming danger.

"Do you know who I am?" I asked, tilting my chin up. I wanted to look down on this man, even if for a moment.

My eyes darted to Sancus and I watched him slip on a set of brass knuckles. *Just in case,* the action said. His focus was trained on Concord, watching for the slightest movement.

Concord's eyes looked up to me, then his face tilted slowly to join them. "You're one of the Psoe Nepsul," he said. "But you don't look like them."

He was referring to my dyed hair and skin. "No, you look different," he mused, slowly, "but you have those eyes—eyes like liquid gold and sun-drenched honey." He spoke beautiful words, for a man who committed genocide. He spoke like he revered me, like there was beauty in the destruction.

"I've come to kill you," I informed him, "but I need information first." I clenched my blade tightly in my hand. Torture was something I had only done once, long ago, back when I was still a kid.

It only worked on certain people. What would I do if it didn't work on Concord?

"Tell me where I can find Ammuru," I ordered, my voice calm and steady. *Show no fear. Show no emotion. Do not let him find a crack in the armor.*

Concord laughed, a sad, wheezing sound. "He's waiting for you. The one in black. The Young Prince of the Eternal Flame. He told me you would ask where he was."

Ammuru knew of me; I was going into the final stretch with a handicap. It didn't matter. I was so close to the end. At this point, I was desperate. I wanted so badly for everything to conclude, to finally let my people be at peace, to wash my hands of the blood.

Concord looked back to the fire. "Forty-six point six-two-four-two degrees North. Eight point zero-four-one-four degrees East. You can find him there."

I looked at Sancus. His eyes were wide as mine felt.

"Why would you tell me that?" I asked. *Why are you so eager to sell out a comrade?*

There was a beat of silence, too short to be filled with thought, too long to be an accident. "All of us are chased by shadows of what we've done." His fingers were bony enough the knuckle showed as he scratched at the wood of the chair. "My shadows have caught me."

I put my knife away. Instead, I pulled out a glass syringe with a thin metal rod coming from the end.

I swallowed hard. I didn't feel like a frigid wasteland now. I didn't feel spirals of ice turning to weaponized shards in me. I felt more like a junkyard, rusting in the rain, weary and creaking.

Concord wasn't fighting me. I couldn't give him the harsh death I had given all the others, even if I knew his docile nature didn't make amends for his past.

My skin crawled and my muscles twitched like something was waiting to pounce on me. It tingled across my stomach and itched at my phalanges. Looking at this wretch of a human gave me nothing but disgusting pity, creeping under my nailbeds and along my throat.

My stomach sank. He looked at me the same way I looked at him.

I was tired of the monotony. There was no veritable impact in what I was doing, beyond keeping the promise I made. I just wanted it over.

I called myself for a god, took her name as my own, as if I carried all her divine purpose in my spirit. What was the end goal, really? None of these lives could bring my Jace back to me. What was that divine rationale I had yet to grasp within my hand? The worst part was that I'd never know. I just had to carry on, until the very end, hoping that I could catch a glimpse of the cosmic scripture that I had never learned to read.

"Any last words?" I asked, pushing aside my guilty mind. I had no reason to feel that way. Concord was the guilty party.

His eyes slipped shut and an upward tilt formed on his lips, in the corners of his eyes. In his final moments, even as I took away Concord's future, he found happiness.

The cold core inside me condensed.

"Yes," he hummed, mulling over his thoughts. "I think I shall say sorry."

My breath caught. I tightened my fist more around the syringe, as I leaned down. I sunk the needle into his skin, right on the top of his hand over the tendon on his left hand that led straight to a vein.

"Sorry?" I asked, betraying no tone. I glanced at Sancus. He looked as confused as I felt. I swallowed. "What are you sorry for?"

Concord opened his eyes slowly, lazily. "For causing you so much pain that you became this."

Arctic fury surged in my body, electrocuting my nerves.

I had learned anger didn't begin alone; I was experienced enough now to understand that. The anger I felt for the demise of my tribe and my family was from grief. The anger I felt from working a case was frustration at the selfish acts that brought the North Wind into being. The anger I felt because of Concord grew from a seed of guilt, endowed with disgust and sorrow at how I had let myself be a monster so that I could keep a promise to people who were no longer alive.

No one could even benefit from that any more.

Stolife vem yujat. *Pity those who remain.*

After a long stretch of silence, I finally said, "I appreciate that."

Concord stared at me, his eyes wet with an emotion I wasn't familiar with, didn't know. When his eyes closed, that emotion was lost to me forever.

"I'm ready," he said.

My mouth felt dry. I looked down to my hand, clasping his wrist. I pressed the plunger, watched as the barrel's space closest to the hub became a fraction smaller. A fraction was all that was needed.

There was no blood.

I stood to full height and dropped the plunger to the floor. I stepped on it with the heel of my sneaker. The glass shattered with a soft crunch. The shards glimmered in the light of the dancing flames.

Glass had a special meaning to me, one of longing and regret and hatred. I think glass represented everything that was taken from me. My tribe's ability as glaziers was prized so highly, I often thought that jealousy was what may have brought about their downfall.

There was something haunting about the way that glass on the floor sparkled, almost like it was laughing at me, asking, after all this time, what had I to show? It laughed because, for all my efforts, my family was still a pile of decaying bones. The glass they had made was still there, outliving its creator, laughing because it was one of the most fragile things, but it still managed to outlive an entire tribe.

Not for the first time, I wanted to yell at the Sun God. I wanted to scream at her. I wanted to ask how she could abandon us. I wanted to tell her that a mother should never tire of her children. I wanted to tell her she was cruel.

When Concord's cardiac arrest ended, I didn't have the energy to cut up him up like everyone else. Why bother? No one would find him here anyway.

"Let's go," I said to Sancus, my eyes not leaving my feet. I didn't just say "let's go" because I wanted to leave. I said let's go because I didn't want to stay. "I can't be in this hell-hole anymore."

We left the creaking marsh shack, walking along the safest pathway, the one with hard looking soil that wouldn't sink beneath our feet. The land slowly became more open, less moist, less hazardous. Away from the marsh and into a foggy temperate forest zone, I found myself calming rapidly.

As Sancus and I trudged along the mossy riverbank, I couldn't help but feel sad. Concord was not like Abran. He took no pleasure in what he had done.

Something about the way he didn't even fight us made my stomach tie in knots and my saliva sour.

"What do you think he meant by that?" Sancus asked. He didn't seem to know what to do with his arms. They hung limp, then touched themselves under his ribs, then clasped.

My shadows have caught me.

"I wish I knew," I admitted.

"Does it get easier?" he asked. "Hurting people with motive instead of…" he trailed off. His voice was not its normal mellow. It was shaky and unsure. *Instead of killing under orders.*

"I wouldn't know." I shrugged. "It never did for me." It seemed to get harder every time, the weight of another life pressing down on me, like gold pulling me down into the depths of the sea.

I hoped it did get easier, eventually.

"You don't have to help me anymore," I informed him.

I stopped walking and he stopped with me.

I searched his face. I thought that it may be the last time I ever got to see it. I looked at the subtle brilliance of his soft smile, the strength of the harsh slope of his nose and the splattering of constellations that spread across it and spilled onto his cheeks, and I drank in the weightless gravity of his warm chocolate eyes.

Eventually, I stopped seeing those things. All I saw was him, Sancus, my brother, my home.

That day, I didn't push away the smile. "Thank you, Sancus… For everything."

He pressed his lips together and nodded resolutely. "So, this is goodbye, then?"

I nodded once. He looked away from me to the east. His tongue darted out to wet his lips and he bounced on his toes. "It doesn't have to be," he rushed. Then he said, "You can still walk away and live for yourself," so quietly it almost escaped my recognition.

I could go back, but I was tired of giving my existence to a cause only for the resources it provided me. I was about to tell Sancus as such, but I realized that he didn't need to know.

I shrugged and shook my head. "Life wasn't meant to be lived for oneself," I stated simply. My life hadn't been my own since the day I was born. I may not believe in gods, but I did believe in fate. I was always meant to be here, to end up like this, to do these things. I was meant to be here because of nature and nurture and the culmination of the record of my life.

Sancus shot me a look with a raised eyebrow and a crooked smile. "All right, Ma'at. Whatever you say. I can't combat stubbornness." His speech was sarcastic and teasing and *Sancus*.

I balled my right hand into a fist and punched his arm lightly. He winced and pretended it hurt, dramatizing the event.

"I'm not stubborn," I argued.

"You're in a catch-22 if you argue with me." He was right.

"Ainsley," I corrected, just as Sancus turned to leave. If I didn't tell him now, I'd never get to. "My name is Ainsley."

I watched Sancus as he twitched in surprise. He turned around to face me. I tried to stain him into my memory again, even his wild hair with the bad dye job... Goodbyes were hard.

He surprised me when he smirked. "I remembered."

I felt my chest tighten. We had met when we were just fifteen and sixteen. It had been six and a half years and he remembered me. Not just my story, not just the sandwich we shared, but my real name.

"Mine is An'Gonye."

An'Gonye. It felt familiar as I reiterated it in my mind. But a question probed at me. "How could you tell I had forgotten?"

"Come on, dude," he said with a shrug. "You're my best friend. And your long-term memory is twice as fallible as your decision-making process."

My face heated.

I didn't deserve An'Gonye. I never did, not once in all our time together.

"Take care of yourself, An'Gonye," I tried. "You and Xbalanque can always depend on me. I'll come running."

He started a backward walk, bouncing slightly on each leg before hopping on the other. "Even if they try to kill you for it?" An'Gonye asked. He was joking, but I heard the change in pitch, the worry hidden in his question.

You made me remember what it meant to care for others, I wanted to say. *I'd come running to you no matter what the consequence.* Instead, I responded, "Even then."

He grinned, brilliantly. I tried, for the third time, for the last time, to remember An'Gonye as he was then. I desperately willed my brain to stain him into my memory so that I didn't have to say goodbye, so that I could keep a little imprint of him with me.

"Let's not try it, dude." He turned and walked off.

It's a weird thing to see the last string of your life being cut before your eyes. Seeing as the scissors rise up to sever the thread, watching it blow away on a breeze, out of sight forever.

I knew I would think of him every day. I was a work of art, a picture comprised of all of the varying hues the people I knew splashed on my canvas. I couldn't just say goodbye to any of those hues, not easily.

It was hard to do nothing and watch Sancus leave, as I clung desperately to the mantra *life wasn't meant to be lived selfishly.*

April 17, 2729

Ammuru

Ammuru was the last person I had to scratch off my list. There was no official record of him in any of my preliminary searches. He was a ghost. But Concord had told me where to find him. 46.6242° North, 8.0414° East.

Things seemed to be coming to a close.

Concord had been so ready, not only to give up his own life, but also the life of his comrade. Maybe he just wanted a quick death. If it had been to ensure a lack of suffering, Concord had sold out his teammate in vain; I had had no bullets to offer.

If it were for atonement, his action would not absolve him. The crimson that stained his nail beds and the stones he carried still drenched his soul in hot, sticky tar. His burden of guilt would cling to his core, even in death, just as my own guilt clung to me.

I knew, without bias, I was no different from these assassins. They had killed for a living, as a means to make ends meet. That, in honesty, was more noble than my pursuit of justice for the dead. Killing would bring the Rabum Giru wages, but my killing would never be able to bring back the dead.

Years ago, the twelve asked if I was certain I did not long for revenge. At the time, blindingly certain, I had answered yes. Now, with many more years and many of those who I had killed permanently residing in the frenzied enclave of my mind, I had a new answer that pierced through the fog: I did not believe there was a difference.

Justice could be revenge and revenge could be justice. The two were entwined as lovers, dancing a macabre waltz.

I tugged the map from my backpack. I had kept that bag all those years. It was worn and tattered and I didn't use it much after I got the standard issue bags from the North Wind. But it was the bag I had used when I first left my region. It had less now, only some water, dried jerky, bandages, and a bronze key with an address dangling off its chain.

I inhaled, deep and slow, twisting the band around my wrist. The air smelled different here. It smelled like a river after fresh snow. It wasn't a bad smell.

I wasn't naive. I knew that the leader of the Rabum Giru must have been more capable than all of the others, whom I had barely survived. I knew it was unlikely I would survive this fight with no aide.

My fingers traced my forearm. The bandages felt sticky and heavy. I pinched the fabric and pulled, watching as the beige cloth unraveled.

I had washed the dye from my hair and scrubbed the tan from my skin with acetone. I had taken out the contacts, too. I think I was being sentimental. Maybe this felt like the end and some part of me didn't want to pretend to be someone else.

The building was an old castle, pressed up into the side of a hill. It looked almost quaint in the early morning, like it was a home of an old widow. Ivy writhed its way through the gaps in the stone and made a mosaic of basil and coin. The sloped roof was a dusty sort of brown, made with little arches to hold it up. Stained glass windows made their home in every inlaid opening.

There was no finesse to my entry. I didn't need it any more. I pressed my hand to the flat of the large oak door, with black, cast-iron bellflowers making their home atop the paneling. The wood was warm. The iron was like me: Cold.

And I could already *feel* the cold coming out of me, different in a way I wasn't able to articulate.

As I pushed open the door, the instantaneous freezing of my core never came. This time, it came upon me slowly, dryly. There was no ice in the cold. It was just a cold. The kind of cold that befell a desert.

The doors were unlocked.

They revealed to a castle of whites and browns. Pillars with ridges lined the walls, dyed a litany of colors by the stained glass casting the beams of light onto them. I was walking through a kaleidoscope of unfinished affairs, an unerring monument to what could have been.

There was no sign of life inside.

A bit of sweat traced the line of my spine. My fingers found their way to the collapsible bo staff on my belt. It seemed too heavy in my hands to pick up, so I let my hand rest there, unmoving.

My breaths came in puffs behind my black mask, hitting my lips and tickling my eyelashes. My core crawled like a serpent, slithering under my skin until the air around me crackled with the stillness of an abandoned Arctic.

It didn't matter to me that the building seemed all too empty. I only needed one person to be here.

I walked across the red carpet that moseyed beneath high stretching ceilings lit by hanging glass chandeliers, checking every dark wood door I found on my way. I climbed wide steps that spiraled into a tower with open windows in which a heady morning chill breezed through, smelling of that same melted snow from before. My skin burst out in a rash of goosebumps.

I followed the hallway out to the second floor, decorated much like the first: A deep red trail carpet leading to brown doors, with hanging chandeliers on the ceiling between the white wedged pillars.

I recognized those chandeliers. There was no mistaking the barrage of razor thin shards that cast light without candles. My throat tightened.

I came to the last room on the floor before I would have to climb the stairs. Back when we had monarchs, this could have been a throne room. The huge doors matched those that lead into the castle, down to the ornate ivy casting.

I held my palm out, but stopped before I touched it. What would I do if this castle were empty?

I took a deep breath and shut my eyes. Ilch ej. *For them.* If this keep was empty, I would keep searching, just as I always had. I pushed my hand forward; the door gave away with a creaking sound.

The room was open, only sparsely held up by four large white marble pillars. They were wrapped in green, living ivy, barely in bloom in the fresh spring. There were no rugs on pristine white marble tile floors. There were no chairs, but there was a set of steps leading to where the throne would sit, at the furthest end of the room for me. There was no wall on that side of the room. It was a missing piece, giving view of a lake below, with clear depths and murky rock covered shores. A figure stood overlooking the view.

It was not who I had expected to see.

My jaw dropped and my head swam. "Xenon?" I asked.

His face was clean-shaven and his hair had been cut since the last time I saw him. Something else was off, too. He didn't look surprised I was here.

You said you never wanted to see me again. My throat swelled.

All the tension leaving my body deluded me into thinking that everything was okay. I was grateful to see him, standing there, truly believing *I no longer have to do this alone.*

When we said goodbye, I thought about the house with the teal color door and how I wanted to live in a place like that with him and stop some wayward kids from making the same mistakes Sancus and I had. That dream had slipped from my grasp. Now, I saw it before me again, a sliver of possibility.

For a delicate moment, I forgot about Ammuru and ran to him. My body slammed into his and knocked the breath out of both of us. I pulled him down to my lips, hoping that even a drop of what I was feeling could push through our contact. He kissed me like he was trying for the same thing.

"I'm done," I told him as I pulled back. My voice was shaky and my thoughts were frazzled, jumping from concept to concept without being able to formulate properly. "I just have one more."

I was here. He was here. This was my chance for a happy ending. I had this chance to be selfish. I was going to be selfish.

His face was pained. He opened his mouth, probably to tell me something I didn't want to hear.

My hands found his own. "Just help me with the last one. Then—then we can run away. Just like you wanted, we could run away." I was, clawing at the idea of starting over because I hadn't realized how much I didn't want to be alone.

Xenon closed his eyes and his head fell to the floor. The air seemed still. Even his ocean scent was muted and off, like tides that had been trapped in a bay for too long.

His Adam's apple moved up and down. "Ainsley, stop." He pulled his hands from my own; the air felt warm in their stead.

Disappointment settled in me like a weight.

"I thought," I stuttered, "I thought that's what you wanted." I thought he loved me. He had said he did. I thought he would go to the ends of the earth for me. He had told me that he would, once.

I could love you, I thought, trying to justify to myself why I deserved his devotion, *I could learn how.*

The teal door fell further and further away from my outstretched fingers.

Xenon took a step back, pulling his cold with him, and opened his eyes.

They were grey, like a light charcoal dust.

A nauseous feeling settled in the pit of my stomach. Those were not the eyes of the man I knew, but they were sickeningly familiar.

"Ainsley, I love you so much," he told me. "I never once stopped. Not after all this time."

A memory burst into my mind, filling up the cracks like water from a dam. "Stop," I ordered. I didn't know if I was telling him or the memory.

The memory of a pulse shattering fear gripping at my core, the feeling of blood pushing against my skin, the feeling of never having enough air. The memory of hiding behind a barrel and looking out of a crack at the man in white and a boy in black with charcoal, dust-colored eyes.

I fought to keep the bile in my stomach, to keep the vertigo from my head.

"I'm not only Xenon. I'm not even just Xenon and Iktomi."

My heart shattered, falling away infinitesimal shards, into the dark recesses of me. Sick overtook me because I must've known, I *should* have known.

"Please," I whispered, my hand already falling to my utility belt. Please, stop. Please, don't say anything more. *Please, don't tell me it's what I'm thinking.*

I didn't really need to hear the words pierce through the air to know they were coming. "I also don the title Ammuru."

I had always considered myself adaptable, but my mind could not adapt fast enough to the new reality I found myself in. No coherent thoughts registered.

What I could register was pain. Not the kind of pain that happened because of injury, but the kind that was intense and overwhelming and made a slow fog obscure the world.

Humans always use metaphors to describe pain. 'It was like a thousand wasp stings' or 'my chest felt like fire raced through it'. The reason for that was apparent to me in that instant. No word I knew could adequately describe the insurmountable sensation of betrayal.

My fingers clenched around the handle of a senbon and I flung it at him. He parried easily, forlornly, like it was a chore and it bored him.

I grabbed for his collar and he shoved his fingers into the juncture of my clavicle. I gasped for air. That was a dirty trick. I taught him that.

My fingers loosened around his shirt and he shoved with an open palm to my sternum. I blinked for a moment and felt searing pain in my left calf.

When I opened my eyes, I reached down and drew out the blade that had made its home in my muscle. My eyes didn't leave his.

"How," I croaked. *How did I not know? How could you lie to me all this time? How could you do this for a living? How could you do this to me? How can I still not hate you for it?* "How could you!" I screamed.

I lunged for him, feeling the ice freeze over inside me once more.

No thoughts ran through my mind, just red. Just crimson staining my vision as I bashed my knuckles against his jaw. No thoughts, just clenched teeth as he kneed my stomach and threw me to the ground. No thoughts, just excruciating pain filling my veins and ripping a hole in my tendons with a serrated blade as I pulled him to the ground and rolled on top of him.

I grabbed the collar of his jacket and pulled my scimitar from my thigh. "Was it all a lie?" I swung down erratically at his head. He moved his chin to the left, dodging where my blade fell by just a hair's width. "Did you have fun using me? Deluding me into thinking that you cared just so you could get close enough?"

We fought brutally, like animals, with neither skill nor technique, only the pure desire to kill.

His fingers went up to grab and pressure my inner bicep. I gasped as his thumb entered the space between my muscle and my bone. My fingers unclenched uncontrollably and my body relaxed and he bucked me from atop him.

I scrambled to my feet and withdrew my staff as Xenon's hands found the handle of my scimitar. He swung it toward the junction of my clavicle and shoulder. I stopped its track with the metal core of my staff. "I bet you were even planning on killing me, weren't you?" I asked through clenched teeth. Before I could extend the weapon, he landed a kick to my sternum that sent me flying back.

My hands unclenched and I heard a metallic *clink* as the weapon hit the ground and my back collided with a pillar. A cracking sound broke from beneath my skin and the air was ripped from my lungs.

"And what about you?" he yelled back, finally responding. "You used me. For years you used me. You thought I couldn't tell, but I knew!"

I ignored the stomach-clenching desire to assure him otherwise. I couldn't assure him; I'd be lying.

I sucked in a sharp breath.

Fights are almost always over in an instant. I'd never won in a fight against Xenon, not when he was really trying. He was angry; I had never fought him when he was angry. There was a very real probability I would lose. As my esophagus clenched around nothing, the looming prospect of failure grated the walls of my gut.

Meriv tke kareic zi'ir jjoiav. *I don't have that option.*

The ground burned the palms of my hands as they pounded against it. My knees ached from the fall.

Black dots encroached upon my vision.

"I could tell I was just another tool in your arsenal." His shattered voice, once so smooth and charismatic, came, "You were too dead to feel anything for me." He was crying, a single wet tract silently making its way down the crest of his cheek. I could have mistaken them for sweat if I didn't know better.

"You died the same day your brother did."

Red and black swarmed the corners of my vision and the cracking ice deafened the rest of the room.

My fingers clenched against nothing. I scrambled to my feet and wrapped my arms around his waist to force him back with as much bodyweight as I could.

I didn't owe him a response, nor a justification for his tears. He knew what he was signing up for when he chose me. His pain was not my responsibility.

Xenon stumbled and we fell to the ground. I heard another clang as my scimitar was dislodged from his grasp. He wrapped his legs around my waist and shifted his weight so I was thrown to the floor with him on top. It was his turn for his hand to hit my jaw. "You don't know anything about my motivations," he hissed as his fist broke through my skin.

My teeth clacked painfully and my brain rattled in my skull. I planted my feet and thrust my hips up. He was dislodged from his position in an instant.

I can win, I thought. *If I don't succeed, I'm not trying hard enough.*

I gripped for the front of his shirt and pulled his torso down and brought my knee up between his legs. An "oof" breezed past my ear.

I shifted my weight and rolled us over. I could hear my breath louder than a jet engine as we both scrambled to right ourselves.

I dug my feet into the ground and pushed up, angling a hook at his jaw.

Just one blow. One blow and I could stab him with the knife my fingers wrapped around.

He dodged. Because, of *course,* he did. He was perfect. He never got caught off guard. I was always going to lose this fight.

I saw Xenon's own knife making a path for my throat. My eyes locked on it, helpless to stop the path it was taking.

Then his right foot scuffed backward against the stone floor and the knife missed.

I blinked.

Then my body was moving. My right foot found its way between his feet and my right forearm thrust into his collarbone, careful to avoid slicing him with my knife's edge. I wasn't ready to kill him yet. I was still angry.

I grabbed ahold of his right arm and pressed down in the forearm at the junction between his triceps and bicep met, my thumb digging straight through to the bundle of nerves there. Xenon dropped his knife.

I pulled back with my right foot and hooked his left shin. We fell to the ground. Xenon let out a breathy hack when his back slammed into the floor.

I threw my knife back into my belt and pulled my elbow up, balling my hand into a fist. My left hand gripped his collar so tightly that my nails pierced my palm through the fabric.

My knuckles split the skin over his cheek bone, leaving a mixture of our blood in its path.

"Then explain," I said with a punch that cracked against skin for a second time. "Explain so that I understand. Explain how you lied to me for months when we met." Crack. "Explain how you told me enough about your past that I thought I knew you, but neglected to tell me that you killed my family." Crack. "Explain how you had chance and chance again to be honest with me, but weren't." Crack!

My right hand found the smooth lacquer handle of my knife, a sliver of dark metal that had taken the lives of so many. My fingers gripped the hilt so tightly that the uneven decorations on its surface drew blood on my palm. I ripped it out of its holster and thrust it down toward his chest, slightly left of center.

I stopped. A millimeter away from his skin, I stopped.

Xenon wasn't looking at me with the markings of anger. His eyes were crinkled like there were more secrets he held, but to speak them would break something tender. He whispered, barely a breath, "I would have lived for you."

"How can I believe that?" I forced out, barely vicious through my panting. *How can I believe* you?

A thin bead of moisture made its way down my neck. I didn't know it was blood until I felt the pinprick of a blade at my throat. Even now, after all this time, after all the effort I had put in, he was better than me.

My own knife was held above his heart. It would be a slow kill, but inescapable. It was the only place I could hurt him physically that may represent a little of the hurt he caused me.

Xenon was breathing heavily, but it wasn't fear.

I was breathing heavily, too. I felt worn and I wanted to collapse here, but I had to outlast him. The one to collapse last would survive. I owed it to my family to be the survivor.

Our gazes locked and his steely eyes matched mine. They were dark grey. And now it made sense. The blue eyes I had come to know were a farce. These were the eyes I had met from behind the barrel. These were the eyes that belonged to a man who took everything I loved and left me alone. He made my world a fantastic hell of solitude.

His lips twitched. They pulled up in a smile. A tragic smile that made my stomach lurch with discomfort.

"What?" I demanded harshly. My wet neck reminded me to maintain my composure.

"In my world, if you get attached, you end up dead," Xenon said, his eyes searching my face for an answer that wasn't there. "I should never have gotten attached to you, Ainsley."

I made sure to keep my face steady and cold. *Resolve will end this.* I said nothing. I didn't know what to say to someone who had made nearly seven years of my life hell.

I heard a clatter. My eyes darted to the noise, briefly. The knife that was once held to my neck had fallen to the right side of his body. Its ivory handle was sticky with my blood. I moved my eyes back to meet his.

There was no schooling my expressions any more, there hadn't been since the moment I saw him. I felt shock, and I was sure that it showed, plain as day, on my face.

The hand that once held the blade was at my face in an instant, smearing my own blood from my busted skin on my cheek. I flinched, but did nothing to remove his hand.

Why wasn't he hurting me?

"I can't," Xenon said, as if he had read my thoughts.

One of the greatest talents I had was the ability to read a person through their eyes. The crinkle, darting, even the amount of light in them could tell me everything I needed to know about a person's honesty. I had never been able to tell with Xenon. His eyes were a wall that I couldn't see through and it had always bothered me. Now, the wall had become glass. I saw, for the first time, he was being honest.

I clenched my jaw and tightened my grip on my own blade. "I want to know when."

He chuckled deeply, the same silken voice returning, without being cut through by anger. It pulled at my chest painfully. "When what? You need to be more specific." He had always had a snarky streak.

"Don't screw with me," I whispered, too drained to be biting. "When did you realize it was me?" *When did you realize I was the kid who you took everything from?* My lower lip felt cold. My left cheek felt warm.

The rough sinews of his palm on my arm made my stomach queasy. I didn't want him to touch me. Xenon was a murderer.

I'm a murderer now, too, I thought. That was why I didn't pull away; because evil thrives upon itself. I thrived on his venom, even after everything.

His smile didn't leave his face once. "Not many people have white hair and gold eyes," he said, as if that explained everything. It explained enough; he knew from the minute he saw me.

His thumb made a light etch across my skin. He wasn't scared. It went against every rule of survival that we had been taught. It was stupid, it was naïve… it was human.

Xenon's pupils were shaking. "I lo—" he said, absentmindedly. Streams of blood from the cuts I had left on his face were diluted with sweat.

Don't say it, I pleaded silently. *Please, anything but that.*

"That day I found you in the cliffs. I was there to kill you. I thought it would save me some trouble if you *fell* from the bluff." His eyes returned to my own. "When I saw you, I couldn't. You were searching the horizon, looking through the world instead of at it."

I didn't say anything. Silence stretched and my pulse thundered.

"I don't know what it was, but I couldn't," he repeated.

I was glad he hadn't said the three words I thought he would. "But I couldn't," was so much better.

My face was damp, a new kind of wet that wasn't sweat or blood. When water fell on Xenon's nose, I knew it was tears. Tears because I had to kill him to keep my promise, but some part of me *still* wanted him alive.

Jace, I steeled myself. *Remember Xenon gave the orders that took your baby brother away. He took away Jace and mom and dad and* everyone.

"A while ago—You owe me a favor. I'm calling it in… Before you do what you need to."

"What?" I demanded.

Xenon closed his eyes. He looked peaceful. "Stay with me until the end. I don't want to die alone."

Murderers shouldn't feel pain. They shouldn't feel longing. They shouldn't feel sorrow. I felt all of these. Perhaps I was not cut out to be the person I had so carefully turned myself into.

"Of course."

I leaned my weight into my right hand and pushed the blade in. It made a squelching sound when it got into the lung, and it made a little pop when it entered the heart. A wheeze of air left his chest. And his hand fell from my arm to cover my own on the blade. His hand was still cold.

Xenon had roughly two and a half minutes to live, less of consciousness.

His body went limp. I rolled off of the top of him to my right as gently as I could, without placing any more pressure on the blade. His hand still gripped mine, and it was difficult for me to pull his head into my lap only using my left arm. He grunted a little at the shift in weight. "I'm sorry," I apologized when the sound came out.

He chuckled again, this time with a hoarse throat. "Strange." He looked through me, seeing something the living could not.

"You're supposed to be dying, not talking," I retorted.

His hand was shaky in mine and growing colder by the second. Its grip was tight, so tight it hurt. I made no move to withdraw my hand from that vice grip. I had taken his life; he could take my hand.

"Do you regret killing my tribe?" I asked. I hadn't needed to ask the others that.

"No," he croaked. I wanted to leave him to die alone, on the dirty floor, covered in his and my blood.

Years prior, Xenon told me he was happy with who he was now, that if anything had changed, he would be a different man. I don't think he wanted to know who that man was.

"Forgive me?" he asked, with a sad tone. His eyebrows were pinched together in pain.

My chest seized and my skull throbbed. It was hard to swallow. The tears and the blood had dried on my face. I hated every second of this waiting.

He killed Jace! I yelled at myself. *He doesn't deserve forgiveness.* I surprised myself when I replied, "Of course," my voice brittle and hollow. I was surprised it wasn't hard to forgive him.

It was silent for some time. I petted his head in the way I had done to the dog I had kept before Jace had been born. That seemed like so long ago, mere seconds compared to the current eternity.

"Do you love me?" came Xenon's shaky whisper. His hand clung tighter to mine, the nails biting into my flesh. Xenon finally looked at me. Really, looked at me. His eyes were truly an ugly color; they were the color of rainy skies and the color of regrets.

No tears came, not to him, nor to me.

I wondered what he saw when he looked at me. Were my eyes the color of grief? The color of revenge? What color were my eyes to him?

I nodded and swallowed the soreness in my throat. "Yeah, Xenon," I whispered the lie as soothingly as I could, slipping my fingers through his hair. "I did."

Looking back, I know I had lied because of the fleeting thought I had earlier: *I could have loved you.*

Xenon's face slipped into tranquility and I knew he was as good as gone. His right hand lifted slowly up toward my face and pushed some white hair from my eyes. "A mess."

Light faded from his eyes like a dried-out leaf. His lips moved one more time, a barely audible, "*Acheron.*" His head lulled and his hands fell from of my own.

Cold. Xenon was cold. With a shaking hand, I pressed my fingers into his pulse point, feeling for a beat. I waited for the rhythm to slow to a stop.

My two and a half minutes were up.

"I'm done."

I really don't know why, but I didn't close his eyes. I didn't want to believe I had killed him, take on that guilt when I had done the right thing.

Tendrils of empty unfurled. There was no more rage to cripple the silence. There was no more resolve to steady my action. There was nothing.

My life until then had been about justice. I had fulfilled my promise. There was nothing left to force my will.

I placed Xenon's head on the ground. I would leave his body here. It would his grave. I wouldn't waste my time burying someone like him.

I pushed myself to stand. Everything ached. It was a dull ache, almost numb, the kind of ache that made it hard to move.

I leaned over to pick up the knife he had held to my throat. I'd swap with him. A little trade to remember one another by. A piece of the man who fucked me over, the man I hated, the man I almost loved, the man I killed.

The body looked peaceful. It was bloodied and had a few rips in the black robes: a tear along the abdomen, the sleeve of the right arm ripped off, holes worn into the knees. The Leather belt around his waist and across his chest were all cut up and had bits of brown leather peeking through the back coating. His black hair stuck to his damp skin. His sweat made it cling to his face and neck. He had a bruise where I punched him in the jaw, along the left side.

"You can rest easy now, Mom."

I touched the lesion on my face that ran down my right cheek. *You gave me a scar.*

A twinge of a smile popped up on the corner of my mouth. The mahogany red of the blade's hilt shined when the light from the sun hit it. *That's only fair, considering my knife is in your chest.*

I rolled up my sleeve on my left arm. It had been a while since I had notched a mark in my skin. I pressed the blade into my arm, making another mark.

Sixty-six. One for my grandfather. Fifty-nine for my tribe. Three for mom, dad, and Jace. One for Gautami. One for Yonten. One for Xenon.

I was going to roll down my sleeve, but I realized one wasn't enough. I pressed the blade in again, making another mark in my scarred flesh of the arm: Sixty-seven.

I would never have my mark on someone's arm. If my purpose had been achieved, it made sense that I mark myself today with the completion of my life.

I crouched down next to Xenon's corpse. "I always hated that phrase 'if things were different.' Things aren't different. We have to make choices based on what really is and live with the consequences of those choices."

It was strangely comforting talking to a corpse. It was familiar enough I felt closure, but my words would never know judgement. His chin was stiff when I grabbed it and tilted his head to the side. "I have to live with the choice to kill you now."

He deserved my softness for what I had done, but I had never been good at being tender. "Goodbye, Xenon."

I stood and turned away from his body. How long it would take for him to become a pile of bones? Would someone find him as bones and bury him? Would they come and rob his grave?

I walked toward the large arching doors that were adorned with wooden columns of sculpted work. Bright orange lit the marble floors and the hanging jeweled lanterns like captured stardust.

I looked back to Xenon's corpse, one last time before rounding the corner. My muscles contracted with the desire to crush his skull in. I wanted to yell, *You turned me into this* at it.

Instead, I said nothing

It wasn't his fault I was a monster. I made that decision myself. I had to live with the consequence of that decision.

April 17, 2729

Xenon

I was born into something I wasn't perfectly suited for, a blacksmith living under the title of prince. I've been wrongly wearing the crown for so long, I wouldn't know what I was truly suited for; I wouldn't know how to pick up a hammer.

I was seventeen when I had my first hunt; it was less of a hunt and more of a slaughter. The people we hunted didn't know how to fight back. It was a bloodbath.

My mother had told me that if I could effectively assassinate the Psoe Nepsul, he would turn over the Rabum Giru to me. I was a child at the time and I wanted *more.* I wanted respect, but respect was hard to earn. Fear was a fine substitute. I could get that by leading the Rabum Giru.

Leave none alive, the squirrely man who hired us warned. *They are the greatest scourge upon this planet and will be our downfall.* I had thought him a crazed fanatic, a zealous relic of a dated line of thought, but following his order would earn me rank and title and I would be a fool to let my own thoughts get in the way of my work.

I took nine with me. We went in daylight. The tribe had a superstition that the daylight would always protect them, and they were less vigilant then. I ordered my men to surround the tribe and hide in the tree line.

When I gave the signal, a bird's whistle, we pounced. My men dispatched their targets. Some were more brutal with their methods than others. Yssir, in particular, loved the smell of blood, and she was unnecessarily savage when she ripped through her victims in a barrage of bullets, her face never once betraying her joy.

I stuck close to Abbadon, the most methodical with his kills.

"There are people inside this one," he had told me, gesturing to a shack. "It is a crime for the Psoe Nepsul to shade their windows unless they wish to hide something inside." He was right; a woman inside brandished a kitchen knife toward us. She was shaking, but her face was contorted with determination. Her eyes were wild with the fury of a cornered beast.

I held up my hand to Abbadon, alerting him I would take her out. She grunted and charged me, holding the knife between her fingers in a savage fashion. I twisted the left side of my body back and grabbed her wrist with my right hand. I rammed my elbow down and snapped the lower humorous. It gave off a crack; she would die from the splintered bone in minutes, the marrow invading her bloodstream, an internal poison.

I swept my foot under her left leg and she tumbled to the ground. I placed my foot on her kneecap and yanked her ankle upward. She screamed, dry and throaty. I grabbed for a pan on the counter close to me and swung it at her head repeatedly. I felt the skull crack and her body flinch. A whimper. I kept smashing until I saw red seep out and the skull collapse upon itself.

When she was good and dead, I wiped the blood from my face on my sleeve. My clothes were black; it wouldn't be noticeable. Her desperation meant that she was hiding something. I gestured to Abbadon to check the home.

When we made it into the cellar, I knew there was someone else there right away. I could feel them watching me, analyzing me. I turned my head slowly, searching for the source.

I almost missed the peek of gold shining through a crack in the wall behind one of the barrels. If the tribe had had darker eyes, normal eyes, I wouldn't have found them.

Those eyes were intense and paralyzed by fear.

I knew the rules of the match: Finish the task and collect the reward. I knew the rules of the game: leave no witnesses because it always comes back around. But I liked what I saw in those eyes too much to follow the rules, that unchecked fear felt only for me. I wanted to keep that fear locked up in my memories, to know that no matter what this person did or how much time had passed, nothing would ever erase the fear I had given.

"Let's go." We left. We collected the reward. The entire tribe was pronounced dead in a few weeks. For years, I didn't think about that flash of gold.

My mother turned over the Rabum Giru and told me that upon her death, I would have to receive special training. She died four years later of advanced liver problems, telling me to go to a forest in the middle of nowhere and hand them a bronze coin.

I disguised myself so that I would be less distinguishable. Blue contacts to cover my ashen eyes. I let my beard grow a little more. I went to the place he told me of, let them chain me up, and waited. My mind was stronger than iron; my father had seen to that in my younger years. I could withstand any form of torture, mental and physical. It was what was demanded of me, my divine task.

A small woman who looked like a fairy came to tell me that I was the only candidate remaining and that they had left me for a day longer than the runner-up. They saw that I would not cede my time and decided not to waste anyone else's.

I was told I was the best; I had the highest potential for greatness. I had already known I would best everyone; I was born for it, after all.

I was asked what I wanted most in this life by Jupiter. I smiled charmingly and lied through my teeth. *I want to feel secure in my abilities.* It was a simple lie, one that not many would catch on to. But Jupiter was not easily deceived. "You shall be Iktomi, the trickster god." Thus, I was named.

Soon, my green robes were ripped from my body and a glowing red iron was held to me. I asked to have my brand over my heart, and the iron was pressed into my flesh, a red tract of flesh rising and scaring over as the hot iron was pulled away. It was a circle, with twelve equidistant notches leading in toward the center. I was glad that the Abi Amurru and the Amurru were not branded when we turned eighteen, as others in the Rabum Giru were; I didn't much enjoy the sensation of burning flesh.

I was led to the room with the other champions. It was dark and cold, but homey at once. I surveyed the others, one in particular catching my eye. I had not seen white hair in many years. I waited until Pluto started speaking to look back to the one with white hair.

It was dark in the room, but I could see the light reflecting from the fire bouncing off golden eyes. I knew who those eyes belonged to: The child from the village was all grown up now, the golden eyes back to haunt me for breaking the rules. The delicious fear I had seen in those eyes was gone, to be replaced by steadfast determination. *Then this person is not of any use to me now,* I rationalized. I would have to finish the job I was assigned to do. I had already taken the pay for it, after all.

We were dismissed and I watched and waited. The survivor didn't run to bed instantly like the rest, but picked up a book and sat down to read.

I introduced myself. "Ma'at," the sole survivor told me.

Ma'at seemed frustrated with me at first. I retained a friendly demeanor, though I wanted to start a brawl. The kid got on my nerves. *Ma'at is no longer a child,* I reminded myself.

I followed Ma'at around the compound for the next few days, watching to see if there was any routine I could discern, any times where we would be alone and I could finish the job.

The week of rest ended and the training started. At first, we learned basic skills.

Deception was taught. Ma'at helped Xbalanque to play the system. It was incredibly naïve; the action earned my grudging respect. It took guts to risk the wrath of the evaluators for someone you barely knew. When Ma'at didn't justify those actions, only mumbled the words, "Don't forget about me," with a confident smirk.

In technical, we focused primarily on Krav Maga, Aikido, Jiu Jitsu, and Tae Kwon Do. I was at an unfair advantage. Most of these were skills assassins already learned.

I felt the satisfying numbness in my fist as it collided with Ma'at's face. I liked that feeling of power I had, knowing that I was laying an inescapable trap. Ma'at didn't seem upset, only suggesting we increase the rigor. I left my mark on Ma'at's brow. I apologized falsely, feigning incompetence. Ma'at's crooked grin lit up a fire in golden eyes; eyebrows furled in a sense of winded determination, despite the blood that dripped through white eyelashes, staining them red. "Never apologize for besting me." For some reason, my heart skipped a beat.

I struggled with pressure points. I had learned a thousand ways to kill, probably more, but I could never quite seem to attack pressure points the way Ma'at could. It made me envious that something would come so easily to someone like *that*. Then I was offered help and the envy faded. Ma'at spent hours late into the night allowing me to practice on a body that I planned to make rigid with death. I heard the grunts of pain that came from Ma'at's chest when I got something right and the controlled congratulations that followed. When I messed up, gentle hands corrected my positioning and I was asked to try again. It was intimate, me being given the power to harm with the belief that I wouldn't. For the first time since I became an assassin, I felt guilt.

Then we were assigned our first mission, an examination of how quickly we could dispatch our duties. We were teamed up with those who most closely matched our skill sets at this phase. Ma'at and I were the top of the curve.

Ma'at had tried to disappear after we got our assignment. It took me a while to follow. I checked all of the usual spots: the training facility, the library, the hall of artifacts… I finally came across Ma'at when I had given up my search. I had walked outside to get some fresh air and compose myself.

Tomorrow, I had thought to myself, I would kill Ma'at in the mission, blame it on an accident. I had gotten rather good at falsifying over the years. No one would know.

Then I saw the figure, perched atop a rock ledge that overlooked the valley. It was hard for me to look at Ma'at then. The sun shone brightly from behind, turning the body in front of me into a darkened silhouette. I knew it may be my last chance to end Ma'at's life, so I drew closer, slowly.

That was the first time that I didn't see that body tense when I stared at it from afar. Instead, Ma'at had a vacant look on that pale face, lit orange by the hue of the sky. The eyes looked off to some place far away, somewhere past the valley and beyond the reach of the human eye. No one was in that body. Ma'at was somewhere far away.

Never in my life had I seen someone look so lonely.

And instead of pushing, letting Ma'at cascade to certain death, I spoke. "I came looking," I had said as I sat down. We watched the sun set behind the horizon in silence.

Often, I've learned, there is much more that is said in silence than there is in words. In that particular silence, I learned a lot about myself. I learned that there was more to life than an endless quest for power; I learned that I was in love with the person sitting beside me.

We went on the mission, my new objective being to protect Ma'at.

We were assigned to get back the money that a high-class banker had stolen from thousands of the poor who had confided in her to invest their savings. Ma'at and I pretended to be wealthy investors, interested in purchasing real estate. We dressed nicely and paraded around a socialite party she would attend. It was at that gala that we saw Reina Vasquez. She was a well-educated and beautiful woman, a charmer of sorts. We spent a day with her, having her show us the land she owned, the land she had bought with the money she had scammed from others.

We agreed to purchase of one of the smaller lots; we were asked to come to her office and sign the papers for the trade and to sign the check. Instead, I held a blade to her neck while Ma'at questioned her for the passwords to all of her bank accounts. Reina told us the information we needed without a fight. Ma'at wired the money to a third-party bank account, to which the victimized families would cash checks for in a week's time.

But I knew people like her. As soon as we left, Reina would be on the phone with her accountants, requesting the wire be reclaimed. I snapped her neck without thinking, a bid to protect against our hard work being in vain. I realized my mistake after it was too late to reclaim. We hadn't been taught how to do that in training.

For a long time, I was happy with fear. I had loved seeing the fear in Ma'at's eyes years ago, too; it had made me feel untouchable. Seeing that fear, watching Ma'at get lost in thought, only to jump when I appeared too close, churned my stomach.

That night, I touched Ma'at's scars. I could say that I did it to provide comfort for that shell-shocked reaction, but I did it because I wanted to feel the warmth of the living.

Ma'at told me they were a burial rite. The dead that I had been responsible for. A litany of scars caused by me.

"I'm sorry," I had choked out. I was sorry for the pain and for the fear. I was a horrible person.

Ma'at and looked at me with undeserved trust and compassion and told me for a second time since we met not to apologize. Ma'at must have believed I was referring to the woman I just killed, because I was certain I wouldn't be forgiven for my actions against the Psoe Nepsul.

I told Ma'at my real name, "Xenon," as a small form of repayment, some cosmic way for me to rebalance the scales and put my life into Ma'at's hands. Ma'at could have reported me and ended my life with that information.

Instead, I learned that Ma'at's real name was "Ainsley." The scales, again, were tipped in my favor, insider information apparent to me on unequivocal terms.

A year later, I found out the name Ainsley meant *lonely*.

After that, I learned to love the small things and useless bits of information. How no matter how hard Ainsley fought to keep that face free of emotions, flattery always stained it pink. How Ainsley hated to have the blanket covering every part of the body during the night. How Ainsley hated glass. How a man with the surname Bahadur had taught Ainsley to fight.

My life became a mantra of *Ainsley*. I held some innate fear within me warned that someone was still coming to finish what I had started years ago. That was absurd, of course, but I was overprotective about my new obsession.

On the night we were sworn into the North, I pulled Jupiter aside and told him who I was. I was released from my obligation to serve them.

Jupiter said it was a pleasure to have trained alongside my father, who was a wonderful man, and to have met me. His words were shallow; I was familiar with shallow words. I smiled and thanked him. My words were shallow, too.

For a moment, I considered telling Ainsley everything. Spilling all the dirty secrets and trying to scrub the blood out from my fingernails with a confession. But when I saw that hopeful smile, heard that hollow sounding whisper asking, "Hey, do you think we will get assigned together again?" I couldn't. It was selfish, but I wanted to preserve whatever we had.

Looking back, I should have said something. Hatred would have been better than indifference. At least then Ainsley would feel something for me.

It was the last night I saw Ainsley for two years.

I went back to the Rabum Giru, in some ways the same as I had left. I was still skilled, logical, calculating… a smooth talker. It aided me well. I killed at my own behest, decided whose life I took. As the commander, I had that discretion.

The clients, were a different beast entirely. They always held an air of superiority, as if they were above those they were putting hits on. I thought they were the worse. But opinions were not friends to assassins; I pushed those thoughts to the back of my mind.

It was when I was out on one such assignment that I first heard the news.

"There's talk of an angel who commits atrocities," it was spoken by a man of ink and mud, overheard by chance.

At first, I was only curious. The man described a monster in human skin, eyes like sundrops. There had been sightings of this "angel" in a few towns, always with a body found in the aftermath, left bloodied and bruised. "Their red water stains it's white hair when it cuts through your throat and wrists. I heard its haunted yellow eyes are the last thing you see before it kills you."

I had frozen then, clenching a pen so tightly that it snapped, spilling black ink onto my hands. It had ruined the letter I was writing.

What had taken ahold of my mind was the newest member of the Rabum Giru, who had come to me with a thin scratch on her neck, saying someone was hunting us, saying she had seen Belig killed with practiced ease. She had remarked she saw nothing beyond glowing demon eyes. I had brushed her warning off, telling her that many people came after assassins and that she had better learn how to protect herself or she deserved to be taken out.

I didn't want to believe it then. I didn't want to believe it in that pub.

Abraham's funeral arrangement came to memory, dressed in his token white suit, surrounded by hyacinth on a table that was meant to display him one last time before we burned him. Abraham had cuts that ran clean through his neck and wrists.

It had seemed weird to me that less than a year had passed Belig died. Belig was a skilled fighter, but he looked like he had been dissected when we found him, emptied of blood and dismantled in the same way as Abran. His fire was lit as well, carrying the smell of flesh up toward the sky in sparks.

Yssir had frequently gone dark, disappearing for weeks when she needed to be alone. But the knowledge that the only mission she, Belig, and Abbodon had shared was the mission to eradicate the Psoe Nepsul, gave me cause to worry about her latest disappearance.

I wiped the spilled ink from my fingers on the cloth napkin at my seat.

I had a fairly good idea of who that person was, the description "demon eyes" settling with guilt in the bedrock of my stomach.

I hoped, to any god that would listen, that Yssir had not met the same fate as Abraham and Belig. If Yssir was alive, that meant it may not be Ainsley. If Yssir was dead, it would be likely six more bodies were to follow, including my own.

Selfishly, I did not want to add any more names to the ledger of lives I was responsible for taking. Selfishly, I wanted to keep my family and

Ainsley, both.

Yssir's body was found four days later.

I sent out letters to five people: Kobe, Maile, Abrán, Tatsu, and Concord. The letters warned that someone was hunting us.

I didn't specify whom. I selfishly withheld that information.

With a heavy heart, I tracked Ainsley down. I mentioned the rumors I had heard and turned my head to gauge the reaction. As usual, there was no visible display of emotion. Even the black eye and busted lip didn't quiver.

I watched delicate fingers trace the edges of the glass mug. That slow trace was enough to tell me that my words were understood, that I had conveyed the danger of the extremely noticeable white hair and golden eyes that genetics had endowed.

I wanted to see the crooked smile that etched a dimple on the left cheek, the smile that was genuine. I didn't get it. "An angel, you say?" Ainsley's lip twitched into that false cocky smirk. "Don't you know better than to believe that stuff?" Deceitful confidence meant to take away my worry.

Maybe not just *my* worry.

My facial muscles tensed and my jaw clenched tight. I had slammed my free fist on the table and a resounding pound came off. I was angry because Ainsley couldn't think past the bogus promise that was made years ago.

"This isn't a game." |My voice had been cold. Guilt ate at me for the rest of my days over the tone I used.

I knew was only upset because I was the reason that promise was made. I had sealed fate for the two of us. I should have killed the kid when I was seventeen. I should have killed Ma'at when I had joined the North Winds. I should have never gotten attached to Ainsley because I was too big a coward to come clean about my crime.

My chest ripped open. I was the reason Ainsley was blinded by revenge that was viewed as justice.

Ainsley turned to look at me then, unnatural liquid gold piercing daggers through me, colder than my voice had been. The bravado was gone and frustration had taken control. I knew I was bigger and stronger, physically, than Ainsley would ever be, but that look made me want to curl in on myself. It made my stomach drop and my brain scream *run*. It was a look that said, *I'm not playing a game. If you are a barrier, I will overcome you by any means necessary.*

I hated that look with such intensity my skin burned. It gnawed at my edges and singed my slopes.

I wanted to beat some sense into Ainsley. My fist clenched.

The face went neutral as quick as it had shifted before. Ainsley sucked in a breath of air and let it out slowly upon turning back to the drink. "I don't want to fight you today," Ainsley admitted, an exhaustion apparent in the intonation of the words.

Ainsley always thought that masking expressions was easy, that no one could tell what thoughts existed in that skull. How wrong that was. Being unexpressive hid nothing; it made the nuances more obvious. I could read every twitch, every quirk, every line, paining that face in a mural of foggy colors.

All of my strength left me in an instant. Overarching numbness and looseness settled within me like dust settles at the bottom of water.

I couldn't say anything else. Nothing would stop Ainsley from hunting the remaining three. Nothing would stop Ainsley from hunting me.

I cared more about Ainsley discovering my secret than about being killed for it.

Of all of the people I could have loved, I had to pick the one trying to kill me. It sucked to be in love. It sucked to betray the person you loved. It sucked not being able to do anything about it.

Ainsley was right next to me, but had never seemed more distant. I wondered if I was the only one who felt that distance. "I know," I punctuated with a soft squeeze. Ainsley felt warm to the touch. *I don't ever want to fight you.* The brave assassin, too much of a coward to tell the truth.

I made the decision to cut ties with Ainsley, then.

When we parted the next day, Ainsley said, "Villains cannot be saviors." Ainsley wasn't talking about me, but those words hit a little too close for comfort.

I tried to give the warning, "You aren't the villain in this story." I don't think it was received. I was grateful it hadn't been. I don't know what I would have done if it were.

For the next year I did my part to ensure the continuance of the Rabum Giru.

I chose and trained my successor, Piper. She was a spitfire, but more than for what she was (competent, talented, dedicated), I chose her because she reminded me of myself. She wanted what I had wanted at the very beginning: respect. If she couldn't have that, she wanted fear. And really, that desire was the only thing demanded of a leader of the Rabum Giru.

We existed to kill. We inspired fear. It only made sense that our leader must inspire that fear with brutality and strength.

I was no longer brutal enough to lead, nor strong enough to put the needs of the guild above my own. I was no longer a suitable Ammuru. I knew that, even if no one else seemed to.

They would not have to ask me to step down. Ainsley was coming; a real leader would take over after that.

Tatsu had been found dead in her home with obvious marks of a struggle and the subsequent post-mortem desecration. I already knew no suspects would be found and the death would be ruled a suicide to save face.

I sent for Concord to meet me the next day, knowing that time was drawing to a close. "Someone will come to you and ask where I am," I told him.

"If that happens?" he had asked me, stoic and loyal.

"Answer." After a moment, I continued, deciding it was fair to give him a warning. "This person will try to kill you."

For the first time in years, I saw Concord smile. "I'm too tired to fight my fate any more, lad." Those were the last words he said to me.

In my final weeks, I trained Piper to take up the mantle. I spent every waking second, training her to lead, to kill, to strategize. I had spent so much time wanting to lead that I had never discovered how much I hated the responsibilities that came along with the title, but my time with Piper, made everything worthwhile.

I gave her a warning: "Do not allow yourself attachments beyond your successor. It will get you killed. My mother was not even attached to me until the day I was chosen. It served her well."

"Yes, Ammuru," she assented. I could have told her to fetch me the stars from the sky and she would not stop trying to do so until she drew her last breath. She looked determined, with her almond eyes scrunched up tight and her ponytail falling from training. I trusted her word. Still, I felt the need to ask if she meant it.

She told me she would not be the one to lead us astray.

She was right, of course, it had been me.

When Ainsley found the keep, a watcher reported a specter around the perimeter. I drew in a cold breath and told Piper to find as many people as she could and leave, that this may be the day that she shed her title of Abi Ammuru for a higher one. She had worn a solemn expression; she had done as she was told.

If I hadn't been so focused on someone else, I may have seen the glint in the corner of her eye as she turned away. If I hadn't been so focused on Ainsley, I may have seen someone who actually loved me cry for me.

I had thought I would be prepared to die. Perhaps I was more of a coward than I gave myself credit for. I wanted to see Ainsley for a little longer. I watched tears make tracks on pulled back cheeks, anger burn in furious eyes, and screams fall from anguished lips. It was a horrendous sight; I still wanted to see it. I wanted to feel the full weight of what I did.

So, I fought, with everything I could to avoid a fatal injury. Ainsley was sloppy, the cuts administered with reckless abandon. It was easy enough to parry the sword slicing from above with my own, it was easy enough to disarm and pin Ainsley down. It was not easy to draw blood. It was not easy to give a bruise. It was not easy knowing my betrayal probably hurt more than anything physical I was doing.

I had been right: Hatred was better than indifference. And Ainsley never loved anything more than they loved hatred.

I was glad Ainsley had come for me without the falsities, the dyes and the contacts. I was glad that when the time came to say goodbye, it wouldn't be to a mask.

But Ainsley made a mistake, and I was presented with an easy target. Just one all too brazen punch to my left jaw was hooked at me from below. It was meant to be a distraction. It would have worked if I hadn't dodged. But I *did* dodge and I had an unimpeded path to Ainsley's jugular.

I couldn't dig my knife into the violently beating pulse point. Instead, I stepped back with my right foot, withdrawing.

Ainsley had always been impulsive and quick to act. A foot was shoved between my legs. Ainsley's right forearm pushed into my collarbone at full force and the left grabbed hold of my upper arm, at the pressure point, was pressed in.

I had lost.

The ground hurt less than I thought it would. The punches that split my skin merely stung. The blade didn't hurt at all when it squelched through my skin and into my heart. My chest *did* hurt when it beat, squeezing around the blade. My face felt wet.

Ainsley looked sad, too. Worry lines etched rivers into a young face, wrinkled by years of stress and adrenaline, and tears dripped through those rivers and fell onto me. It was a pyrrhic victory, I could tell. Revenge is easy enough to attain, but it always hurts.

The tears felt warm. I felt cold.

I always thought Ainsley was a little too striking. A strong jawline that wasn't harsh, a celestial nose, roundish-almond eyes, thin, straight eyebrows, cupid lips. Apparently, trauma grows a child up nicely. I really was shallow for focusing on how Ainsley looked at that moment, but it hurt me to focus on the less superficial stuff, like how gently Ainsley held my head and hand.

Maybe the pain was retribution.

So, I let my mind wander.

I let myself think on the day we met, really met, not just stole glances through a crack behind a wine barrel. I thought of the immense hatred directed at me for disturbing Ainsley's reading that was remedied as soon as I joined in with a book of my own. I thought about training, to the time when Ainsley had stayed awake for nearly thirty-nine hours to master a single-handed hook kick when no one else had even gotten close yet. I thought about the late nights Ainsley would sneak off to look up at the sky when it was storming, just to watch the clouds break above. I thought about the stupid puns Ainsley would make in a hushed tone, thinking no one was paying attention. I thought about the crooked half-smile that Ainsley let slip when the facade of a silent, brooding hero subsided. I thought about the steadfast dedication and loyalty Ainsley always carried in those rough, calloused hands.

Yeah, that stuff hurt too much to think about.

I asked, "Do you love me?" Ainsley responded, "Yeah, Xenon, I did."

I did. Past tense. I wondered if Ainsley stopped loving me because my past was uncovered or if Ainsley used those words because I was a dead man and you can't love the dead.

I could have deluded myself into thinking it was the latter, but a small voice in me said that wasn't true. Ainsley didn't know how to love someone, the voice told me softly. Ainsley never loved me, was never capable of it. "I did," was the first lie Ainsley had ever told without needing to.

I craved that lie, drank it like water in the desert. That's what it means to love someone, to crave anything they decide to give you, no matter how worthless or corrupted.

Loving you is why I'm like this. I couldn't tell if I said those words aloud or not. If I said them aloud, I hoped they came out bitterly.

I moved on and made light of a bad situation with a joke about the new haircut and touched it briefly before my hand was grabbed. It was fluffy. White and fluffy like a cloud.

Darkness encroached on my vision, dissolving the color from the edges. The last thing I saw Ainsley's eyes, looking a little dimmer than I had become accustomed to.

"Acheron," I whispered; the name of the case that started this mess. I could do that one last favor for the person I had taken everything from.

I was so tired of loving Ainsley.

I wished I had been born a blacksmith.

April 17, 2729

Petbe

The only sound that remained was the echoing cadence of footfalls. The keep reminded me of an empty temple for a long-forgotten religion, with only thoughts to fill the chasm left by followers.

Now that I had effectively deprived the Rabum Giru of a leader, I supposed someone else would take up the mantle. Something niggled at the back of my mind, a warning that I should lay in wait to kill the heir apparent and stop the Rabum Giru from continuing its crimson legacy.

I didn't listen. It wasn't my problem to solve.

I was no hero; I was not about to pretend to be one now.

Xenon had whispered, "Acheron." I didn't ask him what he meant; I doubted I would ever know.

My arm quivered as I pushed open the sculpted doors and staggered out into the sun. It was still early, mid-day perhaps. Shadows danced on the west side of the valley's ridges.

I grew up swallowed by tall yellow wheat and dwarfed by encroaching trees of orange and pink. It was different, here. Here was like taking the first breath of air after being under water, with its purple mountains that stretched high into clouds and rolling fields of deep and vivid green.

As I crossed the bridge and took the view in, I felt weightless. It was understandable why assassins would want to have a base here; places like this made sins seem inconsequential.

I took a deep breath.

I was weary. Not weary from fighting, not weary of the stop and go lifestyle. It wasn't that kind of weary. It was a weariness that with deciding I was tired of living. I supposed that is how everyone must feel when there's nothing to live for any more.

What would I do now? I couldn't go back to the North Winds. When I killed the nine members of the Rabum Giru, it constituted as reason for my head, and I had come to quite like having that part of me attached to my shoulders. Even if I were allowed back, I would be asked to kill again. I had taken the lives I needed; I had no desire to take any more.

I would probably spend the rest of my life narrowly avoiding people I had once called friends, as Yonten had.

It didn't feel like I had accomplished much of anything. Yonten had always said that happiness cannot be found in pride. Perhaps I was too prideful that I had been able to resolve my vow, tie it up in a neat little package and say, "Look, it's all done," to truly feel any sense of accomplishment.

Or maybe all of that anger I had inside me didn't know where to go now.

I was away from the keep now, walking in a valley toward a hill. I hoped it was not someone's property. I may have been a mass murderer, but that did not mean I had to act like a heathen.

I crouched down to the grass, prickly and soft at once, neither damp, nor dry. It smelled fresh, and the zephyr that traveled across the tops of the blades made them shift to a brighter shade of green before righting themselves once more. The day was bright and sunny and fluffy white clouds wandered aimlessly across a cornflower sky. The few trees that remained with virid leaves whispered idyllic words in a tongue I was still learning to understand.

I sunk on to both my knees and rolled onto my back, spreading out until I was lying flat on the earth.

My body ached. My left calf stung where a blade had gone in, though I couldn't really remember when; my jaw throbbed; and my ribs cracked when I breathed in too deeply. Despite the pain, my existence was reduced to only the grass and wind that swaddled me.

My mind wandered. It tugged gently, leading back to the day of my naming, where I became Ma'at instead of Ainsley.

That day, one of the twelve asked me, "Justice or vengeance?"

I answered that justice had many forms and had been named for the Egyptian god of justice. Ma'at: the one who weighed the Heart of the Soul and determined if someone was good enough for the afterlife. If I were to weigh my core on her scales of justice, would it be lighter than the feather she compared it to?

As I looked up at the firmament, I thought of Petbe, the Egyptian god of vengeance. Petbe got his name from a corruption of the words meaning

'Soul of the Sky'. I was always confused why someone associated the sky with vengeance.

It occurred to me that I did not feel liberated at all, even though I had killed the Rabum Giru who massacred my tribe. But I did not feel vengeful, either.

I felt nothingness. An all-encompassing empty, settling within me and pushing against my insides, forcing its way to the surface.

I took a deep breath. My ribs cracked once more in protest. I ignored them; I was not fated to die here. There would be time to tend my wounds later.

The warmth of the spring sun gently heated my skin. Pleasant.

What now?

I would like to visit Iibtet, where Yonten had grown up and find what door the key he gave me opened. He spoke fondly of his village on Yamdrok lake, told me of a house on a great mountain bluff that he could not return to. It was too bad I wouldn't meet him there, that I never got to say goodbye.

I was alone.

Sancus had told me goodbye. He wanted to claim ignorance, to save us both the obligation of having to fight. He was a good man, a good friend. I was lucky to have met him.

Xbalanque hadn't known I was leaving. I hugged him tightly the last time I saw him, telling him he was my everything. He was. Even now, if Xbalanque asked me to die for him, I'd ask him to hand me the blade. I loved him as I had loved Jace.

I blinked a bead of moisture out of my eyelashes, where it had gotten stuck.

Xenon was gone, too. I had once told him I wanted to be selfish. Being selfish meant that I wouldn't have killed him today. Being selfish meant that I would have gone on to love him and be loved by him. Being selfish meant forgetting the trail of bodies he left behind and the mistakes that lead me to him.

Vessels aren't selfish; they exist only to serve others. As a vessel, I served my family well.

Mom, Dad, Jace, I thought, hoping it could reach them. *Are you happy now?* They received justice for their deaths. had kept my promise.

Calm settled like water. Not many people can say that they

accomplished what they were meant to accomplish. I could. That, and that alone, provided all of the peace I needed.

It was a beautiful day.

I pushed myself to a sitting position and watched the wind blow sweep the tips of the wild grasses and the splatters of wildflowers growing in patches.

Humans are always searching for something more. My ending didn't feel like it was missing anything; there was no 'more' out there for me. The story had ended.

I smiled to myself. I didn't deserve a happy ending, anyway.

I was sticky with blood and sweat and tears. I was bruised and broken and beaten. I had been a survivor, a harbinger, and an avenger. If I had defined myself by these titles for so long. Who was I without them?

I never stopped being Ainsley. Not really. When it came down to it, I was just wearing the mask of Ma'at in order to make sure I got what I wanted.

I closed my eyes. Honestly, it didn't matter who I was now. I had plenty of time to figure that out.

A gentle breeze pushed at my clothes. I heard the whispers of nature, smelled the fresh air, and watched the spring amble forward.

I guess I could start by choosing a new name for myself.

The ice within me melted, slowly receding away. It would be dormant, slumbering.

I didn't need it any more.

April 16, 2729:

Piper

I clutched the white envelope hard in my hand, feeling it crunch and crumble in my grasp. Ammuru had handed it off to me before we parted. It was sealed and bulged slightly at the center.

I had been asked to mail it. Would Ammuru be mad if I satiated my curiosity and peaked inside? Maybe it didn't matter; I knew Ammuru was dead. There was no other way to interpret someone stating, "When you have completed this final task, you shall be Ammuru."

I sniffed and wiped my nose on my sleeve. Big girls don't cry, so I didn't, but my eyes certainly sweat in the chill of spring.

The letter was addressed to Ainsley Bahadur, who resided in the far east. I doubted whomever this was would mind if I took a quick peek; being the carrier and all, I deserved to sate my curiosity.

I pulled out my lighter and held it adjacent to the seal, careful not to let the flame touch the paper as I clicked it alight. *Piper,* I thought as the flame's heat unsealed the letter, *you have such steady hands.* The envelope was made loose enough to tug back the top fold.

I shook in anticipation. If I thought about it, this was kind of like reading a will. I pulled the folded bundle of papers out from inside the envelope and my heart fell.

It wasn't anything interesting, it was just the official documents detailing the mission that proved Ammuru good enough to hold the title.

OPERATION ACHERON
    DATE: 06/01/2723
    REQUESTED BY: DAINN MACHIAN
    TEAM LEADER: XENON RABUM GIRU

My fingers traced the black ink letters labeling the team leader's name.

I pushed the papers back in before I could read further. My last name had been made to Rabum Giru when Ammuru had adopted me so that I may one day take the title from him.

"Xenon," I whispered to myself. It was the first time I had heard his real name instead of his title. It was nice to have a more intimate name to remember him by.

I resealed the envelope and dropped it in the mailbox. It seemed just like him to use his last days to finish up business matters. Ammuru was diligent, despite the airhead demeanor he chose to portray.

I hoped, for Xenon's sake, that the letter found who it was intended for.

I walked away from the mailbox, away from the last pieces of a man I had called family.

I would honor the name he gave me. I would honor him.

I am Ammuru, now.

April 28, 2731

The dream was always the same.

I was sitting on a bench of stone. The most important people were with me. Xbalanque was there, Gautami and Jace, too, trying to see how high they could climb on the trees, making a contest of it. An'Gonye, Diejiste, and Xenon all stood around the table, stealing spare bites of food. And my parents were there, with Yonten, the three of them laughing over something I hadn't heard.

"Why are you crying?" Jace would ask. He had grown up to look just like our father, with our mother's coloring. He was a handsome lad, and smart, too. He had grown up compassionate and curious.

I would grab his fingers, ground myself with them. "I'm crying because I'm happy," I'd answer. I knew how he would respond, but I never changed my answer.

His nose would scrunch. He'd never lost that trait. "That's a bad reason to cry."

I could only nod. It was a bad reason to cry. Still, I cried because I had had this dream so many times that I knew it would end. Soon I would wake, to the sunlight beaming in through the cracked window, and I would say goodbye to the world in my head.

"Yeah," I admitted, trying desperately to remember how he looked, how they all looked, in this moment. "It is a bad reason, isn't it?"

My eyes opened to the brown plank ceiling of a home that didn't belong to me. The amber morning light leaking into the window showed a flurry of dust in the air. It didn't smell like dust. It smelled like marigolds, warming my lungs with their amber swirl.

I blinked once, twice, before pushing myself up. The covers pooled around my waist. I pulled aside the translucent curtain by the open window; it let in the dewy air, carried on a lazy breeze.

My stomach fluttered. *Today would be a good day to die,* I thought, looking up at the brown plank ceiling. I thought that a lot lately, now that there wasn't much to live for.

I had taken the surname Bahadur and saw it as my responsibility to upkeep the property. There was nothing of my people left to preserve and I had never mastered a glazier's nimble hand, but there may yet be a preservation of Yonten's family.

The ground was cold when my feet touched it, like the porcelain chill of night. *Schuff schuff* my feet sounded as they slid across it.

The Bahadur household was more of a shack than a house; but the yard was a sight to behold.

The house sat atop a lakeside promontory encased within light green brambles that ensured its privacy. On Autumn mornings, fog would settle over the creek that flowed through the property, creating what looked like a bridge to the spirit world. At night, little lightning bugs would flutter around, casting laughing shadows on the orderly stacks of piled grey stone and shiny red shrines.

The shrines, in and of themselves, were beautiful, too. Yonten had carved the names of all of his family members, including his wife and child, into the tablet. His name never made it on.

I didn't know how to fix that. It seemed too personal a thing to ask someone else to do and I couldn't yet do it myself. After two years of living in the area, I was still illiterate.

I slid the white cloth door open and took the first step outside. A rush of the damp morning chill hit me, soothed by the delicate scent of a lotus.

A spring fog settled in the crevices of the valley below, soon to clear out at high noon. The moss-covered ground squished it beneath my feet, as I walked to the edge of the property.

A flat stone, wide enough, but not long enough, to sleep on, was propped atop two other stones, turning it into a bench of sorts. I trailed my fingertips across the surface. The ridges of the stone tickled the grooves of my fingertips. That, too, was cold; so cold it seemed damp at first touch.

I sat on the stone slab and pulled my feet up to press together. I laid my palms gently on my knees and looked out at the lake below and the skyward reaching granite stakes that were covered in deep emerald clusters. The water was deep and dark and when the sun pierced through the mist and reflected it's lapping waves, it shined like dancing night bugs.

I closed my eyes and breathed in the fog, the morning sun, the chirping crickets. The cold pinched my skin through the thin fabric of my sleeping clothes. "Hey, everyone," I said to those who I had loved, knowing I would not be answered. "Today is going to be a good day."

My lips twitched up at the corners.

The town itself was small. There was a population of less than five thousand, which meant that everyone knew everyone and had already passed judgment on them. I'm sure the judgment on me was that I was 'that good for nothing's bastard'. If they knew the kind of man he really was, they'd have thought it an honor to be Yonten's blood, even as a bastard.

The fact remained that the rumor I was Yonten's bastard was almost entirely untrue. I would call him an Uncle Yonten in another life, I supposed, but I merely took his last name for the sake of convenience.

I hiked the strap of my backpack up a little. It rubbed against the flesh of my shoulder, cutting red lines into my skin. My shoes trudged along the dirt, the crimson color getting dyed with oak-colored dust from the town.

Every week, little vendor stalls popped up, tarps with hanging metal signs peeking from their beige entrances to let passers know what goods were inside. Some sold home-made jam, others art, but all were manned by those with little to do, but waste away their remaining days.

I stopped in front of a stall selling woven baskets. The olive-colored leaves that made them were wiry, all of the lines flowing one direction until my fingers brushed the crest of a perpendicular leaf.

"You gonna buy that?" the young man working the stand asked. He smoked so much a gray cloud circled his head like a helmet.

"No," I stated quickly. I moved on.

One of the small wonders of retirement was wasting my time looking at goods I never intended on buying. The Tuesday farmers' market was a good outlet for that. There was always something new to find... which I also had no intention of buying.

I came to a stall with silly hats. There was one in a pleasantly light blue-gray. It had a black ribbon around the crown. I tried it on and looked in the mirror.

I kept up with a spray tan and henna after my last adventure. This time, though, I kept my hair brown rather than black. I wanted to be a little different from what the North Wind would recall.

I didn't change my eyes. They stared back at me, an unrecognizable phantom.

I looked away and took the hat off. Sorrow washed over me, filling my lungs with the salty burn of existence.

I missed them. The ones I lost and the ones I pushed away.

I left the velveteen hat on the rack I took it from and moved on to the next stall. This one had little paper windmills that spun in the afternoon sun. I leaned over and poked a red one with my index finger, watching the spindle rotate rapidly around a plastic button in the center.

A sound came from my left. My eyes darted to where it came from, my fingers twitching to grab the knife that weighed heavily in my brown utility belt.

Another noise. I waited.

The plinking came with greater frequency, becoming a messy, inconsistent melody.

I followed the faint tune, chasing drifting trails of air, carefully assured that there was no threat. I walked down an alley behind the restaurant; there was a door-shaped hole, with curtain flaps covering it.

I pulled back the curtain and peered inside, uninvited and unnoticed. An older man played a harp, plucking incessantly at angel hair chords.

"It's lovely," I said, without thinking. His hands fell away and he started. I never quite learned to stop sneaking around. "Will you allow me to listen?" I asked before he could request I leave.

The middle-aged man nodded slowly and his crow's feet eyes crinkled with acknowledgement. He went back to plucking the little strings.

An empty white working bucket was propped up beside the wall. I picked it up and flipped the plastic over. The metal handle clinked as I did so. The bucket made a weak hollow *clonk* as I set its opening down on the floor.

It bore my weight well enough.

The man wasn't a great player, not by a stretch, but I could tell how much he loved to play. I closed my eyes to hear better. I could feel that love in each discordant plunk.

I heard the curtain shift behind me. I forced myself not to turn and look to it. My heart thudded at the effort.

"May I stay and listen, sir?" a voice came. The words weren't smooth. *Not a local,* my mind kicked into overdrive.

I opened my eyes enough to peer through my lashes at the girl by the door. She looked just barely over half my age. Her green painted fingers clutched desperately at her dingy yellow shirt. Something in my mind recognized that accent with which she spoke, though I couldn't place it; I had been too many places to remember which sounds came from where any more.

Not a local, but familiar. The chill of potential danger spread throughout my spine.

The familiarity gave me cause to be aware of her movements.

The man nodded and went back to playing. She leaned forward and collapsed to the floor to sit. She pulled her green hair back into a sloppy slip knot. The muted green contrasted sharply with her skin.

She had a cut on her lip, I noticed, a scar so faded I almost missed it. Another scar, more noticeable, made its home on the tip of her radius bone, where it met her wrist. Her nose was dainty and upturned, like it had never suffered breakage.

"Excuse me," she whispered to me, trying not to break the sounds that drifted through the air. "You look very familiar. Do we know one another?"

I knew better than to answer that question openly. I gave the fake smile that I often reserved for hiding secrets. "I'm not certain," I responded.

I turned my head back to the man playing the harp, but I was no longer listening to him ; I was listening to the stats rattling off in my head. She was roughly two inches shorter than me, and probably had lower density. Her body was not toned in the way an assassin's was. I could not make out the shape of a bicep or tricep in her arms, just the curvature of her skin. She wasn't pudgy, but she wasn't solid muscle matter either.

Still, I reached back and threaded my fingers through my raggedy hair. It was soft in the way that hair was soft when it hadn't been washed in a day. I tugged the hair tie out and let the hair obscure my face. If she were an operative, I didn't need her looking at me for longer than necessary.

A quick intake of breath. "Ainsley," she whispered. "You're my Ainsley." Her fingers made a home above her dark lips.

I froze. It had been a long time since someone called me that. I turned my head toward her slightly. "I think you're mistaking me—"

"No," she cut me off. "No, I'm sure of it."

She pushed herself to her knees and looked down at the cement floor. "I'm sure of it," she repeated. She didn't sound certain.

My hand reached out of its own accord. I yanked it back to my lap quickly. "What is your name?" I asked.

"Yaya," she responded. My throat went dry. The busted lip, the button nose, the purple swollen eye that a child had nearly a decade ago. Images of the past came flooding back to me, of a little kid in rags and the other kid she clung to so tightly. I remembered that vibrant coloring and the more vibrant smile. She was young woman now, same age as I have been when I left home.

I nodded and ground my teeth together.

I blinked, trying to make certain of what my intuition already knew. "Yaya?" I asked to clarify.

She noted, resolutely.

The harp stopped playing. The man looked at me with impatience. I rolled my lips between my teeth.

"We'll leave," I said awkwardly.

I looked at her. She beamed at me like she was trying to say *Look, look how I've grown up.*

A sharp pressure hit my chest and halted my breath. "Do you want to get some tea?" I asked awkwardly. "I know a place."

"Sure."

She followed me out the door and onto the street. I didn't talk the whole way to the tea shop I frequented, a place marked only by the word 'TEA' on the front door.

She didn't try to make conversation either.

We experienced a silence of two people who had impacted each other profoundly, but did not yet know the other well enough to carry a conversation. We were not old friends. We were something else.

We sat down at a table in the corner and stared at one another until the waitress came to take our order. I ordered for us, since Yaya was fumbling with a translation book.

"How old are you now?" I asked when our drinks had been delivered.

"I'm fifteen, but I already graduated from school, so I'm not ditching, don't worry," she cajoled, as if that had even been a thought in my mind. I hadn't even finished primary school; she had done loads better than I had.

I smiled at her. "Then what do you do now?"

Her smile was made up of two rows of perfectly white teeth sprouting in the valley between two high cheekbones. "I'm a journalist," she told me. "I have five published works, a book and some articles, and I'm working on a sixth now. An article, that is."

I brought my cup to my lips and felt the steam hit my face. "That is quite the accomplishment. Your mother must be very proud." I sipped the tea, scorching my lips and making my throat raw. Lavender and lemongrass danced on my tongue.

She nodded and her finger nails lightly scratched at the surface of her cup. "She is," Yaya whispered. Then, louder, "She told me she didn't expect to live past the last decade. She's very happy to have been here to see it."

"I'm glad she got to." I meant it.

For the first year after I left the North Wind, it felt like all that blood on my hands had begun to drown me, to seep into my throat and choke me while I slept. It felt like I could never atone. Eventually, I learned to ignore it, think only on what I could do now: Help an old woman with her groceries, clean up trash from the streets, offer to fix up broken glasses. Looking at Yaya let me know I hadn't only left carnage in my wake. Somewhere, in the discordant chaos, I had planted a seed for something better than me.

"How did you remember me?" I asked her. "It's been so many years."

"Of course, I remember you," she said, like it was the most obvious thing in the world. A carefully plucked eyebrow arched up the left side of her forehead. "You saved me."

My stomach fluttered. "So, you peeked out of your room, then?" I asked, with the nervousness of a delinquent caught with a can of spray paint.

She nodded, a guilty smile on her face. Her lip had scarred over where it was split on the day I met her. "I was never good at following directions." A pause. "*Still* not good at it."

"And what of him?" I asked. *Your father.* The man with bloodied knuckles and broken metacarpals.

She shook her head and swirled the tea in her mug, her fingers wrapped around the jade-grey ceramic. "Blew his brains out. He hit me one more time a year after your visit and killed himself. Said anything was better than the white-haired bastard with demon eyes. I always assumed he meant you."

I nodded solemnly. "Do you resent me?" I asked quietly, looking down at my own tea.

"I do," she admitted. I winced and looked up. A frizzy strand of hair bounced as she looked down to swish around the cold tea drink in a circle around the edges of the cup again. "But I'm also grateful to you. I'm still trying to reconcile those two feelings."

I sighed, looking to my own tea again, searching the amber liquid for some explanation I didn't know how to give. I finally settled on, "I never wanted you to grow up without a father." Then again, it didn't matter what I wanted. I had no control over how things worked out; that much, I learned over time.

"Ah, it's better now," she said lightly. Her eyebrows raised in excitement. "My mom and I started over across the sea. Now, I spend every day writing for a travel journal. It's a relatively new gig."

I propped my head up on my hand and look at her face. She had grown up free and unrestrained, but more than that, she had grown up happy. The entire world was splayed out before her. She was a lone sailor, surmounting the endless blue horizon before her, with wind in her sails and drive in her gut.

I wished I could catalogue this moment, this version of Yaya, in my mind.

"Where to next?" I questioned.

"I think I'm headed to Senad," she mused. "I heard the food there is bad, but the ruins make it a worthwhile trip."

I nodded. "I went, once," I told her. I didn't mention what I had done there, the horrendous acts of vengeance. "I think you would love it. The vines in the rainforest there match your eyes and hair, actually; you'd have a perfect camouflage, if you wanted."

Her left canine slightly overlapped the lateral incisor, I noticed. "Really?" She sounded so excited as she leaned forward, her shoulders hunching up in anticipation.

"Yeah." I nodded. I hoped she kept that child-like wonder until old age crippled her bones and turned her skin to paper.

"Write some good stories for me when you're there," I requested. "I'd love to read your column."

Her mouth contorted into an O shape and she peeled off her backpack and began digging around inside of it. I tried to look over inside, but she batted me away with a bracelet covered arm. She pulled out a book, with a red cover and little sparrows all over it. *Flight,* it was labeled.

She handed it over to me. "This is my first work, the book," she informed me. "It's yours."

My face contorted. "No," I argued, "No, I ca—I can't take this; it is precious to you." Otherwise, she would not keep it with her, when she only carried around a backpack. I knew as well as anyone how valuable that space was.

I extended the book back to her.

She pushed my hand and the red book into my chest. "I have carried it around all these years because I wasn't ready to say goodbye to it."

"And you are now?" I scoffed, the left side of my mouth tilting up.

"I'm not," she admitted, "but people need to do things we aren't ready for. That's how we grow."

Yaya looked like the first breath you take when you wake up early on a snowy day, before it gets light outside, when you open up the window and let in the biting air just so you can stick out your hand and feel the snow flurries melt on your fingertips. I breathed the icy air into my lungs.

It didn't feel cold. Not cold like I expected. Not cold like me.

"Thank you," I said as my fingers curled around the book.

She nodded.

I looked at the cover more thoroughly. The sparrows were silver, pressed into the thick cover like a stenciled work of art. Yaya Ahmed. All these years, I had never learned her surname.

"I can't wait to read it," I told her.

In that moment, with a crooked smile and a carefree shrug, she reminded me of An'Gonye. A small pang echoed in my chest. I wondered if he still had those stupid dyed tips that he was so fond of.

"Can I ask you a question, Ainsley?"

"Of course," I answered.

"How are you?"

For a second, I didn't understand the question. My brow furrowed. It had been doing that a lot in recent years, since I no longer had to guard my thoughts and intentions.

I opened my mouth and then shut it. My face relaxed and I felt the corners of my mouth tug back. "I'm well," I stated.

I had accomplished my purpose. What more could I ask? I should be happy with that.

Yaya cocked her head to the side and her hand found the back of my own. Her palm was rough with years of use. "Are you sure?" she asked.

"No," I admitted, because in spite of the fact I should be happy, there were days where the world seemed off.

She touched me shoulder. Her hand was big and warm. She had the hands of a worker. "Your scars were raw when we met; they're raw now."

I forced a reassuring smile. She didn't know the scars she saw now were fresher than the ones she had seen when we met. I was quite all right in my little corner of the world, stitching them up slowly, day by day. That was enough for me now.

I grabbed for her right hand. "Take care of yourself, Yaya." I could feel the calluses my own hand rubbing against hers.

Her hand and mine were the same color now. "Travel safely," I advised.

Yaya left much like clouds on a windy day.

I had a lot of things I could've done better, many more that I could've changed entirely. At the least, I didn't completely screw up with Yaya.

I looked into my drink. My fingers traced the ridged rim and the heat seeped into my skin. I reached into my pocket and pulled out three denarii. Yaya hadn't paid for her tea. I wondered if it had been intentional.

"Hey, you're that kid who lives at the Bahadur estate, yeah?" The shop the shop owner interrogated as she wiped down the table where Yaya had once sat. That was a nice way of asking, "You're that Bahadur bastard, yeah?"

I nodded my head. "I call myself Petbe," I explain.

"You have a sibling?"

I shook my head. The shop owner blew a huff of hot air from her mouth and scrunched it closed tight. She scrubbed the stained cloth against the table with a renewed vigor, frustrated.

She reached into her worn black apron, covered with a couple mystery-brown splotches, and pulled out an envelope. She threw it down on the table. I leaned over it to take a look at which departed Bahadur it was addressed to.

My heart clenched. I recognized that writing that sloped the curves of the name *Ainsley Bahadur*. I swallowed. I never should have told him that name.

I looked back up to the woman. She pushed a stray strand of her hair back from her face using the back of her wrist. It was silky.

Yonten's had been different. His was wirier, from his mother, who was from another land. She had given him a darker complexion and no place to call home here, in those times. Maybe that was why Yonten had kept his head shaved; an old habit borne of desperation to belong.

"Where did this come from?" I asked.

She shook her head. "Been sitting here for years. No Ainsley ever came looking. We're the only place in town that handles the post. You'd think the idiot would be able to find us." She paused, thoughtfully. "Hey, care to deliver it for me?" She pushed at my chest with the tips of her fingers.

I had to force myself not to grab her wrist and twist. I swallowed and picked up the yellowed paper in my hands. "Ainsley is blood," I specify, a vague half-truth. "I'll deliver the letter."

The woman's hands were bony and flat, like spatulas or a fish's fin. She picked up the mug Yaya had used and the denarii I had laid out.

I stared at the letter, waiting. I didn't quite know what for. Then I shoveled it into my pocket.

I took another swig of the tea.

Xenon was dead. I killed him. When he had he sent me the letter? For how long had it been at the shop? Last I checked, the dead didn't send letters.

I closed my eyes and propped my forehead on the heel of my left palm. It pressed soothingly into my skull. I took a shaky breath in through my mouth and my chest heaved. I let that same breath out more smoothly through the circle of my lips.

Pity does nothing for the dead, I was always told. But what of us who remain?

It had been a while since I had to fight off an anxiety attack, since I had to calmly force away the oppressive thoughts and the adrenaline running through my veins, thicker than the blood there.

He's dead, I breathed through the logic. *I killed him.*

Years. I had spent *years* trying to forgive myself for that. Now, it was back to poke at the barbwire inside me, making it soil my organs with a litany of imagined abrasions.

I grabbed the warm ceramic ahead of me, threw my head back, and swallowed the rest of the drink. My throat closed around it the way a throat closes when thinking too hard about how to breathe.

I pushed myself back from the counter. "Thanks," I mumbled as I stood and left the teahouse, pushing back the most covered cloth flap that hung in the doorway. My feet shuffled along the stone paved road, heading back to the Bahadur estate.

I didn't do much thinking in the thirty-two minutes it took me to get back. I just kept thinking about Xenon, recycling our conversations in my mind.

"I hate that you're good at everything you do."

"You sound bitter." His voice was like liquid silver, even in my memory.

"I am."

I saw him lying in the spring grass outside, early in the day, pressing his finger to his lips to tell me to be quiet. I saw the outline of his chin and nose and brow as I looked at his profile in the damp of morning, smelled the fresh ocean air sent that came from him, muddled with a mountain scent around us. I could feel the phantom cold of his fingers clutching at mine.

I never got to do that. No, it ended too soon for me to do that. What I regretted most about killing him wasn't actually killing him. It was that I had never taken the time to catalogue our firsts. When did we first hold hands? When did we first talk? I couldn't recall.

Humans place a lot of emphasis on our firsts. We do that because we never know when the lasts are going to happen. We do that because sometimes the lasts suck.

I opened the front gate of the estate and walked the mossy stones to the front door. I entered the wooden building that was always quiet inside. Usually, I didn't mind the absence of noise. Now, with a hollow feeling in my core, the silence seemed to echo indefinitely.

I pulled the paper envelope out of my pocket and set it on the coffee table. I sat down on the floor in front of it, one knee in the air so I could rest my right elbow across it. I chewed on the pad of my thumb.

I'd never been able to make complete amends with what I had done in my life. This letter brought all of those unresolved emotions to the surface.

In the end, night fell and I was still staring at the unopened letter. I left it on the coffee table when I brought myself to bed.

I pulled the covers up to my neck that night, but I still felt cold. I thought of Xbalanque and An'Gonye. Would they open the letter? An'Gonye would. Xbalanque wouldn't.

I couldn't sleep that night, and even the half-hearted "Farrah" I mumbled did nothing to sooth my tensions. I kept rolling over to a different side of my body. The sweat clutched my skin underneath my clothes, sending heated static across me in waves. It was like a foggy nightmare muddling with the fatigue in my skull. My vision blurred and my breathing came in short puffs.

Finally, vibrant beams burst harshly through a gap in the curtains and it hit me directly in the eye. I didn't shy away from it. I blinked and pulled myself from the bed. My eyes were wide and puffy with insomnia.

As I walked back to the table, I could really only see one thing: the letter. That one damned letter with words written by a dead man.

The *schiikk* as the paper tore bashed against the inside of my brain, waging a cataclysmic war against my temples. I peeled back the flap and pulled out the contents. A single slip of paper.

I expected it to be handwritten, but it was typeset. I thought it would be Xenon's last record of thoughts, but it was a documentation of an operation undertaken by the Rabum Giru. It was a document telling me I had taken an undeserved break.

My mission was not yet over.

My fingers lightly traced the scar on by brow. Xenon had left me a trail. I would follow it.

I walked to the kitchen with the letter in my hands and pulled the flint from the drawer beneath the stove. I hit the two stones together until a spark lit the paper. It burned slowly until it was an unrecognizable and illegible carbon sheet. I touched it lightly with my fingers and the grey stained my skin.

Again, I would have to forgo who I was to become who I needed to be.

The name Dainn Machian sat heavy in my throat.

June 1, 2731

Elias

It was a strange thing for me to be on public transport again, after spending two years using only my feet. It was strange to be awaiting arrival in the city of another person that I intended to kill, after thinking I had closed that chapter of my life.

A phantom burning curled around the skin of my left arm.

After I killed Xenon, I never wanted to take another life. For two whole years I had counted myself lucky that it was all over. It was as if glue had adhered itself to my skin once more, sticking me to that heavy weight named Commitment. It was the sensation of suffocation.

The fact of the matter was the same as it ever had been: I was still duty-bound to finish what I had started when I was fourteen years old.

I could no longer call myself a vessel, nor a god. I was someone who took orders from the past, from a version of me who no longer existed.

I closed my eyes and leaned my head against the window of the bus. The amber sun warmed the glass and my temple through it. My head bounced when the bus hit a bump.

Eventually, I grew weary of the jostling and raised my head from the glass. My eyes opened and took in the views through the window.

Funny that it should end here, where it all began, in the region I had called home for fifteen years. Looking at the arid landscape should have filled me with sorrow or longing. When I looked across that gold-drenched long grass and those cascading arches that were dotted with trees of dancing flames, I felt... neither of those things. Because I no longer thought of this place as home.

My village was destroyed by time. My home was silent and empty. My people were gone. There was nothing here for me here.

When the bus stopped, I stood. My fingers trailed across the sea-green cotton seats as I walked to the front and stepped down the ridged black stairs leading out.

The soil was dry and red and puffed up in dry ghost-whisps when I stepped through it. The bus door clicked closed behind me and its engine whirred when it departed, leaving those same ghost-trails in its wake.

How many people took the same bus route as me, stood in the same red dirt as me, and looked at the ruins of genocide like me? Did they think nothing more than how cool it was to see a piece of history? Did they even know they were walking over so many corpses that the entire village main street was filled with mass unmarked graves?

Thankfully, no one else had come to visit the Psoe Nespul today.

How old was I now? How long had it been since I walked this strip? How long did our wooden houses take before they started to fall apart? How many years had passed with the only memory of these people being the names carved in a government ledger?

I looked at the front of my house, standing on stilts, with cotton hanging in the windows and the wind flower Jace and I had made as kids clanging from the top gable. Part of me wanted to walk inside that house, in the unlocked front door and meet the remnants of who I used to be. A larger part of me forced my legs forward and my eyes away; I didn't want to see the dried blood I had never scrubbed from the floor.

I hadn't slept inside during that week I used to bury the bodies. I had slept outside, in the same pile with them. It smelled horrible, but I didn't want the dogs to get them.

I think I was hoping one of them would gasp for air and that I would be there to take them to the hospital. I was hoping I wasn't really alone.

No one gasped.

I walked to the fire-kissed tree that I had broken my arm in. These three were the only graves that really mattered to me.

Grass sprouts and little weeds grew from the ground on top of them so naturally that I wouldn't have been able to find them were it not for the unforgettable memory of pulling limp weight into holes I had dug with bloodied and blistered hands.

I sat down in that red soil with grass and weed sprouts. I took a deep breath and looked up at the cloudless blue above.

"I haven't been very good about visiting," I whispered. The dead wouldn't speak back, but it had never stopped me from talking to them before. "I won't get better about that. Actually, I'll never come back after today."

I pulled my knees up to my chest and crossed my arms across them. A sigh escaped my lungs.

Everything about today was strange and awkward. It was strange and awkward to don a North Wind uniform I didn't have the right to wear any more. It was strange and awkward for me to fill my utility belt with tools of wrath instead of trinkets and candy. It felt strange and awkward to speak to skeletons instead of air.

"This is the last one for real," I said to them. "His name is Dainn. Dainn Machian."

I took a deep breath and rested my chin on my forearms. This was harder than I thought, an arsenal of hornets stinging me inside. "I guess I just came here to say that, after today, I'm done."

A churning sensation wormed inside, every molecule screaming at me about how much of a disappointment I was, how horrible, how useless, how *ungrateful*.

I pushed it away with the words, "I'm going to try living for myself for a while. Do the things I never got to do."

My throat began to constrict around nothing as the tell-tale signs of too much emotion crashed down on top of me, causing my body to shake. I couldn't determine what emotions they were, but they were all encompassing and oppressive.

"I love you guys so much," my voice wobbled. I blinked back the blurriness threatening to spill from my eyelids. I buried my head in my arms and my nose filled with the faint smell of detergent and the overwhelming scent of dry summer heat. "But I can't keep defining myself by others."

I bit my lip so hard I tasted blood. "I can't keep living like I'm not a *person.*"

I could identify what the feeling was now: Shame. I was ashamed of myself.

I kept waiting for them to answer, believing I would hear them respond just like I did in the trials, when I was starved and dehydrated. I only heard psithurism and the occasional chirp of a June-bug. Somehow, that was worse.

A crushing weight heaved down through my chest. I didn't want to be looked at as I confessed, "I don't want to die as your soldier in a war that's already over."

My fingers trailed through to the ground and clutched that canary-hued grass so hard it pricked my palms. The weight of the bandages on my left arm, concealing sixty-seven little slashes felt a little too constricting.

"We already lost."

I pulled my head out of my arms and sucked in a huge breath. I couldn't get enough oxygen. My hands flattened against the ground and I stood to full height, grounding myself in the expansion.

My fingers picked at those bandages on my arm and found the tab to unwrap it. "I want to die as Ainsley." The beige ribbon spiraled off me and landed in a heap on the ground near their graves. *I want to die as Ainsley,* I thought again. All of those marks made up who Ainsley was.

I moved my left foot forward to walk away, but a magnet seemed to pull my foot back. I knew it was just my mind playing tricks on me. It wasn't really happening. It was a figment of my imagination. Still, I felt obligated to say, "Don't worry. I still intend to keep my promise to you," like it would loosen the imaginary pull.

Those were the last words I ever said to my mom and dad. I couldn't say goodbye to Jace so easily. I would carry Jace with me, always.

I had walked to school every day when I was younger. My tribe had to walk into the city, since we were situated on the outskirts. I still remember how Lee, Emil, and Josephine would meet me by the lamp post with the broken light fissure.

It was still painted black, the right light still broken. I grinned when I saw our carved initials in the paint. LH, JAG, EV, and APN.

I looked out to the people that I had never known, the city I had never learned, and the life I never lived, passing in front me.

I no longer wondered how things would have been; they never would be.

"Ma'at."

My head snapped around and my eyes widened. My core immediately tensed and froze over, my hand going to a poisoned dart in my belt.

When my eyes locked in on who was in front of me, my fingers dropped from the dart.

"Xbalanque," I voiced. I never thought I would see him again.

His face was a little fuller now, the lankiness of a child traded for the markings of a man. He was still lean in body, but he had gotten taller. I noticed, when he smiled, it was a smirk that did not reach his eyes.

My chest constricted and my fingertips went numb. Xbalanque looked like the mirror image of myself five years ago. I left him, the little brother that was still around for me to hurt.

My lips shook as I pressed them into a line. "How is everyone?" I asked, to distract from the feeling of regret growing within me, pinching at my gut for leaving him behind. "How is Sancus?"

The smirk fell from his face like mud. His chest puffed and fell and he glanced to the left.

"They started calling us the cursed generation," he answered. His eyes met mine. The cerulean muscle was moist and looked as if light would spill from the corners.

"First Amaethon lost her legs, then Aruna defected. Gautami died. You and Iktomi just dropped off the face off the earth." He wet his lips and swallowed. His voice was pitchy, like he was prepubescent again. "Nyami Nyami lost his mind. Schizophrenia. He thought he could see his wife and all the people he killed. He shot himself."

I swallowed hard. The news of Nyami Nyami was a punch in the throat, but I immediately focused on the fact I had specifically asked of Sancus and had been told nothing. Tar settled inside me, coating my insides with sick terror. The prelude that we were known as the cursed generation did nothing to ease my anxieties, nor did the darting of Xbalanque's eyes.

"And Sancus?" I repeated, my tongue dry as desert grain.

His breath was shaky. I didn't hear what he said, but I could see his lips move. "Sancus died on a grenade," they formed. "He saved everyone when some woman attacked us at Asgard."

My teeth pressed hard against each other and I felt a familiar cold tethering to my core, liquid nitrogen consuming me from within, a long-forgotten ally making me its home. I know in my head. My blood pounded in my eardrums and my tongue tasted iron.

"And the woman?" I asked, my voice falling back to the monotonous pitch it had been in my younger years. It was the voice of a corpse.

There was silence for a moment, like the whole world was awaiting the words, "We killed her."

I nodded.

An'Gonye. I never said goodbye. *It should have been me.* My knife weighed heavy in my belt. My arm tingled.

Xbalanque was all alone. I realized, with guilt, that I had done to Xbalanque what I had feared happening to me. I'd left him alone, with only his longings, regrets, and sorrows to keep him company.

"I'm sorry," he said, squeezing my shoulder with his hand.

I shook my head. I took a deep breath and forced a smile, not to hide how I felt, but to let him know I didn't blame him. If Xbalanque was anything like me, he would've felt it was his fault... And he was a lot like me.

I reached into my pocket, my fingers wrapping around cool metal. "I have something for you," I said it as I pulled out the key. The same one I had gotten in a letter years ago. I held the key out by the ring, the address so dangling from the back on a beige tag.

"A key?"

"A respite," I corrected. "If you ever decide there's no more home for you at Asgard, I hope you'll make this place your new home." Suddenly, I was glad I had written An'Gonye and Xbalanque all those letters I never sent. One day, he could read them.

I resolved myself to keep writing these letters to Xbalanque until he would join me.

If, my mind cautioned, *if he joins you.* I ignored it.

He wrapped his hand around the key. He smirked. "Don't you need this to get in?"

"Nah," I announced with a bittersweet smirk to rival his own, "I'll just break a window or something."

"I assume this is off the record, right?" he asked as he stuffed the object into the pocket of his olive cargo pants. His smirk softened when he caught my gaze again.

He was so grown up. I couldn't help but to reach out and scrub his hair with the tips of my fingers. "It's off the record," I agreed.

I paused. "Be safe," I instructed him more seriously, "You've got to be the oldest man alive one day, okay?"

"Sure, Ma'at, whatever you say," he rolled his eyes. I guessed his attitude had grown up with his body.

"Call me Ainsley," I said, testing the unfamiliar name on my tongue for the first time in years. It felt foreign. I had been so many people in my life.

I didn't know if humans ever stop trying to figure out who we are.

"And Sancus: His name was An'Gonye."

He scoffed. "Well, since it's problematic if I don't report you, and there's no way I'll do that, I may as well tell you my name, too," he amused class being his arms behind his head. He pursed his lips and looked up, pretending he was troubled.

"Nice to meet you, Ainsley," he said, the bravado gone in an instant to make room for a sound I couldn't quite name. "My name is Elias."

Elias. It was strange how much that one word meant to me. A mass of syllables that had no worth other than that which I gave them.

"Nice to meet you."

I paused for a moment. A girl with green eyes and a beauty mark trailing from her neck down to her clavicle came to mind, so did the question she asked me.

"Elias," I probed, "are you happy?"

He tilted his head to the side slightly to indicate he wanted me to elaborate. His face wasn't moving. He was like I had been all that time ago, hiding everything behind a carefully painted mask.

"You've been through so much. Why aren't you crippled by the sorrow?"

Elias looked down at his hands. There was a new scar; it traced along the bridge between his thumb and index finger and crossed to the junction of the wrist, where it cut off in jagged edges.

"Well, I just don't think that I really have the right to be sad," he said, after a moment. He looked up to me and my sight was drawn to his eyes. They always looked cold to me before, vestiges of a closed off soul that could never be reached. Now, they looked like air, floating, open, and unencumbered by the shackles life tried to place on people.

"I've gone through a lot," he continued. "Enough to break a weaker person." His lips twitched. His brows slotted down and his mouth raised in a crooked smirk, all cockiness and confidence. His voice was calm, smooth, and determined as he stated, with all the certainty of the omnipotent, "Even still, this was the life I was given. I'll make the best of it."

In that moment, I wasn't looking at a reflection of myself any more. I was looking at a reflection of An'Gonye. *Good,* I thought, *he took after my better half.*

He embraced me heartily once more. A phrase Sancus used to say came to my mind: The word close and close were spelled the same because everyone craved that someone would close the distance between them and hold them closely. I could hear that desire in Elias when he whispered,

"You, be safe, too."

He released me and turned away.

I gotten quite good at watching others walk away. I was never quite so adept at walking away, myself. I was always stuck in one place, watching the world move on without me. I wondered what they were all walking toward that I could never see. It was beyond my understanding. The funny thing was, I didn't think I'd follow if I could understand.

I stuffed my hand into my belt and pulled out the knife. I press the blade into my arm once more. Sixty-eight. I wiped away the blood. *Goodbye, An'Gonye.*

I took the knife away and began the walk. I knew the way to the building by heart, I'd studied the roads so many times.

I had run the probability and I could say with 97% confidence that Dainn was still in his office. He'd be alone. No one else wanted to spend their Friday evening at work.

Picking locks wasn't hard. It was something any trained monkey with two pins could do. And the locks to the front of the pharmaceutical company were just as easy to crack. No one even looked twice when I was doing it.

There's something about dark and abandoned office buildings that made my heart skip a beat. Transient spaces, they're called: when a place exists as only a means to get you to another place. They have no purpose beyond that. Maybe that heart-skipping was fear, more likely, excitement. I had nothing to fear, after all.

I hopped in the elevator and pushed the button for the eleventh floor. It lit up and the elevator surged upward.

I had nothing to fear.

I had already met the four horsemen. I incubated Pestilence when I was barely old enough to spell the word plague, but could watch just the same, as it ravaged my region in moans and pus-filled boils. I tasted Famine in the depths of alleyways where I huddled for shelter, hoping a trash bin would have enough old potatoes to make my tremors disappear. I shook hands with War every time I heard a loud boom and had to breathe through the phantom feeling of my hand ripping through human flesh, still warm. I met with Death, who looked me in the eyes, every night in my sleep, whispering in that unintelligible, archaic voice, the names of those I had lost to him.

I had met the four horsemen in my life. They told me I had nothing to fear, for there was nothing left for me to lose.

I withdrew the knife from my utility belt. It would be the last time I used it. I stepped from the elevator when the doors opened and walked through the fluorescent-lit halls and came upon the double, wooden doors.

I knew he was behind those doors. I could feel it in my chest, in my lungs, on my skin. The freezing came on steadily at first, slowly. I hadn't felt like this for years. I hadn't felt *cold*. My hatred burned like ice, consuming me.

I'd let it consume every part of me if it could give me what I wanted. I'd die a thousand times for justice or revenge or whatever the fuck I was after. I'd let it eat away at me, because I made a promise and *I keep my promises*.

I took a deep breath and hunched my knees. My arm came up and brandished the knife in front of me. I felt that spiral of cold creak the iron in my veins.

I had nothing to fear.

I pushed open the door.

In my tunnel vision, I saw Dainn sitting at an oak desk with stacks of paper on the sides.

Bang echoed in the room. My fingers went limp and the knife clattered to the floor. My tunnel vision dissipated and I could see the room clearly: the emerald and gold curtains, the encyclopedia covered shelves, the huge leather chairs and the soft fur rugs.

I heard the dull thrum of my heartbeat in my ears. Icy blood rushed through my veins and leaked onto my skin.

The shards inside me fractured.

June 1, 2731

Dainn

I was named after a sword. Dáinn was sword wielded by old Norse Kings. It was said that Dáinn needed to kill before it could be sheathed. That's what I was. Something that needed to kill before I could be put to rest.

Well, that's how my parents told me it was, anyway. Not my birth parents; they cast me out long ago.

I was seen as cursed among the Psoe Nepsul. A baby born to two parents from within the Tribe, but bore only some of the characteristics of the sun. Only one of my eyes was gold. Only a patch of my hair white. Only a few mottled chunks of flesh paled with the sickly pallor they all shared. The sun goddess had rejected me, *that* was why I looked strange. As soon as my fifth year had passed, my parents told me never to come back, that I was unwanted, unwelcome, and unloved.

They weren't my people. My people wouldn't banish me like I was a leper.

When my new parents found me, I was digging in a park garbage can, covered in a layer of dirt and grime, more trash than I was human. I'm still more trash than I am human, but the dirt has long been washed away.

I remember the feeling of the harsh fists, purifying the evil part of me. "Dáinn, we will help you," my dad would say as he grabbed the hair from my head and busted his knuckles on my jaw. Sometimes the purple bruises that showed up after were nice to look at—they only covered the pale parts of my skin. The normal, peach colored parts were unscathed. I think that's what dad was going for: to make me look a little more normal.

I wasn't allowed to cry during these beatings. It would tarnish the ground with my gold eye's dirty tears. When I cried later, in my room, I had to hold a cloth to my left eye. Only my brown, pure, right eye was allowed to fall. I liked watching myself cry in the mirror. I couldn't see the patch of white in the moonlight and the bruises molded perfectly into the untarnished skin. I looked like a kid in these moments, instead of a monster.

I would always thank my dad the next day. He would nod in that gruff way of his. Mom would always give me the lecture the day after. "Remember, Dáinn, you were given just enough good to push back the evil," she would remind me, with a kind look in her eyes. "It's your job to rid the world of the impure part of yourself."

It wasn't until I was sixteen I somewhat understood what she had meant. Every time she spoke of sapping the impurities from the world, my mom was talking about taking away the people who were allowed to hurt me. My birth parents and their tribe.

When my dad died, my mom refused to punish me. She had said that I was old enough to do it myself. Really, I think she didn't want to sully her hands by touching me. Not that I blamed her; I was cursed, after all.

So I went into town the next day and bought myself a leather strap. Every week, I would sit in front of a mirror and flip the strap over my shoulder.

It would sting. It felt like skidding across concrete, skin tearing away from muscle. It would hurt more the thinner my skin got. The slick of the blood made the leather slip from my hands.

I was fascinated by that blood, by the way it dried and flaked from my skin, leaving raised red ridges behind. I thought the crossed pattern of the strikes looked pleasant. I liked how the blood was red, like my mom's was when my dad purified her, too. I had always been told the red blood was a sign the purification was working. It would have been black had I been like the demons who spawned me.

I would look deep into the mirror after I finished, breathless and anxious, hoping to see the marks of a monster fading from me. They never did. I was forced to look at that one foul splotch of shock white hair clawing its way from my brown scalp. Even worse was the ghastly, glowing yellow demon's eye, staring at me. It told me I wasn't normal. It reminded me that, though my blood was red, I still had to atone for being born.

The night I turned sixteen was the night I decided I didn't want to feel that way any longer.

I pushed myself from the ground like a man possessed and rushed down the hall. For the first time in my life, I didn't feel like a burden in those halls. Now, I was endowed with a purpose.

"Mom," I grasped for her attention. She had turned to me, a smile on her lips. She cared for me, in spite of what I was.

"What is it, Dear?" she asked, her fingers making quick work of a yarn scarf.

"I'm going to erase my kind," I informed her, ever so sure of my divine purpose. I had to kill before I could be sheathed and put to rest. "I'll make sure the demons are eradicated."

I watched my mom bite back a smile as she threw her knitting tools up and clasped them back to her lap. Her eyes sparked. She walked up to me, and despite the blood, despite the cursed skin that she used to flinch away from, pulled me into her arms. She stroked my hair and cooed at me about how proud she was my chest swelled. It was the first time she touched me.

"You're such a fine boy," she said. "You aren't a demon, Dainn."

My arms came up to hold her as well. I didn't know how much it would mean to hear those words until I did.

She pulled away and bent to my height. Mom had always been tall. She brushed the sweat slicked hair from my forehead and looked from my right eye to my left. Her voice was cold and deep when she informed me, "But you will be the demon killer."

Be proud was left unsaid.

The world could not be changed by ideals. As much as I wish they could, my feelings alone would not stop the Psoe Nepsul from abandoning another child that didn't fit their standards. If I could stop them from reproducing, no child would ever endure what I did.

I worked hard and studied the sciences, looking for a way to sterilize such hateful people. I couldn't crack it; no amount of time spent hunched over a desk, scribbling formulas got me any closer to a genetic-based sterilizer. I was selective and only wanted to sterilize the Psoe Nepsul; the experimenting was less than successful.

The more I thought about that, the more I believed that it was the mark of the cursed. They stole the DNA of humans and paraded it as if it were their own.

At that point I was in my late twenties, a disgraced geneticist with alcoholism and eyepatch, just waiting for the answer to magically appear in front of me.

Then my mother passed on. She died suddenly. No sickness, no accident, just in her sleep as if she had been old. She was only fifty-two.

I took the plunge into the deeper mahogany, drowning in the liquid fire that ran down my throat and put me to sleep. It hurt less than staying awake.

In fact, it didn't hurt at all to hold her fire blown glass in my hands and pressed the cool and smooth circle to my lips. I fell in love with the woman named Liquor.

I got in the habit of waking up to a home I didn't recognize, missing days, and feeling a robust splitting in my temple. Even when I had those brief moments of clarity once more, I soon found another escape through that same smooth green bottle's rim.

I had let myself go. I still wore the eyepatch, but I hadn't bothered to pay to dye my hair or skin. I caught a glimpse of myself in the mirror, skin a sickly color, hair greasy and long with a very noticeable bunch of white fighting its way through the brown.

I remember thinking to myself as I touched my bloated gut, *I have become one of them.*

That was the day I ended my affair with Liquor.

It was easy to go on as if those months hadn't existed. I went back to my research, thoughts of my mom still playing in my mind. I hadn't done what I told her I would.

I wasn't a demon killer. I was a joke.

I was almost tempted to drink again. I don't know if any thought went through my mind as I drove to the store and purchased another scarlet temptation. I went back to my car, clutching the neck of the bottle through the brown paper. I drove to the top of a seaside promontory, where I turned my car off and stepped out.

I wanted to end it. If I could not be the man I wanted to be, I wouldn't *be.*

I wished, for a moment, that my mom or dad were here to beat the craving out of me, to take away all the impure thoughts racing through my mind. But they couldn't. They were gone.

I raised the emerald circle to my lips tasting the scent of poison on my tongue.

I stood, just as a liquid rose to the rim. I had not yet taken a drink. *They're gone,* I thought. *They can't touch me.*

I pulled the bottle away and emptied the contents onto the dirt shoulder of the road. The red rivulets turned the dirt black.

I got back in my car and drove home. The next day, I turned in my letter of resignation to the University and submitted an application for over fifty pharmaceutical jobs.

I took the first job that was offered to me and climbed the corporate ladder. It was a slow climb. By the time I made it off to the point I needed to, I was an old man, dated in my thoughts for the time.

That didn't matter. The people who preached acceptance didn't know the demons couldn't. They cast out their children; they weren't worthy of acceptance.

I spoke to the Rabum Giru. When they sent a child to collect the payment and the details, I scoffed. He was lithe and didn't look like a famed assassin.

When I looked in his eyes, I lost all the bravery I had. They had no white. They showed no emotion. His eyes were the eyes of a corpse. Never in my life that I felt fear so completely as I did then. If my people were demons, this boy was the devil.

The deal was struck.

A few months later I read about the massacre in the paper. To call it a massacre would be too kind of a word. Punishment was far better suited.

I didn't hear about the Psoe Nepsul for some time after that. Then, one day, I heard about a bloody angel with glowing eyes who left headless corpses in their wake.

I bought a gun.

I was ready when I saw the demon on the security cameras. I almost couldn't recognize it with its dyed hair and skin. But my stomach knew. I felt cool metal in my hand and held the gun forward, waiting for the doors to open.

I squeezed when I saw the flash of gold pop through my office doors.

Bang. One loud sound.

The last of the demons was gone. I could now be sheathed.

It was strange. This demon bled red, same as the rest of us.

I always thought their blood would be the color of tar.

June 1, 2731

Ainsley

I felt the wet slick of blood before I felt the pain. The pain, when it did come, was brief and muted. I looked down at my stomach, watching the blossoming red spider invisibly crawl across my dark clothes.

My mind and body went numb as I lifted up my shirt and reached my finger into the hole the bullet had made. I couldn't find any metal inside the squelching. I withdrew my finger, red slick coating the appendage.

My blood was red, too. I always thought it would be a different color, despite how many times I saw it.

My fingers were too weak to hold onto my shirt any more. I dropped with it. To my knees, then to my stomach. A slight pain slapped my cheek as it pressed hard against the cool quartz floor.

It was a clean shot through the stomach, meaning my stomach acid and bile was spilling onto my other organs. Even if I got to a doctor soon, it would likely leave me with permanent issues.

I sucked in a gasp of air. It hurt to breathe. It was like nails getting driven into me, a hammer clinking away every time I moved.

I always heard that people feel cold when they die. It's because the blood tries to make its way to their vital organs, leaving their appendages without that ninety-eight point seven heat. My fingers weren't cold. It was almost as if someone was holding them, sharing their warmth.

"Not yet," I begged the ice, as it began its slow recession into my body. "I'm not done." I hadn't killed Dainn yet. He was the final piece of the puzzle. He was the *last* person. It couldn't melt. Not yet.

I tried to move my arms, but they only shook in limp protest. My clothes got wetter beneath me. I watched as feet pulled into my line of sight. Dainn's pressed, black shoes clouded my vision. Fingers slid through my hair and tugged, my head surging up with the rough force.

I saw his eyes crinkle in joy and his lips pull into a sneer. The one eye that was like mine gleamed in the setting sun's light, the gold reflecting and making circles of heat on my skin.

I can't die, I didn't finish yet, I thought. "Why?" I croaked.

He leaned close. I could smell the expensive cologne on his neck. "Because we are abominations."

I think he was talking about the whole of the Psoe Nepsul, but all I could think, warm and numb everywhere but the scalp that he tugged up to meet him, was that he was right. He was an abomination and I was, too. A freakshow and a monster.

I searched his face, lined from years of stress, his smile lines non-existent, and his worry lines etched into his forehead and his cheeks. I searched his round eyes and bulbous nose and his effeminate lips for any similarity with myself. There was none. We shared the eye and a patch of hair out of the left side of his head, but that was it. No feature looked similar.

He dropped me to the ground, my head crashing into the flooring, and walked away.

My arms twitched a second time, trying to force myself up again. I tightened my core; my effort only served to push more wet gush from my body.

I was going to die before I could finish what I started.

No, I cried out, lips too tired to move and voice too weak to emit sound. *Please, God, anything to have a little more strength. Just long enough to throw a knife. Just long enough to snap his neck. Just long enough to end things.*

But my body wouldn't move. It just twitched and grew warmer.

I didn't need to hear Dainn call out over his shoulder to me. I didn't need to hear him say the words he did because I was already saying them to myself. *You will never be good enough.* They meant something different to him than to me. Still, their hole was painful than the one in my intestines.

I closed my eyes for a moment. It was hard to keep them open. Sleeping seemed reasonable. No, no it didn't. I couldn't fall asleep yet. I wanted to. My vision was blurred and blinking made my eyes sting less.

I took in a shallow breath of air. Salt. That smell that I hated, clinging to me.

I forced my eyes to open, to stare at the blurry figure of someone who could have been kin if his life had gone differently. "I'm sorry," I mouthed.

I was sorry to Dainn, who had lived a life he thought was impure. I was sorry to my tribe and family, who would never get justice. I was sorry to those who I had killed, just to not carry out the full extent of my task, their lives now in vain.

Some say life flashes before your eyes when you die, your brain trying to search through your memories to find a way to keep you alive. I didn't have that. I was grateful I didn't have to relive my failures.

If I could advise myself how things would turn out, I would have done things differently. I would have stayed in my region, let the cops handle the murdered family mess. If I didn't do that, I would have stayed with Yonten, learned to live simply. I If I didn't do that either, I would have said yes when Xenon asked me to run away together. If I couldn't do any of those things, I would have stopped before I found Xenon and stayed with Sancus at the North Wind.

I closed my eyes again. I gave myself ten seconds to keep them closed before I pried them back open. Breathing got harder, like someone kept adding stones on top my back.

I know none of that was true. I wouldn't have done things any different, even knowing the ending. Younger me would have done things the exact same way and ended up in the exact same position.

Because you're dumb and childish.

Usually I ignored the voice, but today it made a lot of sense. I protested, *I can still kill him, I can still make a difference. Please, please, oh, please hold on just a little longer and my strength will return. Jace, I won't die until I avenge you. I will get you justice if it damns me.*

This time, my eyes refused to open and my strength didn't return. I saw darkness and felt warmth and smelled salt and hated myself because my body didn't do what I wanted it to.

More wet salt tracked down my cheek. I knew I had lied to Jace.

I couldn't do the one thing I had craved for years. I couldn't force the outcome I had centered my thoughts, actions, and intent around. I just *couldn't* do it, no matter how hard I had tried.

Life is like that. Sometimes you never finish what you set out to do.

I remember thinking a while ago, that I was not the main character. That role would have fallen to someone else in my life. Probably Sancus, for his effortless positivity. Perhaps Xbalanque, for his cunning and strength. Perhaps Xenon, who gave everything because he was fool enough to fall in love.

Maybe that's why it didn't work out for me. The main character was already dead. No one cares about side characters once the cover of the book is closed.

Ainsley, I hear a voice call out inside my head, echoing in the recesses of my mind. *What are you doing on the floor? Get up.*

It is Jace's voice. It was different, now, older. It is as if he had gone through puberty and grown into a young man. I try to picture what he would look like now. His jaw would be more angular, his stomach less pudgy. He'd smile a lot; Jace would be a smiler in his older years.

I try flexing my fingers, desperate to do what his voice asked of me. They're twitching minutely. I try again, willing with everything I have to move my hand and push myself up.

"I can't." I can't even open my eyes, let alone stand. I am crushed and disappointed, nothing but the crushing despair of not being able to do what my little brother asked. My baby brother, whom I had taken everything from, by being the one in the hole in the wall after telling him, "You can go play. I'll set the table." An icy tract makes a slow path from my eye across my cheek and down my jaw.

"Did I do right by you all?" I ask, desperate for some answer, some way to make the guilt lessen.

No, not really.

The weight of his words sinks me. It is worse than my ribs breaking, worse than my skin burning, worse than saying goodbye. With a broken voice, I ask, "Why not?"

Jace doesn't answer. I expect him to tell me that they didn't love me anymore, not when I am so useless that I could not even finish off the last piece in the puzzle. I was worthless, *less* than worthless.

This isn't what we wanted, Ains, he finally says, *You knew that and you did it anyway.*

My body turns to ash. "I'm sorry."

The light leaves their place behind my eyelids, sapping from the room slowly, like a candle burning out. *It doesn't matter,* Jace states, bluntly. His words are stoic, but the sound of his voice was soft, like he would break me if he spoke any harsher. Maybe he would. *It's time to go.*

"Where?"

Again, I hear no response.

My hand is warm. Warmer than it was when my blood first started to leave me. Jace is tugging at me, pulling me with him. I know I am hallucinating from the blood loss and that it isn't really Jace. I know the feeling of warmth in my hand is what I want to feel, and not what I actually feel.

I know I am bleeding out on the floor, alone and wasted and that my corpse would end up at the bottom of the ocean, tied in trash bags that are weighed down by rocks.

I have nothing to show for that. Just a bunch of wasted opportunities and a promise left broken. That is my punishment for being a monster: the penalty of failure, weighing upon my soul like hot coals on fresh skin.

At this point, I don't care. I want Jace to be real. I want to know my brother in a way I never got to. I want to be with him again, even if it means an eternity of oblivion.

It takes me a minute to realize I am smiling. It isn't controlled or forced in a certain way. It is soft on my lips and pulls on my cheeks and it clips my brow. I like it.

Well, this is fine. Like Jace said, it doesn't matter.

Are you sure you want to come?

Would it change things if I didn't want to?

No.

Then I will come, without hesitation.

Do you hold regret for what you did?

No. I would do it all again. I would let the hatred consume me and turn my body to ice as many times as it takes to get justice. I only regret I could not finish what I started.

It must have been a lonely existence.

It was.

The thing I remember most is that deafening sound of silence.

01:53 a.m., June 2, 2731

The Bad Liar

My fingers traced the outline of my scarred shoulder—the skin was raised and pink where the sun had been emblazoned, a second piece to the moon I had first gotten there. The second part, my ode to my partner in crime, was more noticeable, just like she always was. Goose pimples raised everywhere on my skin where those lines fell, the silent morning chill settling over my bare arms like an anchor sinking through water.

When I had seen Ma'at—no, Ainsley—it crossed my mind that it wasn't the ones that should last that do. Gautami and An'Gonye should have outlived us both.

They didn't.

"What are you doing out here?" Hephaestus asked. I still wanted to call her Amaethon. The wheels of her chair squeaked against the dew-damp floor. "You'll catch a cold.

Autumn had come once more. The new recruits would be arriving soon.

I sighed and propped my arm up on my raised knee, while my other leg dangled uselessly over the edge I was one poorly-balanced second away from falling off of. "I wonder who we'll lose next."

Hephaestus gasped. "No one," she objected angrily. "Why would you even say that?"

I watched the mist fall off the mossy mountain bluffs and felt an uneasy feeling settle over me. A feeling of loss, like I had been punched clean through my chest, blew through me and my throat was left clenching around an exhale that wasn't there.

I don't know how I knew, but in that moment, I was certain Ainsley was dead, too, the only reminder of existence a small metal key that rested heavily in my utility belt.

I closed my eyes and breathed in. Moss and mulch and cold marble. "I hope I don't lose you, too, Hephaestus," I pleaded, without pleading.

A warm trail slid across my cheek and down my chin, before it was stolen from me by the first breeze of autumn.

"You won't."

I closed my eyes. I had to keep them closed so she couldn't see what I was thinking. "You're right."

I was never any good at lying.